D0040701

UNDER THE
NEVER
SKY

VERONICA ROSSI

UNDER THE
NEVER
SKY

HARPER
An Imprint of HarperCollinsPublishers

Library of Congress Cataloging-in-Publication Data is available.
ISBN 978-0-06-207203-0 (trade bdg.)
ISBN 978-0-06-213195-9 (int. ed.)

Typography by Torborg Davern
12 13 14 15 16   LP/RRDH   10 9 8 7 6 5 4 3 2

First Edition

For Luca and Rocky

ARIA

They called the world beyond the walls of the Pod "the Death Shop." A million ways to die out there. Aria never thought she'd get so close.

She bit her lip as she stared at the heavy steel door in front of her. A display screen read AGRICULTURE 6—NO ENTRY in flashing red letters.

Ag 6 was just a service dome, Aria told herself. Dozens of domes supplied Reverie with food, water, oxygen—all the things an enclosed city needed. Ag 6 had been damaged in a recent storm, but supposedly the damage was minor. Supposedly.

"Maybe we should turn back," Paisley said. She stood beside Aria in the airlock chamber, nervously twisting a strand of her long red hair.

The three boys crouched at the control board by the door, jamming the signal so they could exit without triggering an alarm. Aria tried to ignore their steady bickering.

"Come on, Paisley. What's the worst that could happen?"

Aria meant it as a joke, but her voice sounded too high so she tacked on a laugh. That came out sounding mildly hysterical.

"What could happen in a damaged dome?" Paisley counted on her slender fingers. "Our skin could rot off. We could get locked out. An Aether storm could turn us into human bacon. Then the cannibals could eat us for breakfast."

"It's just another part of Reverie," Aria said.

"An off-limits part."

"Pais, you don't have to go."

"Neither do you," Paisley said, but she was wrong.

For the past five days, Aria had worried constantly about her mother. Why hadn't she been in touch? Lumina had never missed one of their daily visits, no matter how engrossed she was in her medical research. If Aria wanted answers, she needed to get into that dome.

"For the hundredth—wait, thousandth—time, Ag 6 is safe," Soren said without turning from the control board. "You think I want to die tonight?"

He had a point. Soren loved himself too much to risk his own life. Aria's gaze rested on his muscled back. Soren was the son of Reverie's Director of Security. He had the kind of flesh that only came with privilege. He even had a tan, a ridiculous upgrade considering none of them had ever seen the sun. He was also a genius at cracking codes.

Bane and Echo watched at his side. The brothers followed

Soren everywhere. He usually had hundreds of followers, but that was in the Realms. Tonight just five of them shared the cramped airlock chamber. Just five of them breaking the law.

Soren straightened, flashing a cocky smile. "I'm going to have to talk to my father about his security protocols."

"You did it?" Aria asked.

Soren shrugged. "Was there ever a doubt? Now for the best part. Time to turn off."

"Wait," Paisley said. "I thought you were just going to jam our Smarteyes."

"I've been jamming them but that won't give us enough time. We need to turn off."

Aria brushed a finger over her Smarteye. She had always worn the clear device over her left eye and it was always on. The Eye took them to the Realms, the virtual spaces where they spent most of their time.

"Caleb will kill us if we're not back soon," said Paisley.

Aria rolled her eyes. "Your brother and his theme nights." She usually cruised the Realms with Paisley and her older brother, Caleb, from their favorite spot in the 2nd Gen Lounge. For the past month, Caleb had planned their nights around themes. Tonight's theme, "Feeding Friend-zies," began in a Roman Realm where they'd feasted on roasted boar and lobster ragout. Then they'd cruised to a Minotaur feeding in a Mythology Realm. "I'm just glad we left before the piranhas."

Thanks to her Smarteye, Aria had kept daily visits with her

mother, who had followed her research to Bliss, another Pod hundreds of miles away. The distance had never mattered until five days ago, when the link with Bliss broke.

"How long are we planning to stay out there?" Aria asked. She only needed a few minutes alone with Soren. Just long enough to ask him about Bliss.

A grin broke over Bane's face. "Long enough to party in the real!"

Echo pushed his hair out of his eyes. "Long enough to party in the flesh!"

Echo's actual name was Theo but few people remembered it. His nickname suited him too well.

"We can shut off for one hour." Soren winked at her. "But don't worry, I'll turn you on later."

Aria made herself laugh, smoky and flirtatious. "You better."

Paisley shot her a suspicious look. She didn't know Aria's plan. Something had happened to Bliss, and Aria knew Soren could get the information from his father.

Soren shifted his thick shoulders like a boxer stepping into a ring. "Here we go, Glitches. Hold on to your pants. We're shutting off in three, two—"

Aria startled at a shrill ringing that came from deep within her ears. A red wall crashed over her field of vision. Hot needles of pain stabbed into her left eye and then spread over her scalp. They gathered at the base of her skull and then shot down her spine, exploding through her limbs. She heard one of the boys swear stiffly with relief. The red wall vanished as quickly as it had come.

She blinked a few times, disoriented. The icons for her favorite Realms had disappeared. The messages in the queue and the news crawl in the lower part of her Smartscreen were gone as well, leaving only the airlock door, which appeared dull, filtered through a soft film. She looked down at her gray boots. Middle Gray. A shade that covered nearly every surface in Reverie. How could *gray* seem less vibrant?

A sense of loneliness crept over her despite being in the crowded little chamber. She couldn't believe people lived this way once, with nothing but the real. Savages on the outside *still* lived this way.

"It worked," Soren said. "We're off! We're strictly meat!"

Bane hopped up and down. "We're like the Savages!"

"We're Savages!" Echo yelled. "We're Outsiders!"

Paisley kept blinking over and over. Aria wanted to reassure her, but she couldn't concentrate with Bane and Echo blasting around in the small space.

Soren spun a manual release bar on the door. The chamber depressurized with a quick hiss and a rush of cool air. Aria looked down, stunned to see Paisley's hand clasped to hers. She had only a second to absorb the fact that she hadn't touched anyone in months, since her mother left, before Soren slid the door open.

"Freedom at last," he said, and then stepped into the darkness.

In the shaft of light that spilled out of the airlock chamber, she saw the same smooth floors that ran everywhere in

Reverie, but these were coated with a layer of dust. Soren's footprints stamped a trail into the gloom.

What if the dome wasn't secure? What if Ag 6 crawled with outside dangers? A million deaths in the Death Shop. A million diseases might be swimming in the air rushing past her cheeks. Inhaling suddenly felt like suicide.

Aria heard beeps from a keypad coming from Soren's direction. Tracks of lights flickered on with a series of loud clicks. A cavernous space appeared. Farming rows stretched back as even as stripes. High above, pipes and beams crisscrossed the ceiling. She saw no gaping hole or other signs of wreckage. With its dirty floors and solemn quiet, the dome simply looked neglected.

Soren jumped in front of the doorway, bracing the frame.

"Blame me if this turns out to be the greatest night of your life."

The food grew from waist-high plastic mounds. Row after row of decaying fruits and vegetables spread out around her in endless lines. Like everything in the Pod, they were genetically designed for efficiency. They had no leaves, and needed no soil and little water to grow.

Aria plucked a withered peach, cringing at how easily she'd bruised the soft flesh. In the Realms food still grew, or pretended to grow virtually, on farms with red barns and fields under sunny skies. She remembered the latest Smarteye slogan, *Better than Real*. It was true in this case. The real food in Ag 6 looked like old people before aging-reversal treatments.

The boys spent the first ten minutes chasing each other down the aisles and leaping over the farming rows. That turned into a game Soren dubbed "Rotball," which consisted of pegging one another with produce. Aria played for a while, but Soren kept aiming for her and he threw too hard.

She took cover with Paisley, ducking behind a row as Soren changed the game again. He lined Bane and Echo against the wall execution-style and then fired grapefruits at the brothers, who just stood there laughing.

"No more citrus!" Bane yelled. "We'll talk!"

Echo put his hands up like Bane. "We give, Fruit Reaper! We'll talk!"

People always did what Soren wanted. He had priority in all the best Realms. He even had a Realm named after him, SOREN 18. Soren's father created it for his eighteenth birthday a month ago. Tilted Green Bottles played a special concert. During the last song, the stadium flooded with seawater. Everyone had transformed into mermaids and mermen. Even in the Realms, where anything was possible, that party had been spectacular. It had set off the underwater concert craze. Soren had made caudal fins sexy.

Aria rarely meshed with him after school hours. Soren ruled the sports and combat Realms. Places where people could compete and be ranked. She normally kept to art and music Realms with Paisley and Caleb.

"Look at this messy *thing*," Paisley said, rubbing at an orange smear on her pants. "It won't go away."

"It's called a stain," Aria said.

"What's the point of stains?"

"There isn't any. That's why we don't have them in the Realms." Aria studied her best friend. Paisley wore a pinched expression, her brow overlapping the edge of her Smarteye. "Are you all right?"

Paisley waved her fingers in front of her Eye. "I hate this. Everything's *missing*, you know? Where is everyone? And why do I sound so pseudo?"

"We all do. Like we swallowed megaphones."

Paisley lifted an eyebrow. "A what?"

"A cone people used to make their voices louder. Before microphones."

"Sounds mega-regress," Paisley said. She scooted around, squaring her shoulders to Aria. "Are you going to tell me what's going on? Why are we with *Soren*?"

Now that they were shut off, Aria realized she could tell Paisley her reason for flirting with him. "I need to find out about Lumina. I know Soren can get information from his father. He might already know something."

Paisley's expression softened. "The link is probably just down. You'll hear from her soon."

"The link has only dropped for a few hours before. Never for this long."

Paisley sighed, leaning back against the plastic mound. "I couldn't believe it when you sang to him the other night. And you should've seen Caleb. He thought you'd broken into your mother's medicines."

Aria smiled. She usually kept her voice private, something strictly between herself and her mother. But a few nights ago, she made herself sing a sultry ballad to Soren in a Cabaret Realm. In minutes that Realm had reached full capacity, with hundreds of people waiting to hear her sing again. Aria had left. And just as she'd hoped, Soren had been chasing her since. When he'd proposed the idea for tonight, she'd jumped at the opportunity.

"I had to get him interested." She flicked a seed off her knee. "I'll talk to him as soon as he calls off the fruit war. Then we'll get out of here."

"Let's get him to stop now. We'll tell him we're bored . . . which we are."

"No, Pais," Aria said. Soren wasn't one to push into anything. "I'll handle it."

Soren leaped on top of the farming row in front of them, making them both jump. He held an avocado, his arm cocked back. His grays were covered in blotches of juice and pulp. "What's wrong? Why are you both just sitting here?"

"We're bored with Rotball," Paisley said.

Aria winced, waiting for Soren's reaction. He crossed his arms, his jaw working side to side as he stared down at them.

"Maybe you should leave then. Wait. I almost forgot. You can't leave. Guess you'll have to stay *bored*, Paisley."

Aria glanced at the airlock door. When had he closed it? She realized he had all the codes for the door and for resetting their Smarteyes. "You can't trap us in here, Soren."

"Actions precede reactions."

"What's he talking about?" Paisley asked.

"Soren! Get over here," Bane called. "You need to see this!"

"Ladies. I'm needed elsewhere."

He tossed the avocado into the air before he jogged away. Aria caught it without thinking. It popped open in her hand, becoming a slick green mess.

"He means we're too late, Pais. He already locked us out."

Aria checked the airlock door anyway. The panel didn't respond. She stared at the red emergency switch. It was wired directly to the mainframe. If she hit it, Reverie Guardians would come to help them. But then they'd also be punished for breaking out and probably have their privileges in the Realms docked. And she'd lose any chance to speak with Soren about her mother.

"We'll stay a little longer. They'll have to go back soon."

Paisley pulled her hair over one shoulder. "All right. But can I hold your hand again? It feels more like being in the Realms."

Aria stared at her best friend's extended hand. Paisley's fingers were twitching slightly. She took her hand, but fought the urge to pull away as they walked to the far end of the dome together. There, the three boys stepped through a door Aria hadn't noticed before. Another set of lights clicked on. For a moment, she wondered if her Smarteye had reactivated and she was actually seeing a Realm. A forest loomed in front of them, beautiful and green. Then she looked up, seeing the familiar white ceiling above the treetops, run through by a maze of lights and pipes. It was a huge terrarium, she realized.

"I found it," Bane said. "How champ am I?"

Echo jerked his head to the side, his shaggy hair shifting out of his eyes. "Champ, man. It's unreal. I mean, it's real. Zap, you know what I mean."

They both looked at Soren. "Perfect," he said, his gaze intent. He pulled off his shirt, tossed it aside, and ran into the woods. In the next moment, Bane and Echo followed.

"We're not going in, are we?" Paisley asked.

"Not like that."

"Aria, be serious."

"Pais, look at this place." She stepped forward. Rotten fruit was one thing. A forest was a true temptation. "We've got to see it."

It was cooler and darker under the trees. Aria ran her free hand over the trunks, feeling the rough textures. Pseudo-bark didn't grip like it might bite into her skin. She crushed a dry leaf in her palm, creating sharp crumbs. She stared at the patterns of leaves and branches above, imagining that if the boys quieted down, she might be able to hear the trees breathe.

Aria kept track of Soren as they headed deeper into the woods, looking for an opportunity to speak to him, while trying to ignore the moist warmth of Paisley's hand. She and Paisley had held hands before in the Realms, where touching happened. But it felt softer there, unlike the constricting grip she felt now.

The boys were chasing one another through the woods.

They'd found sticks, which they carried as spears, and they'd rubbed dirt on their faces and chests. They were pretending to be Savages, like the ones that lived on the outside.

"Soren!" Aria called as he darted past. He paused, spear in hand, and hissed at her. She jerked back. Soren laughed at her and ran off.

Paisley pulled her to a stop. "They're scaring me."

"I know. They're always massive scary."

"Not the boys. The trees. It feels like they're going to fall on us."

Aria looked up. As different as these woods felt, she hadn't thought of that. "All right. We'll go wait by the airlock," she said, and began to backtrack. A few minutes later, she realized they'd come to a clearing they had already passed. They were lost in the woods. She almost laughed at how unbelievable it was. She let go of Paisley's hand and rubbed her palm against her pants.

"We're going in circles. Let's wait here until the boys come by. Don't worry, Pais. It's still Reverie. See?" She pointed up through the leaves at the ceiling and then wished she hadn't. The lights above dimmed, flickered for a moment, and then came back.

"Tell me that didn't just happen," Paisley said.

"We're leaving. This was a stupid idea." Was this the part of Ag 6 that had taken the damage?

"Bane! Get over here!" Soren yelled. Aria spun, catching a glimpse of his tanned torso jogging through the trees. This was her chance. She could talk to him now if she hurried.

If she left Paisley there alone.

Paisley gave her a shaky smile. "Aria, go. Talk to him. But hurry back."

"I promise."

Soren was hoisting a stack of branches into his arms when she found him.

"We're going to make fire," he said.

Aria froze. "You're kidding. You're not really . . . right?"

"We're Outsiders. Outsiders have fires."

"But we're still *inside*. You can't, Soren. This isn't a Realm."

"Exactly. This is our chance to see the real thing."

"Soren, it's forbidden." Fire in the Realms was a rippling orange and yellow light that gave off a gentle warmth. But she knew from years of Pod safety drills that real fire must be different. "You could contaminate our air. You could burn down Reverie—"

She broke off as Soren stepped closer. Water beaded on his forehead. It cut clear trails through the mud on his face and chest. He was sweating. She'd never seen sweat before.

He leaned in. "I can do anything I want in here. *Anything.*"

"I know you can. We all can. Right?"

Soren paused. "Right."

This was it. Her opportunity. She chose her words carefully. "You know things, don't you? Like the codes that got us here. . . . Things we're not supposed to know?"

"Of course I do."

Aria smiled and slipped around the branches in his arms.

She rolled up onto her toes, inviting him to whisper. "Well, tell me a secret. Tell me something we're not supposed to know."

"Like what?"

The lights flickered again. Aria's heart gave a lurch. "Tell me what's going on with Bliss," she said, making her best attempt at sounding casual.

Soren stepped back. He shook his head slowly, his eyes narrowing. "You want to know about your mother, don't you? Is that why you came here? You've been *playing* me?"

Aria couldn't lie anymore. "Just tell me why the link is still down. I need to know if she's all right."

Soren's gaze dropped to her mouth. "I might let you persuade me later," he said. Then he pushed his shoulders back, shifting the branches higher. "Right now I'm discovering fire."

Aria hurried back to the clearing for Paisley. She found Bane and Echo there as well. The brothers were building up a pile of branches and leaves at the center. Paisley rushed over as soon as she saw Aria.

"They've been doing this since you left. They're trying to make fire."

"I know. Let's go." Six thousand people lived in Reverie. She couldn't let Soren risk everything.

Aria heard the clatter of sticks falling just before something struck her shoulder. She cried out as Soren spun her to face him.

"No one's leaving. I thought I made that clear."

She stared at the hand on her shoulder, her legs softening beneath her. "Let go of me, Soren. We're not getting involved."

"Too late." His fingers dug into her. She gasped at the shock wave of pain that ran down her arm. Bane dropped the large branch he'd been dragging and looked over. Echo stopped midstride, his eyes wide, wild. The lights shone off their skin. They were sweating too.

"If you leave," Soren said, "I'll tell my father this was your idea. With our Smarteyes shut off, it's your word against mine. Who do you think he'll believe?"

"You're insane."

Soren let her go. "Shut up and sit down." He grinned. "And enjoy the show."

Aria sat with Paisley at the edge of the tree line and fought the urge to rub her throbbing shoulder. In the Realms, falling off a horse hurt. Twisting an ankle did too. But pain was just an effect, sprinkled in to boost the thrill. They couldn't actually get hurt in the Realms. This felt different. Like there was no limit to the pain. Like it could go on forever.

Bane and Echo made one trip after another into the woods, bringing back armfuls of branches and leaves. Soren directed them to place more here, more there, as sweat dripped off his nose. Aria eyed the lights. At least they were holding steady.

She couldn't believe she'd let herself—and Paisley—get into this situation. She'd known going into Ag 6 meant risk, but she hadn't expected this. She had never wanted to be part of Soren's clique, though he'd always interested her. Aria liked looking for the fissures in his image. The way he watched people when they laughed, like he didn't understand laughter. The way he curled his upper lip after he said something he thought particularly clever. The way he glanced at her occasionally, like he knew she wasn't convinced.

Now she realized what had intrigued her. Through those fissures, she'd seen glimpses of someone else. And out here, without Reverie Guardians watching, he was free to be himself.

"I'm going to get us out of here," she whispered.

Tears pooled in Paisley's bare eye. "Shhh. He'll hear you."

Aria noticed the brittle crackle of the leaves beneath her and wondered when the trees had last been watered. She watched the pile grow one foot high, then two. Finally, with the pile at nearly three feet, Soren declared it ready.

He reached into his boot and brought out a battery pack and some wire, handing them to Bane.

Aria couldn't believe what she was seeing. "You *planned* this? You came here to make fire?"

Soren smiled at her, his lip curling. "I've got other things in mind too."

Aria sucked in a breath. He had to be kidding. He was just trying to scare her because she'd led him on, but she'd had no choice.

The boys huddled together as Soren muttered, "Try it like this," and "Other end, stupid," and "Just let me do it," until they jumped back, away from the flame that flickered up from the leaves.

"Oh, zap!" they yelled in perfect unison. "Fire!"

2

ARIA

Magic.

That was the word that came to Aria's mind. An old word, from a time when illusions still mystified people. Before the Realms made magic common.

She moved closer, drawn by the gold and amber tones in the flame. By the way it changed shape constantly. The smoke was richer than anything she had ever smelled. It tightened the skin along her arms. Then she saw how the burning leaves curled and blackened and disappeared.

This was wrong.

Aria looked up. Soren had frozen in place, his eyes wide. He looked bewitched, just as Paisley and the brothers did. Like they were seeing the fire without really seeing it.

"That's enough," she said. "We should turn it off . . . or get water or something." No one moved. "Soren, it's starting to spread."

"Let's give it more."

"*More?* Trees are made of wood. It'll spread to the trees!"

Echo and Bane ran off before she'd finished speaking.

Paisley grabbed her sleeve, pulling her away from the burning stack. "Aria, stop or he'll hurt you again."

"This whole place is going to burn if we don't do something."

She glanced back. Soren stood too close to the fire. The flames had nearly reached his height. The fire made sounds now, pops and crackles over a dull roar. "Get sticks!" he yelled at the brothers. "The sticks make it stronger."

Aria didn't know what to do. When she thought of stopping them the ache in her shoulder flared, warning her of what might happen again. Echo and Bane ran up with armfuls of branches. They threw them onto the fire, sending sparks into the trees. A surge of hot air blew past her cheeks.

"We're going to run, Paisley," she whispered. "Ready . . . *go.*"

For the third time that night, Aria grasped Paisley's hand. She couldn't let Paisley fall behind. She wove through the trees, her legs churning, as she tried to keep them on a straight course. She didn't know when the boys started chasing them, but she heard Soren behind her.

"Find them!" he yelled. "Spread out!"

Then Aria heard a loud wailing sound that brought her to a halt. Soren was howling like a wolf. Paisley's hand clamped over her mouth, stifling a sob. Bane and Echo joined in, filling the woods with wild, keening cries. What was happening to them? Aria broke into a run again, tugging Paisley so hard that she stumbled.

"Come on, Paisley! We're close!" They had to be near the door leading back to the farming dome. When they reached it, she'd trip the emergency alarm. Then they'd hide until Guardians came.

The lights overhead flickered again. This time they didn't come back. Darkness slammed into Aria like something solid. She went rigid. Paisley rammed into her back and cried out. They tumbled blindly to the ground, their limbs crashing together. Aria scrambled upright, blinking hard as she tried to orient herself. Eyes opened or closed, what she saw didn't change.

Paisley's fingers fluttered over her face. "Aria! Is it you?"

"Yes, it's me," she whispered. "Quiet or they'll hear us!"

"Bring the fire!" Soren yelled. "Get some fire so we can see!"

"What are they going to do to us?" Paisley asked.

"I don't know. But I won't let them get close enough to find out."

Paisley tensed at her side. "Do you see that?"

She did. A torch wove toward them from the distance. Aria recognized the solid tromp of Soren's stride. He was farther than she expected, but she realized it didn't matter. She and Paisley couldn't move without crawling and feeling along in front of them. Even if they knew which way to go, moving a few feet would hardly help.

A second flame appeared.

Aria groped for a rock or a stick. Leaves disintegrated in her hands. She smothered a cough against her sleeve. Every breath tightened her lungs more. She'd been worried about Soren and the fire. Now she realized the smoke might pose the worst danger.

The torches bobbed across the darkness, drawing closer. She wished her mother had never left. She wished she'd never sung to Soren. But wishing wasn't going to get her anywhere. There had to be something she could do. She turned her focus inward. Maybe she could reset her Smarteye and call for help. She reached for commands as she always had. Even in her mind, she felt as though she were fumbling in the dark. How did you restart something that had never been turned off?

It didn't help her concentration to see the torches closing in, or the fire burning brighter and louder, or to feel Paisley quivering against her side. But she had no other hope. Finally she felt a tap in the depths of her brain. A word appeared on her Smartscreen, blue letters floating against the smoldering woods.

RESTART?

Yes! she commanded.

Aria tensed as hot nails dragged across her skull and down her spine. She gasped in relief as a grid of icons appeared. She was back on, but everything looked strange. All the buttons on her interface were generic and in the wrong places. And what was that? She saw a message icon on her screen labeled "Songbird," her mother's nickname for her. Lumina had sent a message! But the file was stored locally and wouldn't help her now. She needed to reach someone.

Aria tried contacting Lumina directly. CONNECTION FAILURE flashed on her screen, followed by an error number. She tried Caleb and the next ten friends who came to mind. Nothing went through. She wasn't linked to the Realms. She made a final attempt. Maybe her Eye was still recording.

REVIEW, she commanded.

Paisley's face appeared in the playback square on the upper left of her Smartscreen. Paisley was hardly visible, just the contours of her frightened face and the glint of the fire catching on her Smarteye. Behind her a glowing cloud of smoke seeped closer. "They're coming!" Paisley said in a frantic whisper, and the recording ended.

Aria commanded her Eye to record again. Whatever happened, whatever Soren and the brothers did, she'd have proof.

The lights flashed back on. Squinting at the brightness, Aria saw Soren scanning the area, Bane and Echo at his side like a pack of wolves. Their eyes flared as they spotted her and Paisley. She jumped to her feet, pulling Paisley up once more. Aria ran, holding tight to Paisley, tripping over roots and pushing through branches that snagged her hair. The boys' shouts were loud, rumbling in Aria's ears. Their feet pounded right behind her.

Paisley's hand tore from Aria's grip. Aria spun as she fell to the ground. Paisley's hair splayed over the leaves. She reached for Aria, crying out. Soren lay half on top of her, his arms wrapped around her legs.

Before Aria could think, she slammed her foot into Soren's head. He grunted and fell back. Paisley twisted away but Soren lunged for her again.

"Let her go!" Aria stepped toward him, but he was ready for her this time. His hand shot out, clamping onto Aria's ankle.

"Run, Paisley!" Aria yelled.

She struggled to get free but Soren wouldn't let go. He rose to his feet and grabbed on to her forearm. Leaves and dirt stuck to his face and chest. Behind him, smoke tumbled through the trees in gray waves, moving slow and fast at the same time. Aria looked down. Soren's hand was twice the size of hers, rounded with muscle like the rest of him.

"Can't you feel it, Aria?"

"Feel *what*?"

"This." He squeezed her arm so tight she cried out. "Everything." His eyes darted around, not settling anywhere.

"Don't, Soren. Please."

Bane ran up, holding a torch and panting for breath.

"Help, Bane!" she cried. He didn't even look at her.

"Go get Paisley," Soren said, and Bane was gone. "Just you and me now," he said, stroking a hand through her hair.

"Don't *touch me*. I'm recording this. If you hurt me, everyone will see it!"

She hit the ground before she realized what had happened. His weight crushed her, driving the air out of her lungs. He glared down at her as she gasped, struggling to draw a breath. Then his focus moved to her left eye. Aria knew what he was going to do but her arms were trapped, squeezed between his thighs. She closed her eyes and screamed as his fingers dug into her skin, prying up the edges of her Smarteye. Aria's head snapped forward and then slammed back to the ground.

Pain. Like her brain had been torn out. Above her, Soren's face looked red and bleary. Warmth spread down her cheek and pooled in her ear. The pain lessened and became pulses, beating in time with her heart.

"You're crazy," someone with her voice slurred.

Soren's fingers clamped around her neck. "This is *real*. Tell me you feel it."

Aria still couldn't pull in enough air. Spears of pain shot into her eyes. She was fading, powering off like her Smarteye. Then Soren looked up—away from her—and his grip loosened. He cursed and then his smothering weight lifted.

Aria pushed herself to her knees, gritting her teeth at the piercing shriek that erupted in her ears. She couldn't see. She swiped at her eyes to clear the murkiness, her legs quaking as she rose to her feet. Framed against the roaring blaze, she saw a stranger step into the clearing. He was shirtless, but there was no mistaking him for Bane or Echo.

He was a real Savage.

The Outsider's torso was almost as dark as his leather pants, his hair a blond Medusa's snarl. Tattoos coiled around his arms. He had the reflective eyes of an animal. They were bare eyes, both.

The long knife at his side flashed with firelight as he came forward.

3

PEREGRINE

The Dweller girl looked at Perry, blood running down her pale face. She took a few steps, backing away from him, but Perry knew she wouldn't stay on her feet for long. Not with pupils dilated like that. One more step and her legs gave out, bringing her down.

The male stood behind her limp body. He looked Perry over with his odd eyes, one normal and one covered with the clear patch all the Dwellers wore. The others had called him Soren.

"Outsider?" he said. "How did you get in?"

It was Perry's language but harsher. Edged where it should have been smooth. Perry brought in a slow breath. The Dweller's temper hung thick in the clearing despite the smoke. Bloodlust gave a scorching red scent, common to man and beast alike.

"You came when we did." Soren laughed. "You came

after I disarmed the system."

Perry spun his knife for a fresh grip. Didn't the Dweller see the fire closing in? "Leave or you'll burn, Dweller."

Soren startled at hearing Perry speak. Then he grinned, showing square teeth, white as snow. "You're real. I don't believe this." He stepped forward with no fear. Like he held a knife instead of Perry. "If I could leave, Savage, I'd have done it a long time ago."

Perry stood a head taller, but Soren easily outweighed him. His bones were buried deep beneath muscle. Perry seldom saw people that big. They didn't have enough food to grow that thick. Not like in here.

"You approach your death, Mole," Perry said.

"Mole? That's inaccurate, Savage. Most of the Pod is aboveground. And we don't die young. We don't get hurt, either. We can't even break anything." Soren looked down at the girl. When he looked back at Perry, he stopped walking. It happened too fast, his momentum rocking him up on his toes. He'd changed his mind about something.

Soren's eyes flicked past him. Perry drew in a breath. Woodsmoke. Burning plastic. The fire was heating up. He inhaled again, caught what he'd expected. Another Dweller's scent, coming at him from behind. He'd seen three males. Soren and two others. Were they both sneaking up on him, or just one? Perry drew another breath but couldn't tell. The smoke was too dense.

Soren's gaze dropped to Perry's hand. "You're good with a knife, aren't you?"

"Good enough."

"Have you ever killed a person? I bet you have."

He was buying time, letting whoever was behind Perry draw nearer.

"Never killed a Mole," Perry said. "Not yet."

Soren smiled. Then he surged forward and Perry knew the others would be coming too. He spun and saw only one Dweller, farther away than he'd expected, running with a metal bar in his hand. Perry hurled his knife. The blade sailed true and sank deep in the Dweller's stomach.

Soren thundered up behind him. Perry braced as he turned. The blow came from the side, slamming into Perry's cheek. The ground reared up and back. Perry wrapped his arms around Soren as he blurred past. He pushed but couldn't bring Soren down. The Mole was made of stone.

Perry took a shot to his kidney and growled, waiting for the pain. It didn't hurt as much as it should have. Soren hit him again. Perry heard himself laugh. The Dweller didn't know how to use his own strength.

He pushed away, throwing his first punch. His fist smashed into the clear eye patch. Soren seized up, the veins in his neck standing out like vines. Perry didn't wait. He put his full weight behind the next blow. The bone in the Dweller's jaw snapped with a crack. Soren fell hard. Then he tucked in slow, like a dying spider.

Blood ran through his teeth. His jaw hung too far to the side, but he never took his eyes off Perry.

Perry swore, stepping away. This wasn't what he had

wanted when he'd broken in. "I warned you, Mole."

The lights had gone out again. Smoke moved through the trees in rolls, glowing with firelight. He went to the other male to retrieve his knife. The Dweller began to cry when he saw Perry. Blood gurgled from his wound. Perry couldn't look him in the eyes as he slid his blade free.

He came back to the girl. Her hair fanned around her head, dark and shiny as a raven's feathers. Perry spotted her eyepiece resting on the leaves by her shoulder. He prodded it with a finger. The skin felt cool. Velvety as a mushroom. Denser than he'd expected for looking so much like a jellyfish. He slipped it into his satchel. Then he hoisted the girl over his shoulder as he carried larger game, wrapping his arm around her legs to keep her steady.

Neither of his Senses were any help to him now. The smoke had grown thick enough to cloak all other smells and block his vision, making him disoriented. There were no rises and falls in the earth to guide him either. Only walls of flame or smoke wherever he looked.

He moved when the fire inhaled. He stopped when it exhaled in bursts of heat that scorched his legs and arms. Tears streamed from his eyes, making it harder to see. He pushed on, feeling skitty and drunk from the smoke. Finally he found a channel of clean air and ran, the Dweller girl's head lolling against his back.

Perry reached the dome wall, followed it. At some point there had to be a way out. It took longer than he hoped. He stumbled up to the same door he'd come through earlier, stepping into a steel room. By then every breath felt like embers kindling in his lungs.

He set the girl down, closed the door. Then for a good while, he could only cough and pace until the pain behind his nose let up. He swiped at his eyes, leaving a streak of blood and soot on his forearm. His bow and quiver rested against the wall were where he'd left them. The curve of his bow looked stark against the room's perfect lines.

Perry knelt, wobbling as he did, and looked the Dweller over. Her eye had stopped bleeding. She was finely made. Thin, dark eyebrows. Pink lips. Skin as smooth as milk. His gut told him they were close in age, but with skin like that he wasn't sure. He'd been watching her from his perch in a tree. How she'd stared at leaves in wonder. He nearly hadn't needed his nose to know her temper. Her face showed every small emotion.

Perry brushed her black hair away from her neck and leaned close. With his nose blunted by smoke, this was the only way. He drew in a breath. Her flesh wasn't as pungent as the other Dwellers', but it was still off. Warm blood but a rancy, decaying scent as well. He inhaled again, curious, but her mind was deep in the unconscious so she gave off no temper.

He thought about bringing her with him, but Dwellers died on the outside. This room was her best chance to survive the fire. He'd planned to check on the other girl too. No chance of that anymore.

He stood. "You better live, little Mole," he said. "After all this."

Then he sealed the door behind him and stepped into another chamber, this one crushed by an Aether strike. Perry ducked through the crumbling dark corridor. The way grew tighter, forcing him to crawl over broken cement and warped metal, pushing his bow and satchel ahead of him, until he was back in his world.

Straightening, he drew a deep breath of the night. Welcomed the clean air into his singed lungs. Alarms broke the silence, first muted through the rubble, then blaring all around him, so loud he felt the sound thrum in his chest. Perry looped the strap of his satchel and quiver over his shoulder, took up his bow, and pulled foot, sprinting through the cool predawn.

An hour later, with the Dweller fortress no more than a mound in the distance, he sat to give his pounding head a break. It was morning, already warm in the Shield Valley, a dry stretch of land that reached nearly to his home two days to the north. He let his head fall against his forearm.

Smoke clung to his hair and skin. He scented it with every breath. Dweller smoke wasn't like theirs. It smelled like molten steel and chemicals that burned hotter than fire. His left cheek throbbed, but it was nothing compared to the core of pain behind his nose. The muscles in his thighs twitched, still running away from the alarms.

It was bad enough he'd broken into the Dweller fortress. His brother would cast him out for that alone. But he'd tangled with the Moles. Probably killed at least one of them. The Tides didn't have problems with the Dwellers like other tribes did. Perry wondered if he'd just changed that.

He reached for his satchel and rummaged through the leather pack. His fingers brushed something cool and velvety. Perry swore. He'd forgotten to leave the girl's eye patch behind. He brought it out, examining it in his palm. It caught the blue light of the Aether like a huge water droplet.

He'd heard the Moles as soon as he'd broken into the wooded area. Their laughing voices had echoed from the farming space. He'd crept over and watched them, stunned to see so much food left to rot. He'd planned to leave after a few minutes, but by then he'd gotten curious about the girl. When Soren tore the eyepiece from her face, he couldn't stand by and watch any longer, even if she was just a Mole.

Perry slipped the eye patch back into his satchel, thinking to sell it when traders came around in spring. Dweller gadgets fetched a sizey price, and there were plenty of things his people needed, to say nothing of his nephew, Talon. Perry dug deeper into the bag, past his shirt, vest, and water skin, until he found what he wanted.

The apple's skin shone more softly than the eyepiece. Perry ran his thumbs over it, following its curves. He'd bagged it in the farming space. The one thing he had thought to grab as he'd stalked the Moles. He brought the apple to his nose and breathed in the sweet scent, his mouth filling with saliva.

It was a stupid gift. Not even why he'd broken in.

And not nearly enough.

～ 4 ～

PEREGRINE

Perry strode into the Tide compound near midnight, four days after he'd left. He stopped in the central clearing, inhaled the briny smell of home. The ocean was a good thirty minutes' walk to the west, but fishermen carried the scent of their trade everywhere. Perry rubbed a hand over his hair, still wet from his swim. Tonight he smelled a bit like a fisherman himself.

Perry shifted the bow and quiver over his back. With no game slung over his shoulder, he had no reason to follow his usual path to the cookhouse so he stayed where he was, taking in fresh what he knew by heart. Homes made of stones rounded by time. Wooden doors and shutters worn by salt air and rain. As weather-beaten as the compound was, it looked sturdy. Like a root growing aboveground.

He preferred the compound like this, in the dead of night. With winter coming and food in such shortage, Perry had grown used to anxious tempers clotting the air during the day. But after dark, the cloud of human emotions lifted, leaving quieter scents. The cooling earth, opened like a flower to the sky. The musk of nighttime animals, making paths he could follow with ease.

Even his eyes favored this time. Contours were more crisp. Movement easier to track. Between his nose and his eyes, he figured he was made for the night.

He drew in his last breath of open air, steeling himself, then stepped into his brother's home. His gaze swept over the wooden table and the two ragged leather chairs before the hearth, then rose to the loft nestled against the roof timbers. Finally he relaxed as his eyes settled on the closed door that led to the only bedroom. Vale wasn't awake. His brother would be asleep with Talon, his son.

Perry moved to the table and inhaled slowly. Grief hung thick and heavy, out of place in the colorful room. It pressed in along the edges of his vision like a bleak gray fog. Perry also caught the smoke from the dying fire, the tang of Luster from the clay pitcher on the wooden table. A month had passed since his brother's wife, Mila, had died. Her scent was faded, almost gone.

Perry tapped the rim of the blue pitcher with a finger. He'd watched Mila decorate the handle with yellow flowers last spring. Mila's touch was everywhere. In the ceramic plates and the bowls she'd shaped. The rugs she'd woven and the glass jars full of beads she'd painted. She'd been a Seer. Gifted with uncommon sight. Like most Seers, Mila had cared about the looks of things. On her deathbed, when her hands could no longer weave or paint or mold clay, she'd told stories and filled them with the colors she loved.

Perry leaned his weight on the table, suddenly weak and weary with missing her. He had no right to brood, with his brother who'd lost a wife and his nephew who'd lost a mother hurting far more. But she'd been his family too.

He turned to the bedroom door. He wanted to see Talon. But judging by the empty pitcher, Vale had been drinking. A meeting with his older brother now would be too risky.

For a moment, he let himself imagine how it would be, challenging Vale for Blood Lord. Acting on a need as real as thirst. He'd make changes if he led the Tides. Take the risks his brother avoided. The tribe couldn't go on cowering in place for much longer. Not with game so scarce and the Aether storms growing worse every winter. Rumors spoke of safer lands with still, blue skies, but Perry wasn't sure. What he did know was that the Tides needed a Blood Lord who'd take action—and his brother didn't want to budge.

Perry looked down at his worn leather boots. Here he was. Standing still. No better than Vale. He cursed and shook his head. Tossed his satchel up to the loft. Then he pulled off his boots, climbed up, and lay staring at the rafters. It was stupid to daydream about something he'd never do. He'd leave before it came to that.

He hadn't yet closed his eyes when he heard a door whine and then the ladder jostle. Talon, a small, dark blur, catapulted over the top rung, buried himself beneath the blanket, and went still as stone. Perry climbed over Talon to the ladder side. The space was cramped, and he didn't want his nephew taking a tumble in his sleep.

"How come you never move that fast when we're hunting?" he teased.

Nothing. Not even a stir under the blanket. Talon had fallen into long stretches of silence since his mother's death, but he'd never stopped speaking with Perry. Considering what had happened the last time they'd been together, Perry wasn't surprised by his nephew's silence. He'd made a mistake. Lately he'd made too many.

"Guess you don't want to know what I brought you." Talon still didn't bite. "Shame," Perry said after a moment. "You'd have loved it."

"I know," Talon said, his seven-year-old voice bright with pride. "A shell."

"It's not a shell, but it's a good guess. I did go for a swim." Before coming home, Perry had spent an hour scrubbing the scents from his skin and hair with handfuls of sand. He'd had to, or one whiff and his brother would know where he'd been. Vale had strict rules against roaming near the Dwellers.

"Why are you hiding, Talon? Come out of there." He drew the blanket back. Talon's scent came at him in a fetid wave. Perry rocked back, hands fisting, his breath catching in his throat. Talon's scent was too much like Mila's had been when the illness came in force. He wanted to believe it was a mistake. That Talon was well and would grow to see another year. But scents never lied.

People thought being a Scire meant having power. Being Marked—gifted with a dominant Sense—was rare. But even among the Marked, Perry was unique for having two Senses. As a Seer, he made a skilled archer. But only Scires with noses as strong as Perry's could breathe and know despair or fear. Useful things to know about an enemy, but when it came to family felt more like a curse. Mila's decline had been hard, but with Talon, Perry had grown to hate his nose for what it told him.

He forced himself to face his nephew. Firelight from below reflected off the rafters. It outlined the curve of Talon's cheeks with an orange glow. Lit the tips of his eyelashes. Perry looked at his dying nephew and couldn't think of a single thing worth saying. Talon already knew everything he felt. He knew Perry would trade places in an instant if he could.

"I know it's getting worse," Talon said. "My legs get numb sometimes. . . . Sometimes I can't scent as good, but nothing hurts too bad." He turned his face into the blanket. "I knew you'd get wrathy."

"Talon, I'm not—it's not *you* I'm wrathy with."

Perry drew a few breaths against the tightness in his chest, his anger mixing with his nephew's guilt, making it difficult to think clearly. He knew love. He loved his sister, Liv, and Mila, and he could remember feeling love for Vale as nearly as a year ago. But with Talon, love was only part of it. Talon's sorrow dropped him like a stone. His worry made Perry pace. His joy felt like flying. In the span of a breath, Talon's needs became Perry's own.

Scires called it being rendered. The bond had always made life simple for Perry. Talon's well-being came first. For the past seven years that had meant plenty of roughhousing. Teaching Talon to walk and then swim. Teaching him to track game and shoot a bow and dress his kills. Easy things. Talon loved everything Perry did. But since Mila had fallen ill, it wasn't as simple anymore. He couldn't keep Talon well or happy. But he knew he helped Talon by being there. By staying with him as long as he could.

"What's the thing?" Talon asked.

"What thing?"

"The thing you brought for me."

"Ah, that." The apple. He wanted to tell Talon, but there were Audiles in the tribe with hearing as keen as his sense of smell. And there was Vale, an even bigger problem. Perry couldn't risk Vale scenting it. With winter only weeks away, all the trading for the year was done. Vale would have questions about where Perry got the apple. He didn't need any more trouble with his brother than he already had.

"It has to wait until tomorrow." He'd have to give the apple to Talon a few miles away from the compound. For now it would stay wrapped in an old scrap of plastic, buried deep inside his satchel with the Dweller eyepiece.

"Is it good?"

Perry crossed his arms behind his head. "Come on, Tal. Can't believe you asked me that."

Talon muffled a giggle. "You smell like sweaty seaweed, Uncle Perry."

"Sweaty seaweed?"

"Yeah. The kind that's been on the rocks for a few days."

Perry laughed, nudging him in the ribs. "Thanks, Squeak."

Talon nudged him back. "You're welcome, Squawk."

They lay for a few minutes, breathing together in the quiet. Through a crack in the timbers, Perry could see a sliver of the Aether swirling in the sky. On calmer days, it was like being on the underside of waves, seeing the Aether roll and pitch above. Other times it flowed like rapids, furious and blazing blue. Fire and water, come together in the sky. Winter was the season for Aether storms, but in the past years the storms were starting earlier and lasting longer. Already they'd had a few. The last nearly wiped out the tribe's sheep, the flock too far from the compound to be brought to safety in time. Vale called it a phase, said the storms would lessen soon enough. Perry disagreed.

Talon shifted beside him. Perry knew he wasn't asleep. His nephew's temper had grown dark and damp. Eventually it tightened like a belt around Perry's heart. He swallowed, his throat raw and aching. "What is it, Talon?"

"I thought you'd left. I thought you dispersed after what happened with my dad."

Perry let out a slow breath. Four nights ago he and Vale had sat at the table below, passing a bottle back and forth. For the first time in what seemed like months, they'd talked as brothers. About Mila's death and about Talon. Even the best medicines Vale traded for weren't helping anymore. They didn't say it but both of them knew. Talon would be lucky to live through winter.

When Vale started to slur, Perry told himself to leave. Luster sweetened Perry but it did the opposite for Vale. Turned him rabid, just like it had their father. But Perry stayed because Vale was talking and so was he. Then Perry made a comment about moving the tribe away from the compound to safer land. A stupid comment. He knew where it'd lead, where it always led. Arguments. Angry words. This time Vale hadn't said anything. He'd just reached out and cuffed Perry across the jaw. Given him a sharp knock that had felt familiar and horrible at once.

He'd swung back, pure reflex, catching Vale on the nose, starting them both grabbing and swinging across the table. Next thing he knew, Talon stood at the bedroom door, sleepy and stunned. Perry had looked from Vale to Talon. Same serious green eyes, both pairs fixed on Perry. Asking him how could he give a new widower a bloody nose? In his own house and in front of his dying son?

Shamed and still in a fury, Perry had left. He'd gone straight to the Dweller fortress. Maybe Vale couldn't find medicines to help Talon, but he'd heard rumors about the Moles. So he'd broken in, wild and desperate to do something right. Now he had an apple and a useless Dweller eyepiece.

Perry pulled Talon close. "I was stupid, Tal. I wasn't thinking straight. That night should never have happened. But I do need to leave."

He should have done it already. Coming back meant seeing Vale. He didn't know if they could keep pacing around each other after what had happened. But Perry couldn't let that be the last memory Talon had, him slamming his fist into Vale's face.

"When will you go?" Talon asked.

"I thought I'd try . . . maybe I can hang on . . ." He swallowed. Words never came easy, even with Talon. "Soon. Sleep, Tal. I'm here now."

Talon buried his face into Perry's chest. Perry pinned his gaze on the Aether as Talon's cool tears seeped through his shirt. Through the crack above, he watched the blue flows circling, churning in eddies this way and that, like they weren't sure which way to go. People said that the Marked had the Aether flowing through their blood. Heating them up and giving them their Sense. It was just a saying, but Perry knew it had to be true. Most of the time he didn't think he was very different from the Aether at all.

It was a long while before Talon grew heavy in Perry's arms. By then his shoulder had gone numb, pinned beneath Talon's head, but he kept his nephew there and slept.

Perry dreamed he was back in the Dweller fire, following the girl. She ran ahead of him through the smoke and flames. He couldn't see her face but knew her raven-black hair. Knew her off-putting scent. He chased after her. Needed to reach her, though he didn't know why. He was just sure in that certain senseless way of dreams.

Perry woke sweated to his clothes with both his legs cramping. Some instinct kept him still when he wanted

39

to rub the soreness out of his muscles. Dust motes swirled in the dim loft, how he imagined scents must look, always churning through the air. Below, floorboards groaned with the sound of his brother moving around. Adding wood to the hearth. Getting the fire going again. Perry peered at the satchel by his feet, hoping the worn layer of plastic would keep Vale off the scents wrapped within.

The ladder creaked. Vale was climbing up. Talon slept curled against Perry's side, a small fist tucked under his chin, his brown hair wet with sweat. The creaking stopped.

Vale breathed just behind him, the sound loud in the quiet. Perry couldn't scent Vale's tempers. As brothers, their noses skipped past the tones, reading them as their own. But Perry imagined a bitter red scent.

He saw a knife reaching over him. For a panicked, mindless instant, Perry was shocked his brother would go about killing him this way. Challenges for Blood Lord were supposed to be held in the open, before the tribe. There was a way of things. But this had begun over the kitchen table. Wrong from the start. Talon would be hurt, no matter whether Perry left or died or won.

In the next instant, Perry realized it wasn't a knife. Only Vale's hand, reaching for Talon. He rested his hand on his son's head. Vale held it there a moment, brushing Talon's damp hair from his forehead. Then he padded down the ladder and across the room below. The loft flooded with light as the front door opened and closed, leaving the house in silence.

~ 5 ~

ARIA

A ria woke in a room she'd never seen before. She winced, pressing her fingers against the throbbing at her temples. Heavy fabric crinkled over her arms. She peered down. A white suit covered her from neck to feet. She wiggled her fingers inside loose-fitting gloves. Whose clothes was she wearing?

She sucked in a breath as she recognized the Medsuit. Lumina had told her about therapeutic garments like this. How could she be sick? Reverie's sterile environment eradicated disease. Genetic engineers like her mother kept them physically well. But she didn't feel well right now. Gingerly she turned her head left and right. Even the smallest movements brought shocking aches.

She sat up slowly, gasping at the sharp pinch in the crook of her elbow. A tube filled with clear liquid poked out of a patch in the suit by her arm and disappeared into the thick base of the bed. Her head pounded and her tongue was stuck to the roof of her mouth.

She sent a hurried message. *Lumina, something's happened. I don't know what's going on. Mom? Where are you?*

A steel counter ran along one side of the room. A regress screen sat on top, two-dimensional, like the sort used a long time ago. Aria saw a series of lines on it, the vital signals her suit transmitted.

Why was Lumina taking so long to respond?

Time and location, she requested from her Smarteye. Neither came up. Where *was* her Smartscreen?

Paisley? Caleb? Where are you?

Aria tried cruising to a beach Realm. One of her favorites. She stiffened as the wrong images streaked through her mind. Burning trees. Smoke that moved like waves. Paisley's wide-eyed terror. Soren *on top of her.*

She reached toward her left eye and poked herself, jerking back as she blinked. Nothing but a useless eyeball. She flattened her palm over her naked eye just as a slender man in a doctor's smock entered the room.

"Hello, Aria. You're awake."

"Doctor Ward," she said, momentarily relieved. Ward was one of her mother's colleagues, a quiet 5th Gen with a serious, square face. It wasn't unusual to only have one parent, but a few years earlier Aria had wondered if he was her father. Ward and Lumina were similar, both reserved and consumed by their work. But when Aria asked, Lumina had answered, *We have each other, Aria. That's everything we need.*

"Careful," Ward said. "You have a laceration along your brow that's not fully healed, but that's the worst of it. Your tests came out clear on everything else. No infection. No damage to your lungs. Remarkable results considering what you must have gone through."

Aria didn't move her hand. She knew how horrible she must look. "Where's my Smarteye? I can't get to the Realms. I'm stuck here. With no one." She bit her lip to keep from rambling.

"Your Smarteye appears to have been lost in the Ag 6 dome. I've ordered a new one for you. It should be ready in a few hours. In the meantime, I can increase the dosage of sedative—"

"No," she said quickly. "No sedatives." She understood now why her thoughts felt scrambled, like important things had been rearranged or lost altogether. "Where's my mother?"

"Lumina is in Bliss. The link has been down for a week."

Aria stared at him. A beeping from the monitor announced the spike in her heartbeat. How could she have forgotten? She'd gone into Ag 6 because of Lumina. But how could Lumina still be unreachable? She remembered resetting the Smarteye and seeing the "Songbird" file.

"That can't be right," she said. "My mother sent me a message."

Ward's eyebrows drew together. "She did? How do you know it was from her?"

"It was called 'Songbird.' Only Lumina calls me that."

"Did you see the message?"

"No, I didn't have a chance. Where's Paisley?"

Ward drew a slow breath before he spoke. "Aria, I am sorry to have to tell you this. Only you and Soren survived. I know you and Paisley were quite close."

Aria gripped the edges of the bed. "What are you saying?" she heard herself ask. "Are you saying Paisley's *dead*?" It wasn't possible. No one *died* at seventeen. They easily lived into their second centuries.

The monitor beeped. This time it was louder and persisted.

Ward was talking. "You left the secure zone . . . with disabled Smarteyes. . . . By the time we responded . . ."

All she heard was *beep-beep-beep-beep.*

Ward trailed off and looked at the medical screen. At a graph that showed, in rising lines and soaring numbers, the collapsing sensation inside her chest.

"I'm sorry, Aria," he said. The Medsuit stiffened, crinkling as it puffed around her limbs. Cold surged into her arm. She looked down. Blue liquid snaked its way through the tube and disappeared into her Medsuit. Into her. He had ordered the sedative through his Smarteye. Ward stepped closer. "Lay back now before you fall."

Aria wanted to tell him to stay away, but her lips grew numb and her tongue became a strange limp weight in her mouth. The room lurched to the side as the beeping slowed abruptly. Aria fell back, hitting the mattress with a thud.

Dr. Ward appeared above her, his face anxious. "I'm sorry," he said again. "It's the best thing for you now." Then he left, closing the door soundly behind him.

Aria tried to move. Her limbs felt weighted and pulled, like a magnet held her down. It took all her concentration to bring her hand toward her face. She scared herself, not recognizing the gloves over her fingers or the emptiness around her left eye.

She let her hand fall away, unable to control it any longer. Her arm slipped off the edge of the bed. She saw it, but she couldn't bring it back.

She closed her eyes. Had something happened to Lumina? Or was it Paisley? Her mind had filled with a thrumming sound, like a tuning fork deep within her skull. Soon she didn't have a clue what had saddened her.

She didn't know how much time had passed when Dr. Ward returned. Without a Smarteye, Aria felt like she didn't know anything.

"I'm sorry I had to sedate you." He paused, waiting for her to speak. She kept her eyes on the lights above, letting them burn spots into her vision. "They're ready to begin the investigation."

An investigation. Was she a criminal now? The Medsuit slackened around her. Ward stepped forward, clearing his throat. Aria flinched as he removed the needle from her arm. She could stand the pain, but not the feel of his hands on her. She pushed herself upright as soon as he stepped back, her mind reeling with dizziness.

"Follow me," he told her. "The Consuls are expecting you."

"The *Consuls*?" They were the most influential people in Reverie, governing all aspects of life in the Pod. "Consul Hess will be there? Soren's father?"

Dr. Ward nodded. "Of the five, he'll be the most engaged. He's the Director of Security."

"I can't see him! It was Soren's fault. He started the fire!"

"Aria, hush! Please don't say any more."

For a moment, they just stared at each other. Aria swallowed through a dry throat. "I can't tell the truth, can I?"

"It won't do you any good to lie," Ward said. "They have means to get at the truth."

She couldn't believe what she was hearing.

"Come. Any longer and they'll condemn you solely for making them wait."

Dr. Ward led her through a wide corridor that curved, so Aria couldn't see what lay ahead. The Medsuit forced her to walk with her legs and arms slightly apart. Between that and her stiff muscles, she felt like a zombie shuffling after him.

She noticed cracks and streaks of rust along the walls. Reverie had stood nearly three hundred years, but she had never seen signs of its age until now. She'd spent her whole life in the Panop, Reverie's vast and immaculate central dome. Most everything happened there, on forty levels that housed residential, schooling, repose, and dining areas, all organized around an atrium. Aria had never seen a single crack in the Panop, not that she'd bothered to search very hard.

The design was purposely repetitive and uninteresting to promote maximum use of the Realms. Everything in the real was kept bland, down to the grays they all wore. Now, as she followed Dr. Ward, she couldn't help wondering how many other parts of the Pod were deteriorating.

Ward stopped before an unmarked door. "I'll see you afterward." It sounded like a question.

Aria didn't see the five Reverie Consuls when she stepped into the room. That's how they always appeared in public address, the five speaking from a virtual, ancient Senate house. Only one man was seated at a table.

Soren's father. Consul Hess.

"Take a seat, Aria," Consul Hess said, indicating the metal chair across the table.

She sat and looked down, letting her hair fall in front of her bare eye. The room was a steel box, the walls pocked with dents. It smelled strongly of bleach.

"One moment," Consul Hess said as he stared through her.

Aria crossed her arms to hide her trembling hands. He was probably sifting through reports of the fire on his Smartscreen, or maybe talking with an expert on how to proceed.

Soren's father was a 12th Gen, well into his second century of life. She supposed he and Soren resembled each other, both being even-featured and stocky. But their likeness wasn't obvious. Aging-reversal treatments kept Consul Hess's skin as thin and tender-looking as an infant's, while Soren's tan made him look older. But like everyone over a hundred years old, Consul Hess's age showed in his eyes, which were sunken and dull as olive pits.

Aria's gaze moved to the chair next to her. It shouldn't be empty. Her mother should be there instead of hundreds of miles away. Aria had always tried to understand Lumina's dedication to her work. It wasn't easy, knowing as little about it as she did. "It's classified," Lumina said whenever Aria asked. "You know as much as I can tell. It's in the field of genetics. Important work, but not as important as you."

How could Aria believe her now? Where was she when Aria needed her?

Consul Hess's attention closed on her like a focusing lens. He hadn't spoken yet, but she knew he was studying her. He clicked his fingernails on the steel table. "Let's begin," he said finally.

"Shouldn't all the Consuls be here?"

"Consuls Royce, Medlen, and Tarquin are attending to protocol. They'll see our conversation later. Consul Young is with us."

Aria looked at his Smarteye, growing conscious of the missing weight on the left side of her face again. "He's not with me."

"Yes, true. You've been through an ordeal, haven't you? I'm afraid my son bears some responsibility for what happened. Soren's a natural code breaker. A difficult trait at this age, but one day he'll be quite useful."

Aria waited until she knew her voice would be steady.

"You spoke with him?"

"In the Realms only," Consul Hess said. "He won't be capable of speaking aloud for some time. New bones are being grown for his jaw. Much of the skin over his face will have to be regenerated. He will never look the same, but he survived. He was lucky . . . but not as lucky as you."

Aria looked down at the table. There was a long, deep scratch in the metal. She didn't want to picture Soren with disfiguring scars. She didn't want to picture him at all.

"Reverie hasn't suffered a security breach in over a century. It's both absurd and impressive that a group of Second Gens could do what Aether storms and Savages have not accomplished in so long." He paused. "You realize how close you came to destroying the entire Pod?"

She nodded without meeting his eyes. She'd known how dangerous it was to start a fire, but she'd sat and watched it happen. She should have done something sooner. Maybe she could've saved Paisley's life if she hadn't been so scared of Soren.

Aria's eyes blurred.

Paisley was dead.

How was it possible?

"With the nonfunctioning cameras in Ag 6 and your Smarteyes deactivated, we find ourselves in a bit of a primitive situation. We have only your accounts available to tell us what transpired that night." He leaned forward, his chair scraping softly on the floor. "I need you to tell me exactly what happened in that dome."

She glanced up, searching his cold stare for a clue. Had they found her Smarteye? Did Hess know about the recording? "What did Soren tell you?" she asked.

Consul Hess's lips thinned into a smile. "That's confidential, just as your testimony will be. Nothing will be divulged until the investigation is completed. Whenever you're ready."

She traced the scratch on the table with a gloved finger. How could she tell Consul Hess what a monster his son had become? She needed that Smarteye. Without it, they'd believe whatever story Soren gave them. Soren had said it himself in the agriculture dome.

"The sooner we settle this, the sooner you can go," Hess said. "You need time to grieve, as we all do. We've cancelled school and unessential work for the remainder of the week to allow for the healing to begin. I'm told your friend Caleb is organizing a tribute for Paisley." He paused. "And I can imagine how you're anxious to see your mother."

She tensed, looking up. "My mother? Ward said the link was still down."

Hess waved his hand dismissively. "Ward isn't on my staff. Lumina is quite worried about you. I've arranged for you to see her as soon as we're through."

Tears of relief wobbled on her lower eyelids. She was sure now. Lumina was all right. She'd probably tried to reach Aria while she was in Ag 6 and left the message when Aria hadn't been available. "When did you speak with her? Why was the link down for so long?"

"I'm not the one being questioned here, Aria. Your account. From the beginning."

She told him about shutting down their Smarteyes, slowly at first, but gaining confidence as she described the game of Rotball and the fire. Every word brought her nearer to seeing Lumina. When she got to the part where the boys chased her and Paisley, she faltered, her voice cracking. "When he—when Soren—tore off my Smarteye, I guess I went unconscious. I don't remember anything after that."

Consul Hess propped his arms on the table. "Why would Soren do that?"

"I don't know. Ask him."

Hess's dull gaze bored into her. Were the other Consuls feeding questions through him? "He said going there was your idea. That you were after information about your mother."

"It was his idea!" Aria cringed as the ache in her head flared. Sedatives. Pain. Grief. She didn't know what hurt most. "Soren wanted to go on a real adventure. He came ready to make fire. I just went because I thought he'd be able to tell me about Bliss."

"How did you come to be found in the exterior airlock?"

"I was? I don't know. I told you. I blacked out."

"Was someone else in there with you?"

"Someone *else*?" she said. Who else could have been in an off-limits dome? Aria tensed as a blurred image appeared in her mind. Had that truly happened? "There was . . . there was an Outsider."

"An Outsider," Consul Hess said evenly. "How do you think an Outsider came to be in Ag 6 on the same night you went there, at the same time Soren disabled the system?"

"Are you accusing me of letting a *Savage* into Reverie?"

"I'm simply asking questions. Why were you the only one brought to the safety of an airlock? Why weren't you attacked?"

"Your son attacked me!"

"Calm down, Aria. These questions are standard procedure, not intended to upset you. We need to gather facts."

She stared at Consul Hess's Smarteye, imagining she spoke directly to Consul Young. "If you want to gather facts," she said firmly, "then find my Smarteye. You'll see what happened."

Consul Hess's eyes widened with surprise, but he recovered quickly. "So you did make a recording. Not an easy feat with a deactivated Eye. Smart girl. Just like your mother." Hess tapped his fingers on the table a few times. "Your Eye is being searched for now. We'll find it. What did you capture in the recording?"

"Just what I told you. Your son going crazy."

He sat back in his chair, crossing his arms. "This puts me in a difficult position, doesn't it? But be assured that justice will be done. It's my responsibility to keep the Pod safe, above all else. Thank you, Aria. You've been very helpful. Can you manage a few hours of transport? Your mother is eager to see you."

"You mean actually go to Bliss?"

"That's right. I have a transport waiting. Lumina insisted on seeing you in the flesh to be certain you're receiving the proper care. She's quite persuasive, isn't she?"

Aria nodded, a smile stirring inside her. She could just imagine their showdown. Lumina had a scientist's patience. She never stopped until she had the result she wanted. "I'm fine. I can go." She wasn't anywhere close to fine, but she'd pretend to be if it got her to Lumina.

"Good." Consul Hess stood. Two men dressed in blue Reverie Guardian suits entered the room, crowding it with their imposing size, while two more stayed outside. They stared at her face, where her Smarteye should have been. Aria decided there was no use covering her naked eye anymore. She rose from the table, fighting off a riot of aches in her joints and muscles.

"Take good care of her," Consul Hess said to the Guardians. "Get well, Aria."

"Thank you, Consul Hess."

He smiled. "No need to thank me. It's the least I could do after all you've been through."

6

PEREGRINE

Perry pulled his satchel and bow over his shoulder and stepped outside with Talon late the next morning. Fishermen and farmers milled around the clearing. Too many people, mingling like the workday was done. Perry dropped a hand on Talon's shoulder, stopping him.

"Are we getting raided?" Talon asked.

"No," Perry answered. The scents rolling past didn't carry enough panic for a raid. "Must be the Aether." The blue swirls looked brighter than they had overnight. Perry caught glimpses of them stirring above thick rain clouds. "Your father's probably called everyone in."

"But it doesn't look so bad."

"Not yet," Perry said. Like all the stronger Scires, he could anticipate Aether storms. The prickling sensation in the back of his nose told him the sky would still need to take a turn for the worse before it became a threat. But Vale never took chances with the Tides' safety.

At the mercy of his growling stomach, Perry steered Talon toward the cookhouse. He noticed his nephew favoring his right leg. It wasn't a terrible limp. Hardly even obvious. But when a pack of boys came yelling and drumming up dust, Talon stopped walking. The boys shot by. Wiry mutts, lean from work and meager meals, not illness. A few months ago, Talon had been at the head of that pack.

Perry swept his nephew up over his shoulder, hanging Talon upside down and making a show of having fun. Talon laughed but Perry knew he was putting on a show too. He knew Talon ached to run with his friends. To have his legs again.

The smell of onion and woodsmoke hung in the cool dimness of the cookhouse. This was the largest structure in the compound. Where they ate. Where Vale held gatherings in the winter months. A dozen large trestle tables took up one side, with Vale's head table on an elevated stone platform to the rear. To the other, behind a half wall of brick, there was a cooking hearth, a row of iron stoves, and several worktables that hadn't held food with any plenty in years.

The day's haul ended up there, from the fields and the sea. Whatever else Perry and the other hunters managed to bring in. Everything went there to be shared among the families. The Tides were fortunate to have an underground river running through their valley. Made irrigating easy. But having all the water in the world didn't help when the Aether storms came, scorching stretches of land. This year, their scarred fields hadn't yielded nearly enough to fill their stores for the winter. The tribe would be eating because of Perry's sister, Liv.

Four cows. Eight goats. Two dozen chickens. Ten sacks of grain. Five bags of dried herbs. They were just some of the things Liv's marriage to a northern Blood Lord had bought the Tides. "I'm expensive," Liv had joked the day she left, but neither Perry nor his best friend, Roar, had laughed. Half of the payment for her had already arrived. They expected the other half any day, after Liv reached her intended husband. They needed it soon, before winter came in force.

Right away Perry spotted a cluster of Audiles at a table in the back, bent close as they whispered. Perry shook his head. The Ears were always whispering. A moment later, he caught a vibrant green wave, bracing as cypress leaves. Their excitement. Probably someone had overheard his tussle with Vale.

Perry set Talon on the brick bar, ruffling his hair. "Brought you a weasel today, Brooke. Best I could do. You know how it's been out there."

Brooke looked up from the onion she chopped and smiled. She wore one of his arrowheads on a leather cord as a necklace, drawing his eyes down. She looked good today. Brooke always looked good. Her sharp blue eyes narrowed on Perry's cheek for an instant, then she winked at Talon.

"He's a cute little thing. Bet he tastes good." She tipped her head toward the large pot hanging over the fire. "Toss him in there."

"Brooke, I'm not a weasel!" Talon giggled as Perry scooped him up.

"Hang on, Perry," Brooke said. She dished out bowls of gruel for them. "We might as well get him good and fat before we cook him."

He and Talon took a table by the door as always, where Perry could best catch drafts from outside. They might give him a few moments of warning if Vale showed up. Perry noticed that Wylan and Bear, Vale's best men, sat with the Auds. That meant Vale was probably hunting alone.

Perry wolfed down the barley porridge so the flavors wouldn't linger in his mouth. Being a Scire also meant having a great sense of taste. Wasn't always a good thing. The bland mash soaked up traces of other meals from the wooden bowl, leaving the rancy aftertaste of salt fish, goat's milk, and turnips on his tongue. He went back for another helping because he knew Brooke would give it to him, and food was food. When he finished, he sat back and crossed his arms, feeling only mildly hungry and more than a little guilty for filling himself at the price of his sister's happiness.

Talon had stirred his food for a while, making lumpy mounds with his spoon. Now he looked everywhere but at his bowl. It pained Perry to see his nephew looking so drawn.

"We're hunting, right?" Perry asked. Hunting would give him an excuse to get Talon away from the compound. Perry wanted to give him the apple, Talon's favorite. Vale always bought a few in secret just for Talon when traders brought them around.

Talon stopped stirring. "But the Aether."

"I'll keep us clear of it. Come on, Tal. We could go for a bit."

Talon scrunched his nose, leaned forward, and whispered, "I can't leave the compound anymore. My father said."

Perry frowned. "When did he say that?"

"Umm . . . the day after you left?"

Perry pushed down a flare of anger, wanting to keep his nephew from feeling it too. How could Vale deny him hunting? Talon loved it. "We could be back before he knew."

"Uncle Perry . . ."

Perry glanced over his shoulder, following Talon's line of vision to the table in the back. "What, you think the Ears heard me?" he asked, though he knew they had. Perry whispered a few suggestions to the Auds. Ideas for what they could go do to themselves, rather than listen to other people's conversations. His suggestions brought several hard stares.

"Look at that, Talon. You're right. They can hear me. Should've known. I can smell Wylan from here. You think that reek's coming from his *mouth*?"

Talon grinned. He'd lost a few milk teeth. His smile had the look of calico corn. "It smells like it's coming from his south side."

Perry leaned back and laughed.

"Shut up, Peregrine," Wylan called out. "You heard him. He's not supposed to leave. You want Vale to know what you're doing?"

"Your choice, Wylan. Tell Vale or not. You want to deal with him or me?"

Perry knew the answer. Vale's form of punishment meant halved rations. Outhouse duty. Extra rounds of night watch in the winter. Miserable, all, but to a vain critter like Wylan, better than the beating Perry could give him. So when the whole lot of Auds stood and charged him, Perry nearly knocked the bench over getting up. He put himself in the alley between the tables, Talon well behind him.

Wylan, at the lead, stopped a few paces away. "Peregrine, you streaky idiot. Something's going on outside."

It took Perry a moment to understand. They'd heard something outside and were simply heading out. He stepped aside as the Auds poured past him, the rest of the cookhouse hurrying after.

Perry went back to Talon. His nephew's bowl had spilled. Gruel dripped through a knot in the table. "I thought . . ." He glared at the worn planks. "You know what I thought."

Talon knew better than anyone how Perry's blood was primed. He'd always had an edge, but it was getting worse. Lately, if there was a scuffle to be had, Perry found a way to mix himself into it. The Aether in his blood was gathering, growing stronger every year with the storms. He felt like his body had a will of its own. Always looking. Preparing for the only fight that would satisfy him.

But he couldn't have that fight. In a challenge for Blood Lord, the loser died or was forced to disperse. Perry couldn't imagine leaving Talon fatherless. And he couldn't force his brother and his sick nephew out in the open. There were no laws in the borderlands beyond tribe territories, only survival.

That left one choice. He needed to leave. Dispersing was the best thing he could do for Talon. It meant that Talon could stay and live out the rest of his days in the safety of the compound. It also meant he'd never help the Tides like he knew he could.

Outside, people crowded around the clearing. The afternoon air thickened with excited tempers. Brisk scents. But no traces of fear. Dozens of voices chattered, muddled to his ears, but the Auds had surely overheard something to make them dart outside. Perry caught sight of Bear creating a wake as he moved through the crowd. Wylan and a few others followed him out beyond the compound.

"Perry! Up here!"

Brooke stood on the tile roof of the cookhouse, waving him up. Perry wasn't surprised to see her already there. He climbed the farming crates stacked to the side of the structure, pulling Talon up with him.

From the roof, he had a good view of the hills that formed the Tides' eastern border. Farmland stretched back in a patchwork of browns and greens, woven through by a line of trees that followed the underground river. Perry could also see the stretches of Aether-blackened earth where the funnels had struck early in the spring.

"There," Brooke said.

He searched where she pointed. He was a Seer like Brooke, saw better than most during the day, but his real strength lay in seeing in the dark. He knew of no other Seer like him and tried not to call attention to his vision.

Perry shook his head, unable to make out anything distinctive in the distance. "You know I'm better at night."

Brooke shot him a flirty smile. "I sure do."

He grinned at her. Couldn't think of anything to say besides, "Later."

She laughed and turned her keen blue eyes back to the distance. She was a strong Seer, the best in the tribe since her younger sister Clara had disappeared. More than a year had passed since Clara had gone missing, but Brooke hadn't given up on her coming home. Perry scented her hope now. Then how it wilted with disappointment.

"It's Vale," she said. "He's bringing in something big. It looks like a buck."

Perry should have been relieved it was only his brother coming home from hunting. Not another tribe raiding them for food. But he wasn't.

Brooke stepped toward him, her gaze settling on his bruised cheek. "That looks like it hurts, Per." She traced a finger along his face in a way that didn't hurt at all. When her floral scent reached him, he couldn't stop himself from bringing her closer.

Most girls in the tribe were wary around him. He understood, considering his shaky future with the Tides. Not Brooke. More than once as they'd lain together in the warm summer grass, she'd whispered into his ear about them becoming the ruling pair. He liked Brooke, but that would never happen. He'd choose another Scire to be with someday, keeping with his strongest Sense. But Brooke never gave up. Not that he minded.

"So it's true what happened with you and Vale?" she said.

Perry let out a slow breath. There were no secrets with Auds around. "Vale didn't do this."

Brooke smiled like she didn't believe him. "Everyone's down there, Perry. It's the perfect time to challenge him."

He stepped back and swallowed a curse. She wasn't a Scire. She could never understand how it felt to be rendered. No matter how much he wanted to be Blood Lord, he could never hurt Talon.

"I see him!" Talon said from the edge of the roof.

Perry darted to his side. Vale was crossing the dirt field that skirted the compound, near enough for all to see. He was tall, like Perry, but seven years older; he had a man's build. The Blood Lord chain around his neck shone under the light of the sky. Scire Markings coiled around Vale's biceps. One band on each arm, single and proud, unlike the two cluttering Perry's. Vale's Naming Mark cut a line on the skin over his heart, rising and falling like the lines of their valley. He had his dark hair pulled back, giving Perry a clear view of his eyes. They were steady and calm as ever. Behind Vale, on a litter made of branches and rope, rested his quarry.

The buck looked to be well over two hundred pounds. The head was doubled back to keep the enormous rack from dragging. A ten pointer. A huge animal.

Below, the drum began to pound a deep rhythm. The other instruments joined in, playing the Hunter's Song. A song that got Perry's heart pounding every time he heard it.

People ran toward Vale. They took the litter from his hands. They brought him water and praised him. A buck that size would fill all their stomachs. A beast like that was a rare sign of bounty. A good omen for the winter ahead. For the following growing season as well. That was why Vale had called the tribe back to the compound. He wanted everyone there to see him coming home with his prize.

Perry looked down at his shaking hands. That buck should have been his kill. He should be the one hauling in that litter. He couldn't believe Vale's luck. How had he brought in a buck like that when Perry hadn't tracked one all year? Perry knew he was a better hunter. He gritted his teeth, pushing back his next thought, but failing. He'd be a better Blood Lord, too.

"Uncle Perry?" Talon stared up at him, his scrawny chest heaving for breath. Perry saw all the jealous rage inside of him crossing his nephew's drawn face. Tangling up with Talon's fear. He breathed in the desperate mix they made and knew he should never have come back.

7

ARIA

Aria followed the Guardians through the curving corridors. She wanted out of the real, where things rusted and cracked. Where people died in fires. She wished she had her new Smarteye so she could fraction and escape to a Realm. She could be gone right now, somewhere else.

She began to notice more Guardians in the halls and in passing glimpses of chambers that looked like cafeterias and meeting rooms. She knew most of them by face, but they were strangers. They weren't people she meshed with in the Realms.

The Guardians brought her through an airlock chamber labeled DEFENSE & EXTERNAL REPAIRS 2. She stopped in her tracks as she entered a transportation hub larger than any space she'd ever seen. Hovercrafts were lined in rows, rounded iridescent vehicles she'd only seen in the Realms before. The sleek ships looked hunched, like insects poised to take flight. Aerial runways marked by blue beams of light floated in the air above. Laughter erupted from a cluster of Guardians in the distance, the sound small and stifled by the drone of generators. She'd been within walking distance of this hangar her entire life. All of this went on in Reverie, and she'd never known it.

One of the Hovers in the distance lit up with a shimmering glow. It hit her then. She was actually leaving. She never thought she'd leave Reverie. This Pod was her home. But it didn't feel the same. She'd seen its rotten fruit and rusted walls. She'd seen machines that turned her mind blank and her limbs into anchors. *Soren* was here. And Paisley wasn't. How could she go back to her life without Paisley? She couldn't. She needed to leave. More than anything, she needed her mother. Lumina would know how to make things right again.

Eyes blurring, she followed the Guardians to a Dragonwing. She recognized the vehicle. It was the fastest model of Hovers, built for raw speed. Aria climbed the metal steps, hesitating at the top. When would she come back?

"Keep moving," said a Guardian with black gloves. The cabin was surprisingly small, lit with dim blue light, with seats along both sides.

"Right here," said the man. She sat where he indicated and fumbled with the thick restraints, her fingers useless through the Medsuit. She should've asked for grays, but she hadn't wanted to waste time and risk Hess changing his mind.

The man took the straps from her and fastened them with

a series of snaps. Then he sat on the opposite side with five other men. They ran through coordinates using military jargon she hardly understood, falling silent as the door sealed with a sound like a gasp. The craft whirred to life, vibrating, buzzing like a million bees. Near the cockpit, something inside a cabinet shook, creating a metallic chatter. The noise set off her headache again. A cloying chemical taste slid into her mouth.

"How long is the journey?" she asked.

"Not long," said the man who'd buckled her in. He closed his eyes. Most of the other Guardians did too. Did they always do that? Or were they just trying to avoid staring at the blank spot over her left eye?

The lurch of liftoff pressed her down into the seat, then sideways, as the craft thrust into motion. With no windows to peer through, Aria strained to listen. Had they left the hangar? Were they on the outside yet?

She swallowed the bitter taste on her tongue. She needed water and the seat straps were too tight. She couldn't draw in a full breath without pushing against them. She began to feel light-headed, like she couldn't get enough air. Aria ran through vocal scales in her mind, battling against the shrill note of her headache. Scales always calmed her.

The Dragonwing slowed much sooner than she'd expected. Half an hour? Aria knew she wasn't tracking time properly, but it couldn't have been long.

The Guardians pressed at wrist pads on their gray suits and donned their helmets, moving in quick, practiced movements. Soft light glowed from within their visors, shining clear through their Smarteyes. Aria looked around the cabin. Why hadn't she been given a helmet?

The black-gloved man stood and unfastened her seat restraint. She finally drew a deep breath, but didn't feel satisfied. A strange weightlessness had come over her.

"Are we there?" she asked. She hadn't felt them land. The Hover still hummed with noise.

The Guardian's voice projected through a speaker in his helmet. "You are."

The door opened with a blast of light. Hot air gusted into the cabin. Aria blinked furiously, willing her eyes to adjust. She didn't see a hangar. She didn't see anything that looked like Bliss. Empty land ran clear to the horizon. Desert, reaching as far as she could see. Nothing more. She didn't understand. Couldn't accept what she saw.

A hand clamped onto her wrist. She screamed and reeled back. "Let go of me!" She grabbed the seat restraints, clutching them with all her strength.

Hard hands fell on her shoulders, crushing her muscles, tearing her from the straps. They pulled her toward the edge in an instant. She looked down at her cloth-covered feet. They were inches from the metal lip. Much farther below, she saw cracked red earth.

"Please! I didn't do anything!"

A Guardian came up behind her. She caught a glimpse of him as his foot crashed into the small of her back, and then she was falling through the air.

She pressed her lips together as she struck the earth. Pain speared through her knees and elbows. Her temple smacked against the ground. She stifled a cry because making any sound—because even *breathing*—meant death. Aria lifted her head and stared at her fingers splayed on rust-colored dirt.

She was touching the outside. She was in the Death Shop.

She turned as the hatch closed, catching her last glance of the Guardians. Another Dragonwing floated beside it, both glistening like blue pearls. A buzzing sound shook the air around her as they glided away, kicking up clouds of red dirt as they sped across the flat expanse.

Aria's lungs tightened in spasms, aching for oxygen. She covered her mouth and nose with her sleeve. She couldn't fight the need to draw air any longer. She inhaled and exhaled at the same time, choking, her eyes watering as she fought to settle back into her breath. She watched the Hovercrafts blend into the distance and marked the spot where they disappeared. When she could no longer see them, she sat staring at the desert. It looked bleak and barren in every direction. The quiet was so complete she could hear herself swallow.

Consul Hess had lied to her.

He'd *lied*. She'd been prepared for some kind of punishment when the investigation was done, but not this. She realized Consul Young hadn't been watching her interview through Hess's Smarteye. She'd been alone with Hess. His report would probably say she'd died in Ag 6, along with Paisley, Echo, and Bane. Hess would blame her for thinking up the night and letting in a Savage, too. He'd probably tied up all his problems and tossed them out with her.

She stood, her legs trembling as she fought waves of dizziness. The heat of the earth soaked through the fabric of her Medsuit, warming the soles of her feet. As though on cue, her suit blew a rush of cool air over her back and stomach. She almost laughed. The Medsuit was still regulating her temperature.

She looked up. Thick gray clouds blotted the sky. In the gaps, she saw Aether. Real Aether. The flows ran above the clouds. They were beautiful, like lightning trapped in liquid currents, thin as veils in some places. In others, they gathered in thick bright streams. The Aether didn't look like something that could put an end to the world, yet that had nearly happened during the Unity.

For six decades, when the Aether came, it had scorched the earth with constant fires, but the real blow to humanity had been its mutative effect, as her mother had explained to her. New diseases had evolved rapidly and thrived. Plagues had wiped out entire populations. Her ancestors had been among the fortunate few who'd taken shelter in the Pods.

Shelter she no longer had.

Aria knew she couldn't survive in this contaminated world. She hadn't been designed for it. Death was only a matter of time.

She found the brighter patch in the cloud cover, where light shone through in a golden haze. That light came from the sun. She might get to see the real sun. She had to fight off the urge to cry, thinking about seeing the sun. Because who would know? Who would she tell about seeing something so incredible?

She headed toward where the Rovers had disappeared, knowing it was pointless. Did she think Consul Hess would change his mind? But where else could she go? She walked with feet she didn't recognize on earth that looked like giraffe print.

She hadn't taken more than a dozen steps when she started to cough again. Soon she grew too light-headed to stand. But it wasn't just her lungs rejecting the outside. Her eyes and nose streamed. Her throat burned and her mouth filled with hot saliva.

She'd heard all the stories about the Death Shop, like everyone else. A million ways to die. She knew of the packs of wolves as smart as men. She'd heard of the flocks of crows that picked living people to pieces, and Aether storms that behaved like predators. But the worst death in the Death Shop, she decided, was rotting alone.

8

PEREGRINE

Perry watched as his older brother strode into the clearing. Vale paused and lifted his head, scenting the wind. He held the buck's rack in his hand, a huge snarl of horns, thick as a small tree. Impressive. Perry couldn't deny it. Vale searched the crowd and spotted Perry, then Talon at his side.

Perry became aware of a dozen things as his brother came forward. The Dweller device and the apple, both wrapped in plastic, deep inside his satchel. His knife at his hip. His bow and quiver slung across his back. He noticed the way the crowd quieted, easing into a circle around him. He sensed Talon shift at his side, drawing back. And he scented tempers. Dozens of bright scents, charging the air as much as the Aether above.

"Hello, Son." Vale ached, gazing at his boy. Perry saw it in his eyes. He also saw the swelling around Vale's nose, but wondered if anyone else would notice.

Talon raised a hand in reply, keeping back. He didn't want to show weakness in front of his father. How he hurt, both from grief and illness. Once it had been Perry hiding from his father behind Vale's legs. But hiding didn't work around Scires. Scents carried.

Vale raised the rack. "For you, Talon. Choose a horn. We'll make a handle for a new knife. Would you like that?"

Talon shrugged. "All right."

Perry glanced at the knife at Talon's belt. It was Perry's old blade. As a boy, he had carved feathers into the handle, making a design fit for him and later, Talon. He saw no reason for him to have a new one.

Vale finally met his gaze. He looked at the bruise on Perry's face, suspicion flashing in his eyes. Vale would know he hadn't given it to Perry. He hadn't landed any solid punches that night across the table.

"What happened to you, Peregrine?"

Perry went still. He couldn't tell Vale the truth, but lying wouldn't help him either. No matter what he said, people would think Vale had given him the bruise, just as Brooke had. Blaming someone else for it would only make him look weak.

"Thanks for caring, Vale. It's good to be home." Perry nodded at the rack. "Where'd you bring him down?"

"Moss Ledge."

Perry couldn't believe he'd missed picking up the buck's scent. He'd been out that way recently.

Vale smiled. "Fine beast, don't you think, little brother? Best one in years."

Perry glared at his older brother, holding back the bitter words that sprang to his lips. Vale knew it annoyed Perry to be called this in front of the tribe. He was no longer a boy. There was nothing little about him.

"Still think we have overhunted?" Vale added.

Perry was sure of it. The animals had left. They'd sensed the Aether growing stronger each passing year in their valley. Perry sensed it too. But what could he say? Vale held proof there was still game like that out there, ready to be brought in. "We should still move," he said without thinking.

A smile spread over Vale's face. "Move, Perry? Do you mean that?"

"The storms will only get worse."

"This cycle will play out as they all do."

"In time, maybe. But we may not survive the worst of it here."

A stir ran through the crowd. He and Vale might argue like this in private, but no one crossed Vale in front of others.

Vale shifted his feet. "Then tell us about your idea, Perry. About moving more than two hundred people into the open. Do you think we'd be better off *without* shelter? Fighting for our lives in the borderlands?"

Perry swallowed hard. He knew what he knew. He just never said it well. But he couldn't back down now.

"The compound won't hold up if the storms get much worse. We're losing our fields. We'll lose everything if we stay. We need to find safer land."

"Where do you want us to go?" Vale asked. "You think

73

another tribe will welcome us into their territory? All of us?"

Perry shook his head. He wasn't sure. He and Vale were Marked. Worth something, purely for their blood. But not the others, the Unmarked, who weren't Scires or Auds or Seers. Who made up most of the tribe.

Vale's eyes narrowed. "What if the storms are worse in other territories, Peregrine?"

Perry couldn't answer. He wasn't sure if the Aether raged elsewhere as it did there. He only knew that last winter, the storms torched nearly a quarter of their territory. This winter, he expected, would be worse.

"We leave this land, we die," Vale said, his tone suddenly hard. "Try thinking once in a while, little brother. It might serve you."

"You're wrong," Perry said. Didn't anyone else see that?

Several people gasped. He could almost hear their thoughts through their excited tempers. *Fight, Perry. This'll be good to see.*

Vale handed the rack to Bear. It grew so quiet that Perry heard Bear's leather vest squeak as he moved. Perry's vision started tunneling as it did when he hunted. He saw only his older brother, who'd defended Perry countless times as a boy, but who didn't believe him now. Perry glanced at Talon. He couldn't do this. What if he killed Vale right there?

Talon shot forward. "Can we hunt, Father? Can Uncle Perry and I hunt?"

Vale looked down, the darkness in his gaze vanishing. "Hunt, Talon? Now?"

"I feel good today." Talon lifted his small chin. "Can we go?"

"Are you so eager to show me up, Son?"

"Yes!"

Vale's deep laugh roused a few forced chuckles from the crowd.

"Please, Father. Just for a while?"

Vale raised his eyebrows at Perry, like he thought it fitting that Talon had stepped in to rescue him. That look nearly launched Perry forward.

Vale knelt and opened his arms. Talon hugged him, his skinny arms closing around Vale's broad neck. Covering the Blood Lord chain. Stealing it from Perry's sight.

"We'll feast tonight," Vale said, easing back. He cradled Talon's face with his hands. "I'll save the best cuts for you." He straightened and motioned Wylan over. "Make sure they stay close to the compound."

"We don't need him," Perry said. Did Vale think he couldn't protect Talon? And he didn't want Wylan along. If the Aud came, he couldn't give Talon the apple. "I'll keep him safe."

Vale's green eyes settled on Perry's swollen cheek. "Little brother, if you saw yourself, you'd know why I don't believe that."

More laughter, unchecked this time. Perry shifted on his feet. The Tides saw him as a joke.

Talon pulled his arm. "Let's go, Uncle Perry. Before it gets late."

Perry's muscles filled with the need to move, but he couldn't give his brother his back. Talon let go of him and ran ahead in pitiful lurching strides.

"Come on, Uncle Perry. Let's go!"

For Talon, Perry followed.

ARIA

When the coughing fit passed, Aria lay on her side. Her ribs hurt. Her throat was swollen and sore. But she'd survived. Her skin hadn't melted off and she hadn't gone into shock. Maybe the stories were wrong. Or maybe that would come.

She hauled herself to her feet and began to walk again. She'd accepted that she wouldn't get anywhere. What mattered was *pretending* she might. That by taking one step after another, she had a chance of finding shelter. She convinced herself of this so completely that when she saw rough shapes in the distance, she thought she was imagining them.

Aria walked faster, heart pounding as the forms became more distinct and the ground grew uneven with debris. Broken pieces poked through the soles of her Medsuit, hurting her feet. She stopped, scanning a sea of cement.

Pieces of iron stuck out of the rubble, sculptural, bent and rusted. A great city once, she thought. Defiant, here in the middle of nowhere. Now it wouldn't even provide shelter for her. She pointed herself in another direction and set off again.

She avoided her thoughts as long as possible, but they came, stampeding beyond her control. Ward had seen her alive. Had Hess pressured him to keep quiet? Was her mother grieving now? What had Lumina said in the "Songbird" message?

Aria sat down to rest. She remembered the last time she'd been with her mother in Reverie. A Singing Sunday.

At eleven o'clock every Sunday of her life, Aria had met her mother in the Paris Opera Realm, a replica of the lavish Palais Garnier. Lumina was always there first, waiting with her hands folded neatly in her lap, her back straight in her favorite front row seat. She came dressed the same way every time, in an elegant black dress, a thin strand of pearls around her slender neck, her dark hair pulled back in a tight, perfect bun.

For an hour, on a stage built for four hundred performers, Aria sang to her. She became Juliet or Isolde or Joan of Arc, singing about doomed love and grand purpose and resilience in the face of death. Aria let their stories soar on her dark falcon soprano voice, across gilded columns and crimson curtains, up to a fresco of angels. She performed every week for Lumina because her mother was there for that hour, and that was more time than Aria got from her all week.

She did it, though she hated opera. She hated everything about it. The overblown sense of drama. The violence and lewdness. No one had ever died of heartbreak in Reverie. Betrayal never led to murder. Those things didn't happen anymore. They had the Realms now. They could experience anything without taking risks. Now, life was *Better than Real*.

Her last Singing Sunday with Lumina had been different from the start. Lumina's cool hand on Aria's bare shoulder had jarred her awake.

"What is it?" Aria had asked. Her Smartscreen read 5 A.M. "What's wrong?"

Lumina was perched at the edge of the bed. She wore a gray traveling jumpsuit with reflective stripes along the arms, not her usual doctor's smock. Somehow she still looked elegant. "The transport team wants to avoid some weather. I need to leave earlier than planned."

Aria swallowed the tight feeling in her throat. She didn't want to say good-bye. They'd planned to meet every day in the Realms, but Lumina would be far. They wouldn't be in the same Pod anymore.

"Will you sing to me now?"

"Mom, *now*?"

"I look forward to this all week," Lumina said. "Don't make me wait until next Sunday."

Aria flopped facedown on her pillow. Opera first thing in the morning? It seemed criminal. "Why do you have to leave? Why can't you just do your research in the Realms?"

"I need to be in Bliss for this assignment."

"Why can't I go with you?" Aria asked.

"You know I can't tell you why."

Aria pressed her face deeper into the pillow. How could her mother sound so calm? She made it seem so easy to keep things from Aria.

"Please," Lumina said. "I don't have much time."

"Fine." Aria rolled over and glared at the ceiling. "Let's just get it over with." She found the Opera Realm on her Smartscreen. The icon should've showed the columned front facade of the opera house, but Aria had changed it to an image of her pretending to choke herself. She chose it and fractioned, her mind easily opening to another world. She was in two places now. There, in her cramped little room, and in the extravagant, cavernous opera hall.

Aria had chosen to appear behind the main curtain. She glared at the heavy swath of red velvet. Lumina could wait a few more seconds. That would irritate her. When she stepped through, she didn't see Lumina in her usual front row seat. The opera house was empty.

In Aria's bedroom, Lumina leaned forward, resting her hand on Aria's arm. "Songbird. Will you sing to me here?"

Aria yanked herself out of the Realm and sat up, stunned. "*Here?* In *my room?*"

"I won't be able to hear your real voice once I'm in Bliss."

Aria pushed her hair behind her ears, panic coiling in her gut. She looked around the tiny room, at the neat drawers built into the walls and the mirror above her sink. She knew her voice. She knew its power. Her voice would shake the walls in such a confined space. It might carry beyond the small living room outside and make it out to the Panop.

What if *everyone* heard her?

Her heart began to race. This had never happened before. It was too strange. Too big a change from their routine. "You know it's the same as in the Realms, Mom."

Lumina's gray eyes bored into her, urgent and pleading. "I want to hear the gift you have."

"It's not a gift!" Aria cried. It was genetics. Lumina loved opera, so she'd crafted Aria's DNA with enhanced vocal traits to create a daughter who could sing to her. If it was a gift Aria had, then it was a gift Lumina had given to herself. Her own personal songbird, Lumina's pet name for her. Aria had never seen any sense in her upgrade. No one sang outside of the Realms—at least Soren's tan made him look good in the real—but that's what she got for being a geneticist's daughter.

"Please do this for me," Lumina said.

She wanted to ask *why* again. *Why*, when Lumina only seemed to care about work or opera. Why should she do anything for her mother, who was leaving her? Instead she rolled her eyes and threw back the covers.

Lumina held out grays for her, but Aria shook her head. If this was going to be different, then it would be *really* different. She waved a hand over her scant underclothes. "I'll sing like this."

Lumina pursed her lips, unamused. "Will you perform my aria?"

"No, no, Mom. I've got something better," Aria said, hardly able to contain the smirk on her face. Lumina folded her hands together, suspicion lurking in her gaze. Aria drew in a few breaths, and then she sang.

> *Your heart is like cannibal candy*
> *Cannibal candy, cannibal candy*
> *Your heart is like cannibal candy*
> *And I've got a sweet tooth for you!*

She laughed her way through the last lyrics, one of her favorite Tilted Green Bottles songs. But then she felt bad when she saw Lumina's face. Not because her mother looked disappointed. She didn't. But Aria knew she was hiding it, and for some reason that made it worse.

Lumina stood and gave Aria a quick embrace. Her cool hand lingered on Aria's cheek. "That's quite a tune, Songbird," she said, and left.

After that Sunday, something had changed between them. Aria dropped her daily voice lessons, not caring if it upset Lumina. She gave up Singing Sundays, too. She wouldn't give her mother that hour anymore. Lumina had still checked in with her every night from Bliss, as promised, but their visits had been strained. She'd been so stupid. Aria saw that now. She'd wasted the time by acting sullen and bored. All she'd really wanted was for Lumina to come home.

The Medsuit crinkled as she crossed her arms. The light was fading across the desert, but the Aether looked brighter.

It flowed in glowing blue rivers across the sky. Aria's breath came faster as the need to sing built inside her.

She sang the *Tosca* aria—the one she'd refused to sing the morning Lumina had left—but the words came out choked, in crumbling, broken sounds. Sounds that weren't worth hearing. She stopped herself after a few verses and hugged her knees. She'd give anything to be in the opera hall with Lumina now.

"I'm sorry, Mom," she whispered to the emptiness around her. "I didn't know it was the last time."

10

PEREGRINE

Perry set their course toward the ocean and let Wylan pull ahead. He kept his pace slow, not wanting to push Talon. As they crested the last sand dune, the bay unfolded around them. The tide was clear and blue, like it had been when he'd swam last night. People said the water had always been clean before the Unity. Never coated with foam or reeking of dead fish. Plenty of things had been different then.

As soon as they reached the beach, Wylan put on his Aud cap, pulling the padded flaps down over his ears. With the wind and the surf crashing, he apparently had more noise than he wanted, just as Perry had hoped.

Perry staked his quiver in the sand and took his bow. A few seabirds wheeled in the clouded Aether sky. They made meager catchings, scrawny as they were, but good practice for Talon. Timing was important. Gauging the wind. Reading the animal.

Talon did well enough, but Perry saw how he grew tired. The draw weight of Perry's bow was too great, and he wished he'd thought to bring Talon's bow along. Perry took a few shots also. He didn't miss once. His aim was never sharper than when his blood was up. After a time, Wylan grew bored of watching and walked off.

"Want to see what I've got for you?" Perry said, keeping his voice low.

Talon frowned. "What? Oh, yeah."

He'd forgotten Perry had a surprise for him. That raised an ache in Perry's throat. He had a fair idea what was pulling Talon's temper down. Pulling him down too.

"You have to keep quiet about it, all right?" Perry dug inside his satchel for the plastic bundle. He brought out the apple, leaving the eyepiece in the plastic.

Talon stared at it for a few moments. "You saw traders?"

Perry gave a slight shake of his head. "Tell you later." Wylan might have his cap on, but he was one of the keenest Auds Perry knew. "Better get to it, Squeak."

Talon ate half the apple with a smile on his face, pieces poking through the gaps in his teeth. He gave the rest to Perry. Perry finished it in two bites, including the stem and seeds. Seeing his nephew's teeth starting to chatter, Perry pulled off his shirt and dropped it over Talon's shoulders. Then he sat, leaning back on his hands, savoring the sweet aftertaste. Deep on the horizon, clouds lit with flashes of blue. Outside of the winter months, they didn't suffer Aether storms on land, but rogue storms were always a danger out at sea.

Talon rested his head on Perry's arm, drawing in the sand with a stick. He was a born hunter like Perry, but he had his mother's artistic side too. Perry closed his eyes and wondered if this was the last time he'd feel this way. Like he was exactly where he should be. Like for a few minutes everything was in balance. Then he felt the balance shift as a prickling sensation pierced the back of his nose.

Through gaps in the clouds he saw the Aether flowing fiercely, churning like white caps on rough seas. The beach held a blue glow, cast from the light above. Perry drew the cool ocean air down into his lungs, tasting the salt on his tongue. This was it. He could never go back to the compound. He couldn't trust himself to hold back from challenging Vale any longer.

Perry looked down at his nephew. "Talon . . . ," he began.

"You're leaving, aren't you?"

"I have to."

"No, you don't. You don't have to stay here forever. Just until I'm gone."

Perry leaped to his feet. "Talon! Don't talk like that."

Talon scrambled up. His tears came suddenly, rolling down his cheeks. "You can't go!" he shouted. "You can't leave!"

Talon's dark hair blew into his eyes. His jaw trembled with rage. A startling red color bloomed at the edges of Perry's vision. He had never seen this side of his nephew. This sort of fury. He had to work not to let it overtake him. "If I stay, either your father will die or I will. You know that."

"My dad promised he wouldn't fight you!"

Perry froze. "He promised that?"

Talon swiped tears off his face and nodded. "Now *you* promise. You promise and it'll all be fine."

Perry put his hands through his hair, striding upwind so he could think without Talon's anger riling him up. Had Vale really made that promise? It explained why he hadn't made a move earlier in front of Talon. Perry knew he couldn't make the same pledge. The need to take Blood Lord came from too deep.

"Talon, I can't. I have to go."

"Then I hate you!" Talon yelled.

Perry let out a slow breath. He wished that were true. Leaving him would be easier.

"Peregrine!" Wylan's voice sliced above the dull surf. He sprinted toward them on the hard-packed sand by the water, his cap in one hand, his knife in the other. "Dwellers, Perry! Dwellers!"

Perry snatched his bow and quiver and grabbed Talon's hand. Fear poured off Wylan's skin as he ran up, biting cold as it entered Perry's nostrils. "Hovers," Wylan panted. "Coming right at us."

Perry ran up the bank and scanned the distance. A pale glint appeared on the farthest ridge, a plume of sand rising behind it. Seconds later another Hover appeared.

"What's happening, Uncle Perry?"

Perry pushed Talon at Wylan. "Cut up the old fishing trail. Get him home. Stay on him like you're his shadow, Wylan. Go!"

Talon dodged out of Wylan's reach. "No! I'm staying with you!"

"Talon, do what I say!"

Wylan caught him but Talon struggled, digging his feet into the sand.

"Wylan, pick him up!" Perry yelled.

Wylan sank into the sand with Talon's added weight, moving too slowly. Perry ran toward the Hovers. Stopped a few hundred paces away. He had never been this close to them before. Their blue surfaces shimmered like abalone shells.

Talon's screams were terrible, shrill sounds. Perry fought the urge to turn and run for him. As the Hovers sped closer, the charge in the air stung Perry's arms and seared deep into his nose. They were stirring the Aether. Attracting its venom. Perry had an idea for using that to his advantage and hoped it wouldn't kill him first.

From his satchel, he took a thread of copper he used for traps and quickly wound it around the shaft of an arrow. A shock shot up his arm when his fingers brushed the steel arrowhead. Perry nocked the arrow to his bow. He only had the one wire. One shot. He aimed high, so his arrow would soar far enough to reach the craft. Perry imagined the arc he needed. He adjusted for the wind and let it loose.

Things slowed to kill-time after that, crisp and clear. The arrow sailed true. At the highest point, as the arrow began to level, a spool of Aether wove down from the sky, meeting it. Perry winced, shielding his eyes as the arrow dropped, drawing the Aether with it. His shot now carried all the

88

violence of the sky at its tail. It came down with a hellish, gut-grinding scream.

He struck the first Hover clean. The arrow bit into the metal. Then the veins of Aether wrapped around the Hover, strangling the vehicle. Sucking it dry. Perry flinched again as the Aether rejoined in a brilliant ray and shot skyward, diving back into the bright currents above.

The mangled Hover skidded over the dunes like a skipping stone, shaking the ground beneath Perry's feet, until it stopped with a burst of sand. A hot gust blew past, carrying the smells of molten metal, glass, and plastic. More potent was the stench of scorched flesh.

The other Hover slowed right away and settled on the sand. The door slid open, a crack in the perfect shell. Dwellers jumped to the ground. Perry counted six men, helmeted, covered in blue suits. Six against him.

Two knelt immediately. They held weapons Perry didn't recognize. He took out the first man right away. Nocked another arrow and fired again. Perry hit the second Dweller as the man struck him, a blow that felt like a slap to the rib, just under his left arm. He put an arrow in another Dweller, but as the three men who were left came at him, he stumbled, his legs and then his arms going numb. He toppled forward, unable to break his fall, his face thudding into the sand. Perry tried to lift himself up but couldn't move.

"I got him." Someone grabbed his hair, pulling his head up. Sand plugged his nose. Scraped at his eyes. Perry tried to blink but his eyes only twitched.

The Dweller brought his helmeted face close. "Not so dangerous anymore, are you?" His voice sounded metallic and far. "Didn't think we'd forget to pay you a return visit, did you, Savage?"

He let Perry's head drop. Perry took a kick to the ribs, but he didn't feel any pain, only the blow pushing him to the side. Something pressed between his shoulder blades.

"What's this?"

"Some kind of hawk."

"Looks like a turkey if you squint."

Laughter.

"Let's get this done." They rolled him onto his back.

A Dweller pressed a clear sword to his throat. He wore black gloves, the material thinner than the rest of his suit. "I'll take care of him. You get the other ones."

"No!" Perry groaned. He could feel his fingers now, prickling like they were thawing from cold, and pain waking in his ribs.

"Where's the Smarteye, Turkey?"

"The eyepiece? I'll give it to you! You don't need them." His words came out garbled but the Dweller must have understood.

He took the clear sword away. Perry fought to bring his arms back, but his muscles were numb.

"What are you waiting for, Savage?"

"I can't move!"

The Dweller laughed at him. "That's your problem, Turkey."

90

A wave of hatred fueled Perry to battle for control of his limbs. He pushed himself to his feet and turned up the beach, swaying, his legs quaking beneath him. Two Dwellers ran toward Talon and Wylan. One caught Talon, the other swung at Wylan with a short club, catching him on the head and sending him down.

"Uncle Perry!" Talon yelled.

"Move, Savage!" yelled the Dweller with the black gloves. "Get the Smarteye."

Perry stumbled to where he'd left his satchel, falling to his knees twice. He'd regained some feeling, but now he felt the ache in his ribs, threatening to swallow him whole. He turned toward the Dweller with the clear sword, holding up the eyepiece. "Let him go! I have it!"

The two Dwellers had Talon trapped between them. Talon wouldn't stop struggling.

"Stop!" Perry yelled at his nephew.

Talon wrenched an arm free and punched one of the Dwellers in the groin. The man buckled, but the other one reacted quickly, kicking Talon in the stomach. Talon tumbled onto the sand. He came up slow, bearing his knife. Perry's old knife. The Dweller was ready and backhanded him, sending the blade and Talon flying. Eyes blurring, Perry watched his nephew's body go still, the waves breaking against the beach behind him.

A gust carried Talon's temper to Perry, as staggering as any blow he'd ever taken. He couldn't fight the Moles this way, shaking with terror. With legs that couldn't hold him upright.

"Enough! Take it!" Perry threw the eyepiece at the Dweller.

The man caught it in his gloved hand and shoved it into a pocket at his chest.

"Too late," he said. Then he came toward Perry, the clear sword raised and ready. Down the beach, one of the Dwellers picked up Talon and carried him up the bank. Toward the Hover. Perry couldn't believe what he was seeing. They were taking Talon.

"No!" Perry yelled. "I gave it to you! You're dead, Moles!"

The Dweller with the black gloves kept coming. Perry had no weapon and Talon's temper had left him trapped between panic and rage. He backed away, retreating into the sea. The Dweller followed him, stepping unsteadily in the bulky suit as the surf crashed into his knees. A wave rolled past, spraying his helmet. Moles wouldn't know water, Perry realized. He was ready when the next wave came. Perry lunged and tackled the Dweller. They fell together. Saltwater surged into his nose, bringing him a shot of clarity. Back to himself.

He pried the clear sword out of the man's hand as they tumbled into the shallows. The wave slid back to the ocean, leaving them locked together, grappling in a foot of water. The Dweller reached up to shove him off. Perry brought his head down and sank his teeth into the man's gloved hand. His canines punctured the material immediately. He tasted salt and blood and felt the give of muscle. He bit until bone kept him from going further.

The Dweller's scream came garbled through his helmet. Perry rolled to his feet. The Dweller dragged himself out of the water and curled around his hand. Perry slammed his boot down on the Dweller's helmet. It cracked, putting out a burst of air that Perry recognized, noxious and thin. One more kick and the man sagged against the wet sand.

Perry wrenched the eyepiece out of the pocket in the Dweller's suit. Then he lumbered up the sandbank, snatching up his bow and quiver.

"Talon!"

He didn't see his nephew anywhere, only the Hover floating in place. The hatch sealed shut. With a blast of sand, it shot into the distance.

He ran home in a mindless haze, his arm pressed against the spearing pain in his side. He stopped at the top of a ridge. From this far, the compound looked like a circle of stones in the valley below. A sky teeming with Aether flows and dark clouds made night of the late afternoon. Perry tilted his head, searching for scents on the storm winds. No trace of Dwellers that he could tell.

He smelled the sharp tang of bile. Wylan jogged up, a hand pressed to the knot the Dwellers had given him at his hairline. Wylan had vomited twice on the way back. The reek still clung to him.

"Hate to be you right now," Wylan said. He had a dark, feral look in his eyes. "I heard those Moles. They came after you. Vale's going to tear you in half."

"He'll need me to get Talon back," Perry said.

Wylan leaned over and spat. Then he laughed. "Peregrine, you're the last person Vale needs."

Perry found everyone in the clearing, speaking in cheerful tones that mixed with festive music. Torches around the perimeter added a golden glow to the gathering, setting it apart from the cool light surrounding the compound. A few couples danced. Children wove through the crowd, hiding behind women's skirts and laughing. It was a strange scene, as if they didn't see the Aether roiling above them. Didn't care that the sky might rain fire at any moment.

Vale sat on one of the crates by the cookhouse, talking to Bear at his side. He held a bottle in his hand and looked relaxed. Content to watch the celebration.

"Perry!" Brooke called, then she grabbed the arm of the person next to her. Her alarm rippled through the rest of the crowd, bringing the music to a halt. Now Perry heard the frightened brays and bleats of the stabled animals.

Vale stared at Perry, the smile easing off his face. He hopped off the crate and came forward, searching the crowd behind Perry. "Where's Talon? Where's Talon, Perry?"

Perry swayed. He could see the bronze flecks in Vale's green eyes. "The Dwellers took him. I couldn't stop them."

Vale handed his bottle off without looking away. "What are you talking about, Peregrine?"

"The Dwellers took Talon." He couldn't believe he'd spoken the words. That they were true. That he was there, telling Vale his son was gone.

Vale's dark eyebrows drew together. "That can't be. We've done nothing to them."

Perry took in the stunned faces around them. He shouldn't have told Vale here. When the fog of disbelief wore off, the news would destroy him. But Vale, as Blood Lord, as Talon's father, shouldn't have to endure it in front of the tribe.

"Let's go home," Perry said.

Vale hesitated. He looked as though he was going to follow Perry until Wylan spoke up. "Tell him here. Everyone should hear this."

Vale stepped closer. "Start talking, Peregrine."

Perry swallowed hard. "I . . . broke into the Dweller fortress." It sounded ridiculous to him now. Like a prank. "A few nights ago," he added. "After I left."

Vale would know, without Perry saying it, that he'd gone after their fight. That he'd acted like a frustrated child and done something rash, as he always did. In the silence that followed, Perry's breath came fast, like he'd just sprinted. He scented dozens of tempers. Anger. Astonishment. Excitement. The flashing weights and colors and temperatures so potent that he felt sick.

Vale's face tightened with confusion. "They came for my boy because of what you did?"

Perry shook his head. "They came for me. Talon was just there."

He couldn't look at his brother any longer. He stared at the jumble of footprints on the ground. In the next instant, his head rocked to the side and then his shoulder slammed

95

against the earth. He looked up at Vale, a shot of heat flooding his veins. He was at his brother's feet. He should stay there. He deserved this. But he couldn't.

He sprang up. Vale drew his knife. Perry brought out his own blade. People cried out and pushed away from them.

Perry couldn't believe this was happening. Talon should be here, not him. He should be long gone. "I'll get him back," he said. "I'll get Talon. I swear I will."

Rage burned in Vale's eyes. "You can't get him back! Don't you see that? If you go after him, the Dwellers could destroy all of us!"

Perry tensed. He hadn't thought of that, but Vale was right. The Dwellers could have dozens of Hovers like the two he'd just seen. Hundreds of men, ready to fight. He felt stupid for not realizing it sooner. Then worse for not caring.

"It's Talon," he said. "We have to get him back."

"There's no getting him back, Peregrine! You did this! Father was right. You're *cursed*. You destroy everything!"

Perry's legs shuddered beneath him. He couldn't mean it. Perry had survived his father's tirades because of Vale. After all the thrashings, it was Vale and Liv who'd saved him by telling him he wasn't to blame for what happened. For what he considered the greatest mistake of his life. Until now.

"I didn't know. . . . It wasn't supposed to happen." There wasn't anything he could say that would help. He just needed to find Talon.

Vale pressed the back of his hand to his mouth like he might be sick.

"I'm sorry, Vale. . . . I'm—"

Vale lunged at him suddenly. Perry dodged to the side. For the first time in months, he knew exactly what he needed to do. Perry shoved Vale as he blew past, buying a few feet of space. Then he plunged into the crowd.

People cried out in surprise. For all his flaws, he'd never been accused of being a coward. He bore the shame and ran, knocking people down as he fled.

Vale wouldn't fight for Talon, but he would. He was Talon's only hope now.

11

ARIA

Aria walked toward hills in the distance until night forced her to stop. She looked around her. What now? What spot of dirt should she choose to rest against? Would she just end the day where she was?

She sat down, shifting onto her side. Propping herself onto an elbow and then laying on her back. She wanted a pillow and a blanket. Her bed. Her room. She wanted her Smarteye so she could escape into the Realms. She sat back up, hugging her legs. The Medsuit, at least, was keeping her warm.

The Aether looked brighter than it had earlier. It knotted on the horizon in glowing blue waves. She watched the sky until she was sure. The waves were rolling toward her. Aria closed her eyes and listened to the flap of the wind blowing past her ears, rising and falling. There was music somewhere in the wind. She concentrated on finding it, on slowing her racing pulse.

She heard a crunching sound. She tensed, her eyes desperately searching the darkness. The Aether churned in eerie whirlpools above her now, casting rippling blue light across the desert. She'd been in a daze, but she knew she hadn't imagined the sound.

"What are you?" she said, straining to see in the shifting light. No answer came back. "I heard you!" she cried.

A flash of blue lit up the distance. Aether dropped from the sky, whirling and twisting downward in a funnel. It struck the earth with a tremor that rattled the ground beneath her. Frenzied light spread across the empty desert. But it wasn't empty. A human figure charged toward her.

Aria slithered back on her hands, trying to get her feet under her. The funnel spooled back into the sky. Darkness returned just as an immense weight pushed her down. The back of her head struck the dirt and then a hand gripped her jaw.

"I should have let you die. I lost everything because of you."

The Aether flashed again, showing a fearsome face she vaguely recognized. But she knew that wild hair, snarled and streaked through with blond, and those gleaming, animal eyes.

"Get going. And don't try to run. Understand?"

She almost didn't understand him. Words sounded pulled and stretched the way he spoke them. The Savage yanked her up and shoved her without waiting for an answer. She stumbled back, losing sight of him in the marbled darkness. Another funnel came down. In the flash of light, she saw that he was only a few feet away.

"Move, Mole!" he yelled, then turned away from her and swore.

A warm gust rushed past Aria's face. The Outsider collided into her again, crashing into her back and wrapping his arms around her. Fear exploded through her as he muscled her forward. She tried to shove back, but he trapped her in a crouch.

"Don't move," he yelled in her ear. "Close your eyes and put—"

This funnel was much closer. The light blinded her but the sound when it struck the earth was an unbearable horrid shriek. Aria pressed her palms over her ears and screamed as the skin on her face seared with heat. Every muscle in her body seized, gripped by a force far stronger than her.

When the noise and light faded she peered up, blinking furiously as she tried to regain her senses. Wherever she looked, eruptions of light lashed down from the sky, leaving glimmering trails of fire across the earth. She had feared Aether storms all her life from the safety of Reverie. Now she was right in the middle of one.

The Outsider let her go. He turned one way and another, his movements calculating and precise. Aria stepped away from him unsteadily, her mind dazed and slow. She wasn't sure whether her legs or the earth trembled. Her ears felt like they had burst. The horrible scream of the Aether strikes was muted now. She touched the dribbling warmth beneath her nose. The fingers of her glove shone with dark liquid. She was oddly disappointed. Blood was supposed to be bright red, wasn't it? She suddenly realized she shouldn't be taking inventory of her wounds. She needed to get away.

She'd only run a few steps when he caught her, grabbing the back of her suit. Aria tensed, terrified, as she felt a tug. Her Medsuit loosened and then cold air blew across her back. She was just grasping what he'd done when the whole suit fell away. Aria sprang back, covering herself and her thin undergarments. This was not happening.

The Outsider balled her torn suit and hurled it into the darkness. "You were calling the Aether. *Move*, Mole! Now, or we cook!"

She could hardly hear him. Her ears weren't working right and the storm shrieked around her, muffling his voice. But she realized he was right. The Aether funnels appeared to be getting closer and gathering around them.

He grabbed her wrist. "Keep low. If it's close, put your hands on your knees to give the charge somewhere to go. You hear me, Dweller?"

She couldn't think beyond his grip on her wrist. A wave of warm air swept past, heavy, like fingers brushing her face. She recognized the warning. A funnel would strike close. Aria did what he said. She bent low over her knees, saw the Outsider doing the same, folding to half his size, until she had to close her eyes against the glaring light. When the brightness behind her eyelids dimmed, she straightened to a silent flashing world.

The Outsider shook his head, realizing she couldn't hear. She no longer fought when he pointed into the darkness. If he took her away from this place, at least her skin wouldn't burn and her ears wouldn't break again.

She didn't know how long they ran. The funnels never came as close as before. As they moved away from the Aether storm, the rain began, the drops cold pinpricks, so unlike pseudo-rain in the Realms. At first it cooled her skin, but soon the cold numbed her muscles, leaving her shivering.

With the threat of the Aether receding behind them, her focus turned back to the Savage. How could she escape? He was double her size and moved sure-footedly through the dark. She was beyond exhausted, struggling just to stumble alongside, but she had to try something. There weren't any good reasons the Savage could be forcing her to come with him. She needed to find the right moment to get away.

The desert ended abruptly, giving to low hills patched with dry grass. It had grown darker away from the Aether funnels. Aria couldn't see where she set her feet anymore. She stepped on something that stabbed deep into her foot. She stifled a cry of pain, seeing her chance of escape slipping away.

The Outsider turned, his eyes glinting in the dark. "What is it, Dweller?"

She heard him dimly but didn't answer. Rain poured over her as she stood, balancing on one leg. She couldn't put any weight on her foot anymore. He came toward her without any warning and hoisted her against his side. Aria raked her nails into his skin. He lost his footing, nearly bringing them both down.

"Hurt me again, I hurt you back harder," he said through

clenched teeth. She felt the rumble of his voice where their ribs pressed together.

He firmed his grip around her waist and quickened his pace up the slope, his breath a muffled hiss at her side. Warmth gathered where their skin touched, making her nauseous. She didn't think she could bear it anymore when they crested the slope.

By the light of the Aether, she saw a darkened opening in a smooth wall of rock. She'd have laughed if she could. Of course it would be a cave. Rain poured over the mouth in a solid sheet of water. The Outsider set her down inside.

"Back under a rock. Must feel like home." He disappeared into the cave.

Aria limped back out into the pelting rain. She stared down at the way they'd come, a hillside so broken with rock it looked like it had teeth. She saw no other way, downhill or up, that looked manageable. She climbed down anyway, using her hands and her good foot to move over rocks made slick with rain. Aria pushed herself to hurry before the Outsider returned. Her foot slipped, wedging into the space between two large slabs. Aria tugged and turned, but the crack wouldn't let her go and she was fading, the last of her strength seeping into the cold rock against her back.

Aria tucked herself into a ball and had two thoughts. First, she was plunging to a place far deeper than sleep. And second, she hadn't gotten far enough away.

⌁ 12 ⌁

PEREGRINE

The girl had passed out by the time Perry got the fire started. She seemed to do that a lot. He freed her foot from the slabs. Then he carried her into the cave and wrapped a blanket around her. A stone fell out of her hand. He guessed she'd meant it as protection from him. A decent thought. Might have worked for half a second.

He remembered her scent from the night in the Dweller fortress. A rancy mix of must and flesh at the brink of decay. It had surprised him earlier, when he'd come across it in the valley. Led him right to her. Here, in the closed space of the cave, her odor was strong enough to bring a sour taste to the back of his throat. He lay down as far from her as he could without leaving the fire's warmth and slept.

He woke before sunrise to the hush that always followed an Aether storm. The girl hadn't moved. It was a cold morning, the weather heading fast toward winter. Perry got the fire going again, moving slow. Even breathing too deep brought daggers to his side.

He hadn't been in this cave since Vale deemed this area forbidden, but found it well stocked by traders who used the cave as shelter when they came through the valley. He found clothes and jars with nuts. Dried fruits that were still edible. He even found a healing compound. Perry spread it on the girl's feet, seeing that only one cut looked deep. She could use stitches. But he'd never been good with a needle, and she was going to die one way or another. Besides, he didn't need her walking. Only alert long enough to talk.

Perry checked the cut on his side. Only a short slice on his skin where he'd been hit, but he'd bruised a few ribs. He also had five stripes of torn flesh on his chest, thanks to the girl. But his body would heal and grow strong again, unlike Talon's.

He ate, then sat looking at the flames, torturing himself by remembering everything that had happened. He'd lost Talon. Something he thought impossible. Now he needed the impossible to happen again. He needed to get Talon back.

Perry had done what he had to, leaving the Tides. But when he thought of how he'd run, his face went hotter than fire. He had spent his life dreaming of being the Tides' Blood Lord. The tribe would think him a coward now. They'd be glad to have him gone.

When he lay down to sleep, the girl still hadn't moved. He wondered if she'd ever wake.

Perry hunted the next morning. The hurt in his ribs made him sweat cold, but sitting about would've felt worse. He coaxed a rattler from a hole, speared it through with an arrow. He cooked and ate the rich meat, but felt nauseous afterward. Like the snake had come back to life in his gut.

By nightfall the girl began to stir with fever. Perry burned some dry oak leaves to mask her Dweller scent and stayed awake through the night. He needed to be ready if she came around. She might have information about Talon. And there was the eyepiece to find out about. He hoped it would give him a way to contact the Dwellers who'd taken Talon.

She opened her eyes the next afternoon and scurried away from him, pressing her back against the opposite wall. Her legs snapped together beneath the blanket.

Perry smirked. "You've been passed out two days and you're worried about that now?" He shook his head. "Relax, Dweller. Last thing you bring to mind."

She examined the dark granite walls. Then the steel cases of supplies stacked to one side. When she looked at the dwindling fire, she followed the thread of smoke toward the mouth of the cave.

"Yeah," Perry said. "That's the way out. But you're not leaving yet."

She turned to him, her gaze catching on his Markings. "What do you want from me, Savage?"

"Is that what you call us?"

"You're murderers. Diseased. Cannibals." She flung the

words at him like curses. "I've heard the stories."

Perry crossed his arms. She lived under a rock. What did she know about anything? "Guess we're well-named, Mole."

She watched him with a look of disgust. Then she touched her throat with a skitty hand. "I need water. Is there water?"

He took his leather waterskin from his satchel and held it up.

"What is that?" she asked.

"Water."

"It looks like an animal."

"It used to be." The pouch protecting the bottle inside was made of goat hide.

"It looks filthy," she said.

Perry unstopped the cork and drank deeply. "Tastes fine." He shook it so the water sloshed around. "Lose your thirst?"

The girl snatched it from his hand, darted back to her spot. She shut her eyes and drank. When she was done, he raised a hand. "Keep it." No way he'd drink from it now.

"Why were you out in the open?" he asked.

"Why should I tell you?"

"I saved your life. Twice, by my count."

She sat forward. "You're wrong! I'm *here* because of you. Guess who they think let you in?"

That surprised him. He shifted his back on the cool rock, wondering what had happened after he'd left her that night. It didn't matter. He'd done what he could. Now there was only Talon to think of.

Perry slid his knife from the sheath at his hip. He checked

the edge of the blade with his thumb, turning it so it caught the firelight. "I don't have time to waste, Mole. Don't think it would take much to make you talk."

"You don't scare me with that."

Perry inhaled deeply. Her lie was acrid and sharp, bringing a bitter taste to his mouth. She wasn't scared. She was terrified.

"Why are you looking at me like that?" she asked.

"Your scent."

Her lower lip quivered. "You drink from a rabbit and you think *I* smell?"

Perry knew what was coming when she started laughing. He caught the shift in the air like the drag of a dark tide. She wouldn't be laughing for long.

He went outside and sat on a smooth boulder. It was a gray dusk, pulling a cold night in its wake. He sat and breathed and tried not to imagine Talon sobbing for his home like the girl in the cave.

13

ARIA

To calm herself, Aria tried to pretend it was a Realm. A Paleolithic Realm. She was in a cave, after all. With a fire, which she avoided looking at for the memories it brought of Ag 6. But there were also steel cases to one side. And the navy blue blanket around her was made of fleece. And the glass jars lined up near the fire had metal screw-top lids. Too many things that broke the Stone Age illusion.

This was real.

Aria stood and winced at the pain in the soles of her feet. She pulled the blanket around her and listened for the Savage. Only the piercing rhythm of her headache broke the silence. Had she been infected with disease? Would she die in this cave, wrapped in this blue fleece blanket? She drew a few slow breaths. Thinking like that wouldn't do any good.

There were supplies by the Outsider's leather bag, but she wasn't going to touch any of his things. She hobbled to the steel crates. Broken pieces of plastic and glass mixed with bottles of medicine. They were useless to her now. All the expiration dates reached back more than three hundred years, to the time of the Unity, when the Aether had forced people into Pods. She found one sterile bandage that had yellowed with time, but it would serve.

Aria drew up the blanket and gasped. Her feet were already bandaged. The Savage had tended to her feet.

He'd touched her.

She gripped the edge of the case, steadying herself. This was a good sign. If he'd tended to her feet, then he couldn't mean her harm. Could he? The logic was sound, but just thinking of him brought a fresh wave of fear.

He was a beast. Immense. Muscular, but not like Soren. The Savage reminded her of the Equestrian Realms, how every movement in a horse showed a chorus of lean muscles rolling and shifting beneath skin. He had tattoos, just like in the stories. Two patterned bands around each bicep. When he'd turned his back, she'd seen another design on his skin, some sort of hawk with wings spanning shoulder to shoulder. His hair looked like it had never seen a brush. Snarled blond ropes, all uneven in length and color, coiling in every direction. As he'd spoken, she could've sworn she'd glimpsed teeth that were slightly too *canine*. But nothing was more hideous than his eyes.

Aria was accustomed to eyes of all colors. There were fads in the Realms. Purple had been the popular color just last month. The Savage's eyes were bright green but also reflective, like the eerie gaze of a nocturnal animal. And she realized with a shudder, they were real.

She turned, biting her lip as she looked around. A *cave*. What was she doing here? How had this happened? The fire had dwindled. She could no longer see the wall she'd sat against. She didn't want to be in this cave in the darkness, with no noise and nothing to see. She fastened the navy blanket into a toga, belting it with gauze so she could move better, and then went outside.

She found him sitting on a rock at the edge of the jagged slope where she'd fallen. He had his back to her, hadn't yet heard her. Aria stopped within the cave's mouth, a dozen feet away. She didn't want to move any closer so she stood, hugging the blanket close to keep it from shifting with the wind.

He was shaving down a long piece of wood with a knife. Making an arrow, she guessed. A caveman fashioning his weapons. The tattoo on his back was of a falcon, judging by the sleek head. The eyes appeared to be masked with darker plumage. In the Realms people used moving designs. They chose new ones whenever they wanted. She couldn't imagine having an image on her skin forever.

The Outsider turned and glared at her. Aria glared back at him, hiding a jolt of fear. How had he known she was there? He slipped his knife into a leather sheath at his belt.

She stepped closer, careful not to limp and to keep a good distance between them. Aria pushed a strand of her hair back behind her ear. She realized he'd handled the knife with the same habitual ease.

The Aether flowed in gentle ribbons of blue light, swirling above scuttling gray clouds. She wasn't fooled this time. She knew how terrible it could be. Below she saw the valley they'd crossed in the storm, mottled with uneven light.

"Is it twilight?"

"Dusk," he said.

She glanced at him. Wasn't twilight the same as dusk? And how did he manage to drawl such a brief little word? *Dusssk*. Like the word could go on all day. "Why did you bring me here? Why didn't you just leave me out there?"

"I need information. Your people took someone from me."

"That's ridiculous. What use could we have for a Savage?"

"More use than they had for you."

Her breath caught as she remembered Consul Hess's lifeless eyes and empty smile. The Savage was right. She'd served her purpose. She'd taken the fall for Soren and been put out to die. Out here, with this beast.

"So you want to get into Reverie? To save this person? Is that what you were doing that night?"

"I will get in. I've done it before."

She laughed. "*We* disarmed the system. And that dome was damaged. You got lucky, Savage. The walls protecting Reverie are ten feet thick. There's no way you could ever get through them again. What's your plan, anyway? Are you going to hurl dung patties? Or maybe use a slingshot? One well-aimed stone would probably do it."

He spun and came toward her. Aria darted aside, her heart

leaping into her throat, but he strode past her, disappearing back into the cave. Moments later he stalked back out. His eyes gleamed as he held something up.

"Is this better than a dung patty, Mole?"

For long seconds, Aria stared at the curved object in his hand. She never saw Smarteyes off people's faces. Seeing one in the possession of a Savage, she nearly didn't recognize it.

"Is that mine?"

He nodded once. "I took it. After it was torn from you."

Relief shot through her limbs. She could reach her mother in Bliss! And if the recording of Soren was still there, she could prove what he and his father had done to her. She looked up. "It's not yours. Give it to me."

He shook his head. "Not until you answer my questions."

"If I do, then you'll give it to me?"

"I said I would."

Aria's heart pounded. She needed her Smarteye. Her mother would rescue her. She could be on another Hover within hours on the way to Bliss. With Lumina's help, she'd expose Consul Hess and Soren.

She couldn't believe she was considering helping an Outsider get into Reverie. Wasn't that treason? Hadn't Hess practically accused her of that very thing? She'd never do it. Whatever he asked about this missing person, she'd give him false information. She'd tell him what he wanted to hear and he would never know otherwise.

"All right," she said.

His hand snapped shut over the device and then he crossed

his arms. Aria stared in horror. Her Smarteye was buried in a Neanderthal's armpit.

"Why were you out there?" His mouth curved with satisfaction. It was the same question she'd avoided before. But now she'd have to answer him.

She made a sound of disgust. "There were only two of us who survived. One was the son of a Consul—of a very powerful person in our Pod. I was the other."

He grew silent. Her gaze darted to his chest, where she saw the tracks her nails had left on his skin. She looked away quickly, repulsed that she'd touched him. Did he have a problem with clothes? It wasn't exactly warm out. She shivered as a gust swept past, deciding Savages must not feel cold.

"Do you have any allies on the inside still?" he asked.

"Did you just say *allies*?"

"Friends," he said sharply. "People who'll help you, Mole."

Paisley came to mind. Pain came in a wave, threatening to sweep her off. Aria breathed for a few moments, pushing it back. "My mother. She'll help."

The Savage's gaze narrowed. He watched her too closely. She kept herself from fidgeting, but couldn't help adding, "She's a scientist," like it would mean anything to him.

He held out the Smarteye. "You can reach her through this?"

"Yes," she said. "I think so." If Hess was trying to track it, the Eye might have been reactivated.

"Could she learn about a stolen person?" the Outsider asked.

Aria narrowed her eyes. She couldn't see why that would ever happen. Why would anyone want a disease-ridden Savage? But disagreeing wouldn't help. "Yes, she could. She's respected because of her work. She has some influence. She could find out something. If there's anything to find out. Give that to me and I'll help you."

She was proud of herself. The lie slid out smoothly.

He came right up to her, bending close. "You *will* help, Dweller. It's the only way you're going to live."

She leaped back. "I said I would!" What was wrong with him?

He thrust the Smarteye at her. Aria clasped it in both hands and walked away. Just holding the Eye, she felt closer to home. She wondered how much disease she couldn't see on it. The Outsider didn't look terribly filthy, but he had to be.

"Get to it."

She looked over her shoulder. "Who should I ask about when I reach my mother?"

The Savage hesitated. "A boy. Seven years old. His name is Talon."

"A *boy*?" He thought her people had taken *a child*?

"I've waited long enough, Mole."

Aria placed it over her left eye, feeling the tenderness over her eye socket. The biotech worked immediately. The patch suctioned to her skin, the inner membrane loosening and softening. The consistency turning from gel to liquid until she could blink as easily as with her uncovered eye.

She waited for her Smartscreen to appear, her muscles rigid with anticipation. She tried her pass codes. She tried to reset the system, the same thing she'd done in Ag 6. Nothing appeared. No "Songbird" file. No icons. She was simply looking through the clear patch, seeing the bleak earth fading into darkness and the sky moving with Aether.

The Outsider loomed over her. "What's happening?"

"Nothing," she said as a raw ache built in her throat. "It's not responding. I thought . . . I thought they might have linked it back up, but I don't see anything. Maybe it shorted out in the storm. I don't know."

He muttered something, shoving a hand into his hair. Desperately Aria ran through more commands as the Outsider paced. Every failed attempt brought her closer to crying. The Outsider stopped, turning toward her. What now? Was he going to leave her there? Or worse?

"I need that back, Mole."

"I told you it doesn't work!"

"I'm going to get it fixed."

Aria couldn't hold back a sputter of laughter. "*You* know how to fix this?"

His glare was scathing. "I know someone who can."

She still couldn't believe it. "You know a person—an *Outsider*—who can fix this?"

"Do you have to hear everything twice, Dweller? I'll be back in less than two weeks. There's enough food and water in there to last you. Just stay put. No one comes out this way. Not this time of year. Have that thing off by the time I'm done packing." He strode back into the cave.

Aria rushed after him, staying close enough to follow the pale streaks of his hair through the gloom. The fire had dwindled to embers. He tossed a piece of wood onto them, sending a scatter of cinders upward.

"I'm not staying here alone for a week. Or two weeks, or whatever."

He moved to one of the cases and began stuffing things into a leather bag. "You'll be safer here."

"No. I'm not staying! I may not live—" Her voice broke. "I may not have that long. My immune system isn't made for out here. Two weeks might be too late. If you want my help, I need to come."

He considered this awhile. He set his bag on the ground. "I won't slow down for you. That means walking days on those." He nodded at her feet.

"You won't have to slow down," she said, relieved. At least she wouldn't be left alone or separated from her Smarteye.

He sent her a skeptical look and then opened another case. The fire was burning again, illuminating the rough walls of the cave. As he turned away, she noticed he had a patch of blue bruising beneath one arm that spread across his ribs. Aria watched the way the tattoo on his back moved as he moved. She was a falcon too. Her voice had a broad range, but in opera she was categorized as a falcon soprano. That's where Lumina got her nickname. Aria shuddered at the coincidence.

"Does that have some sort of meaning?" she asked.

He took garments from the crate and shook them out.

They were army fatigues from the time of the Unity. Camouflaged cargo pants and button-down shirt. He tossed them to her. "Clothes."

She dodged aside and then peered at the coarse mounds of material. "Can we boil them first?"

No answer again. She slipped into the shadows and pulled them on, moving as fast as she could. They were huge on her, but warmer and easier to move in. She rolled and tied them at her wrists and ankles and used the gauze as a belt again.

She stepped back toward the firelight. The Outsider was sitting where he'd been before. He had on a dark leather vest, similar to the kind boys wore in Gladiator Realms. Another navy blanket like hers was rolled up at his side.

He took quick stock of the adjustments she'd made to the clothes. "There's food in those," he said, nodding to a row of jars he'd set by the fire. "One's filled with water."

"Aren't we leaving?"

"I've seen the way you move through the dark. We'll sleep now and travel by day."

He lay down and closed his eyes as if that were that.

She drank some water but couldn't manage more than a few pieces of the dried fruit. The figs were too grainy, sticking to her throat, and the constant swirl of anxiety in her stomach didn't allow room for hunger. Aria leaned back against the cold granite. The soles of her feet throbbed. She was sure she'd never be able to sleep.

The Outsider didn't seem to have any trouble with it. She

could look at him more closely now that he was asleep. He was covered with imperfections. A faded blue bruise spread over one cheek, matching the one she'd seen on his ribs. Pale scars hashed small lines through the scruff on his jaw. His nose was on the long side and had a bend toward the top, where it had probably been broken more than once. It was a nose fit for a gladiator.

The Outsider peered at her. Aria froze as their eyes locked. He was human. She knew that. But there was something soulless about his bright stare. Without a word, he turned so he faced away from her.

Aria waited for her heartbeat to settle. Then she tugged the blanket over her shoulders and lay down. She kept an eye on the fire and the Savage, not sure which repelled her most. Soon her eyes grew heavy and it occurred to her how often she was wrong. She would sleep.

Even now. Even here.

14

PEREGRINE

Perry woke at first light, second-guessing his deal with the Dweller. How would she make the harsh journey with the cuts on her feet? But she was probably right. He doubted she'd survive the time it took him to get to Marron's and back. He knew one thing for certain: She'd need shoes.

He tore off the first book cover with an impatient tug. The girl shot upright, waking with a startled yelp.

"What is that? Is that a *book*?"

"Not anymore."

She touched the device over her eye a few times, her fingers fluttering and skitty. Perry looked away. The eyepiece was disgusting. A parasite. And it reminded him too much of the men who'd taken Talon. He went back to work, tearing the other leather cover off. Then he took his bag and knelt in front of her. He lifted her foot, pushed the bandage aside.

"You're healing up."

She sucked in a breath. "Let go. Don't touch me."

The cold scent of her fear came at him, flickering blue at the edges of his vision. "Steady, Mole," he said, letting go of her foot. "We have a deal. If you help me, I won't hurt you."

"What are you doing?" she asked, looking at the ripped covers. Her pale skin had nearly gone white.

"Making you shoes. There aren't any in the supplies. You can't travel barefoot."

Cautiously she gave him her foot. Perry set it on the book cover. "Be still as you can." He took Talon's knife and traced the outline of her foot with the tip of the blade. He was careful not to touch her as that triggered her panic.

"You don't have a pen or anything?" she asked.

"A pen? Lost it about a hundred years ago."

"I didn't think Outsiders lived that long."

Perry looked down, hiding his face. Was that a joke? Did Dwellers live that long?

"Are you a shoemaker or something?" she asked after a moment. "A cobbler?"

Did she think this was what he'd come up with if he were? "No. I'm a hunter."

"Oh. That explains a lot."

Perry didn't know what it explained other than that he hunted.

"So you . . . kill things? Animals and things?"

Perry closed his eyes. Then he sat back and gave her a wide grin. "If it moves, I kill it. Then I gut it, skin it, and eat it."

She shook her head, her eyes dazed. "I just . . . I can't believe you're real."

Perry scowled at her. "What else would I be, Mole?"

She kept quiet for a while after that. Perry finished outlining her feet. He cut the impressions out. Poked holes into the binding with the tip of the blade, working as swiftly as he could. This close, her Dweller scent was making him sick.

"My name is Aria." She waited for him to say something. "Don't you think we should know each other's names if we're going to be allies?" She arched a dark eyebrow, mocking his earlier use of the word.

"We might be allies, Mole, but we're not friends." He laced the leather cord through the holes and then tied them around her ankles. "Try those."

She stood and took a few steps, drawing up her pants so she could see her feet. "They're good," she said, surprised.

He swept the leftover scraps of leather cord into his satchel. The covers made perfect soles, just as he'd thought. Tough but flexible. Best use he'd ever seen for a book. They'd last a few days. Then he'd have to come up with something better. If she lived that long.

If she didn't, he'd already decided he would take the eyepiece to Marron's alone. He'd find a way to send a signal to any Dweller who'd hear it. He'd offer himself and the eyepiece in exchange for his nephew.

She lifted a foot and looked at the bottom. "How fitting. Did you choose this one on purpose, Outsider? I'm not sure this bodes well for our journey."

Perry snatched his satchel. Took up his bow and quiver. He didn't have a clue what book he'd chosen. He couldn't read. Had never learned no matter how many times Mila and Talon had tried to teach him. He walked out of the cave before she could see that and call him a stupid Savage.

They spent the morning crossing hills Perry had known all his life. They were nearing the eastern edge of Vale's territory, rolling land that climbed out of the Tide Valley. Wherever he looked he saw memories. The knoll where he and Roar had made their first bows. The oak tree with the split trunk that Talon had climbed a hundred times. The banks of the dry creek that first time with Brooke.

His father had walked this land once. Longer ago still, his mother had as well. It was strange missing a place before having left it. Unsettling to realize he had no loft to climb back into when he tired of being in the open. And he was walking with a Dweller. That cast the day in an odd light as well. Her presence made him shifty and irritated. He knew she wasn't the Mole who took Talon, but she was still one of them.

She jumped at every small sound during the first hours. She walked too slow and made more noise than someone her size ever should. Worst of all, she'd begun to put off a thick black temper as the morning wore on, telling him that grief had followed him. This girl he'd somehow struck a bargain with had suffered and lost and was hurting. Perry did his best to keep upwind from her, where the air was clear.

123

"Where are we going, Savage?" she asked around midday. She was a good ten paces behind him. Walking ahead held another advantage besides avoiding her scent. He didn't have to keep seeing the eyepiece on her face. "I think I'll call you that since I don't know your name."

"I won't answer."

"Well, Hunter? Where are we heading?"

He tipped his chin. "That way."

"That's helpful."

Perry glanced over his shoulder at her. "We're going to see a friend. His name is Marron. He's *that way*." He pointed to Mount Arrow. "Anything else?"

"Yes," she said, frustrated. "What is snow like?"

That nearly stopped him in his tracks. How could a person know about snow without knowing it was pure and silent and whiter than bone? Without knowing how the chill of it stung your skin? "It's cold."

"What about roses? Do they really smell so great?"

"See many roses around here?" He knew better than to give a true answer. From what he could tell, she'd never heard about Scires in her stories. Perry wanted to keep it that way. He didn't trust her. Knew she wasn't planning to help him. Whatever double-crossing she meant to do, he'd figure it out.

"Do the clouds ever clear?" she asked.

"Completely? No. Never."

"What about the Aether? Does that ever go away?"

"Never, Mole. The Aether never leaves."

She looked up. "A world of nevers under a never sky."

She fit in well then, he thought. A girl who never shut up.

Her questions continued through the day. She asked if dragonflies made a sound when they flew and if rainbows were myths. When he stopped answering, she turned to speaking to herself as though it were a natural thing. She talked about the warm color of the hills against the blue cast of the Aether. When the wind kicked up, she said the sound reminded her of turbines. She stared at rocks, wondering at the minerals that made them, even pocketing a few. She'd fallen into a deep silence once, when the sun appeared, and it was then he'd wondered most what she was thinking.

Perry couldn't figure out how a person could be grieving and still manage to talk so much. He ignored her as best he could. He kept an eye on the Aether, relieved to see that it moved in pale drifts above. They'd leave the Tides' land soon so he paid close attention to the scents carrying on the wind. He knew they'd meet with some form of danger eventually. Traveling outside tribe territories guaranteed it. Hard enough to survive alone in the borderlands. Perry wondered how he'd manage it with a Mole.

Late in the afternoon, he found a sheltered valley to lay camp. Night was falling by the time he got the fire going. The Dweller sat on an overturned tree examining the soles of her feet. What healthy skin she'd had left that morning had blistered.

Perry found the salve he'd taken from the cave and brought it to her. She unscrewed the small jar, her black hair spilling forward as she peered at it. Perry frowned. What was she doing? Was her eyepiece some sort of magnifying glass?

"Don't eat that, Dweller. Spread it on your feet. Here." He pushed a handful of dried fruit at her along with a cluster of thistle roots he'd dug up earlier. They tasted like uncooked potatoes, but at least they wouldn't starve. "That you can eat."

She kept the fruit but handed the roots back. Perry returned to the fire, too stunned to be offended. No one handed food back.

"The fire won't burn into these trees," he said when she didn't join him. She was inspecting each piece of fruit before she ate it. "It won't burn like that night."

"I just don't like it," she said.

"You'll change your mind when the cold sets in."

Perry ate his own meager dinner. He wished he'd taken time to hunt. Probably wouldn't have worked even if he had. Her constant blather had scared off game. Nearly scared him off too. He'd need to find food tomorrow. They'd eaten almost everything he'd brought from the cave.

"The boy who was taken," she said. "Is he your son?"

"How old do you think I am, Dweller?"

"I'm a little shaky on the fossil record, but I'd say fifty to sixty thousand years."

"Eighteen. And no. He's not my son."

"I'm seventeen." She cleared her throat. "You don't look eighteen," she said after a few moments. "I mean, you do and you don't."

Perry figured she was waiting for him to ask why. He didn't care.

"I'm feeling fine, by the way. I have a headache that won't

go away and my feet hurt like mad. But I think I'll live to see another day. I can't be sure, though. The stories say diseases can creep up quietly."

Perry bit down into his teeth, thinking of Talon and Mila. Was he supposed to feel sorry for her because she might fall ill? He couldn't imagine a life without disease or illness. He took the two blankets from his bag. Sleep would bring morning and morning would bring him closer to reaching Marron.

"Why do you avoid looking at me?" she asked. "Because I'm a Dweller? Are we ugly to Outsiders?"

"Which question do you want me to answer first?"

"It doesn't matter. You won't answer anyway. You don't answer questions."

"You don't stop asking them."

"See what I mean? You avoid answering and you avoid looking. You're an avoider."

Perry flung the blanket at her. She hadn't been ready. It hit her on the face. "You're not."

She snatched it away, shooting him a fierce look. Perry could see her perfectly, though she sat beyond the circle of firelight.

In the cover of darkness, he let the corner of his mouth lift.

Hours later he woke to the sound of singing. Quiet words, sung in a language he didn't know, but that seemed familiar. He'd never heard a voice like that. So clear and rich. He thought he might still be dreaming until he saw the girl.

She'd moved closer to the fire. To him. She hugged her legs as she rocked back and forth. He caught the salty tang of tears in the air, and a cold slash of fear.

"Aria," Perry said. He surprised himself by using her name. He decided it suited her. There was a curious sound about it. Like her very name was a question. "What is it?"

"I saw Soren. The one from the fire that night."

Perry jumped to his feet and searched into the fog. He'd never liked fog. It robbed him of one of his Senses, but he still had the other, his strongest. He breathed in deeply, careful to keep his movements subtle. Her fear wove with the woodsmoke, but there were no other Dweller scents.

"You dreamed it. There's no one here except us."

"We don't dream," she said.

Perry frowned but decided not to mull over the strangeness of that now. "There's no trace of him here."

"I *saw* him," she said. "It felt real. It felt just like being with him in a Realm." She brushed the blanket over her wet cheeks. "I couldn't get away from him again."

Now he didn't know what to do. If she were his sister or Brooke, he would have held her. He thought about telling her he'd keep her safe, but that wouldn't be entirely true. He would protect her. But only as long as it took to get Talon back.

"Could it have been a message through your eyepiece?" he asked.

"No," she said firmly. "It's still not working. But the strange thing is, I saw what I recorded that night. I recorded

Soren when he was . . . attacking me." She cleared her throat. "And that's what I saw. It's like my mind played the recording back on its own."

That was called a dream, but Perry wasn't going to argue over it. "Is that why the Dwellers want it back? Because of the recording?"

She hesitated and then nodded. "Yes. It could ruin both Soren and his father."

He ran a hand over his hair. Now he understood why the Dwellers wanted the eyepiece. Had they taken Talon as barter? "So we have leverage?"

"If we can fix the Smarteye."

Perry exhaled slowly, feeling a surge of hope. He'd been prepared to surrender himself to the Dwellers in exchange for Talon. Maybe he wouldn't have to. If the Dwellers wanted that eyepiece badly enough, it might be enough to get Talon back.

The girl's temper was beginning to ease. He threw on a fresh piece of wood and sat on the far side of the fire. He couldn't avoid looking at the eyepiece on her face now. "Why do you wear that thing if it's broken?" he asked.

"It's part of me. It's how we see the Realms."

He had no idea what Realms were. He didn't even know what to ask about them.

"Realms are virtual places," she said. "Created with computer programming."

He picked up a stick and poked at the embers. She'd explained without him asking. Like she knew he had no idea. That streaked him a bit, but she kept talking so he listened.

"They're places as real as this is. If my Smarteye was working, I could go to any part of the world and beyond too, from right here. Without going anywhere. There are Realms for times that have passed. Last year the Medieval Realms were champ. You'd be great in one of those. And then there are Fantasy Realms and Future Realms. Realms for hobbies and any kind of interest you can think of."

"So . . . it's like watching a video?" He'd seen those at Marron's. Images like memories playing out on a screen.

"No, that's only a visual. The Realms are multidimensional. If you go to a party, you feel the people dancing around you, and you can smell them and hear the music. And you can just change things, like choose more comfortable shoes to dance in. Or change your hair color. Or choose another body style. You can do anything you want."

Perry crossed his arms. It sounded like she was describing a daydream. "What happens to you when you go to one of these fake places? Do you fall asleep?"

"No, you're just fractioning. Doing two things at once." She shrugged. "Like walking and talking at the same time."

Perry fought back a smile. Her words from yesterday sprang to mind. *That explains a lot.* "What's the point of going to a fake place?" he asked.

"The Realms are the only places we *can* go. They were created when the Pods were built. Without them, we'd probably go insane with boredom. And they're pseudo, not fake. They feel exactly real. Well, some things I'm not sure about anymore. There are a few things out here that aren't what I expected."

She dug into one of her pockets. She'd collected about a dozen rocks yesterday. None of them looked special to him. They looked like rocks.

"Each one of these is unique," she said. "Their shape. Their weight and composition. It's amazing. In the Realms, there are formulas for randomness. I can always pick them out, though. Spot how every twelfth rock is a modified version of the first one's color or density, or whatever the variation might be.

"But rocks aren't the only thing. When I was out in that desert, and then when . . ." The way she looked at him, he knew whatever she'd say next, he was part of it. "I've never felt that way. We don't have fear like that. But if those two things are different, then there has to be more, right? Other things besides fear and rocks that are different in the real?"

Perry nodded absently, imagining a world without fear. Was that possible? If there was no fear, how could there be comfort? Or courage?

She took his nod as encouragement to continue, which he was fine with. She had a good voice. He hadn't realized until he'd heard her sing. He'd rather she sang more instead of talked, but he wasn't going to ask.

"See, it's all energy, like everything. The Eye sends impulses that flow right into the brain, fooling it. Telling it, 'You're seeing this and touching that.' But maybe some things haven't been perfected yet. Maybe they're close to the real thing, but not the same. Anyway, that's not what you asked. I wear it because I'm not myself without it."

Perry scratched his cheek and winced, forgetting about the bruise there. "Our Markings are like that. I wouldn't be myself without them."

Right away he regretted saying the words. Daylight streaked over the ridgeline in long beams, slicing through the fog. He shouldn't be sitting there talking with a Dweller when Talon was dying somewhere, away from home.

"Do your tattoos have to do with your name?"

"Yes," he said, stuffing his blanket into his satchel.

"Are you named Falcon? Or Hawk?"

"No and no." He stood and buckled his belt. Grabbed his bow and quiver. "I'll take the eyepiece now."

Her eyebrows drew together, creasing the pale skin between. "No."

"Mole, if you're seen with that device, there won't be any way to pass you off as one of us."

"But I wore it yesterday."

"Yesterday was yesterday. Here on it'll be different."

"Take your tattoos off first, Savage."

Perry froze, grinding down into his teeth. The funny thing about being called a Savage was that it made him want to act like one. "We're not in your world anymore, Dweller. People die here and it's not pseudo. It's very, very real."

She tipped her chin up, daring him. "You do it then. You've seen how it's done."

132

In a flash of memory, Perry saw Soren ripping the device off her face. He didn't want to do this. He reached for the knife at his hip. "If that's how it needs to be."

"Wait! I'll do it." She turned away from him. When she faced him again seconds later, she had the device in her hand. Her face was tight with fury as she slipped it into a pocket.

Perry took a step toward her. He twirled the knife in his hand like any kid could do, but it worked, drawing her eye to the weapon. "I said I'll take it."

"Stop! Just stay away from me. Here." She flung it at him.

Perry caught it, dropped it into his satchel. Then he walked away, nearly fumbling his knife as he slipped it back into its sheath.

15 ⌒

ARIA

Aria struggled to keep up with the Outsider the second day. Her feet grew worse with every step. *Here on, it'll be different,* he'd said. But it hadn't been. The hours passed much as they had the previous day. Constant walking. Constant pain. Headaches that came and went.

She'd given up speaking with the Outsider. They trudged in silence, with only the sound of her book covers crunching over the earth. She'd almost laughed when she'd read *The Odyssey* on the leather. It wasn't a good omen for their journey. But she hadn't seen any Sirens or Cyclops so far, just scrubby hills with clusters of trees here and there. She'd thought there'd be so much to fear out here, but her companion was the scariest thing around.

They spent an hour digging with flat rocks around midday. Somehow the Outsider had found water a foot beneath the ground. They filled their waterskins and ate in silence. When they were done they sat for a while, the Aether flowing calmly above them. The Outsider looked up, considering the sky. He'd done it often throughout the day. There was something so intent in the way he studied the Aether. Like he found meaning in it.

Aria lined her collection of rocks in front of her. She was up to fifteen. She noticed dirt under her fingernails. Were her nails *longer*? They couldn't be. Nails weren't supposed to grow. Nail growth was regress. Pointless, so it had been eliminated.

The Outsider brought out a flat stone from his leather pack and began to sharpen his knife. Aria watched him from the corner of her eye. His hands were broad and big boned. They drew the blade over the smooth surface in even, sure strokes. The metal hissed a quiet rhythm. Her gaze drifted higher. Daylight caught on the fine blond fuzz over his jaw. Facial hair was another trait genetic engineers had done away with. The Outsider's hands stopped. He peered up, a quick flash of green. Then he put away his things and they walked again.

In all the quiet, Aria was left to circle in her own thoughts. They weren't good ones. Her enthusiasm over finding the Smarteye had worn off. She'd tried distracting herself yesterday by observing the outside, but that no longer worked. She missed Paisley and Caleb. She thought about her mother and wondered about the "Songbird" message. She worried that her feet would get infected. Whenever a headache flared, she imagined that it was the first symptom of an illness that would kill her.

Aria wanted to feel like herself again. A girl who chased the best music in the Realms and bored her friends with facts on inane subjects. Here, she was a girl with leather book covers for shoes. A girl stuck walking across hills with a mute Savage if she had any hope of staying alive.

She made up a tune to match all the fear and helplessness she kept locked inside. A mournful, terrible melody that was her secret, sung only in the privacy of her thoughts. Aria hated the tune. Hated even more how much she needed it. She vowed that when she found Lumina, she'd leave this pathetic part of herself on the outside where it belonged. She'd never sing the sad melody again.

That night, she collapsed before the Outsider had the fire burning, wrapped in the blue fleece blanket. She rested her head on his leather bag, finding that she needed a pillow more than she feared filth.

She had never known this much pain. She had never been this tired. She hoped that was it. That she was tired, and not surrendering to the Death Shop.

On the morning of their third day of traveling together, the Outsider divided the last of the food he'd brought from the cave. He ate, avoiding looking her way, as usual. Aria shook her head. He was rude and cold and eerily animal, with his flashing green eyes and his wolfish teeth, but by some miracle they'd struck a deal. She could've had worse luck than to have crossed paths with him.

Aria chewed on a dried fig as she ran through the inventory

of her discomforts. A headache, muscle pains, and cramps low in her stomach. She couldn't look at the soles of her feet anymore.

"I'll have to hunt later," the Outsider said, poking at the fire with a stick. The morning was cooler. They'd been climbing steadily into higher terrain. He'd put on a long-sleeved shirt beneath the leather vest. It was a tired white color, rife with loose threads and patched holes. It looked like something a shipwreck survivor might wear, but she found it easier to look at him fully dressed.

"Fine," she said, and frowned. Monosyllabicism. An Outsider disease, and she'd been infected.

"We'll be moving onto the mountain today," he said, his gaze darting to her feet. "Well out of my brother's territory."

Aria shifted the blanket tighter around her. He had a brother? She didn't know why it was hard to imagine. Maybe because she hadn't seen any sign of other Outsiders. And she'd had no idea the land out here had any divisions.

"Territory? Is he a duke or something?"

The corner of his mouth lifted in a smirk. "Something like that."

Oh, this was champ. She'd found herself a Savage prince. *Don't laugh,* she told herself. *Don't laugh, Aria.* He was being downright chatty, for him, and she needed to talk. Or listen. She couldn't go another day with nothing but that melody rattling like a ghost in her mind.

"There are territories," he said, "and there's open land where the dispersed roam."

"What are dispersed?"

His eyes narrowed, annoyed at being interrupted. "People who live outside of tribe protection. Wanderers who move in small groups or alone. Looking for food and shelter and . . . just looking to stay alive." He paused, his wide shoulders shifting. "Bigger tribes claim territories. My brother is a Blood Lord. He commands my tribe, the Tides."

Blood Lord. What a horrible-sounding title. "Are you close to your brother?"

He looked at the stick in his hands. "We were once. Now he wants to kill me."

Aria froze. "Are you serious?"

"You've asked me that before. Do you Dwellers only joke?"

"Not only," she answered. "But we do."

Aria waited for his ridicule. She had a fair idea now how hard his life was, if finding a drink of murky water took an hour's worth of digging. There didn't seem to be much to laugh about out here. But the Outsider didn't say anything. He tossed the stick into the fire and leaned forward, resting his arms on his knees. She wondered what he saw in the flames. Was it the boy he looked for?

Aria didn't understand why an Outsider boy would ever be kidnapped. The Pods controlled populations carefully. Everything had to be regulated. Why would they waste precious resources on a Savage child?

The Outsider picked up his bow and quiver, looping them over his shoulder. "No talking once we cross that ridge. Not a word, understand?"

"Why? What's out there?"

His eyes, always bright, looked like green lights in the pale dawn. "Your stories are, Mole. All of them."

As soon as they set off Aria knew this day would be different.

Until that morning, the Outsider had been aloof, light on his feet for all his size. But now he sank into his legs, wary and watchful. The headache that had been coming and going since she'd had her Smarteye ripped off stayed for good, ringing like a shrill whistle in her ears. Her sandals slipped over rocky slopes, chaffing at her blisters. The Outsider kept looking back at her, but she wouldn't meet his gaze. She had promised to keep up, so she would. And what choice did she have?

By midday, her feet had begun to ooze a disgusting combination of blood and pus. Aria couldn't walk without biting the inside of her lip. Eventually her lip started bleeding too.

The way grew less steep as they entered into the woods, giving her feet and muscles a break. She was remembering the last time she'd been beneath trees, with Soren chasing her and Paisley, when they came abruptly to an empty field.

Aria stopped beside the Outsider as they took in a wide patch of earth that was gray, almost silver, and perfectly bare. She didn't see a single twig or blade of grass. Only the golden wink of a few scattered embers and gentle traces of smoke rising here and there. She knew this was the scar left by an Aether strike.

The Outsider put a finger to his lips, signaling for quiet. He reached down to his belt and slowly withdrew his knife, motioning for her to stay close. *What is it?* she wanted to ask. *What do you see?* She forced herself not to speak as they wove through the trees.

She was no more than ten feet away when she saw the person hunched in the knot of a tree, barefoot and wearing tatty, shredded clothes. She did not know if it was a man or a woman. The skin was too drawn and dirty to tell. Owlish eyes peered through yellow-white locks of hair. Aria thought the thing was smiling at first, then realized it had no lips, and so no way to conceal its snaggled brown teeth. It might have been a corpse if it hadn't been for the panicked look in its eyes.

Aria couldn't look away. The creature in the tree lifted its head, daylight glistening on the saliva that ran down its chin. With its eyes on the Outsider, it uttered a strange, desperate wail. An inhuman sound, but Aria understood. It was a call for mercy.

The Outsider touched her arm. Aria jumped and then realized he was just guiding her on. For the next hour, she couldn't get her heart to settle down. She felt those bulging eyes on her and heard the echo of that horrid wail. Questions raced through her mind. She wanted to understand how a person could become that way. How could they survive alone and terrified? But she kept silent, knowing she would endanger them by speaking.

Somehow she'd come to think she and the Outsider were alone in this empty world. They weren't. Now she wondered what *else* was out there.

They found another cave in the late afternoon. This one was damp and crossed with formations that looked like melted wax. It stank of sulfur. Scraps of plastic and bone littered the ground.

The Outsider set his leather bag down. "I'm going to hunt," he said quietly. "I'll be back before it's dark."

"I'm not staying here alone. What was that thing?"

"I told you about the dispersed."

"Well, I'm not staying. You can't leave me here with that dispersed thing out there."

"That *thing* is the least of our worries. Besides, it's well behind us."

"I'll be quiet."

"Not quiet enough. Look, we need to eat and I can't hunt with you skittering all over the place."

"I saw some berries back there. We passed a bush with berries."

"Just stay here," he said, his voice growing harsh. "Rest your feet." He reached into his satchel and handed her a knife, hilt first.

It was a small knife, not the long one she'd seen him sharpening. There were feathers carved into the horn handle. It struck her as absurd to decorate such a sinister tool. "I don't know what to do with this."

"Wave it around and yell, Mole. Loud as you can. That's all you need to do."

It grew dark in the cave well before it did outside. Aria moved to the mouth and listened to an odd quiet with a headache ringing in her ears. The cave sat along a slope. She studied the trees around, straining her eyes as she searched downhill for people huddled in knots. She didn't see any. Some of the trees were leafless and bare. She wondered why some thrived and others died. Was it the soil? Or was it the Aether choosing certain ones to incinerate? She saw no reason in it. No pattern. Nothing made sense out here.

She ached to talk to someone. Anyone. She needed to not be alone right now, thinking of that tree person. When she heard rustlings in the depths of the cave, Aria crawled to the Outsider's leather pack and found her Smarteye. It didn't work, but maybe wearing it would calm her as it had the first day. And it would annoy the Outsider too. That counted for something.

She went back to the mouth of the cave and applied the device. It grabbed tight to her skin, pulling uncomfortably on her eye socket. She held her breath, praying to see her Smartscreen. The message from her mother. Anything. But of course the Eye hadn't fixed itself.

Pais, she pretended to say through the Eye. Paisley was dead. She still couldn't believe it. The tears came out of her in a rush. *Since I'm pretending already, I'm going to pretend you're still alive and that this is a big joke. A Practical Joke Realm. But a really terrible one that should be deleted. I'm in a cave, Paisley. On the outside. You'd hate it. I hate it.* She wiped her tears with her sleeve. *This is the second cave I've been in. It stinks like rotten eggs in here. And there are noises. Weird draggy noises, like something is dragging? But the first cave wasn't so bad. It was smaller and warmer. Can you believe I have a favorite cave? Paisley . . . I'm not doing so great right now.*

Crying had sent her headache piercing through the backs of her eyes and she knew, she just *knew* the tree thing was in the cave shuffling toward her. She pictured that big stare and the gnarled mouth with all the crooked teeth and glistening drool.

Aria grabbed the knife and darted outside.

Silence. She sniffed and looked around. No tree people. Nothing but the woods. The cave loomed behind her. She was *not* going back in there.

She picked her way down the slope, overly aware of the knife in her hand. She found the berry bush without any trouble. Smiling, she stuffed as many berries into her cargo pockets as she could and then made a bowl with her shirt.

She imagined what the Outsider would say when he saw them. It would be one word, no doubt. But he'd see she could do better than *stay.* Aria hurried back uphill, deciding she'd take control over what she could. She was tired of being useless.

She hadn't been gone more than half an hour, she guessed, but darkness was falling fast. She smelled the smoke first and then saw a pale column up ahead, against the deepening blue sky. The Outsider had returned. She almost called out to him, wanting to brag about her berries. She decided to surprise him instead.

Aria came to a dead stop a few feet away from the cave. Smoke tumbled from the top of the wide mouth like a waterfall pouring upward. Several male voices spoke inside. She didn't recognize any of them. She backed away as quietly as she could, her heart thundering in her chest. With her ringing ears, she couldn't tell how much noise she made. She found out when three figures emerged from the cave.

By the failing light, she saw that one man, the tallest, wore a black cape, the hood pulled over a mask with a long, crowlike beak. He held a pale staff with bits of rope and feathers dangling from the top. He stayed by the cave as two other men came toward her.

"Rat . . . is that a Dweller?" said one.

"It is indeed," answered the other. He was slight and bald, with a large pointed nose that left little doubt as to the origin of his name. "You're well gone from home, en't you, girl?"

She heard jingling. Aria's gaze snapped to Rat's waist. Bells hung from his belt, winking in the dim light. They trilled with each step he took.

"Stop there." She remembered she had a knife. She went to raise it, and saw that she already held it in front of her. Aria raised it higher. "Don't come any closer."

Rat grinned, showing teeth that looked like they'd been filed to points. "Easy, girl. We're not going to hurt ya. Are we, Trip?"

"No, we won't hurt you," said Trip. He had intricate tattoos around his eyes, like embroidery. Like something she might see in a Masquerade Realm. "I never thought I'd see a Mole."

144

"Not alive," said Rat. "What're you doing out here, girl?"

Aria's gaze flicked to the crow man, who'd begun to come forward, moving with total silence. As frightened as she was of Rat and Trip, the crow man scared her more. Rat and Trip went still as he approached.

The crow man stood well over six feet tall. He had to look down to see her. The mask was terrifying, the beak angular and pointed, made of leather that had been pulled and stretched over a frame. The smooth parts were the color of skin, but a dirty inky color stained the creases. She could see his eyes through the holes in the mask. They were blue and clear as glass.

"What's your name?" he asked.

"Aria." She answered because there was no way she couldn't.

"Where are you heading, Aria?"

"Home."

"Of course." The crow man tipped his head to the side. "I'm sorry. This must frighten you." He removed the mask, letting it hang by a leather cord that he twisted so it fell over his back. He was younger than she expected. Only a few years older than she was, with dark hair and those clear blue eyes. She realized how much calmer she felt now that she could see his face.

He smiled. "That helped, didn't it? My people bring in the night with ceremony. We use masks to scare off spirits of darkness. My friends aren't initiated yet, or they'd be wearing them too. I'm called Harris. It's good to meet you, Aria."

His voice was a beautiful, smoky baritone. He sent Trip and Rat a pointed look.

"Yes. Good to meet you," they said, tipping their heads and setting the bells ringing again.

"Bells are another part of our ceremony," Harris said, following her gaze.

"Ancient cultures used bells," she said, hating herself for knowing stupid things and for not being able to keep quiet when she was nervous.

"I've heard that Tibetans did."

"Yes. They did." Aria couldn't believe he knew that. A Savage who knew more than just digging holes and starting fires. A spark of hope lit inside her. "They believed bells represented the wisdom of emptiness."

"I've known a few people with empty minds, but I wouldn't call them wise." Harris smiled, his eyes flicking to Trip. "To us, bells are noises of lightness and good. Are you alone, Aria?"

"No. I'm with an Outsider."

It was darker now, but by the soft light of the Aether, she saw his eyebrows furrow.

"I meant one of you," she said, realizing they wouldn't call themselves Outsiders.

"Ah . . . that's good. This is dangerous land. I'm sure your companion told you."

"Yes. He did."

Trip snorted. "Nearly soiled myself when I heard you sneaking up on us."

Rat lifted his big nose and sniffed the air. He shoved Trip in the shoulder. "Nearly?"

Harris smiled apologetically. "We have enough food to share and a fire going. Why don't you and your companion join us tonight? If you think you can put up with these two."

"I don't think so. But thank you." She realized she was gripping the handle of the knife so tight her knuckles throbbed. Why did she have a knife? She lowered it. As frightening as he'd looked with the mask on, Harris seemed friendly now. Far more than her Outsider, whose name she didn't even know. And Harris *talked*.

"Well," she said, reconsidering. "I could see what he says."

"I say no."

They all turned sharply toward the voice uphill. It was her Outsider. He was barely visible in the faint light of dusk.

Aria was just going to call out to him when she heard a sound like a wet slap, followed by the ringing of bells. Rat tripped and fell backward. At least, this was what Aria thought until she saw a stick—no, an arrow—lodged in his throat.

She didn't think. She spun and ran. Trip caught her arm and trapped it, twisting the knife from her fingers. Then he laid the blade on her neck and thrust her arm behind her. Aria gasped at the burst of pain in her shoulder. His stench brought a sickening roll to her stomach.

"Lower your bow or I'll kill her!" Trip's voice exploded by her ear.

She saw him now. The Outsider had come closer. He

stood by the cave, his legs and arms lined up with his bow, a weapon he had been carrying for days but that somehow she'd forgotten about. He'd taken off his white shirt, and his skin blended into the murky woods.

"Do what he says!" Aria cried. What was he doing? It was too dark. He would hit her instead of Trip.

She saw movement to her left. Harris started up the hill toward the Outsider. He no longer held the staff but a long knife that reflected the Aether light. He drew closer in determined strides. The Outsider kept still as a statue, either not seeing Harris or not caring.

Trip's panicked breath pumped hot foul air against her cheek. "Lower your bow!" he yelled.

She didn't see anything this time either, but she knew he'd fired another arrow. Aria heard a pop and then she jolted backward. She tumbled over Trip. Momentum carried her down the slope. Her knee struck something sharp as she hit the ground. She sprang to her feet despite the stab of pain that shot down her leg.

Trip lay twitching on his side, an arrow stuck in the left part of his chest. She turned uphill, terror like a shriek in her ears. She'd seen people wrestle and fence in the Realms. She had some idea of what a true fight might look like. Parrying and deflecting. Footwork and guards. She couldn't have been more wrong.

Harris and the Outsider swept past each other in streaks of movement, one bare-skinned, the other draped in black cloth. She could just make out the flash of a knife or the twisting crow mask. She wanted to run. She didn't want to see this. But she couldn't bring herself to move.

It took no more than seconds, though it felt much longer. Their bodies slowed and parted. The cloaked figure, Harris, hit the ground in a black heap. The bare-skinned Outsider stood above him.

Then she saw something roll downhill as if it had been bowled toward her. It hit a bump that shook loose a pale mask, and now she saw clear blue eyes and a nose and white teeth and black hair, tumbling over the dirt and trailing red.

PEREGRINE

"No, no, no." Aria shook her head, her eyes were wide with terror. "What just happened?"

Perry skidded over loose gravel as he sprinted downhill to her. "Are you hurt?"

She leaped back. "Stay away from me! Don't touch me." Her hand came to her stomach. "What just happened? What did you just do?"

Every scent came to Perry clear and strong on the cool night air. Blood and smoke. Her fear, like ice. And something else. A pungent bitterness. He inhaled, scanning, and saw the source. Dark patches stained the front of her shirt.

"What is that?" he asked.

Her head whipped to the side like she expected to see someone. Perry grabbed a fistful of her shirt. She grazed him with a punch to the chin.

"Hold still!" He trapped her wrist and brought the shirt

up, drawing the scent in. He couldn't believe it. "That's why you left? You left for those berries?"

Then he saw that she was wearing the device over her eye again. Those men could have taken the eyepiece. Then how would he have gotten Talon back? She pulled out of his grasp.

"You slaughtered them," she said, her lips trembling. "Look what you did."

Perry pressed his fist to his mouth and stalked away, not trusting himself to be near her. He'd crossed the Croven's scent soon after he had left her. Perry knew they were heading toward the shelter of the cave. He'd taken another path, had sprinted to get there first, only to find the cave empty. By the time he'd picked up her trail and followed it, he'd been too late. She had brought him right back to the cave.

Perry rounded on her. "Stupid Dweller. I told you to stay here! You left to pick *poisonous* berries."

She shook her head, turning a stunned look from the Croven's dead body to him. "How could you? They wanted to share their food with us . . . and you just *killed* them."

Perry was coming off the rush and beginning to shake. She didn't know what he had scented from those men. Their ache for her flesh had been so potent it had nearly scored his nostrils. "Fool. You were going to *be* their food."

"No . . . no. . . . They didn't do anything. You just started shooting at them. . . . *You* did this. You're worse than the stories, Savage. You're a *monster*."

He couldn't believe what he was hearing. "This is the third time I save your life and that's what you call me?" He had to get away from her. He jabbed a finger into the dark, pointing east. "Mount Arrow is on the other side of that ridge. Head three hours that way. Let's see how you do on your own out here, Mole."

He spun and broke into a run, plunging swiftly into the woods. He pounded his rage into the earth but slowed after a few miles. He wanted to leave her, but he couldn't. She had the Smarteye. And she was a Mole who lived in fake worlds. What did she know about surviving out here?

He circled back and found her, keeping far enough away that she wouldn't see him. She had Talon's knife in her hand. Perry cursed at himself. How had he forgotten that? He watched as she picked through the woods with surprising quiet and care. After a while, he realized she was managing to keep a straight course too. He'd wanted to see her panic. She hadn't, and that streaked him even more. With only a short distance left to go, he pulled ahead and ran the rest of the way.

It was still dark when he reached the Blackfins compound. Perry caught his breath as he absorbed the shocking scene around him. The compound looked nothing like the bustling settlement he'd seen a year ago. Now, it was crushed. Abandoned. All its scents faded and old. A picked-over carcass at the foot of Mount Arrow.

Aether storms and fires had leveled all but one of the homes, but one was all he needed. There was no door and only part of a roof. He dropped his satchel at the threshold so she'd know where to find him. Then he went inside and sank onto a battered straw mattress. Above him the broken roof's timbers stuck out like ribs.

Perry dropped his arm over his eyes.

Had he left her too soon?

Had she gotten lost?

Where was she?

Finally he heard faint footsteps. He looked toward the door in time to see her rest her head on his satchel. Then he closed his eyes and slept.

He stepped outside quietly the next morning. Her small camouflage-clad form was curled against the wall, lit by the hazy light of a clouded sky. Aria's black hair fell over her face, but he could see she'd taken off the device. She held it in her hand like it was one of the rocks she collected. Then he saw her bare feet. Dirty. Wet with blood. Raw flesh showing where the skin had peeled back or fallen off completely. The book covers must have broken after he'd left her.

What had he done?

She stirred, peering at him through her lashes before she sat up against the house. Perry shifted his weight, wondering what to say. He didn't mull it over long before her temper came at him, bringing him a rush of alarm.

"Aria, what's wrong?"

She stood, moving slow and defeated. "I'm dying. I'm bleeding."

Perry's gaze traveled down her body.

"It's not my feet."

"Did you eat any of those berries?"

"No." She held out her hand. "You might as well have this. Maybe it'll still help you find the boy you're looking for."

Perry closed his eyes and inhaled. Her scent had changed. The rancy Dweller musk was almost gone. Her skin breathed a new scent into the air, faint but unmistakable. For the first time since he'd known her, her flesh smelled like something he recognized, feminine and sweet.

He smelled violets.

He took a step back, swearing silently as it hit him. "You're not dying. . . . You really don't know?"

"I don't know anything anymore."

Perry looked down at the ground and drew another breath, no doubt in his mind.

"Aria . . . it's your first blood."

ARIA

Since she had been thrown out of Reverie, she'd survived an Aether storm, she'd had a knife held to her throat by a cannibal, and she'd seen men murdered.

This was worse.

Aria didn't recognize herself. She felt like she'd donned a pseudo-body in a Realm and couldn't get out of it.

Her mind ran in circles. She was bleeding. Like an animal. Dwellers didn't menstruate. Procreating happened through genetic design, then a special course of hormones and implantation. Fertility was used strictly when needed. How terrifying to think she could *conceive* at random.

Maybe the outside air was changing her. Maybe she was breaking down. Malfunctioning. How would she explain this to her mother? What if she couldn't be fixed and this happened to her again, what, every month?

She'd been prepared for death. Death was to be expected

on the outside. A normal consequence of being tossed into the Death Shop. But no matter how she looked at it, menstruating was utterly barbaric. She lay down on the filthy mattress, feeling much the same. Filthy. She closed her eyes, hoping to shut out the horrible outside world. She imagined lying on the white sand of her favorite beach Realm, listening to the soft lapping of the waves as she began to relax.

Aria tried to restart her Smarteye again.

It worked flawlessly.

All her icons were back, exactly where they should be. The icon of Aria strangling herself slid to the center of her screen, flashing a reminder.

SINGING SUNDAY. 11 A.M.

She chose it and fractioned instantly. Swaths of the Opera House's crimson curtain billowed in front of her. Aria reached out, touching the thick velvet. She'd never seen it move like this, in rolling waves. She stepped forward, feeling through the heavy cloth for the center seam. She felt the curtain shift as it surrounded her. She turned in circles and saw no way out. Panicked, she pushed out her arms, but the material grew coarse as gravel beneath her touch.

Lumina! Aria yelled, but no sound came from her. *Mom!* she tried again. Where had her voice gone? She grabbed hold of the curtain and pulled with all her strength. It came loose with a lurch and began to spin, turning around her in a funnel, blowing her hair into her eyes and drawing closer with every second. She wouldn't let herself be swallowed by it. Aria counted to three and dove into the whirling mass.

Instantly she appeared at center stage. Lumina sat in her usual seat in the front row. Why did she seem so far, like she was a mile away? What kind of Realm was this?

Mom? Aria still couldn't hear her voice. *Mom!*

"I knew you'd come," Lumina said, but her smile faded quickly. "Aria, is that another joke?"

A joke? Aria looked down. She was in camouflaged army clothes. Here, in the formal opera hall. *No, Mom!*

She wanted to tell Lumina what had happened. About Soren and Consul Hess and being thrown out with the Savage. But the words wouldn't come. Tears of frustration blurred her vision. She looked down, not wanting her mother to see, and noticed a small book in her hands. A libretto. The lyrics of an opera. She didn't know where she'd gotten it or when. Flowers drawn in ink scrolled across the faded parchment, twining together to form letters.

ARIA

Dread seeped through her. Was this her story? She opened the book and recognized the image inside instantly. A double-helix spiral turned on the page. DNA.

"It's a gift, Aria." Lumina smiled. "Aren't you going to sing, Songbird? No Cannibal Candy this time, please. Though it was certainly amusing."

Aria wanted to scream. She needed to tell her mother that she was sorry and that she was furious at her and where was she? Where *was* she? Aria tried again and again, but she couldn't make a sound. She couldn't even hear herself breathe.

"I see," Lumina said. She rose and smoothed down her tailored black dress. "I'd hoped you'd changed your mind. I'll be here when you're ready," she said, and vanished.

Aria blinked at the gilded hall. "Mom?" Her voice startled her. "Mom!" she yelled, but it was too late. For long moments, she stood on the stage, feeling the vastness of the hall, the emptiness of it, as a feeling built in her as if she might explode. She didn't know when she started screaming. And then she didn't know how to stop. The sound coming out of her grew louder and louder, like it would never end. The Grand Chandelier began to shake first and then the gilded columns and box seats. And then, at once, the walls and seats shattered, sending gold and plaster and crimson velvet everywhere.

Aria flew upright, gasping, clutching the ratty mattress beneath her. Her Smarteye rested in the palm of her hand, moist with the sweat of her nightmare.

The Outsider strode into the house a moment later. He peered at her suspiciously as he handed her a chunk of meat and then left. Aria ate, too numb to make any sense of what had just happened. She'd dreamed. Now both her body and mind felt foreign.

She heard the Outsider moving through the rubble outside. She sat back and listened to the thud of rocks hitting earth, or clacking sharply as they struck other rocks. Hours had passed when he returned carrying the navy blanket cinched like a sling.

He set it down without a word and spread it out, revealing a pile of odd things. A ring rolled over the fleece before it settled to a stop. She noticed a blue gemstone set into the thick gold band just as he swept it up and dropped it into his satchel. He sat on his heels and cleared his throat.

"I found a few things for you. . . . A coat. It's made of wolf fur. It'll get colder as we move farther up the mountain so it'll keep you warmer." He glanced at her, then back at the pile. "Those boots are in fair shape. A touch big but they should work. The cloths are clean. Boiled." A fleeting smile crossed his lips, though his eyes remained downcast. "They're for . . . whatever you want to do with them. There are a few other things. I brought what I could find."

She looked at the random assortment, emotion sticking like glue in her throat. A ragged old leather coat with holes she could poke her fingers through but lined with thick silvery fur. A black knitted cap with a few feathers slipped into the woven wool. A piece of leather with a buckle that looked like it had once been a horse bridle but would serve better as a belt than the gauze she used now. He'd spent hours locating these things. Digging them up, as he had their water and the thistle roots. Like most things needed to be on the outside.

"What you said about my Markings . . . my tattoos," he continued. "You were on the right track." He looked up, meeting her eyes. "I'm called Peregrine. Like the falcon. People call me Perry."

He had a name. Peregrine. Perry. New information to

consider. Did it suit him? Did it mean something? But Aria found she couldn't even look at him. A Savage had needed to explain to her that she was menstruating. She bit into her raw inner lip and tasted blood. Her eyes blurred. She had never thought so much about blood before. Now she couldn't get away from it.

"Why did you do this?" she asked. "Find all this stuff for me?" Pity. It had to be out of pity that he'd gathered all of this and told her his name.

"You needed it." He rubbed a hand over the back of his head. Then he sat down, propping his long arms over his knees and lacing his fingers together. "You thought you were dying this morning. But you brought me the eyepiece anyway. You were going to give it to me of your own will."

Aria picked up a rock. She'd developed a habit of lining them up. By color. By size. By shape. Making sense of the randomness she'd admired at first. Now she just looked at the conglomerate chunk in her hand, wondering why she'd ever bothered pocketing such an ugly mixed-up thing.

She didn't know if she'd brought the Smarteye back to be noble, exactly. Maybe so. But maybe she'd done it because she knew he'd been right about the cannibals. And she owed him for saving her life. Three times.

"Thank you." She didn't sound very grateful and wished she had. She knew she needed these things, and needed his help. But she didn't want to need anything.

He nodded, accepting her thanks.

They fell into silence. The Aether light seeped down into the decrepit house, washing away the shadows. As tired as she was, her senses filled with the chill of the air against her face. With the weight of the rock resting in her hand and the dusty smell he'd brought in with him. Aria heard her own breathing and felt the quiet power of his attention. She felt completely where she was. There with him. With herself.

She'd never felt anything like it.

"My people celebrate the first blood," he said after a moment, his voice soft and deep. "The women in the tribe prepare a feast. They bring gifts to the girl—woman. They stay with her that night, all the women in one house. And . . . I don't know what happens after that. My sister says they tell stories, but I don't know what they are. I think they explain the meaning of it . . . of the change you're going through."

Aria's cheeks went hot. She didn't want to change. She wanted to go home perfectly preserved. "What meaning can there be? Seems like a horrible thing no matter how you look at it."

"You can bear children now."

"That's completely primitive! Children are *special* where I come from. They're created carefully, each one. It's not a random experiment. There's so much thought that goes into every person. You have no idea."

Too late, she remembered that he was trying to rescue a boy. Making her shoes. Murdering three men. Saving her life. The Outsider had done it all for the boy. Obviously children were cherished here as well, but she couldn't take the words back.

She wasn't sure why she cared. He was a killer. Scarred. Covered with signs of violence. What did it matter that she'd been insensitive to a murderer?

"You've killed before, haven't you?" She already knew the answer. Still, she wanted to hear him tell her *no*. Tell her something that would take away the queasy feeling she got every time she remembered what he'd done to those three men.

He didn't answer. He never answered, and she was tired of it. Sick of his quiet, watchful eyes. "How many men have you killed? Ten? Twenty? Do you keep some sort of count?" Aria had raised her voice to let some of the poison out. He rose and moved to the threshold, but she didn't stop. She *couldn't* stop.

"If you do, you shouldn't add Soren. You didn't kill him, though I know you tried. You shattered his jaw. Shattered it! But maybe Bane and Echo and Paisley brought your numbers up."

He spoke through a clenched jaw. "Do you have any idea what would've happened if I hadn't been there that night? And yesterday?"

She did. And here it was. The fear she'd pressed back. Of those men, who'd seemed friendly but who ate human flesh. Of the terrible hours she'd spent running alone, searching for glimpses of Mount Arrow, hoping she was headed the right way in the dark. She was lashing out recklessly but she knew the true source of her anger. She didn't trust her own judgment anymore. What did she know out here? Even *berries* might kill her.

"So what!" she yelled, scrambling to her feet. "So what if you saved my life! You *left*! And do you really think it makes you a good person? Saving one person when you kill three others? And bringing these things for me? Saying things, like it's an honor what's happening to me? It's not an honor! This shouldn't happen. I'm not an animal! I haven't forgotten what you did to those men. I won't forget."

He laughed bitterly. "If it makes you feel better, I won't forget either."

"You have a conscience? That's touching. My mistake. I had you figured wrong."

He crossed the distance between them in a flash. Aria found herself looking up, right into furious green eyes. "You know nothing about me."

She knew his hand was on the knife at his hip. Aria's heart pounded so hard she could hear it drumming in her ears. "You would've already done it. You don't hurt women."

"You're wrong there, Mole. I have killed a woman before. Keep talking. You might be the second."

A choked sob burst through her lips. He was telling the truth.

He turned his back on her and stood there a moment. "The Croven will retaliate," he said. "If you're coming, we travel now. In the dark."

After he left, she stood breathing hard for a few moments, absorbing what had just happened. What she'd said, and what he'd admitted to. She didn't want to think of what cannibals did to retaliate, or of the Outsider taking a woman's life.

Aria looked down at the navy blanket. She stared at it as her breath calmed and the urge to scream and cry receded.

Boots. At least she had boots now.

— 18 —

PEREGRINE

They kept a good pace despite traveling at night. They needed to. Three slain Croven would bring out their tribesmen in search of revenge. The Croven would surely have a Scire among them who'd latch on to Perry's scent. It was only a matter of time before they came after him in their black cloaks and masks.

Perry had committed the greatest possible wrong against the Croven, who believed they brought the spirits of the dead into themselves by eating flesh. By leaving those three men out for scavenging animals, he would be seen as a murderer not of men but of eternal souls. The Croven wouldn't stop in their quest for vengeance until they found him. He should have burned the bodies or buried them, both of which could've bought him time. He glanced at Aria, walking ten paces away from him. He should have done a few things differently.

She met his eyes for an instant before looking away. Beast, she'd called him. Monster. Her temper told him she felt the same way toward him now. He'd lost his mind, hearing those things. Scenting her reaction to what he'd done. To what he'd had to do, because of her. He didn't need anyone telling him what he was. He knew. He'd known what he was since the day he was born.

The air became cool and sharp as they climbed into the mountain. As the pine forest grew thicker, Perry saw the power of his Sense diminish. Pine blasted his nose, shrouding subtler scents and stunting his range. He knew he'd adapt in time but it worried him, not having his ability at its strongest. They were well into the borderlands now. He needed both his Senses at their best to steer clear of the Croven and other dispersed who hid out in these woods.

Perry spent the morning adjusting to the change and searching for game trails. He'd shared a lean little rabbit he had caught with Aria yesterday, along with some more roots he'd dug up, but his stomach still growled. He couldn't remember the last time he'd filled it.

Thoughts of Talon grabbed hold of him. What was his nephew doing now? Were his legs bothering him? Did he hate Perry for what had happened? He knew he was avoiding tougher questions. Things too painful to even consider. That maybe Talon hadn't survived. To think that way would've laid him out for good. Nothing would matter if that were so.

They took a short rest at midday. Aria leaned against a tree.

She looked drawn, the skin beneath her eyes pale purple. Even tired she had a face made to be looked at. Finespun. Delicate. Beautiful. Perry shook his head, surprised by his own thoughts.

Late in the afternoon, they stopped for a drink by a creek that cut a lazy, winding path through a ravine. Perry washed his face and hands, then drank deeply from the icy water. Aria stayed where she'd dropped along the bank.

"Is it your feet?"

Her eyes turned to him. "I'm hungry."

He nodded. He was hungry too. "I'll find us something."

"I don't want your food. I don't want anything else from you."

Bitter words but her temper, sluggish and dank, spoke of deep despair. Perry watched her for a moment. He understood. This, at least, wasn't about him. He wouldn't want to ask to eat every time his stomach felt empty either.

They walked on, following the creek up the mountain. This was decent land, kept green by snowmelt. Too hilly for farming, but the hunting would be better than at home. He searched for animal scents, hoping to find anything but the musk of wolves. With night a few hours off, he knew they'd have to rest soon and eat, too. Just as he was growing frustrated with his pine-fettered nose, he crossed a sweet scent that set his mouth watering.

"Rest for a bit." He jogged off a couple of paces. "I'll be right back."

Aria sat right away and shrugged. He waited, expecting her to say something. Wanting her to, but she didn't say a word.

He came back a few moments later and knelt in front of her on the gravelly bank. With the pine trees towering over them, it was growing dark already, though night was still a good hour off. Behind him the creek gurgled softly. Her eyes narrowed when she saw the leafy branch in his hand, spotted with dark red berries.

"What are you doing?"

"Teaching you so you can find your own food," he said, looking down at the branch, wondering if she'd laugh at him in the next moment and call him a Savage. "Soon you'll recognize what's safe to eat by knowing where things grow, and recognizing the shapes of the leaves. Until then, the first thing is to crush a small piece and smell it."

He peered at her. She sat up, looking more alert. Relieved, he plucked a berry and handed it to her. "If it smells nutty and bitter, don't eat it."

Aria broke it open, dipped her head to sniff it. "It doesn't smell like either."

"Good. That's right." The blackberry, a lucky find buried in a patch of brambles, smelled sweet and ripe. Perry could scent it perfectly. This close, he also caught Aria's scent again. Violets. A scent he could never get enough of. And then there was her temper, clear and strong. For the first time today, it wasn't full of anger or repulsion. The tone that came off of her was bright and alert, like mint.

"Look at the color next. If the berry's white or has white inside, it's safer to toss it."

She examined the berry. He could see her mind working, memorizing the information. "This looks dark red."

"Yeah. So far, it's looking good. Next you'd want to rub it on your skin. Tender skin is best." He went to take her hand and remembered how she hated being touched. "The inside of your arm. Right here." He showed her where on his own arm.

She drew the berry over the inside of her wrist. It left a smooth line of juice on her skin. Perry frowned at the stumble in his heartbeat, then made himself not frown.

"So, you'd want to wait a while. If you didn't see a rash creeping on, you'd put a bit on your lip."

He watched as she pressed the berry to her lower lip. He kept looking at her mouth after she'd done it. He knew he should look away, but he couldn't. "Right. Good. If there's no stinging, you'd put it to your tongue."

Perry shot to his feet before he finished the words, nearly tripping over himself. He ran a hand over his head, feeling skitty, like he needed to laugh or run or do something. He picked up a stone and tossed it into the creek, trying to get the image of her tasting the berry out of his mind. Trying to keep from pumping her scent into his nose like he wanted to.

"Is that it?" she asked.

"What? No." All he could think about was the way she'd looked the night of the Aether storm. The curves of her bare skin, pressed at his side. "You'd swallow a small amount and wait a few hours, see how it sits. Now you know how to find berries. We need to pull foot."

He crossed his arms and stood there, still unsure what to do. He knew he was giving her a strange look. He felt strange. He felt *a lot* of strange. He hadn't seen her as a girl before now. He'd seen her as a Mole. Now he couldn't stop seeing all the girl about her.

Aria gave him the same look right back—eyebrows drawn down, mouth twisted to the side, a mixy, strained look—mocking him.

Perry laughed. A ripple ran through his shoulders at the feeling of laughing. When was the last time someone had joked with him? The answer came easily. He'd been with Talon.

"So is this one good?" she asked, holding up the berry.

"Yeah. It's good."

She popped it into her mouth and swallowed. Then she smiled, extending the branch out to him.

"Go ahead," he said, and set to tightening the string on his bow.

When she was finished, she looked over and smiled. "Seems easier if I just find them and ask you whether they're edible or not. Faster than the rubbing and tasting process."

"Sure," he said, feeling like a fool. "That would work too."

19

ARIA

They decided to take turns sleeping, right there by the creek. She was supposed to take her turn first, but when she lay down, she couldn't keep her eyes closed. Dreams were unsettling things, and she wasn't up for another one just yet. So she sat, shivering despite her thick coat and the blue blanket wrapped around her. The Aether moved in thin sheets, slow and wispy as the clouds. Gusts rustled through the pine needles, setting branches swaying around her. There were people who lived in trees and cannibals who dressed as crows out here.

Yesterday she'd seen them both.

"How far away is Marron's?" she asked.

"Three days or so," Peregrine said. He held the small knife with the carved feathers, twirling it absently. Spinning it once. Catching the handle. Spinning it. Catching it.

Peregrine or Perry? She didn't know what to call him. Perry made her shoes from book covers and taught her how to find berries. Peregrine had tattoos and flashing green eyes. He twirled a knife without fear of cutting himself and put arrows through people's necks. She'd seen him *decapitate* a man. But then, the man had been a cannibal who'd been after her. Aria sighed, her breath fogging lightly in the cool air. She wasn't sure what she thought of him anymore.

"Will we get there in time?" she asked.

His lips turned up like he'd been expecting the question. "The Croven aren't close, as far as I can tell."

It wasn't the exact answer she'd wanted, but good to hear nonetheless. "Who is he—Marron?"

"A friend. A trader. A ruler. A bit of everything." His eyes dropped to her shaking shoulders. "Can't have a fire."

"Because someone would see the smoke?"

He nodded. "Or scent it."

She looked at his restless hands. "You don't sit still much, do you?"

He slid the knife through a leather strap at his boot. "Being still makes me tired."

That made no sense, but she wasn't going to ask and risk upsetting what felt like a fragile truce.

He crossed his arms and then uncrossed them. "How do you feel?"

A tingle ran down her back. This was so strange. Him, asking her this. Far more intimate than it should have felt. Because she knew he wanted to know. He didn't ask empty questions or waste words.

"I want to go home."

It was a weak answer and she knew it, but how could she explain? Her body was changing, and it wasn't just that she was menstruating. Her senses were filled with the trickle of the creek and the smell of pine in the air. Her whole awareness was shifting. Like every cell in her body was stretching its arms and yawning off sleep. Sure, she ached in her feet. And she still had the headaches and a dull pain low in her stomach. Yet in spite of all her ailments, she didn't feel like a girl whose life was slipping away.

Perry stood. Perry, she realized. Not Peregrine. It seemed her subconscious had decided what to make of him. She unwrapped herself from the blanket, her muscles aching and reluctant to move again. They might as well walk, she supposed, if they weren't going to sleep. Then she noticed the way Perry stared into the darkness.

"What is it?" she asked, shooting to her feet. "Is it the Croven?"

He shook his head, still gazing into the woods. Perry cupped his hands around his mouth. "Roar!"

The sound of his raised voice made her heart stop.

"Roar, you rancy bastard! I know you're out there! I can smell you from here!"

A moment later, a whistle broke into the air, echoing through the mountain pass.

Perry looked down at her, a striking grin on his face. "Our luck just turned."

He devoured the hillside in big, loping strides. Aria ran to keep up, her heart racing faster than her feet. At the top,

172

they reached an outcropping of boulders that looked blue in the failing light, like whales breeching from the sea. A dark figure stood there, his arms crossed over his chest as though he'd been waiting. Perry tore over to him. Aria watched as they locked into a fierce embrace, then began to shove at each other playfully.

She picked her way closer, taking in this new Outsider. Everything about him looked refined under the cool light. His lean build and sharp features. The cut of his dark hair. He wore fitted clothes. Black from head to toe, with no frayed edges or holes that she could see. This was someone she could easily see in the Realms. Polished and too handsome to be real.

"Who's this?" he asked, seeing her.

"I'm Aria," she answered. "Who are you?"

"Hello, Aria. I'm Roar. Do you sing?"

It was a surprising question, but she answered on reflex. "Yes, I do."

"Excellent." Up close, she saw the gleam in Roar's gaze. He had a prince's looks but a pirate's eyes. Roar smiled, an appealing, clever flash. Aria laughed. Definitely more pirate. Roar laughed at her laugh, and she decided on the spot she liked him.

He looked back at Perry. "Have I gone dull, Per, or is she a Dweller?"

"Long story."

"Perfect." Roar rubbed his palms together. "We'll settle into a few bottles of Luster. Long stories are the best sort for cold nights."

"How'd you come up with Luster out here?" Perry asked.

"Swoggled a bottle a couple of days ago, along with enough bread and cheese to keep us from starving. Let's celebrate. With you here, it won't be long before we find Liv."

Perry's smile vanished. "Find Liv? She's not with the Horns?"

Roar cursed. "Perry, I thought you knew. She ran! I sent word to Vale. I thought you'd come to help find her."

"No." Perry closed his eyes and tipped his head up, the muscles in his neck tight with anger. "We never got word. You stayed with her, right?"

"Of course I did, but you know Liv. She does what she wants."

"She can't," Perry said. "Liv can't do what she wants. How will the Tides survive the winter?"

"I don't know. I've got my own reasons for being streaked about what she's done."

A dozen different questions cropped up in Aria's mind. Who was Liv? What was she running from? She remembered the gold ring with the blue stone that Perry had stashed away. Was the ring for her? She was curious, but it seemed too personal to pry.

Roar and Perry set to work building a screen with leafy branches to form a bulwark against the wind. Whatever had happened with the girl, Liv, had left them quiet. They worked quickly together despite their silence, like they'd done this sort of thing a hundred times. Aria copied the way they wove the branches together and found that for her first-ever screen, she did a respectable job.

They couldn't have a fire, but Roar produced a candle that gave them a flickering light to gather around. Aria had just begun devouring the bread and cheese Roar brought out when she heard the snap of a twig. It sounded close in the quiet. She turned, seeing only the screen of pine branches as she heard footsteps scuttling off in retreat.

"What was that?" She'd just started to relax. Now her heart was pounding again.

Perry bit into a piece of hard bread. "Your friend have a name, Roar?"

Aria scowled at him. How could he dismiss this lurking stranger after what they'd been through with the cannibals?

Roar didn't answer right away. He stared off like he was still listening for movement. Then he unstopped a black bottle and took a long drink, settling back against his bag. "It's a kid, and he's more a pest than a friend. His name is Cinder. I found him sleeping right in the middle of the woods about a week ago. No thought to being seen or sniffed out by wolves. I should've let him be, but he's young . . . thirteen maybe . . . and he's in bad shape. I gave him some food and he's been trailing me since."

Aria peered at the pine screen again. She'd gotten a taste of being alone out there the night Perry had left her behind. Those hours had been filled with nothing but fear. She couldn't imagine a boy living like that.

"What tribe's he from?" Perry asked.

Roar took another drink before he answered. "I don't

know. He has the look of a northerner." He glanced her way. Did *she* look like she was from the north? "But I couldn't get it out of him. Wherever he's from, believe me, I'd love to send him back. He'll show up. He always does when his hunger gets the better of him. But don't expect much from his company."

Roar handed her the black bottle. "It's called Luster. You'll like it, trust me," he said with a wink.

"You don't look very trustworthy."

"Looks can be misleading. I'm reliable to the core."

Perry grinned. "I've known him his whole life. He's full of something else to the core."

Aria froze. She'd seen a glimpse of Perry's smile earlier when he'd heard Roar, but now she saw it in full, directed completely at her. It was lopsided and punctuated by canines that couldn't be ignored, but it was this fierce quality that made it so disarming. Like seeing a lion smile.

She suddenly felt like she was staring at him. She took a hasty drink from the bottle. Aria sputtered into her sleeve as the Luster rolled down her throat like lava, spreading heat across her chest. It tasted like spiced honey, thick and sweet and pungent.

"What do you think?" Roar asked.

"It's like drinking a campfire, but it's good." She couldn't look at Perry. She took another drink, hoping this one would go down without all the hacking. Another wave of fire seeped through her, heating her cheeks and settling warm in her stomach.

"You going to keep it all to yourself?" Perry asked.

"Oh. Sorry." She handed it to him, her face growing hotter.

"How's Talon?" Roar asked. "And Mila? She and Vale have any luck making Talon a brother?" His voice held a hint of wariness beneath the lighthearted words.

Perry sighed and set the bottle down. He ran a hand over his hair. "Mila got worse after you left. She died a few weeks ago." He looked at Aria. "Mila is . . . was my brother Vale's wife. Their son is named Talon. He's seven."

Blood rushed in Aria's ears as she put the information together. This was the boy taken by her people. Perry was trying to rescue his nephew.

"I didn't know," Roar said. "Vale and Talon must be in hell."

"Vale is." Perry cleared his throat. "Talon's gone. I lost him, Roar." He brought his knees up and bowed his head, lacing his fingers behind his neck.

Even by the soft candlelight, Aria saw the color drain from Roar's face. "What happened?" he asked quietly.

Perry's wide shoulders drew together like he was containing something vast, keeping it trapped inside him. When he looked up, his eyes were glazed and red. In a hoarse voice, he told them a story Aria had been part of but had never heard. Of how he'd come into her world for medicines, to help a sick boy. A boy who'd been kidnapped by her people. He told Roar about their deal. Once Marron fixed her Smarteye, she'd reach her mother. He'd get Talon back and Lumina would bring Aria into Bliss.

They sat in silence after he'd finished. Aria heard only the stir of leaves when a breeze swept past. Then Roar spoke.

"I'm in. We'll find them, Perry. Both Talon and Liv."

Aria turned her face toward the shadows. She wished Paisley was there. She missed having her friend at her side.

Roar muttered a soft curse. "Prepare yourselves. Cinder's back."

A few moments later, the screen of leaves rustled then parted. A boy stood in the gap, his eyes dark and feral. He was shockingly thin. No more than a skeleton in filthy baggy clothes. He had fair skin. Nearly as fair as hers, Aria realized.

Cinder dropped beside her with a thump and leered at her through matted strands of dirty blond hair. His shirt hung so loose that Aria could see the way his collarbones stuck out like sticks.

Cinder's gaze roamed over her face. His eyes were half-lidded with fatigue. "What are you doing out here, Dweller?" he asked suspiciously.

He sat too close. Aria scooted back. "I'm on my way home. To my mother."

"Where's she?"

"In Bliss. It's one of our Pods."

"Why did you leave?"

"I didn't leave. I was thrown out."

"You were thrown out but you want to go back? That's barmy, Dweller."

She guessed by Cinder's expression that *barmy* meant

something close to *crazy*. "I guess, when you put it like that."

Roar tossed a piece of bread onto the ground. "Take it and be gone, Cinder."

"It's all right," Aria said. Cinder might lack manners, but it was a cold night and where would he go? Out there by himself? "He can stay. It's fine with me."

Cinder picked up the bread and bit off a piece. "She wants me to stay, Roar."

Aria could see his jawbone moving up and down as he chewed. "My name is Aria."

"She even told me her name," Cinder said. "She likes me."

"Not for long," Roar muttered.

Cinder looked at her, gnashing at the bread with his mouth open. Aria looked away. He was being crude on purpose.

"You're right," he said. "I think she already changed her mind."

"Shut your mouth, Cinder."

"How am I supposed to eat?"

Roar sat up. "That's *enough*."

Cinder's smile was full of challenge. "What are you going to do? Stop feeding me? You want this back?" He held the half-eaten bread out. "Take it, Roar. I don't want it anymore."

Perry reached out and plucked the bread from his hand.

Cinder turned a stunned look on him. "You shouldn't have done that."

"You didn't want it." Perry brought the bread to his mouth. He stopped with it inches from his lips. "Did you?

Or were you lying?" His eyes gleamed in the dark. "If you tell them you're sorry, I'll give it back."

Cinder snorted. "I'm not sorry."

The corner of Perry's mouth lifted into a smile. "You're still lying."

Cinder suddenly looked panicked, his eyes darting to her and then Roar and finally back to Perry. He scrambled to his feet. "Stay away from me, Scire!" He grabbed the bread out of Perry's hand and barreled through the gap in the screen.

A cool feeling crept up Aria's neck as the sounds of Cinder's getaway faded. "What just happened? Why did he call you 'Scire'?"

Roar's eyebrows lifted in surprise. "Perry . . . she doesn't know?"

Perry shook his head.

"What don't I know?"

He looked up at the night sky, avoiding her gaze, and took a deep breath. "Some of us are Marked," he said softly. "That's what the bands on my arms are. Markings. They show that we have a dominant Sense. Roar is an Aud. He can hear things more clearly and from farther away. Sometimes miles off."

Roar gave her an apologetic shrug.

"What about you?"

"I have two Senses. I'm a Seer. Night-Sighted. I can see in the dark."

He saw in the dark. She should have known with his reflective eyes. With the way he never stumbled at night. "And the other?"

180

He looked right at her, his gaze brilliant green. "I have a strong sense of smell."

"You have a strong sense of smell." Aria tried to process what this meant. "How strong?"

"Very. I can scent tempers."

"Tempers?"

"They're emotions . . . impulses."

"You can scent people's feelings?" She could hear her voice rising.

"Yes."

"How often?" she asked. She'd started to tremble.

"Always, Aria. I can't avoid it. I can't stop breathing."

Aria went cold everywhere. Instantly. Like she'd just taken a plunge in the ocean. She shot through the path Cinder had cleared, diving into the darkened woods. Perry came right behind her, calling her name and asking her to stop. Aria spun.

"You've been doing that all this time? You've known how I've felt? Have I entertained you? Has my misery amused you? Is that why you kept it to yourself?"

He pushed his hands into his hair. "Do you know how many times you've called me a Savage? You think I wanted to tell you I can smell better than a wolf?"

Aria's hand shot up, covering her mouth. He could smell better than a wolf.

She thought of all the horrible feelings she'd had over the past days. Days she spent with that pathetic, sad melody going round and round in her mind. The shame she felt at menstruating. Of being terrified, a stranger in her own skin.

Was he smelling the way she felt *right now*?

He tipped his head to the side. "Aria, don't be embarrassed."

He was. He *did* know.

She backed away, but his hand closed around her wrist. "Don't go. It's not safe. You know what's out there."

"Let *go* of me."

"Perry," said a smooth voice. "I'll stay with her."

Perry looked down at her, frustration plain on his face. Then he let go of her arm and stalked off, branches snapping in his wake.

"You can cry if you like," Roar said when Perry was gone. He crossed his arms. In the darkness, she could just make out the glint of the black bottle of Luster propped on his elbow. "I'll even offer up my shoulder to the cause."

"No, I don't want to cry. I want to hurt him."

Roar laughed softly. "I knew I liked you."

"He should have told me."

"Probably, but what he said is true. He can't help knowing tempers. And would it have changed your agreement?"

Aria shook her head. It wouldn't. Before long, she knew she'd be back to walking endless miles with him.

She sat against a tree and picked up a pine needle, breaking it into tiny pieces. It seemed obvious once she thought it out. Basic genetics. The population of Outsiders was small. Any shifts had the possibility of running rampant in such a limited pool. A drop of ink in a bucket was more potent than a drop in a lake. And with the Aether accelerating mutations, the Unity had created an environment ripe for genetic jumps.

"I can't believe this," she said. "You're a subspecies. Is there anything else? Are there any other traits that have drifted? Like . . . like your teeth?"

Roar sat beside her against the same large trunk. He wasn't as tall as Perry, she noticed. Aether light fell across the smooth planes of his profile, all straight lines and perfect proportions. He didn't have scruff over his jaw like Perry, either.

"No," Roar said. "Our teeth are all the same. Yours are the ones that are different."

Aria pressed her lips together on reflex. It hadn't occurred to her before, but he was right. Before the Unity, teeth had been uneven. Roar smiled and kept talking.

"There are some differences between the Senses. Scires tend to be tall. They're the rarest Marked. Seers are the most common. Seers are good at looking *and* good-looking, but before you start wondering, no, I'm not a Seer. Just lucky."

Aria smiled despite herself. She was surprised by how at ease she felt in his company. "What about your kind?"

"Auds?" He flashed a mischievous grin at her. "We're said to be sly."

"I could've guessed that." She looked down at his bicep, imagining the tattoo hidden beneath his dark shirt. "How well can you hear?"

"Better than anyone I know."

"Can you hear emotions?"

"No. But I can hear a person's thoughts when I touch

them. That's just me, not all Auds. And don't worry, I won't touch you. Unless you want me to."

She smiled. "I'll let you know." This was unreal. There were people who could smell emotion and hear thoughts. What was next? Aria cupped her hands, blowing warmth into them. "How can you be friends with him, knowing he . . . knows everything?"

Roar laughed. "Please don't ever say that in front of him. He's cocksure enough as it is." He tilted the bottle and drank. "Perry and I grew up together, along with his sister. When you know someone that well, it's something like being a Scire."

She supposed it was true. She'd been sensitive to some of Paisley's moods. Caleb's too. "But it feels . . . imbalanced. He never talks but he gets to know what other people are feeling?"

"He's quiet because he's scenting tempers. Perry doesn't trust words. He's told me before how often people lie. Why would he bother listening to false words when he can breathe and get right at the truth?"

"Because people are more than emotions. People have thoughts and reasons for doing things."

"Yes, well. It's hard to follow a person's logic if you don't know how they feel. And you're wrong. Perry does talk. Watch him. You'll see he says plenty."

She knew this. For days she'd been translating his actions into meaning. Noticing how he walked in a dozen different ways. With utter quiet. With barely contained violence. With easy animal grace.

"What about his sister?" she asked.

"Olivia," Roar said, and then added more softly, "Liv."

"Is she a *Scire* also?" Aria didn't even like the word. It sounded like a warped version of *scare.*

"As strong as Perry if not more. We never could decide who has the keener nose."

"What happened to her, Roar?"

"She was betrothed to someone else. Someone who wasn't me."

"Oh." Roar was in love with Perry's sister. She sucked on her bottom lip, tasting the sweetness of the Luster. She didn't want to be forward and ask too many questions, but she was curious. And Roar didn't seem to mind. "Why not you?"

"She's a strong Scire. She's too valuable. . . ." Roar stared at the bottle in his hand like he was searching for the right explanation. "Blood is our currency. As Marked, we make the most skilled hunters and fighters. We overhear plans for raids and sense shifts in the Aether. Blood Lords surround themselves with people like me and Perry and Liv. When it comes to mating, they choose the strongest of their kind. If they don't, they risk losing the Sense. Some say they risk worse."

Aria had a hard time with how casually he'd said *mating.* "Couldn't a child get two Senses with different parents? Is that what happened with Perry?"

"Yes. But it's rare. What Perry is . . . it's very rare." After a pause, he added, "It's best you don't ever mention his parents."

She slipped her hands into the sleeves of her coat, digging her fingers into the fur. What had happened to Perry's parents?

"So as a Scire, Liv has to marry a Scire?" she asked instead.

"Yes. It's what's expected." Roar shifted against the trunk. "Seven months ago, Vale promised her to Sable, the Blood Lord of the Horns. They're a large tribe to the north. Ice-cold people, Sable the coldest of the lot. Vale was to receive food for the Tides in exchange for her. Half of which they may never get."

"Because she didn't go."

"That's right. Liv ran. She disappeared the night before we'd have crossed into Horn territory. It was exactly what I had wanted us to do together. I'd been thinking about it the whole way there. She left before I could ask." Roar paused and cleared his throat. "I've been searching for her since. I've come close to finding her. A few weeks ago, I heard a couple of traders speaking of a girl who could track game better than any man. They'd met her in Lone Tree. I'm sure it was her. Liv's not one you easily forget."

"Why?"

"She's tall—barely shorter than me. And she has the same hair as Perry, only longer. That alone is enough to draw attention, but she has this quality. . . . You watch her because just that will fascinate you."

"They sound very alike." Aria couldn't believe she'd said that aloud. It had to be the effect of the Luster, loosening her tongue.

White teeth appeared in the dark. "They are, but thankfully not in every way."

"Did you go to Lone Tree?"

"I did. By the time I got there, she was long gone."

Aria let out a slow breath. Though she felt sorry for Roar, this was exactly what she'd needed. A break from her own mind and body. A chance to forget for a few moments about fixing the Smarteye and reaching Lumina. She had the urge to reach for Roar's hand. She would have, if they'd been in the Realms. Instead she dug her fingers deeper into the fur of her sleeves.

"What are you going to do, Roar?" she asked.

"What can I do but keep looking?"

20

PEREGRINE

Having Roar along changed everything. They walked through the morning and though Perry hadn't caught any traces of the Croven, he knew they weren't clear of danger. It worried him that they hadn't been confronted yet, but with Roar's help, they could make better time to Marron's. Whatever signs of danger Perry missed with his pine-dulled nose, Roar would catch with his ears.

Aria hadn't spoken to him since he'd told her about his Senses. She'd been hanging back all morning, walking with Roar. Perry had strained to hear what they were saying. Even found himself wishing he was an Aud. That had been a first. When Perry heard her laugh at something Roar said, he'd decided he'd heard enough and pulled out of earshot. In the span of a few hours, Roar had spoken with her more than he had in days.

Cinder kept his distance, but Perry knew he was there.

The kid was so weak that he walked in noisy, dragging steps. It didn't take being an Aud to hear him shuffling in the woods behind them. Something about the boy's scent had set the back of Perry's nose thrumming last night. It stung, just as it did when the Aether became agitated, but when Perry had looked up, he hadn't seen the sky churning. Just the wispy streaks that still held above. He wondered if the Luster had muddled him, or if it'd just been the pine messing with his Sense.

He hadn't had any trouble picking up the boy's temper, though. Cinder's wrathy attitude might throw Roar and Aria off, but Perry knew the truth. The icy fog of fear clung to him. Roar had guessed him to be thirteen, but Perry put him at least a year younger. Why was he on his own? Whatever the reason, Perry knew it couldn't be good.

Around midday he picked up a boar's trail, the animal's smell strong enough to cut through his stunted nose. He headed downhill, then he told Roar the best path for driving the animal to where he waited.

They had hunted this way their whole lives. Roar could hear Perry's directions clearly from that far, but it was more complicated for Roar to communicate with him. Mimicking natural sounds came easily to Auds, so over the years they had adapted the calls of birds, turning it into a language between them.

Perry heard Roar's whistle now, alerting him. *Be ready. He's coming.*

Perry got a shot right into the boar's neck and then another into its heart after it fell. As he knelt and retrieved his arrows, it struck him that this was the purest use of his abilities. He'd missed the rush of doing something simple and doing it well. But his satisfaction didn't last. As soon as Roar jogged up, Perry knew something was off.

Roar was normally a real rooster after they made a kill together, showing off and claiming he'd done all the work. Now he glanced at the boar and then closed his eyes. Angled his head in quick, sharp movements. Perry knew what was coming before he spoke.

"The Croven, Perry. A whole piss barrel of them."

"How far?"

"Hard to tell. Seven miles or so on the wind."

"Could be more on land, most of it hill."

Roar nodded. "We're looking at half a day's lead at best."

Perry cut the boar into strips and seared them over a fire. The Aether had roused, flowing in agitated rivers. Setting off the sting in the back of his nose. A storm would complicate things. He ate with Aria and Roar, the three of them hardly bothering to chew the meat. They'd need the strength of a meal in their stomachs to outrun the Croven. Marron's compound was still two days away, and he knew they couldn't stop until they reached it.

He built up the fire before they set off, adding a stack of green wood. Smoke would help mask their scents for a while. Then he staked a cut of meat he'd set aside with a stick and told Aria and Roar he'd catch up.

He found Cinder curled against the root of a tree. Dappled light shifted across the boy's dirty face as he twitched in fitful sleep. He looked smaller. More frail without the sneering look on his face. Perry pinched the bridge of his nose as the stinging sensation flared. "Cinder."

He shot up, disoriented, blinking and rubbing at his eyes. When he finally focused on Perry, panic flashed across his face.

"Leave me alone, Scire."

"Steady," Perry said. "It's all right." He held the stick out. Cinder glanced at it, his Adam's apple bobbing as he swallowed. He wouldn't take it, so Perry wedged the stick into the ground. He backed away a few steps. "It's yours."

Cinder snatched it up and sank his teeth into the meat, ripping at it in a fury. Perry's gut clenched at the desperation in the boy's face. This was nothing like the meal he'd just rushed through with Aria and Roar. This was true hunger. Fierce as any fight for life. Perry remembered Cinder gnawing at the bread rudely last night. He realized the boy had just been hiding the depth of his need.

He should tell Cinder what he had to say and leave. Perry didn't want Cinder pulled into the mess he was in with the Croven. He glanced east, toward Marron's. Roar and Aria wouldn't get too far ahead. He could spare a few moments. Perry slid his bow off his shoulder and sat.

Cinder's black eyes darted up, but he kept attacking his food. Perry took a few arrows from his quiver. Checked the fletching as he waited. He'd been wondering why Roar had helped Cinder. But now he understood, seeing the boy this way. Would the Tides end up like this without the second shipment from Sable?

"Why is that girl with you?"

Perry looked up, surprised. Cinder was still chewing, but the stick was clean. Not a scrap of meat left. His eyebrows were drawn together in a dark scowl.

Perry lifted his shoulders, allowing himself a smug smile. "Isn't it obvious?" The boy's black eyes went wide. "I'm kidding, Cinder. It's nothing like that. We're helping each other out of some trouble."

Cinder swiped a grubby sleeve over his face. "But she is pretty."

Perry grinned. "Really? I hadn't noticed."

"Sure you haven't." Cinder smiled like they'd agreed on something important. He pushed his hair away from his face, but it fell back into his eyes. It was a mess of knots. Like his own hair, Perry realized.

"What kind of trouble?" Cinder asked.

Perry let out a long breath. He didn't have the time or energy to tell their story again. But he could skip to the part that mattered now. He sat forward, propping his arms over his knees. "You've heard of the Croven?"

"The flesh eaters? Yeah, I've heard of them."

"A couple of nights ago, I got in a mix with them. I'd left Aria to hunt. When I came back, they'd found her. Three of them. They had her cornered." Perry slid his hand down to the arrowhead. Pressed his finger against the sharp point.

This story wasn't easy to tell either. But he noticed the way Cinder's expression had opened. The mask of scorn was gone. He was just a boy now, drawn in by a thrilling story. So Perry kept on.

"They were blood hungry. I could almost taste their hunger for her. Maybe because she's a Dweller . . . different . . . I don't know. But they weren't going to walk away. I took two down with my bow. The third with my knife."

Cinder licked his lips, his black eyes rapt. "So now they're after you? You were just helping her."

"That's not how the Croven will see it."

"But you *had* to kill them." He shook his head. "People don't ever understand."

Perry knew he looked stunned. There was something in the way he'd said it. Like it was a burden he knew. "Cinder . . . do *you* understand?"

Wariness crept into the boy's gaze. "Can you really tell when I'm lying?"

Perry shifted his shoulders, his heart beating hard. "I can."

"Then my answer is maybe."

Perry couldn't believe it. This kid . . . this pathetic boy had killed someone? "What happened to you? Where are your parents?"

Cinder's mouth twisted into a snide smile, his temper a cool, sudden drift. "They died in an Aether storm. It happened about two years ago. Poof, and they were gone. It was sad."

Perry didn't need his Sense to know he was lying. "Were you forced out here?" Blood Lords exiled murderers and thieves into the borderlands.

Cinder laughed, a sound that belonged to someone much older. "I *like it* out here." His smile faded. "This is my home."

Perry shook his head. He slipped the arrows back into his quiver, grabbed his bow, and stood. He had to get moving. "You can't keep tailing us, Cinder. You're not strong enough and it's too dangerous. Head off while there's still time."

"You can't tell me what to do."

"You have any idea what the Croven do to kids?"

"I don't care."

"You *should*. Head south. There's a settlement two days from here. Climb a tree if you need to sleep."

"I'm not afraid of the Croven, Scire. They can't hurt me. No one can."

Perry almost laughed at him. It was an impossible claim. But Cinder's temper was cool and sharp and clear. Perry inhaled again, waiting for it to sour with his lie.

It never did.

Perry's mind was racing as he caught up to Aria and Roar. He hung back a ways, needing some space of his own, too absorbed by what Cinder had said. *They can't hurt me. No one can.* He'd been *sure* when he had said those words. But how could Cinder believe something like that?

Perry wondered if he'd read the boy's temper wrong. Was

it the pine or Cinder's strange Aether scent throwing off his nose? Or was Cinder mentally wounded? Had he convinced himself he was untouchable in order to survive alone? The afternoon hours passed, silent and swift, and Perry still struggled to understand.

At dusk they emerged from a dense grove of pines to a rugged basin. A range of sharp peaks framed the northern horizon. Roar left Aria's side, dropping back to get a better sense of the distance between them and the Croven.

Perry fell in step with her. He counted twenty paces before he spoke. "Do you want to rest?" He wondered how she was managing. His own feet ached, and they weren't cut and blistered.

Her gray eyes turned to him. "Why do you even bother asking?"

He stopped. "Aria, that's not how my Sense works. I can't tell if you're—"

"I thought we weren't supposed to talk out here," she said without breaking her stride.

Perry frowned as he watched her go. How had it happened that now he wanted to talk but she didn't?

Roar came back a short while later. "It's not good news. The Croven have broken into smaller groups. They're coming right around us. We're losing our lead, too."

Perry shifted the bow and quiver on his back, eyeing his best friend. "You don't need to do this. Aria and I have to get to Marron's, but you don't."

"Sure, Per. I'll just go then."

He'd expected the answer. Perry would never leave Roar in trouble either. But Cinder was another matter. "Did the kid leave?"

"Still on our tail," Roar said. "I told you he's a burr. Your little talk with him earlier didn't help. He'll probably never leave now."

"You heard us?"

"Every word."

Perry shook his head. He'd forgotten the strength of his friend's ears. "You ever get tired of eavesdropping?"

"Never."

"What do you think he's done, Roar?"

"I don't care and neither should you. Come on. Let's catch up to Aria. She's that way."

"I know which way she went."

Roar thumped him on the shoulder. "Just making sure you noticed."

Late into the night, with the miles blurring together, Perry's thoughts took on the vividness of dreams. He imagined Cinder on the beach, being dragged into a Hover by Dwellers. Then Talon, surrounded by black-caped men with crow masks. By daybreak, the Croven were closing on them like a net, and Perry had decided to do whatever it took. He would not hold Cinder's life in his hands.

"I'll be back," he said. He turned downhill, letting Roar and Aria pull ahead. Cinder wasn't in eyeshot, but Perry knew he wasn't far. He let the stinging sensation in his nose lead him to the boy.

When he found Cinder, Perry kept back for a moment and watched him through the woods. He had a lost, sorrowful look about him when he didn't think he was being watched. It was harder to see him this way than when he sneered.

"Last chance to leave," Perry said.

Cinder jumped back, swearing. "You shouldn't sneak up on me, Scire."

"I said it's time for you to go." The terrain ahead opened into a broad plateau. Cinder wouldn't have the cover of the woods to help him make a break on his own. He would be trapped with them if he didn't leave now.

"This isn't your territory," he said, spreading his bony arms wide. "And I'm not pledged to you."

"Get out of here, Cinder."

"I told you before. I go where I want."

Perry slid off his bow, nocked an arrow, and aimed at Cinder's throat. He didn't know what he planned to do, only that he couldn't watch this scrawny boy die because of him. "Be gone before it's too late."

"No!" Cinder shouted. "You need me!"

"Leave *now*." Perry brought the bowstring back to full draw.

Cinder made a low, growling sound. Perry sucked in a breath as the prickling sensation behind his nose sharpened, turned to stabbing.

A blue flame lit in Cinder's dark eyes. For an instant, Perry thought it was the Aether reflecting in his black eyes, but it grew brighter and brighter. Glowing blue lines crept up from Cinder's sagging collar, winding up his neck. Snaking over his bony jaw and face. Perry couldn't believe what he saw. Cinder's veins lit like they ran with Aether.

Splinters of pain flushed across Perry's arms and face. "Stop what you're doing!"

Roar and Aria ran up to them. Roar had his knife in his hand. They froze when they saw Cinder. Perry's heart drummed wildly. Cinder's glowing eyes stared through him, vacant and bright.

Perry gritted his teeth as his muscles began to twitch painfully. "Cinder, stop!"

The boy put his palms up, showing hands webbed with Aether. The charge in the air surged, sending another stabbing wave over Perry's skin.

What *was* he?

Heat flared across the knuckles of Perry's forward hand, gripping the bow. The steel arrowhead inches away began to glow orange. Reflex took over. He made a quick adjustment off his mark and loosed the arrow.

An explosion of light blinded Perry, keeping him from seeing what he'd struck. He didn't feel himself drop onto the dirt or ball up around his arm. He lost time. Knew only that something terrible had happened. The scent of his own cooked flesh brought him back to a world where pain was everything. Terrible animal groans filled his ears. They came from him.

"Stay back!" Cinder yelled. Through squinted eyes, Perry saw Roar and Aria uphill, both motionless and stunned.

Scorched smells flooded Perry's nose. Burnt hair and wool and skin.

Cinder dropped to his knees at his side. "What happened?" he asked. "What did you make me do?" The blue of Cinder's eyes was fading. His veins melted back into his skin.

Perry couldn't answer. He didn't know if he still had a hand. He couldn't bring himself to look.

Cinder trembled. His entire body was quaking. "What did I do? You fired. . . . You were going to shoot me."

Perry managed to shake his head. "Just needed you to go."

Cinder looked stricken. He climbed to his feet, his balance weaving wildly. "I don't have anywhere to go," he said, his words choked. Stooping, bent over his stomach like he'd been punched, he staggered into the woods.

Roar and Aria thundered up. Roar took one look at Perry's hand and went white.

Perry met his eyes. "Help him. Bring him back."

"Help him? I'm going to slit his throat."

"Just get him back here, Roar!"

When he was gone, Perry lay back and stared through the trees. The Aether swirled above. He closed his eyes. Concentrated on breathing.

"Perry, can I see?"

Aria knelt at his side. "Let me see," she said softly, reaching for his hand.

He sat up, a groan tearing through his throat. Then he looked at his left hand for the first time. It had swollen to twice its normal size. The skin over his knuckles looked like blackened meat. Big, red blisters crowded the flat of his hand, making a trail down his wrist. Perry's stomach twisted. Stars burst before his eyes. He swallowed back the sour rush in his mouth. He was going to vomit or pass out. Maybe both.

"Put your head down and breathe. I'll be right back."

She handed him the bottle of Luster when she returned. Perry drank. Didn't stop until he'd drained what was left. He dropped the bottle to the side. Aria had taken his burnt hand into her lap and pushed his sleeve up. She held a long strip of gauze. Her belt once, he realized. She poured water over it.

"I should wrap it, Perry. So it doesn't get infected."

Cold sweat broke out over his back. Perry met her eyes for only a second, afraid she'd see his fear. He nodded and let his head fall forward again.

Her first touch over his knuckles was feather soft, but chills came over him, shaking his shoulders. Aria's hands went still.

"Keep going," he said, before he could change his mind and rip his arm off. It might have hurt less. He kept his head down. Watched the dark spots his tears made as they fell on his leather pants. He wanted to ask her to sing. He remembered her voice, how it had carried him away. He couldn't form the words. But then the Luster kicked in, saving him by dulling some of the pain. Perry pushed the wetness off his cheeks and straightened, swaying unsteadily.

Aria wrapped the long strip of gauze around his wrist, and then wove it up, looping it through each of his fingers. She was calm now. Focused. He watched her as he sank deeper and deeper into the mind-numbing fog of Luster.

She was touching him. He wondered if she realized it too. "Have you ever seen someone like him before?" she asked.

Cinder. A boy with Aether in his blood. "No. Never seen that," he slurred. Perry wondered how it was possible, but he couldn't deny what he'd seen. Not with proof moving through him in agonizing waves. How many times had he looked up and felt connected to the sky himself? Like it wasn't just some faraway force? Like his own mood ebbed and flowed with the Aether? He should've trusted his Sense. Cinder set off the same stinging sensation in his nose. And he'd known the boy was hiding something.

"I was trying to help. . . . The more I try to catch up, the farther I fall behind." The words slipped out, clumsy but true.

Aria looked up from his hand. "What did you say?"

Her face blurred left and right. Finally his focus pinned on her.

"Nothing. Nothing. Just stupid things."

Roar came back carrying Cinder across his neck in a hunter's hold, legs to one side, arms to the other.

"Is he dead?" The question came out of Perry in one sound, all of the words sliding together.

"Unfortunately, no," Roar said, out of breath.

Cinder balled up as soon as Roar set him down. He was shaking worse than before. He turned his face into the earth. Perry saw wide patches of bare scalp. They hadn't been there before. His clothes were blackened. Almost falling off completely.

"We have to leave him, Perry. He's too weak."

"We can't."

"Look at him, Peregrine. He can barely hold his head up."

"The Croven will come through here." Perry gritted his teeth as stars bloomed before his eyes. Fewer words, he told himself. Less movement. Just breathing.

Aria draped a blanket over Cinder. She bent close. "Is it the Aether?"

Perry peered up. The Aether had a soft, washed-out look. It had waned back to the wisps of earlier that day. He was in so much pain, he hadn't noticed. Then he realized the sting in his nose was faint. Hardly there. Cinder had to be linked to the Aether tides.

"Just leave," Cinder rasped.

"Listen to him, Perry. It's a haul to Marron's, and we've got twenty Croven on our heels. Are you really going to risk our lives for this fiend?"

Perry didn't have the strength to argue. He climbed to his feet, concentrating on hiding his unsteadiness. "I'll carry him."

"*You* will?" Roar shook his head, his laugh dry. "He's not Talon, Perry!"

Perry wanted to punch him. He tried to get himself over to Roar, but his legs took him sideways. Aria jumped up, darting toward him, but he found his balance. For a moment, he was staring down into her eyes. Seeing her worry. She turned to Roar.

"He's right, Roar. We can't leave him like this. And we're only wasting time arguing."

Roar looked from Aria to him. "I can't believe I'm doing this." He went to Cinder and hoisted the boy roughly onto his shoulders, cursing viciously as he turned up the mountain and set off.

They traveled in a close pack now. Aria walked to Perry's right, the blisters and cuts on her feet hidden by boots. Roar trudged to his left, breathing hard, making the climb to Marron's with a hundred extra pounds on his shoulders. Perry tucked his arm close to his chest, but it didn't help. He felt his heartbeat thumping in his hand with every step. Thirst gripped him. He emptied every one of their skins within the first hour but found no relief.

When the Luster wore off, he battled waves of pain that threatened to drop him. But he noticed something else, too. The pine shroud had lifted. Scents came with familiar clarity, isolated and sharp. His nose had finally adjusted.

The Croven's fetid scents carried to him on the wind. He counted more than two dozen individual scents. Stronger, closer, were Aria's and Roar's tempers.

From them he scented only fear.

ARIA

Aria stared into the woods with burning eyes, searching for crow masks and black capes. They were moving too slow and stopping too often for Roar to catch his breath. When they did rest, she didn't miss the look of relief on Perry's ashen face. Somehow, despite the state of her feet, she'd become the fastest one among them.

Her gaze fell to Perry's bandaged hand. The white gauze, bright in the fading daylight, was spotted with blood. She'd never seen a wound like that. She couldn't imagine the pain he was in. She couldn't believe what had happened.

Who *was* Cinder? How could a human have that kind of power? Aria knew about animals that used bioelectricity. Rays and eels. But a *boy*? It was like something from a Realm. But then hadn't she just learned about Scires and Auds and Seers? Couldn't Cinder's ability be just another mutation? Harnessing the Aether seemed like a massive genetic break. But it was possible.

She lost herself in the rhythm of picking her feet up and setting them down until Roar stopped suddenly and dropped Cinder on the dirt, making no effort at gentleness.

"I can't carry him anymore."

Night had fallen but a full moon shone, bold and bright in the sky. The Aether had weakened, fading to a wash of pale light. They'd reached a stretch of flat land. The mountain climbed up ahead, growing thickly wooded again.

Cinder lay in a heap, his eyes closed. He wasn't shivering anymore. Perry swayed beside her.

"We're almost there," he said, tipping his head toward the wooded slope. "It's just there."

Roar shook his head. "My legs."

Perry nodded. "I'll take him."

Cinder's eyes opened to slits, searching for Perry. *"No."* His voice was small, a whimper. He rolled to the side, turning his back to them.

Perry stared at him for a moment. Then he took Cinder's wrist, pulling the boy's arm across his shoulder. Perry's wounded arm wrapped around Cinder's waist as he hauled Cinder up. They began to walk together, Perry bending forward to bring himself closer to Cinder's height.

Cinder glanced up as they passed her, his black eyes sparkling with the sheen of tears. With shame, Aria realized. He'd torched the hand that now held him upright.

Aria whirled around. "What is that?" The night had a new noise. A faraway hum.

"Bells," Roar said, glaring at the woods.

She remembered Harris's words. "To drive away dark spirits," she said.

"To drive me mad." Roar took something from his bag. A black hat that he pulled over his head. Heavy flaps came down to cover his ears. "They disorient me."

Perry turned. He lifted his head slightly, his eyes scanning as he drew a breath through his nose in a natural, wild gesture. This was him. The Scire. The Seer. He met Roar's gaze, a silent message passing between them.

"We have to run," Roar said.

Terror shot through her. She looked at Cinder, hanging at Perry's side. "How are you going to run with him?"

He was moving before she'd finished asking the question. Aria reached into her pockets and scooped out the rocks she'd collected. She let them scatter on the ground.

Minutes after they started running, her muscles cramped. Nausea rose up in her, which she didn't understand, as she hadn't eaten in a day. She pushed on. Her boots caught on every small stone. Every step stabbed the bottoms of her feet. Trees loomed up ahead, shadowed shapes on the hillside. The trees would hide them. She ran and ran and still they seemed no closer.

"They're running too," Perry said after another stretch. An hour? A minute? All the color had drained from his face. She could see that even in the dark.

She didn't notice when dawn came, gray and misty. Or when they'd made it to the incline where the trees began. She appeared beneath the pines suddenly, like she'd fractioned into a Realm.

"Move, Cinder. Run," Perry told him.

Cinder's feet dragged. He was barely supporting his own weight anymore.

Aria bit her lip, searching desperately into the woods for the Croven. The bells were loud now, disorienting like Roar said. "Let me take him, Perry."

Perry slowed. His hair was slick and darkened with sweat. His soaked shirt sucked to his frame. He nodded, letting her take Cinder. Cinder was freezing to the touch. His eyes had rolled to the back of his head. Roar appeared at his other side. Together, they dug in, pushing, carrying Cinder between them as the slope grew steeper and the bells rang louder.

Roar stopped. "Straight uphill. Can you manage without me?"

"Yes." She turned and her heart seized. "Where's Perry?"

"Slowing the Croven down."

He'd *left*? He'd gone back?

Roar drew his knife. "Keep moving. Get to Marron's. Get us help."

He tore down the slope, his black clothes fading into the shadows. Aria firmed her grip around Cinder's bony ribs and pressed on, her every step weighted by terror. She couldn't push back the thought . . . What if she never saw them again? What if that was the last time she'd see Perry? She wouldn't let it be.

"Help me, Cinder."

"I can't." The words were softer than a whisper at her side.

She was close when she noticed the stone wall. It was so unexpected, rising amid the evergreens. It soared to high above, many times her height. Aria hobbled up with Cinder, flattening her free hand on the rough surface. She had to feel it to be sure it was real. She followed it, keeping close enough that her shoulder dragged against the wall, until she came upon a heavy wooden gate. A screen was embedded in the mortar to the side. She gasped, seeing a device from her world here on the outside.

She swiped her hand across the dusty screen. "I need help! I need Marron!" Her breath came in ragged sobs. She tipped her head up to a tower high above her.

"Help!"

Someone peered down, a dark figure against the bright morning sky. She heard distant shouts. A few moments later, the inset screen flickered on. A man appeared, his face plump and fair and blue-eyed. His damp, butter-blond hair showed the traces of a thorough combing.

A disbelieving smile broke over his face. "A Dweller?"

The gate opened with a rumble that clattered in her kneecaps.

Aria wobbled into a broad grass courtyard, her shoulders screaming with the effort of keeping Cinder on his feet. Cobbled streets linked stone cottages and garden plots. In the distance, still within the wall, she saw pens with goats and sheep. Smoke drifted skyward from several chimneys.

A few people glanced at her, more curious than surprised. It looked like a keep in a Medieval Realm, except the enormous structure at the center resembled a gray box, not a castle.

Ivy grew along its walls but did nothing to soften the cement structure. There was only one entry, heavy steel doors that slid open smoothly as she watched. The round-faced man from the screen emerged. He was short and portly but graceful as he hurried toward her. A young man followed close at his side. She'd been standing there long enough that the gate behind her began to close.

"No!" she said. "There are two more people coming! Peregrine and Roar. I was told to find Marron."

"I'm Marron." He turned his blue gaze toward the door. "Perry is out there?" By then, shouts of "Croven" rained down from the wall. Marron gave quick orders to the lanky young man at his side, directing people to take posts on the wall, others to head downhill to help Perry and Roar.

Two men came forward and took Cinder from her side. Cinder's head fell back limply as they picked him up.

"Have him taken to medical," Marron told them. When he looked back to her, his expression softened. He pressed his hands together beneath his soft chin, a smile lighting in his eyes. "Blessed, blessed day. Look at you."

He tucked her neatly under his arm and ushered her toward the square structure. Aria didn't protest. She could hardly walk. She let herself be cushioned to his soft side. Perfume flowed into her nose. Sandalwood. Citrus. Clean smells. She hadn't smelled perfume since she'd been in the Realms.

She rushed through an explanation of the Croven as he led her inside. They crossed an airlock chamber that had been left open, no longer serving the purpose for which it had been designed. A wide cement hall brought them to a large room.

"I sent my best people to help. We can wait for them here," Marron said.

It was only then she realized Marron was wearing Victorian clothes. A black tailcoat over a blue velvet vest. He even had a white silk puff tie and spats.

Where was she? What kind of place had she stumbled into? She turned, searching the room for understanding. Three-dimensional wallscreens, like people had before the Unity, framed two sides of the room. They showed images of forests, green and lush. Birdsong twittered through hidden speakers. The other walls were covered in richly patterned fabric. Every few feet, glass cases housed collections of odd items. An Indian headdress. A red old-fashioned sporting jersey with the number forty-five in block numbers across the back. A paper magazine, the dinosaur illustration on the cover framed by a yellow border. Spotlights showcased everything, like in ancient museums, so that Aria's eyes traveled from one burst of color to another.

At the center of the room, several lush couches were ordered around an ornate coffee table with curved legs. Aria's brain flashed with recognition. She'd seen a table like that in a Baroque Realm. A Louis XIV piece. She peered at Marron. What kind of Outsider was he?

"This is my home. I call it Delphi. Perry and Roar call it the Box," he added, with a quick, affectionate smile. "There's so much I want to know, but it'll have to wait, of course. Please have a seat. You look so very tired, and standing won't bring them here any faster, I'm afraid."

Aria moved toward the couch, suddenly feeling self-conscious. She was filthy and Marron's home looked rich and immaculate, but the need to get off her feet overpowered her. She sat down, a gasp of relief escaping from her lips. The plush couch gave beneath her weight, melting against her back and her legs. She brushed her hand over the chocolate-colored fabric. Unbelievable. A silk couch. Here, on the Outside.

Marron sat opposite her, twisting a ring around a pudgy finger. He appeared to be a 4th Gen, but there was a childlike curiosity in his eyes.

"Perry is hurt," she said. "His hand is burned."

Marron issued more orders. Aria hadn't even realized there'd been other people in the room until they sped off. "I have a facility here. We'll take care of him as soon as he's inside. Slate will see that it gets done."

She guessed Slate was the tall young man who'd just been outside. "Thank you," she said. Her eyes were closing on their own. "I didn't know. I wouldn't have left him. But he was gone before I knew it." She spoke without realizing it.

"My dear . . . ," Marron said, looking at her with concern. "You need rest. What if I have you informed the moment they arrive?"

She shook her head, fighting off a wave off exhaustion. "I'm not going anywhere until they get here." She folded her hands in her lap, recognizing the gesture as her mother's.

Any second, Perry would get there.

Any second.

~ 22 ~

PEREGRINE

The bells rang everywhere. Perry couldn't tell where the sound was closest. He scanned the woods. "Where are you?"

His eyes locked onto movement. Downhill two Croven stalked toward him, their capes dragging along the earth. They didn't wear masks. Perry knew the exact moment they saw him. Fear slashed across their faces and then they dove behind a tree.

Perry pulled his bow off his shoulder, but he couldn't move the fingers of his burnt hand. How was he supposed to draw his bow? The Croven peered around the tree, testing for danger. Sure, they crept onward in quick bursts, clutching their knives.

He had to do something. Aria and Roar were moving too slowly with Cinder. They wouldn't make it to Marron's unless he held off the Croven.

Perry sat where he was and wedged the bow stave across his feet. With his good hand, he fumbled to nock an arrow to the string. Then he pushed his legs out, drawing the string back and loosing it. It was a clumsy shot—he hadn't fired an arrow using his feet since he was a boy sneaking off with his father's bow—but the arrow flew, forcing the Croven to scramble for cover again.

"Perry, your bow!"

Roar pulled the quiver off Perry's back as he ran up. He took Perry's bow, nocked an arrow, and fired. Perry shot to his feet and drew his knife, and realized that it was backward—Roar with a bow and him with a knife—but they were moving. Keeping the Croven back as they worked their way up to Marron's. He became Roar's eyes, spotting whenever one of the Croven made a reckless charge. He found them. Roar fired.

Perry sensed movement at his back, and spun. A dozen men sprinted downslope toward them. Perry gripped the knife tighter. There were too many and too close. Then he realized they weren't Croven.

"Marron's men, Roar!"

Roar spun, his eyes wide, sweeping. Arrows sliced past them, flying at the Croven. They ran, legs tearing into the slope. They didn't stop until they'd crossed the gate into Marron's courtyard.

People surrounded him, telling him to follow. Perry did what they asked. He could barely speak. He stumbled into the Box and through Marron's halls, not thinking beyond moving his legs.

He was taken through a heavy steel door into a wide, empty hall with gleaming tile floors. Repellent smells surged into his nose. Alcohol. Plastic. Urine. Blood. Disease. The medical facility's scents had reminded him of Mila last year. Now he thought of Talon, and his legs almost gave out beneath him.

He'd gotten here. Marron would fix the Smarteye and he'd find Talon.

A man in a doctor's coat asked Perry something about his hand, jumbled words Perry couldn't focus on. Perry looked at Roar, hoping he knew the answer, when shouts burst across the hall.

"Cinder," Roar said, but Perry was already running, pushing past the knot of people clustered by a door. He scanned the room. Cloth partitions divided it into smaller areas with cots. Cinder slumped against the far left corner, a feral look in his black eyes. His noxious scent burst in the back of Perry's nose, followed by the icy burn of his fear.

"Don't come near me! Stay back!"

"He was unconscious," said one of the doctors. "I was trying to give him an IV."

Cinder hurled curses at them.

"Easy," Perry said. "Settle down, Cinder."

"We need to tranquilize him," someone said.

Cinder's eyes snapped over Perry's shoulder and he yelled, "Get back or I'll torch you!"

The sting in Perry's nose surged as the lights flickered and then went out. Perry blinked hard, willing his eyes to adjust, but he was no good in pitch-black. "Get out," Perry said, spreading his arms. He couldn't let Cinder burn them, too. "Roar, get them out."

Fumbling, feeling through the dark, he and Roar herded everyone outside. Then Perry shut the door, leaning against it as he caught his breath. He couldn't see anything. For long seconds, all he heard were the muffled voices in the hall. Then Cinder spoke.

"Who's there?"

"It's me. Perry." Perry frowned. Had he even told Cinder his name until now?

A sliver of warm light peeked beneath the door. Candlelight out in the hall. Enough for the room to take shape before him.

"You like getting hurt?" Cinder asked. "You want me to burn your other hand?"

Perry didn't have any fight left in him. He didn't think Cinder did either. The kid was still shoved against the corner, barely keeping himself upright. Perry walked to the cot nearest to Cinder. It creaked as he sat down.

"What are you doing?" Cinder asked after a moment.

"Sitting."

"You should leave, Scire."

Perry didn't respond. He wasn't sure he could leave. The last bit of strength drained out of him, leaving his muscles twitching. The sweat that covered his shirt was cooling.

"Where am I?" Cinder asked.

"A friend's. His name is Marron."

"Why are you here, Scire? You think you can help me? Is that it?" He waited for an answer. When Perry didn't give him one, Cinder slid to the floor.

In the low light, Perry saw that Cinder had dropped his head into his hands. His temper sank, growing cool and dark, until it was a blackness so complete and cold that Perry's heart began to pound. There was something familiar about it. About a temper like this.

"You should've just left me. Didn't you see what I am?" The boy's voice broke, and then Perry heard soft whimpering sounds.

Perry swallowed the tight feeling in his throat, keeping still and quiet on the cot as salt mixed with all the scents in the room. Slowly, he told himself. This boy had a rip in him. A wound that ran soul deep. Perry knew what that was like. This would take time.

"Can you . . . can you move your fingers?"

Perry looked down at his hand. "Not much. But it'll be easier when the swelling goes down, I think."

Cinder let out a moan. "I could have killed you."

"You didn't."

"But I could have! It's just in me and then it's out and people get hurt and die and *I* did it. I don't want to be like this." Cinder buried his face as he fell into harsh, raw sobs. "Get out. Please go."

Perry didn't want to leave him this way, but he was sure of one thing. Cinder was filled with shame. If he stayed there now, Cinder would never look him in the eye again. And he wanted that. He needed to talk to this boy again. Perry slid off the cot onto weary legs.

He would go for now, but he would return.

23

ARIA

"Aria?"

Aria pushed herself out of the deepest sleep she'd ever been in. She blinked until the blurriness cleared.

Perry sat at the edge of the bed. "I'm here. Marron . . . he said to tell you."

She knew he'd gotten there safely. She'd been with Marron when Slate came with the news. But seeing him, she was rocked again by relief. "You took so long. I thought the Croven had gotten you."

His eyes glinted with amusement. "No wonder you were sleeping so well."

She smiled. When Slate had shown her to the bedroom, she'd only planned to wash her hands and get off her feet until Perry's hand was treated. But she'd had no hope of staying awake when she saw the bed.

"You're all right?" she asked. Mud crusted to the side of

his jaw. His lips were dry and cracked, but she didn't see any new injuries. "How's your hand?"

He lifted his arm. A white cast reached from his fingers to his elbow. "It's soft inside and cool. They gave me some pain medicine, too." He smiled. "Works better than Luster."

"What about Cinder?"

Perry looked down at his cast, his grin fading. "He's in the medical ward."

"Do they think they can help him?"

"I don't know. I haven't said anything about him, and Cinder won't let anyone near him. I'll go see him later." He sighed and rubbed tiredly at his eyes. "I couldn't leave him out there."

"I know," she said. She couldn't either. But she also couldn't deny the danger in bringing Cinder around other people. He was a boy, but she'd seen what he did to Perry's hand.

Perry tipped his head to the side. "I gave Marron the Smarteye. He's working on fixing it. He'll let us know when there's news."

"We made it, ally," she said.

"We did." He smiled. It was the lion grin she'd only seen a few times. Sweet and engaging, with a hint of shyness. It showed a whole part of him she didn't know. Heart pounding, she looked down and saw that they were on the same bed. Alone.

He tensed like he'd just noticed the same thing and then his gaze flicked to the door. She didn't want him to leave. He was finally talking to her without the grit of anger between them. Without any help from Luster or Roar's easy chatter. She said the first thing that came to mind. "Where's Roar?"

His eyes widened slightly. "Downstairs. I can go get him—"

"No . . . I just wondered if he'd made it back safe."

It was too late. He'd already reached the door. "Not a scratch on him." He hesitated for a moment. "I'm going to go pass out somewhere," he said, and left.

For a few moments, she stared at the spot where he'd been. Why had he hesitated? What had he wanted to say?

She burrowed back into the warm covers. She was still in her filthy clothes, but she felt the soft pressure of bandages on her feet. Vaguely she remembered answering Slate's question about her limp.

A lamp on the bedside illuminated soft cream walls. She was in *a room*, four solid walls around her. It was so quiet. She didn't hear the rustling wind, or the Croven's bells, or the sound of her running feet. She looked up and saw a ceiling that was still. Perfectly still. She hadn't felt this safe since she'd last been with Lumina.

The bed was low to the ground and sleek, but covered in heavy luxurious damask. A Matisse hung on one wall, just a simple sketch of a tree, but the lines brimmed with expression. Her eyes narrowed. Was it a *real* Matisse? An oriental rug spread autumn colors across the floor. How had Marron collected all of these things?

Sleep came, tugging at her again. As she drifted off, she

wished for another dream of Lumina. A better one than the last. In this one, she'd sing her mother's favorite aria. Then Lumina would leave her seat, come up to the stage, and hug Aria close.

They'd be together again.

When she woke again, she unwrapped the bandages from her feet and headed to an adjoining bathroom, where she showered for the next hour. She almost wept over how good the hot water felt cascading over her tired muscles. Her feet were a mess. Bruised. Blistered. Scabbed. She washed them and wrapped them in towels.

She was surprised to find the bed made when she returned to the bedroom. A small bundle of folded clothing rested on the duvet, along with soft silk slippers. A red rose sat on top of the stack. Aria picked it up gingerly and breathed in the fragrance. Beautiful. Softer than the scent of roses in the Realms. But roses in the Realms didn't make her heart race. Had Perry remembered her asking about their scent? Was this his answer?

The clothes were pure white, the kind of white she hadn't seen since she'd left Reverie, and far more fitted than the camos she'd worn for the past week. She pulled them on, noticing the change in the shapes of her legs and calves. She'd grown stronger despite eating such meager amounts.

She heard a knock at the door. "Come in."

A young woman entered, dressed in a white doctor's smock. She was striking, dark and long-limbed, with high cheekbones and almond-shaped eyes. A braid wove back from her forehead, ending in a rope that swung in front of her as she knelt by the bed. She set down a steel case and unsnapped the thick buckles.

"I'm Rose," she said. "I'm one of the doctors here. I'm here to have another look at your feet."

Another look. Rose had already tended to her while she'd slept. Aria sat on the bed as Rose unwrapped the towels. The medical implements in the steel case were modern, similar to what they had in the Pod.

"We provide medical services," Rose said, following Aria's gaze. "It's one of the ways Marron sustains Delphi. People travel weeks to receive care here. These look much better already. The skin is closing nicely. This will sting for a moment."

"What is this place?" Aria asked.

"It's been many things. Before the Unity it was a mine and then a nuclear shelter. Now it's one of the only places to live in safety." Rose's eyes flicked up. "We avoid trouble with the outside most of the time."

Aria couldn't say anything to that. They had shown up wounded, and with cannibals chasing after them. Rose was right. They hadn't exactly made a graceful entrance.

She watched quietly as Rose applied a gel to the bottoms of her feet. A cool, tightening sensation came, followed by relief from pain that had haunted her for a week. Rose pressed a device that resembled a vitals reader to Aria's wrist. She checked the small screen on the back after it beeped, frowning. "How long have you been out here?"

"Eight—I mean *ten* days," she answered, adding the two days she'd been unconscious with fever.

Rose's eyebrows lifted in surprise. "You're dehydrated and undernourished. I've never treated a Dweller before, but as far as I can tell you're otherwise in good health."

Aria shrugged. "I don't feel like I'm . . ."

Dying.

She couldn't finish the sentence. No one was more surprised than she was about her health. She remembered laying her head on Perry's satchel early in their odyssey. She'd been so tired and sore to the bone. She still felt that way, like her muscles and her feet needed to heal, but now she had the sense they *would* heal. She didn't feel cramps anymore, or headaches, or the grip of illness.

How much longer would her health hold? How long would it take to fix the Smarteye and reach Lumina?

Rose returned the reader to the case.

"Did you treat Peregrine?" Aria asked. "Who I came here with?" She could too easily picture the blisters across the solid bones of his knuckles.

"I did. You'll heal faster than he will." She rested her hand on the opened lid, ready to close it. "He's been here before."

Aria knew she was being baited. "Has he?"

"A year ago. We grew close," Rose said, leaving no room for misunderstanding. "At least, I thought we did. Scires will do that. They know exactly what to say and how it affects you. They'll give you what you want, but they won't give you themselves." She pushed up her sleeve, showing unmarked skin around her biceps. "Not unless you're one of them."

"That was so . . . *open* of you," Aria said. She couldn't help imagining Perry with her. Beautiful. A handful of years older than Aria and Perry both. She felt her face go hot but couldn't stop herself from asking the next question. "Do you still love him?"

Rose laughed. "It's probably best if I don't answer that. I'm married now and with child."

Aria stared at Rose's flat stomach. Was she always this candid? "I don't know why you're telling me all of this."

"Marron told me to help you so that's what I'm doing. I knew what I was getting into. I knew it would never work. I think you should know too."

"Thanks for the warning but I'm leaving. Besides, Perry and I are just friends. Even that's questionable."

"He wanted me to see to you first until he learned you were asleep. He told me you walked a week on those cuts without once moaning about it. I don't think there's much question at all." Rose shut the case with a loud snap, the hint of a smile on her lips.

"Tread carefully, Aria. And try to stay off your feet."

24

ARIA

Aria stepped into the hallway, Rose's words still echoing in her mind. Tapestries hung on smooth turquoise walls, the color picking up the rich threads that wove an ancient battle scene. A lighted alcove to one end housed a life-size marble statue of a man and woman locked in either a fierce struggle or a passionate embrace. It was hard to tell. To the other end of the hall, stairs with a gilt-leafed banister swept downward. Aria smiled. Everything in Delphi came from a different time and place. Marron's home felt like being in a dozen Realms at once.

Perry's voice drifted up the stairs. For a moment, she closed her eyes and listened to his deep drawl. Even among Outsiders, he had a distinctive, unhurried way of talking. He spoke of his home, the Tide Valley. Of his worries about Aether storms and raids by other tribes. For someone who hardly said anything, he was a compelling speaker. Concise but sure. After a few minutes, she shook her head at her own shameless eavesdropping.

The stairs took her back down to the room with the couches. Roar sat on one, Perry sprawled across another. Marron perched by Roar, one rounded leg bouncing over the other. She didn't see Cinder but that didn't surprise her. Perry stopped speaking and sat up when he saw her. She tried not to think of what that meant, that he didn't want to continue in her presence.

He wore new clothes like she did. A shirt the color of sand. Leather pants that were closer to black than brown and weren't patched and re-patched. His hair had been pulled back and it gleamed under the lights. He was drumming the fingers of his good hand against his cast. He was also pointedly not looking her way.

Marron came over and took her hands into his, the action so full of affection Aria couldn't bring herself to pull away. He wore what Aria could only call a smoking jacket, a ridiculous burgundy velvet affair, trimmed and belted with black satin sashes.

"Ah," he said, his cheeks plumping with a smile. "You received them. Not a bad fit, I see. I have other clothes being readied for you, my dear. But this will do fine for now. How are you, darling?"

"Good. Thank you for these. And for the rose," she added, realizing it had come from Marron, along with the clothes.

Marron leaned in, giving her hands a squeeze. "A small gift for a great beauty."

Aria laughed nervously. In Reverie, she wasn't anything unusual. Only her voice set her apart from other people. To be praised for something she'd had no say in seemed odd, but it also felt nice.

"Shall we eat?" Marron asked. "We have much to discuss and might as well fill our stomachs as we do it. I'm sure you're all quite hungry."

They followed him into a dining room as lavishly decorated as the rest of Delphi. The walls were covered in crimson and gold fabric and hung floor to ceiling with oil portraits. Candlelight caught on crystal and silver, filling the room with sparkling light. The opulence sent a pang of sorrow through her. It reminded her of the Opera House.

"I've traded over my lifetime for these treasures," Marron said at her side. "But meals should be revered, don't you think?"

Roar pulled out a chair for her as Perry headed to the far side of the rectangular table. They'd hardly sat down when people arrived to pour them water and wine. They were well-dressed and fastidiously groomed. Aria was beginning to see what Marron had done in his compound. Work in exchange for safety. But the people who served him didn't appear distressed. Everyone she had seen within Marron's walls seemed healthy and content. And loyal, like Rose.

Marron lifted his glass, his soft bejeweled fingers fanning like a peacock's feathers. Aria locked onto a flash of blue. Marron was wearing the ring with the blue stone that Perry had stashed away. Aria smiled to herself. She should stop making assumptions about roses and rings.

"To the return of old friends and to an unexpected but most welcome new one."

Soup was brought out, the smell stirring her appetite to life. The others began to eat, but she set down her spoon. It was dizzying, going from the harsh outside world, from the sprint for their lives, to this sparkling feast. She should have adjusted faster, having fractioned through Realms her entire life. But she savored the moment, despite its strangeness, appreciating all that she saw before her.

They were safe. They were warm. They had food.

She picked up the spoon again, welcoming the weight of it in her hand. When she took her first sip, tastes burst like tiny fireworks over her tongue. It had been so long since she'd eaten anything rich. The soup, a creamy mushroom concoction, was delicious.

She glanced at Perry. He sat at the head of the table, opposite Marron. She'd expected to find him out of place. He belonged in the woods; she knew that with every certainty. But he looked comfortable. Clean-shaven, the angles of his jaw and nose seemed sharper, his green eyes brighter, catching as much candlelight as the chandelier above.

He motioned for one of the servants. "Where did you find morels this time of year?"

"We grow them here," said the young man.

"They're very good."

Aria's gaze fell to the soup. He knew there were morels in it. She'd tasted mushroom but he identified them exactly.

Smell and taste were related senses. She remembered Lumina telling her that once. They were the last senses to be incorporated into the Realms after sight, sound, and touch. Smell was the hardest sense to replicate virtually.

She looked back at Perry, watching as his lips closed over the spoon. If his sense of smell was so strong, was his sense of taste heightened too? For some reason, the thought made her blush. Aria took a few sips of water, hiding her face with the crystal.

"Marron has been working on your Smarteye," Perry said. He was calling it a Smarteye. Not a device. Not the eyepiece.

"Since the minute Perry gave it to me. It's largely undamaged, from what we can tell so far. We're working on restoring power to it, touchy without setting off a locating signal, but we'll get it. I'll know how long that should take soon."

"There should be two files," Aria said. "A recording and a message from my mother."

"If they can be found, we'll find them."

For the first time, Aria felt hope. Real hope that she'd reach Lumina. That Perry would find Talon. Perry met her eyes and smiled. He felt it too.

"I don't know how I can thank you," she said to Marron.

"I'm afraid it's not all good news. Restoring power will be the easy part. Linking the eye to the Realms to contact your mother will be far more difficult." Marron cast an apologetic look her way. "I've tried to breach the security protocols for the Realms before. I've never managed it, but I've never tried with a Smarteye or with a Dweller before."

Aria had worried about this. Hess had surely blocked her access into the Realms, but she hoped the "Songbird" file might help them reach Lumina.

Marron asked questions about the Pod as they moved from soup to beef stewed in rich wine sauce. Aria explained how most everything, from the production of food to the recycling of their air and water, was automated.

"People don't work?" Roar asked.

"Only the minority do in the real." Aria glanced at Perry, looking for signs of disgust, but he was tucked into his food. A meal like this had to be a rarity for him, not just something he'd missed on their journey.

She told them about the pseudo-economy, where people amassed virtual wealth, but that there were black markets and hackers. "None of it changes what happens in the real. Aside from the Consuls, everyone is entitled to the same living quarters and clothes and diet."

Roar leaned across the table and smiled at her seductively, his dark hair falling into his eyes. "When you say everything happens in the Realms, do you mean *everything*?"

Aria laughed nervously. "Yes. Especially that. There are no risks in the Realms."

Roar's smile widened. "You simply think it and it happens? And it actually feels *real*?"

"Why are we talking about this?"

"I need a Smarteye," he said.

Perry rolled his eyes. "There's no way it's the same."

Marron cleared his throat. He'd gone a little red in the face. Aria knew she had too. She didn't know if it was the same, real or Realms, but she wasn't about to tell them that.

"What happened with the Croven?" she asked, anxious to change the subject. Surely by now they had disappeared.

She looked around the table. No one answered. Finally Marron wiped his mouth neatly with a napkin and spoke. "They're still gathered in the plateau, from what we can tell. Slaying a Blood Lord is a grave offense, Aria. They will stay as long as they can."

"We slew a Blood Lord?" she asked, hardly believing she'd just used the word *slew*.

Perry's green eyes flicked up. "It's the only way to explain their numbers. And I did it, Aria. Not you."

Because of what she did. Because she'd left the rotten cave and gone searching for berries. "So they're waiting?"

Perry sat back in his chair, his jaw tight. "Yes."

"We're safe here, I assure you," Marron said. "The wall is fifty feet at the lowest point, and we have archers posted day and night. They'll keep the Croven from coming too close. And soon the weather will turn. With the cold and the Aether storms, the Croven will leave in search of shelter. Let's hope that happens before they do something rash."

"How many are there?" she asked.

"Near forty," Perry said.

"*Forty?*" She couldn't believe it. Forty *cannibals* were after him? For days, she'd imagined reaching her mother in Bliss.

She imagined Lumina sending a Hover for her. With the footage of Soren, she'd clear her name of any wrongdoing and start over in Bliss. But what about Perry? Would he ever be able to leave Marron's? If he did, would he always have to run from the Croven?

Marron shook his head at his wine. "In these harsh times, the Croven fare well."

Roar nodded. "They destroyed the Blackfins a few months ago. They're a tribe west of here. They'd suffered a few lean years, like most. Then the Aether storms came and hit their compound directly."

"We were there," Perry said, glancing at her. "It was the place with the broken roof."

Aria swallowed through a thick throat, imagining the power of the storm that had leveled that place. Perry had found her boots and coat there. She'd worn the Blackfins clothes for days.

"They took a cruel hit," Perry said.

"They did," Roar agreed. "They lost half of their number to the storms in one day. Lodan, their Blood Lord, sent word to Vale, offering to pledge what was left of his tribe to the Tides. This is the highest form of shame to a Blood Lord, Aria." He paused, his dark eyes darting to Perry. "Vale refused the offer. He claimed he couldn't take on any more hungry mouths."

Perry looked stung. "Vale didn't tell me."

"Of course not, Perry. Would you have supported his decision?"

"No."

"As I heard it," Roar continued, "Lodan was heading toward the Horns."

"To Sable?" Marron asked.

Roar nodded. "There's a place people speak of," he told Aria. "A place free of the Aether. They call it the Still Blue. Some say it's not real. Just a dream of a clear sky. But from time to time, people get to whispering about it."

Roar looked back at Perry. "There's more noise than I've ever heard out there. People are saying Sable's discovered it. Lodan was convinced."

Perry sat forward. He looked ready to spring from his chair. "We need to find out if it's true."

Roar's hand settled on his knife. "If I go to Sable, it won't be to ask questions about the Still Blue."

"If you go to Sable, it will be to deliver my sister as you should have." Perry's tone had grown cold. Aria's eyes darted from Roar to Perry.

"What happened to the Fins?" Marron asked. He calmly cut his meat into a perfect square, like he had no idea of the sudden tension in the room.

Roar took a long drink before he spoke. "The Fins were already weakened when illness hit them in the open. Then the Croven came and took the strongest children into their fold. To the rest . . . well, they did what the Croven do."

Aria looked down. The sauce on her plate had begun to look too red.

"Terrible," Marron said, nudging his plate away. "The

stuff of nightmares." He smiled at her. "You'll soon leave this all behind, my dear. Perry told me your mother is a scientist. What sort of research does she do?"

"Genetics. I don't know much beyond that. She works for the committee that oversees all the Pods and the Realms. The Central Governing Board. It's high-level research. She's not allowed to talk about it."

Aria was embarrassed at how it sounded. Like her own mother couldn't trust her with information. "She's very dedicated. She left to work in another Pod a few months ago," she added, feeling the need to say something more.

"Your mother is not in Reverie?" Marron asked.

"No. She had to go to Bliss to do some research."

Marron set his wine down so fast it spilled over the edges of the crystal, soaking into the cream table linen.

"What is it?" Aria asked.

Marron's rings winked red and blue as he gripped the arms of his chair. "There's a rumor from the traders who came around last week. It's only a rumor, Aria. You heard what Roar said about the Still Blue. People talk."

The room turned around her. "What's the rumor?"

"I'm so sorry to tell you. Bliss was struck by an Aether storm. They said it was destroyed."

25

PEREGRINE

Perry stood outside Aria's door, his lungs pumping air like a bellows. There was plenty to like about Marron's. Food. Beds. Food. But all the doors and walls gave him a pathetic range on tempers. He thought of all the times over the past week he'd wanted a break. Just an hour without breathing in Aria's ache, or Roar's. Yet here he was, practically sniffing under Aria's door.

He didn't catch anything. Perry put his ear to the wood. Fared no better. Swearing under his breath, he jogged downstairs. He entered a room on the first floor, bare save for a large painting that looked like accidental splatter, and the heavy steel door of an elevator. Perry punched at the buttons. Paced until the door slid open. There were no buttons inside. The steel box dropped to only one place. Marron called it the Navel.

Ten seconds in, he started to sweat. He continued to drop,

deeper, deeper, imagining all the steps he'd taken to climb the mountain in reverse. The elevator slowed and stopped, though his stomach kept going for a moment or two. He remembered the feeling from his first visit. A hard one to forget. Finally the door opened.

A smell as damp and thick as breathing dirt came to him. He sneezed a few times, striding through a wide corridor toward the source of light at the end. Crates were piled high along the walls. Even on top, they were littered with odd things. Dusty vases and chairs. A mannequin arm. A thin paper screen painted with images of cherry blossoms. A harp with no strings. A wooden box full of doorknobs and hinges and keys.

He had explored every one of those crates the last time he'd come. Like everything at Marron's, the bits and pieces stashed in the Navel had taught him about the world before the Unity. A world Vale had discovered years before him in the pages of books.

Perry followed the clutter to the end of the corridor, nodding to Roar and Marron as he entered a large room. A bank of computers took up one side. Most were ancient, but Marron had a few pieces of Dweller equipment, sleek as Aria's Smarteye. There was also a wall-sized screen, like in the common room above. The image he saw on it was of the plateau they'd crossed before the final climb to Marron's. The colors were odd and the image was murky, but he recognized the caped figures moving around tents.

"I had a microcamera set up," Marron said from a wooden desk. He controlled the images on the wallscreen from a thin control palette. Aria's Smarteye was on his desk on a thick black board that looked like a piece of granite. "It won't last long with the Aether, but it'll help us see what they're doing until then."

"They're setting up to stay, that's what they're doing," Roar said. He sat on the lone couch, his feet kicked up onto a small table. "Another ten added since the last count, I'd say. You've finally got a tribe following you, Per."

"Thanks, Roar. But it's not the kind I wanted." Perry sighed. Would the Croven ever leave? How was he going to get out of here?

Marron guessed his thoughts. "Perry, there are old tunnels that run deeper into the mountain. Most of them are impassable, but we might find one that's held up. I'll have them explored in the morning."

Perry knew Marron had meant to be reassuring, but it only made him feel worse for all the trouble he was creating. And tunnels? He dreaded to think of leaving that way. Just being in this room was making him sweat. But unless the Croven gave up and left, he couldn't think of another way out of Delphi.

"What's the news on the Smarteye?"

Marron's fingers glided over the palette. The image on the wallscreen changed to a series of numbers. "By my estimate, I could have it decrypted and running in eighteen hours, twelve minutes, and twenty-nine seconds."

Perry nodded. They'd have it sometime early tomorrow night.

"Perry, even if I can get it powered, I think the two of you should be prepared for any outcome. The Realms are even better protected than their Pods. Walls and energy shields are nothing by comparison. There may not be anything I can do to get you connected with Talon. Or to link Aria with her mother."

"We have to try."

"We will. We'll try our best."

Perry tipped his chin at Roar. "I need you." Roar followed him without question. He explained what he wanted in the elevator.

"I thought you'd already gone to her," Roar said.

Perry stared at the metal doors. "I haven't. . . . I did, but I didn't see her."

Roar laughed. "And you want *me* to go?"

"Yes. You, Roar." Was he going to have to explain that Aria talked to him more easily?

Roar leaned against the elevator and crossed his arms. "Remember that time I was trying to talk to Liv and I fell off the roof?"

In the cramped elevator car, he couldn't escape picking up the shift in Roar's temper. The scent of longing. He'd always hoped Roar and Liv would outgrow their crush, but they'd always been wrapped up in each other.

"I was talking to her through that hole in the timbers, remember that, Perry? She was up in the loft and it had just rained. I lost my balance and slid right off."

"I remember you running away from my father with your pants around your ankles."

"That's right. I tore them on a tile on the way down. I don't think I'd ever seen Liv laugh so much. Almost made me want to stop running just to see her like that. Hearing it was pretty good, though. Best sound in the world, Liv's laugh." Roar's smile faded after a moment. "He was fast, your father."

"He was stronger than he was fast."

Roar didn't say anything. He knew how it had been for Perry growing up.

"Was there a point to that story?" Perry stepped out as soon as the elevator doors parted. "Are you coming?"

"Fall off your own roof, Perry," he said as the door slid closed.

The elevator dropped back to the Navel, carrying away the sound of Roar's laughter.

Aria was sitting at the edge of the bed when Perry stepped into her room. Her arms were crossed low, over her stomach. Only the small lamp by the bedside was lit. The light came off the shade in a perfect triangle, falling across her folded arms. The room held her scent. Violets of early spring. The first bloom. He could've gotten lost in that scent if it weren't for the dankness of her temper.

Perry closed the door behind him. This room was smaller than the one he'd been given to share with Roar. He saw nowhere to sit but the bed. Not that he felt like sitting. But he didn't want to stand by the door, either.

She looked over, her eyes swollen from crying. "Did Marron send you again?"

"Marron? No . . . he didn't." He shouldn't have come. Why had he closed the door like he'd meant to stay? Now leaving would be strange.

Aria wiped the tears from her face. "That night in Reverie? I was in Ag 6 trying to find out if she was all right. The link with Bliss was down, and I was so worried. When I saw the message from her, I thought she was fine."

Perry stared at the empty space by her side. Just four steps away. Four steps that looked like a mile. He took them like he was going to launch himself off a cliff. The bed rocked as he sat. What was wrong with him?

He cleared his throat. "They were just rumors, Aria. The Auds just spread things."

"It could be true."

"But it could be false, too. Maybe only part of it is destroyed. Like the dome that night? It was crushed where I came in."

She turned to the painting on the wall, lost in thought. "You're right. The Pods are built to break down in parts. There are ways of containing damage."

She pushed her hair behind her ear. "I just want to know. I don't feel like she's gone. . . . But what if she is? What if I should be mourning her right now? What if I do and she's not? I'm so afraid of guessing it wrong. And I hate that I can't do anything about it."

He bent over his knees and pulled at the edge of his cast.

"This is what you've felt about Talon. Isn't it?"

He nodded. "Yes," he said. "Exactly." He'd been avoiding the fear that he might be doing everything in vain. That

Talon was gone. He hadn't allowed himself to think about that. What if Talon had died because of him? Where *was* Talon? Perry knew she understood. This Dweller girl knew what it was like to feel the torture of loving someone who was lost. Maybe gone forever.

"Marron says he'll have the files and the link working by tomorrow."

"Tomorrow," she said.

The word hung in the quiet of the room. Perry drew a slow breath, working up the courage to say what he'd wanted to for days. Everything could change when they fixed the Smarteye. This could be his last chance to tell her.

"Aria . . . everyone feels lost and low. It's how a person acts that makes them different. These last days you kept going despite those feet. Despite not knowing your way . . . Despite me."

"I can't tell if that was a compliment or an apology."

He peered at her. "Both. I could've been kinder to you."

"You could have at least said a little more."

He smiled. "I don't know about that."

She laughed, and then her eyes turned serious. "I could have been kinder too."

She scooted herself back against the headboard. Her dark hair fell straight to her shoulders, framing her small chin. Her pink lips turned up in a soft smile.

"I'll forgive you on two conditions."

Perry leaned back on his good arm and stole a look at her. Her body belonged in tight clothes, not in camos. He felt guilty looking, but he couldn't help it. "Yeah? What are they?"

"First, tell me what your temper is like right now."

He covered his surprised gasp with a cough. "*My* temper?" No way this was a good idea. He searched for a gentle way to say no. "I could try," he said after a moment, and then pushed a hand through his hair, shocked at what he'd just agreed to do.

"All right. . . ." He fiddled with the edge of his cast. "Scents, the way I get them, are more than smells. They have weights and temperatures sometimes. Colors, too. I don't think it's like that for others. My bloodline on my father's side is strong. Probably the strongest line of Scires." He stopped himself, not wanting to sound boastful. He realized his thighs were flexed tight. "So, my temper right now is probably cool. And heavy. That's what sorrow is like. Dark and thick, like stone. Like the scent coming off a wet rock."

He glanced at her. She didn't look like she wanted to laugh so he kept going. "There'd be more. Most of the time, a lot of times . . . there are a few scents in a temper. Nervous tempers are sharp scents. Like laurel leaves? Something bright and tingling like that? Nervous tempers are hard to ignore. So there'd be some of that probably."

"Why are you nervous?"

Perry smiled down at his cast. "That question makes me nervous." He made himself look at her. Looking at her wasn't working either, so he pinned his gaze on the lamp. "I can't do this, Aria."

"Now you have an idea how it feels. How exposed I feel around you."

242

Perry laughed. "That was tricky of you. You want to know what I'm nervous about now? That you have a second condition."

"It's not a condition. It's more of a request."

Every part of him was locked tight, waiting for what she'd say next.

Aria pulled the covers over her, hugging them close. "Will you stay? I think I'd sleep better if you stayed here tonight. Then we could miss them together."

His impulse was to agree. She was beautiful sitting against the headboard, her skin looking smoother, softer than the sheets pulled up around her. But Perry hesitated.

Sleeping was the most dangerous thing a Scire could do with another person. Tempers mixed in the harmony of sleep. They tangled up, forming their own bonds. Scires became rendered that way, as had happened with him and Talon.

He didn't know why he thought of this only now, but he didn't need to worry. Scires seldom rendered to anyone outside their Sense. And she was a Dweller. The furthest thing from being a Scire. Besides, he'd been sleeping within feet of her for more than a week. What difference would another day make?

Perry's eyes flicked to the soft carpet, then back to Aria. "I'll be right here."

26

ARIA

Marron had a running countdown to when they could safely power up her Smarteye. He showed it to Aria in the morning, when he took her down to the Navel.

Seven hours, forty-three minutes, and twelve seconds.

It was an estimate, but Aria knew enough about Marron to take the numbers for their worth. The room was spare and cold compared to the rest of Delphi. A collection of computer equipment. A desk and a couch. It had a sacred air. She had the impression no one came down there except Marron. Aria noticed a vase of roses sitting on a little coffee table.

"You liked the other one so," Marron said, beaming, then he quietly set to work on her Smarteye at his desk.

Aria sat on the couch, her stomach rolling with nerves. She couldn't tear her eyes from the numbers on the wallscreen. Was the recording of Ag 6 still in the Eye? Was the "Songbird" file? Would she be able to find Lumina and

Talon? Only an hour had passed when Marron invited her on a walk outside. She agreed right away. Her feet were still sore, but she'd go crazy down here all alone. Time had never moved more slowly.

She searched for Perry as they moved through Delphi's halls. She'd stayed awake listening to the steady rhythm of his breathing during the night. But when she'd woken that morning, he hadn't been there.

Aria immediately noticed a change in the courtyard as she stepped outside with Marron. Only a few people were moving about, compared with the bustle she'd seen when she stormed in with Cinder.

"Where is everyone?" Aria glanced at the sky. She'd seen much worse than the veinlike flows above.

Marron's expression sobered. He looped her arm through his as they continued on the cobblestone path. "We had a few arrows over the wall early this morning from the Croven. They were careless shots fired before daylight. Aimed to strike fear more than anything else. In that, they were successful. I was hoping they'd have relaxed by now, but it appears . . ."

Marron trailed off as he looked toward Delphi. Rose and Slate hurried toward them, Rose's dark braid swinging behind her. She was talking before she'd even stopped.

"The boy, Cinder, is gone."

"He left through the east gate," Slate added quickly. He looked furious with himself. "He was already out when the tower spotted him."

Marron's arm tensed around hers. "This is intolerable under the circumstances. It *cannot* happen. Who was on that post?" He strode off with Slate, still ranting.

Aria couldn't believe it. After everything, after carrying him there, Cinder had gone? "Does Perry know?" she asked Rose.

"No, I don't think so." Rose pursed her lips in disapproval. Then she rolled her eyes. "You should try the roof first. That's where he usually is."

"Thank you," Aria said, and then dashed for Delphi.

Rose called out behind her, teasing. "Your feet look like they're healing!"

Aria took the elevator to the top of Delphi and stepped onto the roof, a vast stretch of cement with only a wooden rail framing the perimeter. Perry sat against it, gazing up at the Aether, his wounded arm propped onto his knee. He smiled when he saw her and strode over.

When he reached her, his smile fell. "What happened?"

"Cinder's gone. He left. I'm sorry, Perry."

His face tightened, and then he looked away and shrugged. "It's all right. I didn't even know him." He was quiet for a moment. "Are you sure he's gone? They looked for him?"

"Yes. The guards saw him leave."

They walked to the edge of the roof. Perry propped his arms on the rail, lost in thought as he stared across the trees. Aria took in the long sweep of the wall, curving wide around Delphi. She saw the gate she'd run through just yesterday, and the towers, evenly spaced around the perimeter. Some seventy feet below, animal pens and gardens made neat geometric patterns of the courtyard. She'd just been down there.

"Who told you I was up here?" Perry asked. The disappointment had faded from his face.

"Rose." Aria smiled. "She told me lots of things."

He cringed. "She did? What did she say? No, don't tell me. I don't want to know."

"You really don't."

"Ahh . . . that's cruel. Now you're just kicking me while I'm down."

She laughed and they fell quiet again. The silence between them felt good.

"Aria," he said after a while. "I want to wait for the Smarteye with you but I can't stay in the Navel. Not for long. Makes me skitty being that deep underground."

"It makes you *skitty*?" For a lethal creature, sometimes he used words that struck her as utterly childish.

"Shaky? Like you can't be still?"

She smiled. "Can I wait with you up here?"

"Yeah," he said, grinning. "I was hoping for that." He threaded his legs beneath the wooden rail, letting them hang over the edge. Aria sat cross-legged beside him.

"This is my favorite place in Delphi. It's the best spot to read the wind."

She closed her eyes as a breeze swept past, searching for what he meant. She smelled smoke and pine on the cool wind. The skin along her arms tightened.

"How are your feet?" he asked.

"They're still a little sore, but much better," she said, moved by the simple question. With him, it wasn't small talk. He was always looking after people. "Talon's lucky to have an uncle like you," she said.

He shook his head. "No. It's my fault he was taken. I'm just trying to fix it. I've got no choice."

"Why?"

"We're rendered. There's a bond between us through our tempers. I feel what he feels. I don't just scent it. Same for him."

She couldn't imagine being linked with a person that way. She thought of what both Roar and Rose had said about Scires keeping to their kind.

Perry leaned forward, crossing his arms over the rail. "Being away from him, it's like part of me is gone."

"We'll find him, Perry."

He rested his chin on the rail. "Thanks," he said, his eyes fixed on the courtyard below.

Aria's gaze moved to his arm. He'd pushed his sleeves up above his elbows because of the cast. A strong vein laced the swell of his bicep. One of his Markings was a band of angled slashes. The other was made of flowing lines like waves. She had the urge to touch them. Her eyes trailed up to his profile, following the small rise at the top of his nose, finding the thin scar at the edge of his lip. Maybe she wanted to touch more than his arm.

Perry's head snapped over to her and she realized *he knew*. Heat bloomed across her cheeks. He'd scent her embarrassment, too.

She scooted to the edge and swung her legs over the side of the roof like him and tried to look interested in the goings-on below. The courtyard showed more signs of life. People were moving here and there. A man split firewood with practiced thwacks of an ax. A dog barked at a young girl who held something high, out of its reach. As much as she concentrated on what she saw, she still felt Perry's attention on her.

"What are you going to do after you find Talon?" she asked, switching tactics.

He relaxed over the rail again. "I'll get him home, then form my own tribe."

"How?"

"It's a matter of winning men. You get one who's either willing or forced to follow your lead. Then another and so on. Until you have a group big enough to stake out some land. Fight for it, if need be."

"How are they forced?"

"In a challenge. Winner either spares the loser's life and earns fealty that way, or . . . what you'd imagine."

"I see," Aria said. Fealty. Allies. Oaths taken at the point of death. They were ordinary concepts in his life.

"Maybe I'll head north," he continued. "See if I can find my sister and get her to the Horns. Maybe I can fix that ruffle before it's too late. And I want to see what I can find about the Still Blue."

Aria wondered where that would leave him and Roar. It didn't seem fair to keep two people who loved each other apart.

"What about you?" he asked. "When we find your mother, will you go back to those virtual places? The Realms?"

She liked the way he'd said *Realms*. Slow and resonant. She liked even better the way he'd said *when* we find your mother. Like it would happen. Like it was inevitable.

"I think I'll get back to singing. It was always something my mother made me do. I never . . . I never really *wanted* to sing. Now I have the urge to do it. Songs are stories." She smiled. "Maybe I've got my own stories to tell now."

"I've been thinking about it."

"You've been thinking about my voice?"

"Yeah." He gave a shrug that managed to seem both shy and offhand. "Since that first night."

Aria had to rein in a ridiculously proud smile. "That was from *Tosca*. An ancient Italian opera." The song was for a male tenor. When Aria sang it, she brought it up just enough to get it into her range, but still kept its lost, mournful quality. "It's about a man, an artist who's been sentenced to die, and he's singing about the woman he loves. He doesn't think he'll ever see her again. It's my mother's favorite aria." She smiled. "Besides me."

Perry pulled his legs around and sat against the rail, an expectant smile on his face.

Aria laughed. "Seriously? Here?"

"Seriously."

"All right. . . . I have to stand. It's better if I stand."

"Then stand."

Perry rose to his feet with her, leaning his hip against the rail. His smile was distracting, so she gazed up at the Aether for a few moments, breathing the cool air into her lungs as anticipation stirred inside of her. She'd missed this.

The lyrics flowed out of her, springing straight from her heart. Words full of drama and wild abandon that had always embarrassed her before, because who flung themselves at raw emotion like that?

She did it now.

She let the words fly across the roof and past the trees. She lost herself in the aria, letting it carry her off. But even as she sang, she knew the man below had stopped cutting wood and the dog had stopped barking. Even the trees hushed to hear her sing. When she was done, she had tears in her eyes. She wished her mother could've heard her. She'd never sounded better.

Perry closed his eyes when she was finished. "You have a voice as sweet as your scent," he said, his words deep and quiet. "Sweet as violets."

Her heart stopped in her chest. He thought she had a scent like violets? "Perry . . . do you want to know the words?"

His eyes flew open. "Yes."

She took a moment to think through the lyrics, and then to muster up the courage to tell him—everything—without looking away.

"How the stars shone. How sweet the earth smelled. The orchard gate creaked, and a footstep pressed on the sand. And she entered, fragrant as a flower, and fell into my arms. Oh, sweet kisses, lingering caresses. Slowly, trembling, I gazed upon her beauty. Now my dream of true love is lost forever. My last hour has flown, and I die, hopeless, and never have I loved life more."

They reached for each other then like some force had pulled their hands together. Aria looked at their fingers as they laced together, bringing her the sensation of his touch. Of warmth and calluses. Soft and hard together. She absorbed the terror and beauty of him and his world. Of every moment over the past days. All of it, filling her up like the first breath she'd ever taken. And never had she loved life more.

27

ARIA

When she went back to the Navel with Perry, only forty-seven minutes remained on the time counter. Roar was at the control table with Marron. She had a vague notion of them speaking together quietly, and of Perry pacing behind the couch. She couldn't focus on anything beyond the numbers on the screen.

Mom, she pleaded silently. *Be there. Please be there. I need you.*

Perry and I need you.

She expected fanfare when the counter reached zero. An alarm or some sort of noise. There was nothing. Not even a sound.

"I have the two files here," Marron said. "Both stored locally on the Smarteye."

Marron pulled them up on the wallscreen. One file had a date and a timer on it. The readout showed twenty-one minutes of recorded time. The other was labeled SONGBIRD.

Aria didn't have any memory of Perry joining her on the couch or taking her hand. She didn't know how she hadn't noticed. Now that she did, he felt like the only thing keeping her from drifting off the couch.

They'd decided to check the files before trying to contact Lumina. Aria asked to see the recording first. This was the file they both needed. Barter for Talon. Evidence that would clear her name. Then she braced herself for fire and Soren. For the sounds of Paisley dying. She couldn't believe she actually *wanted* it to be there.

A smoldering forest appeared on the wallscreen. Paisley's panicked voice burst across the room. Images Aria had seen through her eyes played out on the screen. Her feet blurring beneath her. Flashes of Paisley's hand linked with hers. Shuddering images of fire and smoke and trees. When it came to Soren grabbing Paisley's leg, Perry spoke at her side. "You don't have to watch all of it."

She blinked at him, feeling like she'd stepped out of a trance. There were still six minutes left, but she knew how the recording ended. "That's enough."

The wallscreen went dark and silence came. They had the recording. It should have felt more like a victory, but Aria felt like crying. She could still hear the echo of Paisley's voice.

"I need to see the other file," she said.

Marron selected "Songbird." Lumina's face took up most of the wallscreen. Her shoulders reached from one end of the room to the other. Marron adjusted the image to half the size, but she remained larger than human.

"That's my mother," she heard herself say.

Lumina smiled at the camera. A quick, nervous smile. Her dark hair was fastened as she always wore it, pulled back from her face. Behind her there were rows of shelves with labeled boxes. She was in some sort of supply room.

"This is strange speaking to a camera and pretending it's you. But I know it's you, Aria. I know you'll be watching this and listening."

Her voice was loud, everywhere in the room. She reached up and smoothed the collar of her doctor's smock.

"We're in trouble here. Bliss has suffered serious damage in an Aether storm. The Consuls estimate forty percent of the Pod has been contaminated, but generators are failing and the number seems to be climbing every hour. The CGB has promised help. We're waiting for them. We haven't given up. Neither should you, Aria.

"I wanted to tell you when it happened, but the CGB shut down our link with other Pods. They don't want panic spreading. But I found a way, I hope, to get this message to you. I know you must be worried."

Aria's heart had stopped beating. Lumina sat back. Her hands were offscreen but Aria knew they'd be folded in her lap.

"I need to tell you something else, Aria. Something you've wanted to know about for so long. My work." She sent a fleeting smile toward the camera. "You must be happy to hear that.

"I have to begin with the Realms. The CGB created them to give us the illusion of space when we were forced into Pods during the Unity. They were only meant to be copies of the world we left behind, as you know, but the possibilities proved to be too enticing. So we gave ourselves the ability to fly. To travel from a snowcap to a beach with a single thought. And why feel pain if you don't have to? Why feel the brunt of real fear if there's no danger of becoming hurt? We increased what we deemed good and removed the bad. Those are the Realms as you know them. *Better than Real*, as they say."

Lumina stared at the camera a few moments. Then she reached forward, pressing something beyond the camera's view. A colorful scan of the human brain appeared in a quadrant over her left shoulder.

"The central area in blue is the oldest portion of the brain, Aria. It's called the limbic system. It controls many of our most basic processes. Our drive to mate. Our comprehension of stress and fear and reaction to it. Our quick decision-making capability. We say a gut reaction, but actually these reflexes come from here. Simply put, this is our animal mind. Over generations in the Realms, the usefulness of this part of our brain has vastly diminished. What do you think, Daughter, happens to something that goes unused for time too long?"

Aria let out a sob, because this was her mother. This was how she'd always taught her, asking her questions. Letting her form her own answers.

"It's lost," Aria said.

Lumina nodded as though she'd heard her. "It degenerates. This has catastrophic consequences when we do need to rely on instinct. Pleasure and pain become confused. Fear can become thrilling. Rather than avoid stress, we seek it and even revel in it. The will to give life becomes the need to take it. The result is a collapse of reason and cognition. Put simply, it results in a psychotic break."

Lumina paused. "I have spent my life studying this disorder, Degenerative Limbic Syndrome. When I began my work two decades ago, incidents of DLS were isolated and minor. No one believed it would amount to a real threat. But in the past three years the Aether storms have intensified at an alarming rate. They damage our Pods and cut off our link to the Realms. Generators fail. Backups fail. . . . We're left in dire situations that we're incapable of handling. Entire Pods have fallen to DLS. I think you can imagine, Aria, the anarchy of six thousand trapped people who have come under this syndrome. I see it around me now."

She looked away from the camera for a moment, hiding her face.

"You will hate me for what I will say next, but I don't know if I'll ever see you again. And I can't hold this knowledge from you anymore. My work has led me to research Outsiders in search of genetic solutions. They don't have the dangerous response we do to stress and fear. In fact, what I've seen is the reverse effect. The CGB makes arrangements for us to bring them into our facility. That's how I met your father.

I work with Outsider children now. It's easier for me after what happened."

Aria's heart tightened and tightened, twisting, the pain unbearable.

This couldn't be happening.

She was not an Outsider.

It couldn't be true.

Lumina reached up, pressing her fingers to her lips as if she couldn't believe what she'd said. Then she brought her hands back down. When she spoke again, her voice was hurried and raw with emotion.

"I never viewed you as being inferior in any way. The Outsider half of you is the part I love most. It's your tenacity. Your curiosity about my research and the Realms. I know your fire comes from that part of you.

"You'll have a thousand questions, I'm sure. What I haven't shared is for your own protection." She paused, giving the camera a teary smile. "And it's always better, isn't it, when you discover answers on your own?"

Lumina reached forward, ready to shut off the recording. Her pained expression filled the screen. She hesitated and sat back, her small shoulders shifting nervously, her petite frame rocking, like she couldn't stop herself. Seeing her that way, tears streamed from Aria's eyes.

"Do me a favor, Songbird? Sing the aria for me? You know which one. You sing it so beautifully. Wherever I am, I know I'll hear it. Good-bye, Aria. I love you."

The screen went dark.

Aria had no limbs.

No heart.

No thoughts.

Perry appeared in front of her, his eyes flashing with rage and hurt. What had just happened? What had Lumina just said? She studied Outsider *children*?

Like *Talon*?

Perry picked up the small coffee table, upending the vase of roses. With a guttural cry, he hurled the table at the wallscreen. The vase broke first with a hollow pop at her feet. Then the screen shattered with a terrible explosion of glass.

Long after he'd left, shards still rained on the floor.

She watched her mother's message three more times in the upstairs common room. Marron stayed with her, patting her knee and making soft comforting sounds.

She looked down at the handkerchief wadded in her hand. Her heart ached, like it was ripping inside of her. The pain only seemed to get worse.

"It happened in Ag 6," she said to Marron. "This thing. DLS." Aria remembered Soren's wide, glazed eyes as he'd stared at the fire. How intent Bane and Echo had been. How even Paisley had been afraid the trees might fall on her. "The only difference is that we shut off on purpose that night."

Aria pressed her eyes closed, fighting the image of the chaos in Ag 6 on a grand scale. A Pod-wide riot where her mother was. A thousand Sorens starting fires and ripping off Smarteyes. What chance did Lumina have, between the Aether and DLS?

Marron's eyes were full of compassion. He looked worn from the day, his hair mussed, his shirt wrinkled and damp from when he'd held her and let her cry. "Your mother knew about this condition. She sent you this message. She had to have been prepared for something like this."

"You're right. She would have. She's always prepared."

"Aria, we can try the Smarteye now. If you're ready, we can try getting you into the Realms. We might be able to reach her."

She nodded to Marron quickly, her eyes filling again. She wanted to see her mother. To know she was alive, but what would she say? Lumina had kept so much from her. She'd kept Aria from knowing herself.

She was half Outsider.

Half.

She felt that way. Like half of her had just disappeared.

Marron brought her the Smarteye. Aria's hands shook as she held it. "What if there's nothing? What if I can't get her?"

"You can stay here as long as you like."

He said it so quickly, so readily. Aria looked into his round, kind face. "Thank you." She couldn't speak the next question that came to her mind.

What if I find out she took Talon?

She needed to know. Aria placed the Smarteye over her left eye. The device pulled uncomfortably tight on her skin.

She saw the two local files on her Smartscreen. Soren's recording. Her mother's message.

She ran through the mental commands to bring up the Realms as Marron monitored everything on the palette on his lap.

WELCOME TO THE REALMS! flashed across her Smartscreen, followed by BETTER THAN REAL!

After a few moments, another message appeared.

ACCESS DENIED

She took the Eye off quickly, not wanting to see those words. "Marron, we failed. I'm not going to go home. Perry's not getting Talon back."

He squeezed her hand. "It's not the end of the road yet. It didn't work for you, but I have something else in mind."

28

PEREGRINE

The Croven were chanting when Perry strode out to the roof. He braced the rail with his good hand and looked out across the pine forest, listening to the distant ringing of their bells. His legs twitched with the need to run. To escape. Even now, with nothing between him and the sky, he felt trapped.

It couldn't be true. He had blamed himself for Talon's kidnapping. He'd taken the Smarteye, and the Dwellers had come after him. Now he wondered—was it possible the Dwellers had Talon for an *experiment*? Was he suffering at the hands of Aria's mother? A woman who stole innocent *children*?

He yanked an arrow from his quiver and fired it toward the Croven, not caring that he was too far. That he couldn't even see them. Cursing, he loosed one arrow after another, letting them sail over the wall and past the treetops. Then he slumped against the elevator box, cradling his throbbing hand.

He spent the rest of the night staring at the Aether, thinking of Talon and Cinder and Roar and Liv. How everything was about searching and *missing*. How none of it was coming together the way it should. By dawn, with daylight creeping to meet the Aether, all he could think about was Aria's face as her world had shifted around her. It had torn her open to learn she was like him. He'd scented it. Her temper had slammed into him, fire and ice, shooting into his nose. Straight to his gut.

He couldn't have slept more than an hour when Roar came up to the roof. He perched on the rail with the cat's balance of an Aud, no trace of fear at the huge drop behind him. He crossed his arms, a cold edge in his eyes.

"She didn't know about the work her mother does, Perry. You saw her. She was just as stunned as you."

Perry sat up and rubbed his tired eyes. His muscles were stiff and sore from sleeping on cement. "What do you want, Roar?" he asked.

"I'm delivering a message. Aria said to come down if you want to see Talon."

Aria and Marron were in the common room when he and Roar got there.

She rose from the couch when she saw him. Purple shadows darkened the skin beneath her eyes. Perry couldn't help but breathe in deeply, searching the room for her temper. He found it. The hurt she felt. A deep, raw thing. Anger and shame at being an Outsider. At being a Savage, like him.

"This is working now," she said, holding out her Smarteye. "I tried it but I couldn't get into the Realms. My signature didn't work. They've blocked me."

Perry's knees almost buckled. That was it. He'd lost his chance to find Talon. Then why had they brought him down here? Confused, he turned to Roar and found him fighting a smile.

"I can't," Aria said, "but you might be able to, Perry."

"Me?"

"Yes. They've only blocked me. The Eye still works. I can't go in. But you might be able to."

Marron nodded. "The device reads a signature in two ways. DNA and brain pattern recognition. Aria's signature was denied right away. But with you, I can try to create some static, some noise in the authentication process. We ran some tests overnight. I think we could steal some time before you're identified as an unauthorized user. It could work."

It made no sense to him. All he heard was the last bit. *It could work.*

"My mother's file had the security codes to her research," Aria said. "If Talon's there, we might be able to find him."

Perry swallowed hard. "I can find Talon?"

"We can try."

"When?"

Marron raised his eyebrows. "Now."

Perry headed to the elevator, suddenly weightless on his

legs, until Marron held his hand up. "Wait, Peregrine. It's better if we do this up here."

Perry froze. He'd forgotten about what he did downstairs. Shamed, he had to force himself to hold Marron's gaze. "I can't fix it. But I'll find a way to pay you back."

Marron didn't answer for a long moment. Then he tipped his head. "No need to, Peregrine. One day I think I'll be glad you owe me a favor."

Perry nodded, accepting the agreement, and strode to one of the display cases on the rear wall. He pretended to observe a painting of a lone boat moored on a gray beach as he tried to collect himself. He'd made more than a few promises lately. *I'll find Talon. I'll get Aria home.* What had he done but bring a tribe of cannibals to Marron's door and then break a valuable piece of equipment? How could Marron have faith in him?

Behind him, Aria and Marron talked about the problems of presenting him with the task of gliding through something he wasn't even sure he understood. Perry had begun to sweat. It rolled down his spine, along his ribs.

"You all right, Perry?" Roar said.

"Hand hurts," he said, lifting his arm. It wasn't entirely a lie. They all looked at him, then at the dirty cast like they'd forgotten about it. Perry couldn't blame them. If it didn't hurt so badly, he'd probably have forgotten about it too.

Within a few minutes, Rose arrived and pulled Aria aside, speaking with her quietly. Rose handed Aria a metal case and left.

Aria sat next to Perry on one of the couches. He watched her cut through the cast on his left hand, her fingers trembling slightly. He drew in her temper. She was just as scared as he was about what they'd find in the Realms. And he knew Roar was right. She hadn't known anything. Not the truth about herself, or about her mother's work.

Perry remembered what she'd said in her room.

We could miss them together.

She'd been right. It had been easier with her. Perry placed his right hand on hers.

"Are you all right?" he whispered. It wasn't what he wanted to know. Of course she wasn't all right. What he wanted to know was if the *together* part still mattered to her. Because even though he was confused and sorry and angry, it still mattered to him.

She looked up and nodded, and he knew she agreed. Whatever else came, they'd face it together.

His hand looked more like a hand. The swelling had gone down. The blisters had flattened. The patches that looked wrinkled and dark worried him most, but he could move his fingers and that was all he'd hoped for. He sneezed at the caustic scent of the gel Aria spread over the charred skin, and then he sweat even more at the cool burn that seeped deep into his knuckles. It was a strange thing, sitting on a silk couch and sweating in place. Not something he liked.

Marron came over as Aria rewrapped his hand with a soft bandage. He moved to put the Smarteye on him and then handed it to Aria. "Perhaps you can do it."

First Rose. Now Marron. Perry could no longer deny that it was common knowledge. Aria was the safest path to him. He wondered what he had done that sent that message so loudly. Wondered how after a lifetime of scenting others' feelings, he could be so poor at shielding his own.

Aria took the device. "We're going to do the biotech first—just applying the device. You'll feel pressure, like it's sucking up your skin. But it lets up and then the inner membrane will soften. You'll be able to blink again when that happens."

Perry nodded stiffly. "Right. Pressure. Can't be that bad." Could it?

He held his breath as Aria brought the clear patch to his left eye, digging his fingers into the soft arm of the couch as he struggled to keep from blinking.

"You can close your eyes. It might help," Aria said. He did and saw a shimmer of stars telling him he was about to pass out.

"Peregrine." Aria placed her hand on his forearm. "It's all right."

He focused on her cool touch. Imagined her delicate, pale fingers. When the pressure came, he sucked in a breath through his teeth. The force reminded him of an undertow. How it felt bearable at first, but then came stronger and stronger until you feared being carried off. On the edge of pain, it let up suddenly, leaving him panting.

Perry opened his eyes, blinked a few times. It felt similar to walking with one shoe. Feeling and movement on one side. On the other, a heavy sense of protection. He could see clearly through the eyepiece, but he noticed differences. Colors were too bright. The depth of things seemed off. He shook his head, clenching his teeth at the added weight on his face. "Now what?"

"A moment, a moment." Marron fuddled with the palette as Roar watched over his shoulder.

"We'll go to a forested Realm first," Aria told him. "There won't be anyone else there and it'll give you a few seconds to adjust. We can't have you calling attention to yourself once you're in the CGB's research Realms, and we'll have to move fast. While you're getting used to fractioning, Marron will check to see if the link with Bliss is back. He'll do all the navigating for you. Everything you see, we'll see on the wallscreen."

Ten different questions popped into his mind. He forgot them all when Aria smiled and said, "You look handsome."

"What?" He couldn't think about a comment like that now.

"Ready, Peregrine?" Marron said.

"Yes," he answered, though everything in his body said *No.*

A hot sting ran up his spine and over his scalp, ending with a burst in the back of his nose. On his right, he saw the common room. Aria staring at him with concern. Roar close over her shoulder, bracing the back of the couch. Marron saying, "Easy, Peregrine," over and over. On his left a wooded evergreen forest appeared. The scent of pine burned deep into his nostrils. The images blurred and flashed before his eyes. Perry looked one way and the other, but he couldn't make anything stick. Dizziness came hard and fast.

Aria squeezed his hand. "Calm down, Perry."

"What's going on? What am I doing wrong?"

"Nothing. Just try to relax."

The images shook before his eyes. Trees. Aria's hand grasping his. Pine branches swaying. Roar leaping over the couch to stand in front of him. Nothing was still. Everything moved.

"Take this thing off. Take it off!"

He pulled at the Smarteye, forgetting to use his good hand. He couldn't get it off. Pain burst across the back of his burnt hand, but it was nothing compared to the daggers that stabbed deep into his skull. Saliva coursed into his mouth in a warm rush. He shot to his feet and darted to the bathroom. Or thought he had, because he was dodging trees as well as walls, and poorly at that. He ran smack into something hard, shoulders and head connecting with a solid thud. Roar caught him as he fell back. They exploded into the bathroom together, Roar holding him upright, for Perry no longer trusted his balance.

He felt cold beneath his hands. Porcelain. No more trees.

"I've got it."

He was alone with the toilet now and that was how he stayed for a good long while.

When it was over, he pulled his shirt off and draped it over his head. It hung heavy and damp with his sweat. He still felt dizzy and queasy, like he was coming off the worst seasickness he could imagine. How long had he lasted in the Realms? Three seconds? Four? How would he find Talon?

Aria sat beside him. He couldn't summon the courage to come out from hiding. A glass of water appeared in front of him.

"I felt the same way when I first came to your world."

"Thank you," he said, and drained it.

"Are you all right?"

He wasn't. Perry took her hand and turned his face into her palm, resting his cheek. He breathed in her violet scent, drawing strength from it. Letting it settle the trembling in his muscles. Aria's thumb ran back and forth over his jaw, making a soft brushing sound over his scruff. There was something dangerous about this. About the power of her scent on him. But he couldn't think about it. This was what he needed now.

"How'd you like the Realms?" Roar asked.

Perry peered from beneath his shirt. Roar stood at the bathroom door, and he could see Marron out in the hall.

"Not very much. Try again?" he said, though he seriously doubted whether he could manage it.

When he returned to the common room, the lighting had been dimmed. Someone had brought in a fan. The efforts embarrassed him even though he found they did help settle his nerves. Perry tried to explain what he felt.

"You need to try to forget about here," Aria said. "About

this physical space. Turn your focus toward the Smarteye and it'll start to feel right."

Perry nodded like that made sense, as she and Marron continued to instruct him. Relax. Try this. Or maybe try that.

Then Roar said, "Per, act like you're sighting down the length of an arrow."

He could do that. Shooting an arrow had nothing to do with his stance or his bow or his arms. Not for a decade had he thought about any of those things. He thought only of his target.

They brought up the forest again. The images battled for his attention like before, but Perry imagined aiming at a curled piece of bark that shuddered past. The woods fixed around him, bringing a sudden, shocking stillness. Somehow the others must have known because he heard Marron say, "*Yes.*"

The longer he focused on the woods, the more he felt them settling in place. Perry's body cooled under the current of a soft breeze, but this wasn't from the fan. This breeze carried a pine scent. Cone pine, though all he saw were spruces. And the odor was too strong. He scented fresh sap, not just the breath of the trees. The air held no traces of human or animal scents, or even the cluster of mushrooms he spotted at the base of a tree.

"The same but different, right?"

He turned, looking for Aria in the woods. "It sounds like you're in my head."

"I'm next to you out here. Try to walk, Perry. Take a few more seconds."

He found that doing so took only the thought of walking. It wasn't like being in his own skin. He was still dizzy and unsure, but he was moving, one step after the other. He was in the woods now. It should've felt like home, but his body held on to the feeling he'd had since he'd come to Marron's. The same feeling that drove him up to the roof at every chance.

Then he remembered something and knelt quickly. With his good hand, he swept aside the dry pine needles and scooped up a handful of dirt. It was dark and loose and fine. Not the hard-pack earth he usually saw in pine forests. Perry shook his hand, letting the dirt sift through his fingers until a few rocks rested in his palm.

"Do you see?" Aria said softly.

He did. "Our rocks are better."

29

ARIA

On the wallscreen, Aria watched through Perry's eyes as he stood and brushed dirt from his palms like it was real. Like it would stay with him.

Aria met Marron's gaze. He shook his head, his signal to her that he hadn't detected a link to Bliss. She wouldn't find Lumina today. She'd been prepared for that. Aria pushed down the blow of disappointment. They had to find Talon.

"We're going to take you into the research Realms, Perry. It's a little strange hopping to another Realm. . . . Just try to stay calm."

DLS 16 appeared in red lettering on an icon, suspended in front of the woods. She and Marron had spent the night hacking into her mother's files, organizing everything. She knew Perry couldn't read, so Marron was controlling Perry's location through the palette. Perry turned his head, the icon tracking with his movement.

"Here we go, Peregrine," Marron said.

Perry swore at her side as the image on the wallscreen rearranged itself into a tidy office. A small red couch with neat proportions and square cushions sat opposite the desk. A fat fern rested on a low coffee table. To one side of the office, a glass door gave to a courtyard with boxwood hedges and a fountain at the center. To the other, evenly spaced along the wall, there were four doors: Lab, Conference, Research, Subjects.

Aria felt light-headed. She'd never seen her mother's office before. Her gaze lingered on the empty chair behind the desk. How many hours had Lumina spent in that chair?

"Perry, step through the fourth door," she told him. "The one on the right. Subjects."

He walked through it, arriving at the end of a long corridor lined on both sides with more doors. He ran to the nearest one.

"Amber." Aria read the name on the small screen. He moved on to the next. "Brin." And then to the next. "Clara."

Perry didn't move. He stayed in front of the door marked CLARA. Aria couldn't tell what was happening. She was looking through his eyes. She couldn't see his face in the Realms. Beside her, he looked calm but she knew he wasn't. "What's going on?" she asked.

Roar cursed at her side. "She's one of us. A girl who disappeared from the Tides last year."

Marron sent her an urgent look. "Aria, he has to keep going. We have little time."

Perry sprinted now, past Jasper. Past Rain. To Talon. He burst through the door, into a room with walls covered with animated drawings of soaring hawks, swirling blue skies, and fishing boats casting in the sea. Two comfortable stuffed chairs sat at the center. They were empty.

"Where is he?" Perry asked desperately. "Aria, what have I done wrong?"

"I'm not sure." She had thought that opening the door would summon the children into that Realm, but she didn't know. All of this was new.

She was right. Talon fractioned at that moment, appearing on one of the chairs. His eyes flew open and he shot across the room, away from Perry.

"Who are you?" he said. He had a commanding voice for such a young boy. A voice full of fire and daring. He was a rangy little thing. He had green eyes, the color deeper than Perry's, and dark brown hair that fell in the same twisting locks. He was a striking child.

"Talon, it's me."

Talon peered at him suspiciously. "How do I know?"

"Talon . . . Aria, why doesn't he know me?"

She scrambled for an answer. These were the Realms. You could never trust anything. It was too easy to become something else. Someone else. Talon knew that already. "Tell him something," she said, but it was too late.

Perry was wild, cursing. He turned to the door. "How do I get him out of here?"

"You can't. You're with him only in the Realms. He's

somewhere else. Ask him where he is. Ask him anything else you want to know. Quickly, Perry."

Perry dropped onto one knee, his eyes falling to his burnt hand. "He should know me," he said under his breath.

Talon came closer, tentative. "What happened to your hand?"

Perry wiggled his swollen fingers. "You could call it a mix-up."

"Looks like it was bad. . . . Did you win?"

"If you were really Talon, you wouldn't ask me that."

Aria knew Perry had smiled at his nephew. She could picture his crooked smile, a blend of shy and fierce.

Recognition sparked in the boy's eyes, but he didn't move.

"Talon, it looks like you, but I can't get your temper."

"There're no tempers in here," he said, full of righteousness. "All the scents are off."

"That's eight. They're faded but strong. . . . Squeak, it's me."

The suspicion left the boy's face and he threw himself against Perry.

Aria watched Perry's hand on the wallscreen, stroking the back of Talon's head. "I was so worried about you, Tal." Beside her, on the couch, he shifted, dropping his head into his hands. He was growing used to being in the two places at once. Aria put her hand on his shoulder.

Talon squirmed out of the embrace. "I wanted you to come."

"I got here as soon as I could."

"I know," Talon said. With a gap-toothed grin, he reached out for a tendril of Perry's hair and rubbed the streaked gold between his thin little fingers. Aria had never seen anything so tender in all her life.

Perry took him by the shoulders. "Where are you?"

"In the Dweller Pod."

"Which one, Talon?"

"Rev. That's what the kids here call it."

Perry patted Talon's arms, took hold of his chin, touching his small neck. "They're not hur"—Perry's voice caught— "hurting you?"

"Hurting me? I get fruit three times a day. I can run in here. *Fast.* I can even fly, Uncle Perry. All we do is go around in these Realms. They even got hunting Realms, but a lot of them are too easy. You just—"

"Talon, I'm going to get you out of here. I'll find a way."

"I don't want to leave."

Perry's shoulder tensed beneath Aria's hand.

"This isn't where you belong," Perry said.

"But I feel good here. The doc says I need medicine every day. It makes my eyes water, but my legs don't even ache anymore."

Aria exchanged a worried look with Roar and Marron.

"You want to *stay*?" Perry said.

"Yeah, now that you're here."

"I'm still on the outside. I'm only here this once."

"Oh . . ." Talon's lower lip pushed out in disappointment. "It's good for the tribe, I guess."

"I'm not with the Tides."

Talon frowned. "Then who's Blood Lord?"

"Your father, Talon."

"No, he isn't. He's here with me."

Beside Aria, on the couch, Perry's body jerked. Roar hissed nearby.

"Vale's there?" Perry asked. "He was captured?"

"You didn't know? He was trying to come rescue me and they got him. I've seen him a couple of times. We've gone hunting together. Clara's here too."

"They caught your father?" Perry asked again.

Marron sat up sharply. "They've found him! We need to shut off."

Perry yanked Talon against him. "I love you, Talon. I love you."

The drawing of a hawk flying against the Aether sky flickered out.

The screen went dark.

For a second, no one moved. Then the couch shook as Perry jolted back, cursing. "Get this thing *off*!"

"You have to do it, Perry. You need to be still—"

He was gone, across the room in a few strides. He stopped in front of the wallscreen and dropped to his knees. Aria didn't think. She went to him, wrapping her arms around him. Perry cinched her into his own arms, uttering a strangled sound as he buried his head into her neck. His body was a tight coil of pain around her, his tears cool feathers on her skin.

30

PEREGRINE

Aria guided him upstairs and pulled him into her room. Perry had a vague thought that maybe he shouldn't be there, but his feet never slowed. He walked in and sat heavily on the bed. Aria turned on the lamp, keeping the light dim. Then she sat beside him and wove her fingers through his.

Perry flexed the fingers of his wounded hand. The surge of pain felt reassuring.

He was still there.

He could still feel.

"Talon didn't look harmed," he said after a while. "He looked all right."

"He did." She bit her lip, frowning in thought. "I knew they wouldn't be hurting him. I knew my mother would never do that. We're not cruel."

"Taking innocent kids isn't cruel? They have Talon, Aria! And my *brother*. They don't belong there. They're not Moles."

Right away he knew it was a stupid thing to say. She'd been kicked out of her home. Cut off from everyone, even her mother. Where did *she* belong? A cold wave rolled through him. Perry winced, not sure if he'd inhaled her temper or if it was his own regret, his own sorrow. "Aria, I shouldn't have said that."

She nodded, but didn't say anything. Just stared at their joined hands. Perry drew in a breath. Her sweet violet scent was everywhere. His gaze drifted to the smooth skin along her neck. He wanted to breathe there, just below her ear.

"He's a lot like you, Perry. The way he moves. The way he acts. He adores you."

"Thank you." His throat began to tighten as he thought of Talon. He let go of her hand and lay back on the bed. Dropped his arm across his face. He'd just been wrapped up with her in front of the wallscreen. The bandage on his hand was still damp with their tears. But it felt different now. He didn't want her seeing him like this.

She surprised him by lying down next to him, resting her head on the same pillow. Perry's heart started pounding. He peered over at her. "I haven't even asked how you feel."

She smiled sadly. "That's a funny question."

"I mean what you're thinking."

Aria stared up at the ceiling, her eyes narrowing in thought. "A lot of things make sense now. I thought I was going to die when I was dropped out here. Everything felt wrong. Being in pain. Being lost and alone."

Perry shut his eyes, pulled into the feeling of what it must have been like. He'd been there. He'd scented her fear and grief. He'd known it then. He felt it now.

"Now what I feel most is this . . . this *relief*. I know why I'm alive. And why my body started changing. Now . . . it's like I have the day ahead of me again. Like I can take a breath and know for sure it's about *living*. But there's so much more I need to work out. I never thought my mother would be capable of lying to me. I can't figure out how she did it." She turned her head, looking at him. "How do you hurt someone you love like that?"

"People can be cruelest to those they love." He saw a flicker in her eyes. A question he didn't want her to ask. Not now, when he was raw like this. Not ever. But then her curiosity faded and he let out his breath.

"You don't hate it, then?" he asked after a while. "Knowing you're half . . . Savage?"

"How could I hate what's kept me alive?"

He had no doubt the words were meant for him. Without thinking, he reached for her hand. Tucked it against his chest, feeling that was where it should be. Her eyes went from their hands to his Markings. Perry's heart slammed against his ribs. She had to feel it.

"Will you be the Tides' Blood Lord?" she asked.

"I will." His own words amazed him. He'd wanted to be Blood Lord for so long. He'd never have imagined it happening this way. But he knew in every part of him that he needed to go home and win the right to lead the Tides. They couldn't spend the winter hungry, with infighting and people vying for Blood Lord. They'd need him. Then he remembered the Croven, camped in the plateau. Waiting for him. How would he get out of Marron's before winter came?

Perry looked down at the small hand pressed against his skin. He knew where he had to go, but what about her? "Aria, what are you going to do?" Somehow, in asking the question, he felt like he was failing her.

"I'm going to Bliss. I need to find out if my mother is alive. Marron and I talked last night. When the Croven leave, he's going to let me take some of his men. I can't just wait for news that might not ever come."

"Aria, I'll take you. I have to go home. I can take you to Bliss first."

Perry tensed. What had he just said? What had he just offered?

"No, Perry. Thank you, but no."

"We had a deal. Allies, remember?" he heard himself say.

"Our deal was to come here and fix the Smarteye."

"It was to find Talon and your mother. We haven't done that yet."

"Bliss is south, Perry."

"It's not far. Another week. Doesn't matter. I'll get you better shoes this time. And I'll carry your rocks for you. I'll even answer all your questions."

Perry didn't know what he had just done. Where was the wisdom in heading a week out of the way when his tribe needed him? There was no sense in it, and recognizing that, his blood went cold.

"Will you answer a question now?" Aria asked.

"Yes." He suddenly couldn't keep still. He had to leave. He needed to think.

"Why did you really offer to take me to Bliss?"

"I want to," he said. Even as he spoke, he wasn't sure if he'd told the truth. It hadn't felt like a *want*. It felt more like a *need*.

Aria smiled, turning toward him, her eyes dropping to his mouth. The room sweetened with her violet scent, drawing him in, becoming everything, and he felt it. A shift deep within him. The seal of a bond he'd only known once before. And suddenly he understood why he'd promised something he shouldn't have.

Perry pressed a hasty kiss to her hand. "I need some time," he said, and then bolted out of the room. Perry shut the door and fell back against the wall, stifling a curse.

It happened.

He had rendered to her.

31

PEREGRINE

"We might be able to handle a dozen," Roar said, "but fifty?"

Perry paced in front of the glass cases in the common room, eyeing the image of the Croven's camp on the wallscreen. In morning light, the image was much clearer than when he'd seen it last. Black-cloaked figures moved around the cluster of tents in the plateau. Red tents. A fitting color. He wanted to draw his bow and fire at them right through the screen.

"There are more than fifty Croven out there, Roar," he said. The camera only showed some of them. Early that morning, he and Roar had been up on the wall, moving from tower to tower, using all the power of their Senses. It had taken them hours, but they'd detected another dozen Croven scattered around the perimeter. Sentinels, there to sound an alarm should he try to escape.

Roar crossed his arms. "*Sixty* Croven then."

Marron turned a ring around his finger. "One of the old mining tunnels looks promising, but it'll take weeks to excavate safely."

"That's well into winter," Perry said. By then the storms would be moving in constant sets across the sky. Travel would be too dangerous.

"I can't wait that long," Aria said.

She'd been quiet, her legs tucked beneath her on the couch. What a fool he must seem to her, peeling for the door with barely a word in parting. She had no idea what had happened last night. Perry pinched the bridge of his nose, remembering the weakness rendering had brought him with Talon. Not being able to choose with freedom. Thinking of his needs as an afterthought. He couldn't have that spell cast over him now. He'd do what he promised. He'd take her to Bliss, then do what he *should* and get to the Tides. They'd part ways soon enough. Until then, he'd just keep his distance. And try not to breathe when he was around her.

"I can give you some of my men," Marron said.

Perry looked up. "No. I can't have your people dying for me." He'd put Marron through enough. "We won't meet them head-to-head." On the screen, the plateau spread around the Croven, wide and open. He wanted to be there. Outside. Moving free under the Aether. That was when it hit him.

"We could leave during a storm."

"Peregrine," Marron said. "Leave during an *Aether storm*?"

"The Croven are out in the open. They'd need to take

285

shelter. It would put them off their guard. And I can keep us away from the worst of the Aether."

Roar pushed himself off the wall, his smile eager. "We could clear the sentinels and head east. The Croven won't follow us."

Aria's eyes narrowed. "Why won't they follow us east?"

"Wolves," Roar said.

"Our best choice is to leave during an Aether storm and head toward wolves?"

Roar grinned. "That or sixty Croven."

"All right," she said, lifting her chin. "Anything but the Croven."

That afternoon, Perry strode across the roof with Roar. They'd spent the morning plotting their route and readying their packs. Now there was nothing to do but wait for a storm to build. The Aether moved in steady streams above. They wouldn't see a storm today, but maybe tomorrow. It couldn't come soon enough.

How was he going to wait? Waiting meant stopping. It meant *thinking*. He didn't want to think about what was happening to Talon and Vale, stuck inside the Dweller Pod. How could Talon want to stay there? How had Vale been captured? Why was Liv roaming the borderlands when she *knew* what the cost was to the Tides?

Roar caught him hard across the shoulders, tackling him. Perry thudded onto the cement before he knew what had happened.

"One to nothing," Roar said.

"You jaggy bastard." He pushed Roar off and the game was on.

He usually had the upper hand when they wrestled, but he took it easy because of his hand, and that kept them more evenly matched.

"Talon wrestles better than you, Ro," he said, helping Roar up after earning a point. Perry's mood had begun to lift. He'd been idle too long.

"Liv's pretty good too."

"She's my *sister*." Perry lunged for him but broke away the instant Aria stepped out of the elevator. No way he'd let Roar in on his thoughts when she was around. He couldn't help noticing that she'd changed into fitted black clothes and pulled her hair back. Roar looked from him to Aria, a knowing grin spreading over his face. Perry knew he was in trouble.

"Did I interrupt something?" Aria said, confused.

"No. We were done." Perry grabbed his bow and stalked away. Earlier he'd dragged a wooden crate across the roof to serve as a target. He took aim, pain thudding dully in his hand.

"Perfect timing, Aria," Roar said behind him. "Watch this. You know, Perry's known for his skill with the bow."

Perry fired. The arrow bit into the pine with a crack.

Roar whistled. "Impressive, isn't he? What a great shot."

Perry spun, halfway between laughing and wanting to kill Roar.

"Can I try it?" Aria asked. "I should know how to defend myself when we get out there."

"You should," he agreed. Anything she learned would help them all when they ventured beyond the wall.

Perry showed her how to hold the bow and set her feet, keeping himself upwind where he could avoid her scent. When it came to nocking an arrow, it wasn't enough for him to tell her what to do. Drawing a bow smoothly took strength and calm. Rhythm and practice. To him, it was no more difficult than breathing, but he saw right away the only way to teach her was to guide her through the motion.

He stepped behind her, bracing himself. When he inhaled, her temper shot through him, her nerves adding to his own. Then came her violet scent, drawing his focus completely to her, to the way she looked this close, just in front of him. He fumbled with how to hold the bow. Her hand was where his usually was and he didn't want the bowstring to snap back on her.

Roar didn't help. "You need to get closer to her, Peregrine," he called out. "And her stance is all wrong. Turn her hips."

"Like this?" Aria asked.

"No," Roar said. "Perry, just do it for her."

He was sweating by the time they got themselves set. On their first try shooting together, the arrow clattered to the cement a few feet in front of them. On the second, it landed just in front of the crate, but the bowstring grazed her forearm, raising a red welt on her skin. By the third, Perry wasn't sure which one of them was making the bow shake.

Roar hopped to his feet. "Not your weapon, Halfy," he said, striding over. "Look at his shoulders, Aria. Look how tall he is." Perry shot away from her and then shifted on his feet, self-conscious at the way she sized him up. "A bow like that has a draw weight of ninety pounds or so. It's made for small giants, like him. He's a Seer on top of it. All the best archers are. It's his weapon, Aria. Suited for him. For who he is."

"It's second nature to you, isn't it?" she asked him.

"First. But you can learn it. I can make a bow for you. Your size," he said, but he could see and scent that she was disappointed.

Roar slid his knife out of its sheath. "I could teach you this."

Perry's heart stopped cold. "Roar . . ."

Roar knew exactly what he was thinking.

"Knives are dangerous," he told Aria. "You can do more harm than good if you don't know how to use one. But I'll teach you a few things. You move easily and you have good balance. If a situation comes up, you'll know what to do."

Aria handed Perry his bow. "All right," she said. "Teach me."

Perry had to come up with something to do while he watched them. He found a branch from a tree inside the courtyard and cut it down. Then he sat against the crate making practice blades as Roar showed Aria the different ways to hold a knife. Roar had a passion for the knife. He gave her too much information about the advantages of each

289

grip, but she listened, rapt, absorbing it all. After an hour of constant talk, they settled on a hammer grip as the best for her, which Perry had known from the start.

Next they covered stances and footwork. Aria was a quick learner and her balance was good, just as Roar had said. Perry watched them moving past each other, his gaze turning from Aria to the Aether. From the flow of her footwork to the flow of the sky.

By the time Roar asked for the carved practice knives it was late in the afternoon. Roar showed Aria the best places to strike, angles to strive for, and bones to avoid, fluttering his eyes when he told her the heart was as worthy a target as any.

And then she was ready.

Perry stood as they began to move, their wooden knives held at guard. He told himself that it was Roar. That he'd made the edge of the practice knives as dull as his thumbs. But his heart was beating too fast for just watching simple drills.

They prowled for a bit; then Aria made the first move. Roar darted past her and struck, drawing the blade firmly across her back. Aria jerked back and whirled, her knife falling out of her hand.

Perry shot forward, lunging for Roar. He pulled up short a few steps away, but Roar glared at him, his eyes full of suspicion.

Aria was breathing hard, her temper bright red, pure wrath. Perry's muscles shook, wound tight with surprise and rage.

"First rule: Knives cut," Roar said, his tone brutally cold. "Expect it to happen. Don't freeze up when it does. Second rule: Don't *ever* drop your weapon."

"All right," Aria said, accepting the lesson. She picked up the blade.

"You staying, Scire?" Roar asked him, lifting an eyebrow. He knew Perry had rendered to her.

"Why would he leave?" Aria said. "You're staying, right, Perry?"

"Yeah. I'm staying."

Perry crossed the roof and then climbed on top of the elevator box, the highest point on Delphi, and watched her train in stunned silence. He shook his head. How had he ended up rendering to a Dweller?

Aria was a quick study, daring and confident with the blade, like she'd only been waiting for a chance, a method to bring that out into the open. He'd been a fool, teaching her to find berries when this was what she'd needed. The knowledge to protect herself.

Darkness forced them to stop. The Croven's bells rang in the distance. Perry took a final glance at the sky, disappointed when he saw no change. He climbed down, careful to keep upwind and well back as she and Roar came toward him.

Roar crossed his arms in front of the elevator. "Fine work, Halfy. But you can't leave without paying me."

"*Pay* you? With what?"

"A song."

She laughed, a chirky, happy sound. "All right."

Roar took the wooden blade from her. Aria closed her eyes, turning her face up to the Aether as she drew a few slow breaths. Then she treated them to her voice.

This song was softer, quieter than the last one. He couldn't understand these words either, but the feel of it, he thought, was perfect. A perfect song for a cool night on a roof surrounded by pines.

Roar didn't blink as he watched her. When she finished, Roar shook his head. "Aria . . . that was . . . I can't even . . . Perry, you have no idea."

Perry forced himself to smile. "She's good," he said, but he wondered how her voice would sound to Roar, who heard infinitely more tones.

When they stepped into the close space of the elevator, Aria's scents flooded into his nose, a combination of violets and sweat and pride and power. He felt it all like a surge of strength inside him. He breathed again and soared with his feet on the ground. Perry couldn't stop himself from putting his hand on the small of her back. Told himself he'd do this just once. Then he'd stay away.

She looked up at him. Her face was flushed. Strands of her dark hair clung to her sweated neck. Roar was with them, and a good thing, too. He'd never been as tempted by her, by the warm muscle he felt beneath the palm of his hand.

"You did well today."

She smiled, fire in her eyes. "I know I did," she said. "And thanks."

32

ARIA

Aria spent two days training with Roar as they waited. Knots of Aether threatened in the distance, but the flows above Delphi held in steady streams. Another reason to call it the never sky, she thought. It never did what you wanted.

With every passing hour, her hope of finding Lumina alive dimmed, but she wouldn't let it go. She couldn't let herself believe she was alone. She would never stop hoping, and that meant she'd never stop worrying, either. The only way out of the agony was to go to Bliss and find out the truth. Learning the knife became the only source of relief. When she was moving across the cement with Roar, there was no room for worry or hurt or questions. So she practiced with him from morning until night, ending with her payment in song. Aria knew the Croven were still out there, but at least no one heard the ringing of their bells at dusk anymore.

They heard opera.

On the third morning, she stepped out of the elevator to a new sky, shot through with swirls of blue light. The eddies ran calm above her, but turned brighter and faster on the horizon. It was Van Gogh's *Starry Night*, right before her eyes.

She had a feeling this was the day they'd leave.

She picked up the wooden knife. Yesterday she'd struck Roar twice. It wasn't much, especially compared with the hundreds of times he'd struck her, but in a fight, one good hit was all it took. Roar had taught her that.

She had no illusions of becoming a master knife fighter. This wasn't the Realms, where a thought delivered a result. But she also knew she'd given herself a better chance. And in life, at least in her new life, chances were the best she could hope for. They were like her rocks. Imperfect and surprising and maybe better in the long run than certainties. Chances, she thought, *were* life.

On the horizon, the mass of Aether began to drop blue flares she recognized as funnels. Aria watched, mesmerized, as something roused deep within her, whirling and heating through her limbs, bringing her strength as fierce as the never sky.

She decided to go through some maneuvers on her own since she'd arrived early. Gusts whipped up over the roof, the sound lulling her, as she lost herself in movement. She didn't know how long Perry had been standing there when she finally saw him. He rested a hip against the wooden rail, his arms crossed as he stared across the treetops. She was surprised to see him. Perry had come to her training sessions with Roar, but he'd kept a distance. And she'd hardly seen him inside Delphi. She was starting to think he'd changed his mind about taking her to Bliss.

"Is it time?" she asked.

"No." He tipped his chin. "But that looks promising. Tonight, I'd say." He picked up the other practice knife. "Roar's still asleep, but I'll train with you until he gets here."

"Oh," she said, because it was better than blurting *You?* Like she'd almost done. "All right." Aria drew a slow breath, her stomach suddenly buzzing with nerves.

As soon as they squared up, she knew this wouldn't be the same at all. Perry was much taller and broader than Roar. Fearless and direct. Nothing like Roar's light-footed grace. And it was *Perry*.

"Is that the hand you usually fight with?" she asked. He had the knife in his good hand, the bandaged one held out for balance.

He grinned. "Yeah, but I may change my mind if you beat me."

Her cheeks caught on fire. She couldn't look at him but she *had* to look at him. *Be ready. Light on your feet. Watch for the signs.* Roar's lessons flew from her mind. What she thought as she stared into his eyes was how green they were. How strong his shoulders looked. How, really, he was *grand*. Finally she couldn't stand her own giddy thoughts anymore.

She lunged. He blew past her right side, his movement shifting more air and light than Roar.

Perry smiled as they faced each other again.

"What?" she asked.

"I don't know." He wiped his sleeve over his forehead.

"Are you laughing?"

"I was, yeah. Your fault, but I apologize anyway."

"It's *my* fault you're laughing?" Did he think she was that easy an opponent? She made a gut-quick move forward, drawing the wooden blade in a low arc. Perry leaped to the side, but Aria grazed him on the arm.

"That was nice," he said, still smiling.

Aria swiped her sweaty hand on her pants. Perry got back into his stance, but only for a moment before he straightened and tossed his blade aside.

"What are you doing?" she asked.

"I can't concentrate. I thought I could do this." He put his hands up in defeat. "Can't." Then he came closer. Aria didn't think her heart could beat any faster, but then it did, faster with every step he took toward her, until it hammered against her chest, making her breathless when he stopped right in front of her. Her wooden blade rested on his chest. She stared at it, her heart in her throat. She stared at the way it pressed into his shirt.

"I've been watching you and Roar. Wanting it to be me training with you." His shoulders came up. "I don't want to do it now."

"Why?" Aria's voice was high and thin.

He smiled, a flash of shyness, before he leaned close.

"There are other things I'd rather do when I'm alone with you."

Time to step off the edge. "Then do them."

His hands came up, cradling her chin. Rough skin on one side, soft gauze on the other. He lowered his head and brought his lips to hers. They were warm and softer than she had ever imagined they would be, but not there nearly long enough. He backed away from her before she knew it.

"Was that all right?" he whispered, close. "I know touching isn't . . . this has to be your lead, your pace——"

Aria rolled up onto her toes. She wrapped her arms around his neck and kissed him. The soft warmth of his mouth sent a wave of fire through her. Perry froze, then his arms tightened around her ribs as he deepened their kiss. They molded together, fitted against each other with stunning perfection. Aria had never felt as she did now, exploring the taste of him. Feeling the strength of his arms around her. Inhaling sweat and leather and woodsmoke. His scents. She felt as though she'd found a moment of forever. Like this was how they should've always been.

When they finally drew apart, the first thing she saw was the grin she always savored.

"I guess you're fine with touching." His tone was light but his arms shuddered around her. He shifted them, his hands rubbing up her back, sending ripples of heat through her.

"That was my first kiss," she said. "My first real one."

He brought his head close, resting his forehead on hers. Blond waves fell around her face, soft against her cheeks. His chest rose and fell as he drew in a breath. "Felt like the first real one for me, too."

"I thought you were avoiding me. I thought you'd changed your mind about going to Bliss."

"No. I haven't changed my mind."

She slipped her hands into his hair. She couldn't believe she was touching him. He smiled and his lips found hers again and she thought there could never be enough of this. Of him.

"Well, I can't say this is a surprise," Roar said, strolling out onto the roof.

"Rot," Perry muttered, drawing back.

"Fine close-quarter work, Aria. Nothing you learned from me, but you handled yourself well. I think you won."

Aria glared at him, but couldn't keep the smile off her lips. Perry bent close and brushed back her hair. "He's got a weaker parry on his left side." His voice rumbled right by her ear.

Roar rolled his eyes. "That is untrue. Traitor."

She was terrible as she began to train with Roar. Worse than the first day. She battled with her peripheral vision, which wanted Perry front and center. Even when he lay back on the roof and draped an arm over his eyes, she couldn't stop looking at him. It was absurd how the shape of his thighs drew her interest. Ridiculous that the sliver of his stomach where his shirt had crept up fascinated her.

Every move she made had too much behind it. Every step went too far. Roar pushed her further than ever. He didn't say it, but Aria could almost hear his lesson point. *In real situations, you'll have distractions. Learn to ignore them.*

Eventually she reined in her focus and lost herself in jabs and parries. In the simplicity of action and reaction. She was pure movement until Perry stood. Then she noticed him, and the roiling sky and the lashing wind.

"Better stop," he said. "It's time to go."

33

PEREGRINE

"It'll be so dull without you," Marron said. Behind him, the wallscreens in the common room were black. His camera had finally given out.

Aria took his hand. "I'm so envious. A dull day sounds wonderful."

They were ready. Perry had checked and rechecked their packs. He'd given Aria Talon's knife. Tonight a wooden one would do her no good. And he had run through the plan with Gage and Mark, two of Marron's men. Marron had insisted they come on the journey. Gage and Mark would bring Aria back to Delphi if they discovered the rumors about Bliss were true.

Marron embraced Aria. His hair looked almost white against hers. "You're always welcome here, Aria. Whatever happens, whatever you find, you always have a place here."

Perry turned to the painting of the boat on the gray beach, the sea a broad stretch of blue behind. Looking at it, he could almost smell home. What if she was forced to come back here? Marron's was just a week's travel from Tides land. Would it matter? Perry shook his head at himself. It wouldn't. The Tides would never accept a Dweller once they learned about Vale, Talon, and Clara. They wouldn't have beforehand. And he wouldn't make the same mistake his father and brother had made. Nothing good ever came of mixing blood. He knew that better than anyone.

Roar strode up. "As Blood Lord, you could strike a new deal with Sable. You could get Liv back."

Perry just looked at him for a moment. Partly because the question came out of nowhere. Partly because he realized he could do that as Blood Lord. It would fall within his duty. But it didn't mean he would do it. It wasn't a simple decision. "Don't ask me that now."

"I'm asking now." Roar tipped his head toward Aria. "I thought you'd see things differently."

Perry glanced at her. She was still talking with Marron. All he could think about was the way she'd felt against him when they had kissed. "It's not the same, Roar."

"Isn't it?"

Perry pulled his satchel over his shoulder. Grabbed his bow and quiver. "Let's go."

He wanted the earth blurring fast beneath his feet. The night flowing into his nostrils. He always knew what to do with a weapon in his hand.

They left through a small gate on the north wall. Perry brought in all the scents, letting earth and wind tell him what they'd find. His nose hummed with the strength of the Aether. He glanced up. Vast spools crowded the sky.

He eased smoothly into the woods, finally shedding the feeling of being bound. They broke into two groups to lessen the sounds of their movement. He prowled uphill with Aria, choosing every step with care, scanning the canopy. He had no doubt the Croven's sentinels were Marked, probably Auds. They would sleep in the treetops, the safest place at night.

Perry glanced over his shoulder. Aria had her hair pulled under a black cap and her face darkened with charcoal, as he did. Her eyes were wide and alert. She had a satchel of her own now. A knife. Clothes that fit. It struck him in that instant how much she'd changed. He'd wondered how it would be, doing this with her. She could have weakened his concentration. She was afraid. No question of that. But this was different than their journey to Marron's. She was trapping the nerves and making them work. When he breathed, he knew the strength of her control.

Delphi's walls receded as they crept deeper into the mountain. Judging by the look of the Aether and the burn in his nose, they still had time. An hour maybe, before the funnels rained down.

Aria's hand at his back stopped him. She pointed to a large tree forty paces ahead. A fresh scatter of branches littered the ground below. Looking up, he saw a figure nestled in the crook of a branch. The man bore an ivory horn. The signaler. Perry looked higher and spotted another man. A pair, tasked with sounding the alarm.

He didn't know how he'd missed them. Even more, he wasn't sure how Aria had spotted them first. The men spoke quietly, a conversation Perry only caught as faint sounds. He met Aria's eyes and then straightened slowly, nocking an arrow in place. He knew he wouldn't miss the first man. Perry's challenge was to kill him soundlessly. If he could keep the man from falling from the tree, that would be even better.

He took his aim and drew a few breaths. It should be easy. He wasn't far. But one yell from the man, or one blast of his horn, and all the Croven would be on them.

A wolf howled in the distance, the perfect sound cover. He straightened the two fingers that held the bowstring, loosing the arrow. He struck the man's neck, pinning him to the trunk. The horn slid off his lap but didn't fall to the ground. It remained slung around his arm by a strap, hanging just below the branch. A pale crescent hovering in the darkness.

Perry nocked another arrow but the other man, definitely an Aud because he'd heard the noise, called out desperately for his friend. When he got no answer, he climbed down the tree, fast as a squirrel. Perry loosed another arrow. He heard a crunch as his shot sank into bark. The Aud scampered to the opposite side of the thick trunk, giving Perry no clear shot. Perry dropped his bow, pulled his knife, and ran.

The Aud saw him and veered toward a dense knot of brush. He was slight, closer to Aria's size than Perry's, and quick as he threaded around the thick undergrowth.

Perry didn't slow down. He crashed through the branches, hearing them snap and break around him. The man turned downhill, scampering in panic, but Perry knew he had him. He lunged, covering the final paces in the air, slamming into the Aud's back.

Perry jerked up as soon as they hit the ground, making a clean swipe with his blade across the man's neck. The wriggling body beneath him went slack as the rich scent of hot blood shot into his nose. Perry wiped his blade on the man's shirt and stood, his lungs working for breath. Killing a man should be more difficult than killing game. It wasn't. He looked at the knife in his trembling hand. Only the aftermath was different.

A stab deep inside his nose had him looking up. The Aether had begun to take the shape of a massive whirlpool. The storm would come soon and it would strike hard.

He slid the knife back into his sheath, his muscles seizing as he heard a muffled cry.

Aria.

34

ARIA

A ria pulled into a crouch as a third man appeared, dropping from another tree close by, only twenty paces off. She clutched Talon's knife, ready to fight, but he didn't run toward her. He darted toward the tree where the dead man hung. Fear shot through her. He wanted the horn. If he alerted the rest of the Croven, it wouldn't just be her death. It would be Marron's men. Roar. And Perry.

She waited until he neared the base of the tree before she ran after him. Aria didn't feel her legs moving beneath her. She knew she'd picked the right moment. He was climbing, his hands occupied, and his back turned to her. She'd used speed and surprise to her advantage just as Roar had taught her.

It should have been perfect. But with steps to go, she realized the only lethal targets she knew were along the front of the body. She thought of reaching around for his jugular, but he was too far off the ground.

She couldn't turn back. He heard her, his head whipping around. For an awful second, their eyes met. Roar's voice burst into her mind. *Strike first and fast.* But where? On the leg? His back? Where?

The man pushed off the tree, falling toward her. She tried to raise her blade. She intended to do it. But he came down on her in a blur.

Aria landed on her back, the air driving out of her chest in one heave. A muffled groan burst out of her. He was on top of her. She braced for a knife in her side. For a blow across the face. She was ready, but he shuddered and then went limp.

She'd killed him.

Waves of panic blared through her at the feel of his hair strewn over her eyes, at his weight pressing down on her. It took three tries to bring air into her lungs. When she finally did, the odor of him was so foul, she choked back a rise of nausea. Warmth seeped across her stomach. She couldn't move.

A face appeared above her. A girl. She was a wild-eyed thing, but pretty. She scrambled up the tree, slipped the horn around her neck, jumped to the ground, and ran off.

Aria pushed her shoulder back with all the strength she had. It was enough to free her arm. With another push, she rolled the man off. She wanted to shoot away from him. She couldn't do anything except feed her starved lungs.

Another Croven came, a larger figure, suddenly there, crouching at her side. Aria groped through the dirt for her knife, hearing Roar in her mind again. *Never let go of your blade.*

"Steady, Aria. It's me."

Perry. She remembered he was wearing a cap, hiding his gold-streaked hair.

"Where are you hurt?" His hands ran over her stomach.

"It's not me," she said. "It's not mine."

Perry pulled her into his arms, cursing softly, saying he'd thought it had happened again. She didn't know what he meant. She wanted to stay pressed close to him. She'd just killed a man. His blood was all over her, making her stomach shake. But she pulled away.

"Perry," she said. "We have to find Roar."

Before they were on their feet, the blast of the horn shattered the silence.

They ran through the darkened woods together, knives in hand, coming upon a body lying facedown. Aria's knees weakened. She knew Roar's proportions well, had spent the past days watching him, measuring him so she could dodge his strikes.

"It's not him," Perry said. "It's Gage."

Roar called softly from a distance. "Here, Perry."

They found him sitting against a tree, one leg outstretched, an arm propped on his other knee. Aria fell to her knees at his side.

"There were five of them. They got Mark right away. Gage and I managed four. He went after the one who ran off."

307

"Gage is dead," Perry said.

A pool of blood glistened beneath Roar's leg. Aria saw the tear in his dark pants at his thigh. The skin was split open, the muscle beneath as well. Blood leaked steadily out of the wound, shiny under the blue Aether light. "Your leg, Roar." She pressed her hands on his leg to stop the flow of blood.

Roar's face twisted with pain. Perry pulled a lash of leather from her satchel and tied it above the wound, his hands moving swiftly. "I'll carry you."

"No, Peregrine," Roar said. "I hear them. The Croven are coming."

Aria heard it too. The bells were ringing. The Croven were moving, chasing them, undeterred by the storm.

"We're getting you back to Marron's first," Perry said.

"They're too close. We won't get there in time."

Cold raced down Aria's neck. She stared into the trees, imagining sixty cannibals sweeping toward them in black cloaks.

Perry swore. He handed Aria his satchel, bow, and quiver. "Don't fall more than three feet behind me." He hoisted Roar up, slinging an arm over his shoulder as he'd done with Cinder. They ran, Perry half carrying Roar, as the bells trilled in her ears. She stumbled downslope, the pealing of the bells maddening.

Perry scanned the trees, his eyes bright and wide. "Aria!" he yelled, turning toward an outcropping of rocks. He set Roar down and took his bow and quiver from her.

She crouched behind the rocks, breathless, shoulder-to-shoulder with Roar. Perry stood at her other side, unleashing a barrage of arrows, one after another, never stopping. Shouts of alarm erupted from the night. The Croven flung their last words at the sky. But still the bells rang louder.

Aria couldn't tear her eyes away from Perry. She'd seen him this way before, almost serene as he dealt death. He'd been a stranger then. But this was *Perry*. How could he bear to do it?

His bow landed with a soft, surprising thump on the pine needles by her feet.

"I'm out," he said. "I've run out of arrows."

$$\sim 35 \sim$$

PEREGRINE

The Croven's putrid scents coated Perry's throat. The bells at their belts glinted in the Aether light. They rang softly now. The chase was over. They were surrounded.

At some signal, they donned their masks and pulled on the hoods of their black cloaks. Soon it was all Perry saw. Dozens of beaked faces hovering in the gloom of the forest. Aria stood beside him, her knife out. Roar rose to his feet and leaned against the rock behind him.

The Croven had their own archers, Perry saw. Six men with bows trained on them. None of them more than thirty feet away. Would this be the way he died? It would be a fitting death. How many men had he just killed with his bow?

A heavily built man stepped forward. His mask wasn't made of bone and skin but silver. It shone, reflecting the Aether as he lifted his head to the wind in a way Perry knew well.

"Lay down where you are, Blood Lord."

His voice was loud and deep. A voice for ceremony. In any other situation, Perry might've appreciated that this man assumed him a Blood Lord. Now he only saw the sad truth in it. That he should hear himself addressed this way for the first and last time together.

"I will not," Perry said.

Silver Mask kept silent for a long moment. Then he called one of the archers. "Strike him through the leg. Muscle only. Don't pierce the arteries."

Perry had come close to dying several times. But at those words, he knew this was his time. It wasn't fear that struck him, but a crushing disappointment at all the things he hadn't done. At all the things he knew he could do.

The archer raised his bow, his eyes steady, aiming through the Croven mask.

"No!" Aria stepped around Perry.

"Get back, Aria." He said this, but when she took his hand, he accepted it. She moved to his side, somehow understanding that he needed her. Needed Roar there too. With the two of them, he could stand there and wait for an arrow to strike him down.

The archer hesitated, seeing their joined hands.

"Perry . . . ," Roar said hoarsely, behind them. "Get down."

The charge of the Aether burned in the back of Perry's nose. It buzzed over his skin, grating and alive. A stir ran through the Croven. They lifted their masks, yelling in terror as they saw Cinder.

He strode through the Croven. Shirtless, his veins created glowing lines over his skin. He came forward, searching with his Aether blue eyes. The Croven darted out of his way with a sudden eruption from the bells.

"Cinder," Perry said.

The boy's eyes found him and held for a moment. Then he turned his back to Perry and raised his palms. Perry felt an updraft like the intake before a scream. He grabbed Aria by the waist and leaped over the stone outcropping, landing on Roar, as Cinder lit the night with liquid fire.

Searing flashes rolled past as the Aether let out its horrid shriek, drowning the Croven's screams. Perry pressed his eyes closed against the burning streaks. He covered Roar and Aria as best he could, his fingers gripping the earth like they might be carried off.

Quiet came with a suddenness that thundered emptily in his ears. The night returned with a cool drift over Perry's arms. Long seconds passed before he could lift his head. The pungent scent of burnt hair mingled with charred flesh and wood. Perry tried getting to his knees but ended up rolling to the side.

Stars. He saw stars through a vast hole in the Aether. Clear, bright stars. Around the hole, the Aether rippled in circles. Like a pebble thrown in a pond but working closer. Tightening instead of spreading. Slowly covering one star after another with its blue light.

Aria appeared over him. "Perry, are you all right?"

He couldn't speak. Perry tasted ash and blood.

"Roar!" Aria said. "What's wrong with him!" She thrust Roar's hand onto Perry's forehead.

Now Roar stared down at him. "Where are you hurt, Perry?"

Everywhere, Perry thought, knowing Roar could hear him. *But mostly my throat. You?*

"I'm good enough." Roar turned to Aria. "He's all right."

With Aria's help, Perry sat up. As far as he could see, the trees were burned to black stalks of carbon. The earth glittered with embers, but he saw no fire. No bodies anywhere. Everything had already burned. Cinder had bled the life out of everything except a crow mask that lay in the ash, the silver warped. Dripping like melted wax.

Nearby a half-starved figure with a shorn head lay within a circle of fine gray dust. Perry climbed to his feet. Cinder was curled into himself. He was bare. His clothes gone to ash. Not a single hair was left on his scalp. The glow of his veins faded before Perry's eyes, seeping back into his skin.

His eyes opened to dark slits. "Did you see what I did?"

"I saw," Perry said, his voice in shreds.

Cinder's gaze fell on Perry's hand. He stared at the spoiled flesh. "I couldn't help it."

"I know," Perry said, seeing himself in Cinder's black eyes. He understood the terror of being good at ending lives.

Cinder groaned, clutching at his stomach as he began to shake. His breath came in gasps as he convulsed in a tight ball. Perry took a blanket from his satchel and covered him.

Then he stashed the rest of their things in the rocks. Aria took Roar as he had done earlier, supporting his injured side. Perry lifted Cinder into his arms, stunned by the coldness of the boy's skin.

"I made it right," Cinder said through trembling lips.

They came upon a pair of Croven huddled together in the shadow of a tree. At the sight of Cinder, they scurried away. Perry swallowed against the rawness in his throat. Had the boy ever known anything beyond fear and pity?

They rushed into Delphi, bursting into the courtyard. Perry set Cinder down next to Roar right on the cobbles. People were gathered inside the gate, armed with weapons, braced for war, for an invasion, for anything. The Aether continued to seal above. Whatever break Cinder had brought them was vanishing.

Marron cut through the gathered crowd. "Mark and Gage?"

Perry shook his head, then he staggered off a dozen paces, turning his back. He pressed his fist to his lips to hold back the guilt and everything else that threatened to come up. Behind him, Aria told Marron what had happened. People cried and cursed Perry. They were right. He'd brought the Croven here. Mark and Gage had died because of him. Perry saw no way of escaping that blame.

Marron came up to him. "You have to go. The Croven might return. Get home, Peregrine. Get Aria to her mother."

Clarity returned with those simple words. He had no time to spare. He went to Roar. "You'll come in the spring."

Roar took Perry's offered hand in a firm grip. "As soon as I can get there."

Perry moved to Cinder. He knew he couldn't command the boy, whose power was far greater than his own. But he also knew Cinder needed him. Needed someone to help him make sense of what he'd done, and what he could do. Maybe Perry needed that too.

"Will you come with Roar?" It was a bigger question than what it appeared to be on the surface. The true question was whether he'd pledge himself to Perry.

Cinder answered right away.

"Yes."

PEREGRINE

Perry and Aria stepped through the gate together. They collected their belongings from the rocks and ran. The Aether came screaming, dropping funnels that shook the ground beneath them. Smoke thickened the cool air as the woods ignited. Perry steered around the flames, holding tight to Aria's hand.

They moved swiftly, driven by the need to put Delphi behind them. They cleared the worst of the storm in a few hours and then spent the rest of the night traveling in silence. Descending slopes with locked arms. Passing water back and forth between them, and sharing touches. Her hand holding his for a dozen paces. His, resting on the small of her back for a moment. Touches that had no real purpose but to say *I'm here* and *We are together still*.

By dawn, Perry couldn't ignore the scents that clung to them any longer. Blood and ash crusted to their clothes and skin. The smoke from the Aether storm was thinning. He could no longer count on it to mask their scents and keep the wolves at bay. They stopped by a river that rushed over a cascade of gray boulders and washed quickly, shivering at the icy water, and then set off again. He hoped they'd done enough.

Hours later, Aria grasped his arm. "I hear barking, Perry. We need to find someplace safe." Her words fogged in the cool afternoon.

Perry strained to listen. He heard only the lull after a storm, but the musk of the animals was strong, telling him a pack couldn't be far. Scanning the woods for a sturdy tree where they could shelter, Perry saw only pines with high, slender branches. He quickened their pace, cursing himself for not grabbing more arrows from Marron when they'd taken Cinder and Roar back. He had only his knife to protect them. A knife wouldn't last long against wolves.

Aria looked back sharply, her eyes wide. "Perry, they're right behind us!"

Moments later, he heard the wolves himself, two sharp barks that sounded far too close. Desperate, he ran for the nearest tree, a poor choice. The branches too low and brittle. Then he saw a game trail, a worn dirt path weaving to a tree up ahead. He spotted a wooden shack set up in the branches of the massive pine. He ran, Aria beside him, as the snarling grew louder. Claw marks shredded the trunk around the base. A rope ladder hung from a thick branch.

He lifted Aria onto the ladder.

"They're coming!" she yelled. "Perry, climb!"

He couldn't. Not yet. Didn't trust the brittle rope to hold both of their weight. He drew his knife.

"Go! I'll be right behind you."

Seven wolves prowled into view. Huge animals with glinting blue eyes and silver pelts. Their musk came at Perry in a red wave of blood hunger. They raised their shining snouts, reading scents as he did, then laid back their ears and bared their teeth, their hackles rising.

Aria reached the top and called out to him. Perry spun and leaped, grabbing the highest rung he could reach. He pulled his legs up and slashed with his knife as their jaws snapped at him. He kicked one wolf on the ear. It yelped and fell away, giving him an instant to find a rung with his foot and push. He launched himself up, pulling himself to the top.

Aria grabbed him, steadying his balance. They followed the wide branch to the shack. The two outfacing sides were boarded solidly. On the other two sides, every other board had been left off, giving it the look of a cage.

Aria slipped right in. He couldn't squeeze his shoulders through so he smashed one of the boards with his foot. The wood groaned beneath him, and he couldn't stand at his full height, but the floorboards were sturdy. For a few seconds, he and Aria looked at each other, panting for breath, as the wolves barked below them, claws ripping at the tree. Then he kicked off a layer of leaves and set his satchel down. The last of the daylight came gray and blurred through the slats, like light moving through water.

"We'll be safe up here," he said.

Aria peered out of the shack, her shoulders drawn tight with strain. The rabid sounds continued. "How long will they stay?"

He saw no point in lying to her. The wolves would wait, just as the Croven had. "As long as it takes."

Perry ran a hand through his hair as he considered his options. He could make new arrows, but that would take time and he'd dropped his bow somewhere below. For now, there was nothing he could think to do. He knelt and took the blankets from his satchel. They'd been running for their lives. They didn't feel the cold now, but they would soon enough.

They sat together as night fell over the shack, the darkness amplifying the snapping sounds from below. Perry brought out water, but Aria wouldn't drink. She covered her ears and pressed her eyes closed. Her temper seethed with anxiety and he knew—*felt*—how the sounds brought her physical pain. He didn't know how to help.

An hour passed. Aria hadn't moved. Perry thought he might go mad when the barking stopped unexpectedly. He sat up.

Aria uncovered her ears, hope a passing flicker in her eyes. "They're still here," she whispered.

He eased back against the board, absorbing the quiet. The howl sent a sudden chill down his spine. He tensed, listening to a wail unlike anything he'd ever heard. Like being rendered, it pulled him into the deepest, heaviest feeling, trapping his breath in his throat. Other wolves joined in, creating a sound that raised the hair on his arms.

After a few minutes, the howls died off. Perry waited, hoping, but then the barking and scraping began again. The boards shifted beneath him as Aria stood and moved to the edge, the blanket sliding off her shoulders. Perry watched as she stared down at the wolves. Then she cupped her hands around her mouth and closed her eyes.

He thought it was another wolf howling. Even watching her, he couldn't believe she'd made the sound. The barking below ceased. When she finished, her gaze darted to his for a moment. Then she let out an even richer, mournful sound, her singer's voice carrying more power, more reach than any of the wolves below.

Quiet fell over them when she was done. Perry's heart pounded.

He heard a soft whine and a wet sneeze. And then, after a moment, the patter of paws retreating into the night.

With the wolves gone, they sat and shared water. Perry's fear was wearing off, leaving a heavy fatigue. He couldn't stop looking at Aria. He couldn't stop wondering.

"What did you say to them?" he finally asked.

"I have no idea. I just tried to copy their howls."

Perry took a drink of water. "It's a gift you have."

"A gift?" She looked lost in thought for a while. "I never thought so before. But maybe it is." She smiled. "We're alike, Perry. My voice is called a falcon soprano."

He grinned. "Birds of a feather."

With their nerves settling, they ate a quick meal of cheese and dried fruits they'd packed from Marron's. Then they wrapped themselves into their blankets and sat against the planks, listening to the wind stir the branches around them.

"Do you have a girl in your tribe?" Aria asked.

Perry peered at her, his pulse picking up. It was just about the last question he wanted to answer. "No one important," he said carefully. That sounded terrible, but it was the truth.

"Why isn't she important?"

"You know what I'm going to say. Don't you?"

"Rose told me. But I want to hear it from you."

"Mine is the rarest Sense. The most powerful. It's even more important for us to keep our bloodline pure than it is for other Marked." He rubbed his tired eyes and sighed. "Crossing Senses brings a curse. It brings misfortune."

"A curse? That sounds archaic. Like something out of the Middle Ages."

"It's not," he said, trying to keep the edge out of his voice.

She thought for a moment, her small chin jutting out. "What about you? You have two Senses. Was your mother a Scire?"

"No. Aria, I don't want to talk about this."

"Actually, I don't either."

They fell into silence. Perry wanted to reach for her. He wanted to feel like he had for the past day, with her hand in his. But her temper had become weighted, cool as the night.

Finally she spoke. "Perry, what would I scent now if I were a Scire?"

Perry closed his eyes. Describing their differences wouldn't bring her any closer. But neither would refusing to answer. He inhaled and then he told her what his nose told him. "There are traces of the wolves. The scents of the tree carrying a winter tone."

"The trees have a winter smell?" she asked.

"They do. Trees know first what the weather will do."

He already regretted speaking. Aria bit her lip. "What else?" she said, but he scented how it hit her, all the things he knew that she didn't.

"There's resin and rust on the iron nails. I scent the remnants of a fire, probably months old, but the ash is different from yesterday, with Cinder. This is dry and has a taste like fine salt."

"And yesterday?" she asked softly. "What did that ash smell like?"

He peered at her. "Blue. Empty." She nodded like she understood, but she couldn't. "Aria, this isn't a good idea."

"Please, Perry. I want to know what this is like for you."

He cleared his throat against a sudden tightness. "This shack belonged to a family. I scent traces of a man and a woman. A stripling—"

"What's a stripling?"

"A boy on the cusp of becoming a man. Like Cinder. They have a scent that can't be ignored, if you get what I mean."

She smiled. "Would that be your scent?"

He put his hand to his heart, pretending to be stricken. "That hurt." Then he grinned. "No doubt, yes. To another Scire, my appetites must raise one skunk of a reek."

She laughed, dropping her head to the side. Her black hair spilled over her shoulder. Just like that the night cold vanished.

"I would know all that if I were a Scire?" she asked.

"That and more." Perry drew a shuddering breath. "You'd have a fair idea of what I want right now."

"What would that be?"

"You nearer."

"How near?"

He lifted the edge of his blanket.

She surprised him by folding her arms around his waist and embracing him. Perry looked down at the top of her dark head as she burrowed against his chest. Something heavy and cold at his core lightened. Hugging wasn't what he'd had in mind, but maybe it was better. It shouldn't surprise him, her knowing what he needed more than he did.

After a moment, she drew back. Tears pooled in her eyes. She was so close, her scent moving through him, filling him. He found his eyes pooling too.

"I know we only have this time, Perry. I know it'll end."

He kissed her then, parting her soft lips with his. She tasted perfect. Like fresh rain. He deepened their kiss, his hands finding her, bringing her closer. But then she drew away and smiled. Without a word, she kissed the bridge of his nose, then the corner of his lip, and then a spot on his chin. His heart stopped when she tugged his shirt up. He helped her, yanking it over his head. Her gaze ran over his chest and then her fingers trailed over his Markings. He couldn't slow down his breathing.

"Perry. I want to see your back."

Another surprise, but he nodded and turned away. Dropped his head forward and took the moment to try and calm his breath. He jerked when she traced the shape of the wings on his skin, a groan sliding out of him. Perry silently cursed himself. He couldn't have sounded more Savage if he'd tried.

"Sorry," she whispered.

He cleared his throat. "We get them when we turn fifteen. All Marked do. A band for your Sense and one for your name."

"He's magnificent. Like you," she added softly.

That was what did it. He spun and caught her up, pulling her down onto the boards, possessing just enough of his wits to soften their fall with his arms.

Aria gave a startled laugh. "You didn't like that?"

"I did. Too much." With some quick shifting, he pulled a blanket beneath them, another one over. And then she was his. He kissed her and lost himself in the silk of her skin, and in her violet scent.

"Perry, if we . . . couldn't I get . . . ?"

"No," he said. "Not now. Your scent would be different."

"It would? How?"

Questions. Of course with her. Even now. "Sweeter," he said.

She pulled him closer, wrapping her arms around his neck.

"Aria," he whispered, "we don't have to do this if you're not sure."

"I trust you and I'm sure," she said, and he knew it was true.

He kissed her slowly. Everything went slowly so he could follow her temper, and search into her eyes. When they joined, her scent was brave and strong and certain. Perry took it into himself, breathing her breath, feeling what she felt. He'd never known anything as right.

~ 37 ~

ARIA

The next morning, Perry told her the wolves' scents were faint. He didn't think the pack was close, but they traveled with more care than ever, relaxing only when they had left that territory behind.

He was different with her. He spoke to her quietly as they walked. He answered every one of her questions, even things she didn't ask, knowing she'd want to know them. He told her about the plants they passed. Which ones were edible or had medicinal uses. He showed her the animal tracks they came across and explained how to navigate by the shape of the hills.

Aria memorized every word he said and savored every smile he gave her. She found excuses to bring him close, pretending interest in this leaf or that rock. Nothing fascinated her more than him. When Perry told her it would take them six days to reach Bliss, she gave up on excuses. Six days was too long to wait for news of Lumina. It wasn't long enough to be with him.

In the afternoon, they stopped to eat on a rocky outcrop. Perry brushed a kiss on her cheek while she was chewing, and she learned that it was the loveliest thing to be kissed for no reason, even while chewing food. It brightened the woods, and the never sky, and everything.

Aria embraced this tactic, calling it the Spontaneous Kiss, and soon learned how difficult Scires were to surprise. Whenever she tried the Spontaneous Kiss in return, Perry smiled with heavy-lidded eyes and opened his arms. She kissed him anyway, not caring, until it hit her that he'd someday choose a girl who was like him. A Scire who would also be immune to the Spontaneous Kiss. Aria wondered if they would know every emotion that ran through each other. She found it curious and frightening that she could deeply dislike someone she didn't even know. It wasn't her. At least, it wasn't how she used to be.

That night Perry devised a hammock from their blankets and rope. Pressed together in a cocoon of warm fleece, his heart pounding solidly beneath her ear, she wished for what she'd always had in Reverie. A way to exist in two worlds at once.

The next day she spent hours thinking, turning her inquisitiveness inward. She liked what she was discovering about herself. Aria, who knew that birds should be plucked while they were still warm so the feathers came out more easily. Aria, who could start a fire with a knife and a piece of quartz. Aria, who sang wrapped in the arms of a blond-haired boy.

She didn't know where this side of her would fit with what lay five days ahead. How would it be going back to the Pod? Knowing how utterly visceral and terrifying and euphoric these days had been, how would she return to simulated thrills? She didn't know, but thinking of it worried her. As to her biggest question—what would happen when she reached Bliss—she did something new. She withheld her questions and fears and trusted that she'd know what to do when the time came.

"Perry?" she whispered late that night. His arms immediately tightened around her ribs and she knew she'd woken him.

"Hmm?"

"When did you get your Senses?"

In the quiet, she could practically hear him sinking into his memories.

"My sight came first. Around age four. For a while no one knew that it was different . . . even I didn't. Most Seers see better in the light, but I thought everyone saw like I did. When it came out that I was Night-Sighted no one made much of it. At least not around me. I was eight when I started scenting tempers. Eight exactly. That I remember."

"Why?" Aria asked. But there was something about the way he'd said it. She wasn't sure she wanted to know.

"Scenting tempers changed everything. . . . I realized how

often people say one thing and mean another. How often they want what they can't have. I saw all these reasons for everything. . . . I couldn't avoid knowing things people hid."

Aria's heartbeat quickened. She found his burned hand. He'd stopped using the bandage the night they left Marron's. The skin at the top had patches that were too rough and patches that were too smooth. She brought it close and kissed the marbled skin. She'd never have dreamed a scar could be something worth kissing, but she loved every scar on him. She'd found them and kissed them all, and asked to hear each and every story that had left its mark on him.

"What did you learn?" she asked.

"That my father drank so he could bear to be around me. I knew he felt better still when his fists found me. For a while, anyway. Never for long."

Her eyes filling with tears, Aria pulled him close, feeling how tense he was against her. She'd sensed this piece of him. Somehow she had known. "Perry, what could you have possibly done to deserve that?"

"My . . . I've never talked about this before."

When he sniffed, Aria felt a sob catch in her throat. "You can tell me."

"I know . . . I'm trying. . . . My mother died birthing me. She died because of me."

She leaned back so she could see his face. He closed his eyes.

"That wasn't your fault. You can't really blame yourself. Perry . . . do you?"

"He did. Why shouldn't I?"

She remembered what he'd said about killing a woman. She realized he'd been speaking of his *mother.* "You were an infant! It was an accident. It's just a horrible thing that happened. It's a horrible thing your father did to make you feel like that."

"He just felt what he felt, Aria. There's no disguising a temper."

"*He* was wrong! Did your brother and sister blame you too?"

"Liv never did. And Vale never acted like it, but I can't be sure. I can't scent his tempers just like I can't scent my own. But maybe he did. I'm the only one who carries her Sense. My father gave up everything to be with her. He built a tribe. He had Vale and Liv. And then I came and stole what he loved most. People said it was the curse of mixing blood. They said it finally caught up to him."

"You didn't steal anything. It's just something that happened."

"No. It's not. The same thing happened to my brother. Mila was a Seer too, and she's . . . she's gone. Talon's sick. . . ." He exhaled a shuddering breath. "I don't know what I'm saying. I shouldn't be talking about this with you. I've been talking so much lately. Maybe I forgot how to stop."

"You don't have to stop."

"You know what I think of words."

"Words are the best way I have to know you."

His hand slid under her jaw, his fingers threading into her hair. "The best way?"

330

His thumb ran back and forth across her chin. It was distracting, and she knew that was what he wanted. Maybe all he'd ever done was move forward. Try to save the people he could. Try to make up for something he'd never done.

"Perry . . . ," Aria said, covering his hand. "Peregrine . . . you are *kind*. You put your life at risk for Talon and Cinder. For me. You did it when you didn't even like me. You worry about your tribe. You ache for Roar and your sister. I know you do. I saw it in your face every time Roar spoke of Liv." Her voice was shaking. She swallowed the lump in her throat. "You are *good*, Peregrine."

He shook his head. "You've seen me."

"I have. And I *know* your heart is good." She put her hand over it and felt all the life that drummed through him. A sound so strong, so loud, as if she'd rested her ear against his chest.

His thumb stopped. His hand moved to the back of her head. He drew her toward him until their foreheads touched. "I liked those words," he said.

In his glinting eyes, she saw tears of gratitude and trust. She also saw the shadow of what neither of them would dare say to each other, with only days left together. But for now, for tonight, they were done with words.

PEREGRINE

Aria made him forget to eat. It was as real a sign as any that he was in trouble. They'd finished the small provisions they had brought from Marron's. Today he'd need to hunt. Perry made a few quick arrows in the morning using shoots he'd been collecting, deciding to track for game as they went. It would slow their pace, but he couldn't ignore the cramping in his stomach any longer.

They were working down into the foothills when he scented a badger in a wide glade that gave to a river. The animal's odor wafted out of its underground tunnels. Supper, he decided.

Perry found the entry hole and another one, farther back. He set a fire on one end and had Aria wait there with a leafy branch. "Fan the smoke into the hole. It'll come to me. Animals don't run toward fire."

The badger saw Perry as it came up from its hole. It spun

and did exactly what he said it wouldn't do. Perry ran toward Aria. "Your knife! He's coming to you!"

She was ready, staring down into the opening as Perry reached her. But the badger didn't come up. Aria straightened from her crouch and began walking. She stopped every few steps, changing directions as she stared at the river-moist soil. Perry had an idea what this was. He'd been wondering since the day they'd seen the wolves. Finally she stood in place and met his eyes.

"He's right underneath me," she said, smiling wide, surprised.

Perry slid his bow off his shoulder.

"No. I'll get him. But I need your knife."

Perry gave it to her and backed away, afraid to blink.

She waited for a few moments, the long blade clutched in both hands. Then she brought it over her head and thrust it deep into the muddy earth.

Perry heard a faint squeal but Aria, he knew, had heard it clearly.

Later, in the same glade, they sat against a stump. Aria lay back against his chest. A fire trailed a line of smoke up into the trees. There were a few more hours left in the day, but with a full stomach and Aria's contented temper sating him, Perry let his head fall back. He watched the glow of Aether dance behind his eyelids as Aria described the sounds she heard.

"They aren't louder . . . I don't know how to explain it.

They've just become richer. Sounds that were simple are so intricate now. Like the river. There are hundreds of small sounds coming from the water. And the wind, Perry. It's constant, moving through the trees, making the bark groan and the leaves rustle. I can tell exactly which way it's coming. It's almost like I can *see* it, I hear it so clearly."

Perry tried in vain to hear what she heard, feeling an odd sense of pride over her newfound ability.

"Do you think it's being out here—under the Aether—why this has all happened to me? Like the Outsider part of me is waking up?"

Perry heard her, but he was so content that he'd started to drift asleep. She pinched his arm. He startled. "Sorry. The Outsider in me was falling asleep."

She glared at him, her eyes shining with cleverness. "Do you think I'm related to Roar?"

"Maybe generations back. Not closely. Your scents are too different. Why?"

"I like Roar. I was thinking that if he didn't find Liv, you know . . . we are both Audiles. Never mind. Roar will never get over Liv."

Perry sat up. "*What?*"

She laughed. "You're awake now. Did you think I was serious?"

"Yes. No. Aria, there's truth there. Roar would be better suited for you." Perry sighed, shoving his hand into his hair. He peered at her. There was another reason too, and he might as well just tell her since he was getting good at telling her everything. "Liv says . . . she says he's a feast for the eyes." He tried to say it without sounding envious, but doubted it would help. Surely she'd hear the emotion in his voice.

Aria smiled. She took his scarred hand and ran her thumb over his knuckles. "Roar is very handsome. In Reverie most people look like him. Or close."

Perry cursed. His fault for bringing it up. "And here you are. Holding hands with a crooked-nosed Savage who's been burnt and beaten in—how many places did you count?"

"I've never seen anyone as beautiful as you."

Perry looked down at their hands. How did she do that? How did she make him feel weak and strong? Thrilled and terrified? He couldn't find a way to return what she'd given him. He didn't have the gift she did with words. All he could do was take her hand and kiss it, and bring it to his heart, and wish she could scent his temper. He wished it was all easy between them. At least now she'd come to understand. She was learning the power of a Sense.

He pulled her back into his arms, resting her along his chest. "I can tell you one thing about your father," he said, because he knew she wondered. "He's probably from a strong line of Auds for you to be as keen as you are."

She squeezed his hand. "Thank you."

"I mean it. That was no small trick, hearing through dirt that thick."

Perry kissed the top of her head as they fell into silence. He knew she was listening. Hearing a new world. But her good mood didn't pull him along anymore.

For days he'd had a shifty, anxious feeling in his gut. A feeling like the instant after a cut, before the pain came. He knew when the hurt would hit him. Three more days and they'd reach Bliss. And she'd go back to her mother. He didn't know what he'd do if they didn't find Lumina. Bring her to the Tides? Take her back to Marron's? He couldn't imagine doing either. He tightened his arms around her. Brought in her scent, breathing deep, letting it mellow him. She was here now.

"Perry? Say something. I want to hear your voice again."

He didn't know what to say but he wasn't going to disappoint her. He cleared his throat. "I've been having this dream since we started sleeping together up in the trees. I'm in this grassy plain. And there's this blue sky stretching out over me. No Aether in it at all. And the breeze is moving the grass in waves, stirring up bugs. And I'm just walking, my bow sort of combing the tall grass behind me. And there's not a thing I'm worrying about. It's a good dream."

She squeezed him. "Your voice sounds like a midnight fire. All warm and worn in and golden. I could listen to you talk forever."

"I could never do that."

She laughed at him. He brought his lips to her ear. "Your scent is like violets in early spring," he whispered. Then he laughed at himself because though it was true, he sounded like the worst kind of fool.

"Was Vale a good Blood Lord?"

Aria was too eager to learn about her Sense to sleep so

they walked into the night.

"Very good. Vale is calm. He thinks things through. He's patient with people. I think . . . I think if it weren't a time like this . . . he would be the best man to lead the tribe."

Maybe that had held him back from making a challenge for Blood Lord, as much as his fear of hurting Talon, Perry realized. He still couldn't believe his brother had been captured. "He wasn't going to go after Talon," he said, remembering the last time they'd been together. "Vale said it meant risking the tribe's safety. It's the reason I left."

"Why do you think Vale changed his mind?"

"I don't know," he said. Vale had never put anything above the good of the tribe before, but Talon was his son.

"They're together. Will you still try to bring them to the outside?"

He looked at her.

"Talon is being cared for," she said. "You saw him. He has a chance to live in there."

"I'm not giving up."

Aria slipped her hand into his. "Even if it's better for him?"

"Are you saying I should let him go? How could I do that?"

"I don't know. I'm trying to figure out the same thing."

Perry stopped. "Aria . . ." He was going to tell her he'd rendered to her. That nothing was the same anymore because of her. But what difference would it make? They only had three more days together. And he knew she had to go home. He knew exactly how much she needed her mother.

337

She took his other hand. "Yes, Peregrine?" After a moment, she smiled.

He found himself smiling too. "Aria, I don't understand how you can be so chirky right now."

"I was just thinking. Soon you'll be Peregrine, Blood Lord of the Tides." She swirled a hand in the air as she said it. "I just love how it sounds."

Perry laughed. "Spoken like a true Aud."

~ 39 ~

ARIA

A ria heard song everywhere.

Shifting in the trees. Rumbling in the earth. Drifting on the wind. It was the same terrain, but she saw it differently. When she looked into the distance, where she'd seen nothing before, she now imagined the father who might be there. A man who would hear the world as she did, in endless tones. He was an Audile. That was the only thing she knew about him. Strangely, it felt like a lot.

A day after she'd discovered her ability, she noticed her own footfall growing quieter. Somehow, without consciously thinking of it, she'd begun to choose her steps with greater care. When she mentioned it to Perry, he grinned.

"I noticed that too. Easier to hunt," he said, patting a hare strung over his shoulder. "Most Auds are quiet as shadows. The best end up as spies or scouts for the larger tribes."

"Seriously? Spies?"

"Seriously."

She practiced sneaking up on Perry, determined to succeed where she'd failed before. The morning before they were to reach Bliss, she pounced on him, throwing her arms around his neck as she planted a kiss on the blond scruff over his jaw. Finally she had accomplished the Spontaneous Kiss. She expected him to laugh and kiss her back. He didn't do either. He wrapped his arms around her and rested his head on top of hers.

"Should we rest?" she asked, feeling his weight settle onto her shoulders. She could see the hills where Bliss was supposedly nestled on the horizon.

Perry straightened. "No," he said. His green eyes were tight, like the day was too bright for him. "We have to keep going, Aria. I don't know what else to do."

Neither did she, so they walked.

They reached the hills late in the afternoon. They climbed one and another, and then almost suddenly, there stood Bliss, a man-made mountain amid earthen hills. Aria had never seen a Pod from the outside but knew the largest dome at the center would be the Panop. The off-shooting structures were the service domes, like Ag 6. She'd spent seventeen years in Reverie's Panop. Contained in one place. It seemed unbelievable to her now. With daylight fading, the Pod's deep charcoal shape was fast blending into the night.

Perry shifted his weight at her side, silent as he took in the scene. "Looks like a rescue. There are Hovers . . .

thirty or so, and a bigger craft. At least fifty people out in the open."

To her, what he described was just a smattering of dots next to Bliss, lit within a circle of light. The soft drone of engines carried to her ears.

"What do you want to do?" he asked.

"Let's get closer." They moved quietly across the dry grass, stopping when they reached a rocky perch. Now Aria saw a large square opening in Bliss, a wide-open cavity on the smooth walls of the Pod. The Guardians who came and went wore sterile suits. She knew what that meant. The closed environment was compromised. She'd expected this, but numbness seeped through her limbs.

Perry cursed softly beside her.

"What is it?" she asked.

"There's a black cart down there," he said, his expression pained. "Some sort of truck, close to the Pod." She saw it. It was in miniature, but she saw it. "There are people—bodies on board."

Her eyes blurred. "Can you see any of their faces?"

"No." Perry wrapped his arms around her. "Come here," he whispered. "She could be anywhere. Don't give up now."

They sat on the rocks side by side as she forced herself to think. She couldn't walk out of the darkness and announce herself a Dweller. She needed to come up with a plan. She took her Smarteye from her satchel. It hadn't helped her reach Lumina at Marron's, but it would be useful now.

Aria stared at the small black point in the distance. She'd

341

waited enough. She knew what she needed to do. "I have to get down there."

"I'm coming with you."

"No. You can't. They'd kill you if they saw you."

He groaned like the words hurt him physically.

"The Tides need you to be Blood Lord, Perry. I have to go alone. And I need your help up here."

She told him her idea, describing the disguise she hoped to find and the way she would slip back in. He listened, his jaw rigid, but he agreed to do his part. Aria stood and handed him Talon's dagger.

"No," he said. "You might need it."

She looked at the knife, her throat tight with emotion. No roses or rings with him, but a knife with feathers carved into the handle. A knife that was part of him. She couldn't accept it.

"This won't help me down there," she said. She didn't want to hurt anyone. She just wanted to get back in.

Perry slipped the knife into his boot, but he wouldn't look at her when he straightened. He crossed his arms and uncrossed them, and then brushed the back of his hand across his eyes.

"Perry . . . ," she began. What could she say? How could she possibly describe what she felt for him? He knew. He had to know. She hugged him, pressing her eyes closed as she listened to the solid beat of his heart. His arms tightened as she drew away.

"It's time, Perry." He let her go. She took a step back,

taking in his face one last time. His green eyes. The bend in his nose and the scars on his cheek. All the tiny imperfections that made him beautiful. Without a word, she turned and made her way downhill.

She felt like she was floating as she skimmed over the grass toward Bliss. *Don't stop,* she told herself. *Keep going.* She was downslope in an instant, taking cover behind a row of large crates labeled CGB RESCUE & RECOVERY in reflective lettering. Engines buzzed loudly in her ears. She couldn't catch her breath. *Don't turn around.* She forced herself to focus on the scene before her.

Lights erected on cranes electrified the area with a sharp glare. To her right, she saw the massive mobile structure that appeared to be the heart of the operation, an angular and clumsy craft compared to the pearl blue Hovers nested around it. The curving gray walls of Bliss soared skyward to the left, smooth, broken only by the gaping rift she'd seen from above. A dozen Guardians roamed in the dirt field between. Then she spotted her target. The black truck was parked by several Hovers that sat in the darkness.

Her mother *couldn't* be there.

She couldn't be.

Aria needed to know.

~ 40 ~

PEREGRINE

Perry's eyes locked onto Aria as she huddled by a line of crates in the darkness below. He couldn't breathe. He couldn't blink. What had he done? How could he let her go alone? He knew she was waiting for the right moment to move, but every second that passed, he came closer to sprinting down to her side.

The Guardians retreated into the rescue center, their work winding down as the night deepened. Perry tensed when the perimeter lights shut off, leaving only an illuminated path to the rescue center. He hadn't expected that, but it would help them. Finally, when everything was still, Aria straightened from her crouch and dashed through the darkness toward the black truck.

His gut twisted as he watched her climb into the bed. Perry could see the tangle of limbs clearly. A dozen people, by his guess. He watched her search through the dead for her mother. He watched with his legs shaking and an ache like a rock caught in his throat. Was this it? Was she going to find Lumina like this? A body, left out in the cold?

He cursed the part of him that wished she'd find her mother this way. It was the only chance Aria would ever return to him. But then what? Wasn't this what he wanted? For her to go home so that he could return to the Tides?

He couldn't bear it, standing there, doing nothing. What was happening? How was she feeling? He'd known every small shift in her temper for days. Now he didn't know anything.

Aria dropped something over the side of the bed. A bulky suit like the Guardians wore. Boots. A helmet. Then she hopped down to the ground and scurried under the truck. He couldn't see her now but he knew she was undressing in the cramped space, putting on the Dweller clothes. He knew what that meant. She hadn't found her mother.

She crept from beneath the truck in the suit, a Dweller again. Aria pulled on a helmet and then wove her way through the darkness, drawing as close as she could to the rescue unit. Perry moved within range. There were only two men there now, standing by the entrance ramp. He knew it was as good a chance as they'd ever get, and so did she.

Aria crawled closer, only a few paces away from the ramp, then she turned uphill toward him and signaled that she was ready. It was his move now.

Perry nocked the arrow, his arms steady and sure as he aimed high, to the spotlight that shone down on the entrance. He wouldn't miss. Not this time.

He let the arrow go.

41

ARIA

The spotlight exploded with a deafening pop that burst through the speakers of Aria's helmet. The two Guardians by the rescue center ramp startled at the sudden darkness. In seconds, a dozen men flooded down the ramp to see what had happened. Aria slipped from the shadows into the commotion and then darted toward the rescue center, her shoulders brushing against Guardians who were hurrying outside.

She put one foot in front of the other through a long metal corridor, passing a pair of Guardians. They barely glanced at her. She wore their clothes. She had a helmet and a Smarteye. She was one of them.

Aria strode with purpose, though she didn't know where she was going. Her eyes searched frantically as she passed opened doors along the hall. She glimpsed cots and medical equipment. This part of the rescue center nearest the entrance held triage chambers, which didn't surprise her, but the stillness in the rooms did. Where were the survivors?

Were there any?

How was she going to find her mother?

She slowed as she approached the next chamber, listening first and then peering inside. Aria stepped into the room, her gaze sweeping, making sure she was alone.

She wasn't.

People lay in stacked bunks along the walls. Not wearing helmets. Unmoving. Aria walked farther into the room, taking in their open wounds and the dark bloodstains that seeped into their grays. They were dead. Every one.

Suddenly she couldn't escape the stench that clung to her hair, of the bodies she'd had to crawl through outside. Every breath she took, she smelled the odor of death. Desperate now, she searched for Lumina's face, moving from one row of cots to the other. From one lifeless body to the next. The marks of brutality were everywhere. Mottled yellow bruising. Scratches and ripped flesh. Bite marks.

She couldn't help imagining what had happened. So many people, turning on each other like rabid animals. Like Soren in Ag 6. Her mother had been trapped in this.

Where was she?

Aria heard a faint voice and spun. Someone approached. She tensed, ready to hide, but then she recognized the voice and froze. Was that Doctor Ward? Lumina's colleague? He entered the room, glancing through his visor in her direction, and then stopped. Hope surged through her. He would know how to find her mother.

"Doctor Ward?" she said.

"Aria?" For a moment they stared at each other. "What are you doing here?" he asked, and then answered his own question. "You've come for your mother."

"You have to help me, Doctor Ward. I need to find her."

He came toward her, leveling his intense gaze on her. "She's here," he said. They were the words she'd wanted to hear, but the tone was all wrong. "Come with me."

Aria followed him through the metal halls. She knew what was happening. She knew what he was going to tell her. Lumina was dead. She had heard it in his voice.

She followed him, her head spinning with dizziness, her legs heavy and slow. This wasn't real. It couldn't be. She couldn't lose Lumina, too.

He took her into a small, bare room with a heavy airlock door that hissed as it closed behind her.

"The storms kept us away," Ward said. A muscle by his Smarteye twitched. "We were too late."

"Can—can I see her? I need to see her."

Ward hesitated. "Yes. Wait here."

When he left, Aria staggered back. Her helmet clacked against the wall. She slid to the floor. Every muscle shook. Tears ached behind her eyes. She tried to press her palms into them, but her hands smacked into the visor. She panted, her breath loud to her own ears.

The airlock door slid open. Ward pushed a gurney into the small chamber. A long black bag made of thick plastic lay on top. "I'll be outside," he said, and left.

Aria stood. Cold emanated from the bag, rising like wisps of smoke. She opened the seal around her gloves and pulled them off. She unfastened the helmet, letting it clatter to the floor. She had to do this. She had to know. Her fingers trembled as she fumbled for the zipper. She braced herself for an opened gash. Bruises. Something terrible, like what she'd seen outside. Then she drew the zipper down, exposing her mother's face.

She saw no horrible wound, but the pallor of Lumina's skin was worse, nearly white, but deeply shadowed with purple around her eyes. Her hair fell in messy strands across her closed eyes. Aria brushed it away—Lumina would never have tolerated hair like that—and sucked in a breath at the coldness of her mother's skin.

"Oh, Mom."

Tears pushed from the edges of her Smarteye and ran down her cheeks.

She rested her hand on Lumina's forehead until her skin burned with cold. She had so many questions. Why had Lumina lied about Aria's father? Who was he? How could she have left Aria and gone to Bliss when she'd known the danger of DLS? But she needed one answer most.

"Where am I supposed to go, Mom?" she whispered. "I don't know where to go."

She knew what Lumina would say. *That's a question for you to answer, Songbird.*

Aria closed her eyes.

She knew she *could* answer it. She knew how to put one foot in front of the other even when every step hurt. And she knew there was pain in the journey, but there was also great beauty. She'd seen it standing on rooftops and in green eyes and in the smallest, ugliest rock. She would find the answer.

She bent close to her mother's face. Quietly she sang the *Tosca* aria, her voice warbling and breaking, but she knew it didn't matter. She'd promised Lumina this aria—*their* aria—so she sang.

The door slid open as she finished. Three Guardians strode into the chamber.

"Wait," she said. She wasn't ready to say good-bye. Would she ever be?

One man zipped the bag closed with a quick tug and then wheeled the gurney out. The other two Guardians stayed behind.

"Give me your Smarteye," said the one closest to her.

Behind him, the other Guardian held a white baton that made a fizzing electrical sound.

Aria lunged for the door on instinct.

The Guardian with the baton blocked her.

Light flashed before her eyes and then everything went black.

42

PEREGRINE

Perry couldn't leave. He stayed on the overlook, waiting for her to come back. What was happening? Had she found Lumina? Was she all right? He watched as the Guardians fixed the light below. He watched as they made their way back into the rescue center and as the night grew still again.

She didn't come back out, and he realized she never would.

He spun and ran, tearing into the darkness. He should've headed west, toward home. But his legs followed the trail of smoke carrying on the wind. Soon he saw the glow of firelight flickering through a stand of trees. Heard the soft pluck of a guitar and men's voices. He approached, counting six men gathered around the fire.

The guitar went silent as they spotted him. Perry slipped Talon's knife from his belt. He held it out, bringing a few men to their feet. "A trade. For drink." He nodded toward the bottles by the fire.

"It's a fine blade," said one man. He turned to another man who'd stayed where he sat across the fire. He had braided hair and a long scar from the bottom of his nose to his ear. He watched Perry for a long moment.

"Make the trade," he said.

Perry handed the knife off, wanting to be rid of it and all its memories. He was given two bottles of Luster. One more than anyone should drink in one night. He took them and moved away from the fire. The guitar picked up its song again. Perry set the bottles down beside him. He'd take his father's cue tonight.

An hour later, the first bottle stood on end beside him. It wove back and forth on the dirt, riding some invisible tide. Perry started on the other bottle. He should have known it wouldn't be enough. His body was numb, but not the ache deep inside him. Aria was gone, and no amount of Luster would change that.

The braid-haired man kept looking across the fire at him. *Come on,* Perry pleaded silently, his hands curling into fists. *Get up. Let's get it over with.* It took Braids a few more minutes to come over. He squatted a few feet away, sitting on his heels.

"I heard of you," he said. He looked sturdy, thick, but Perry sensed he could be quick as a trap. The scar cut a deep line across his cheek.

"Good for you," Perry slurred. "I got no idea who you are. Nice hair, though. My sister does hers like that."

Braids looked right at Perry's burnt hand. "Dispersed life

not suiting you, Tider? No elder brother to look after you? To keep you out of trouble?" Braids set a hand down on the dirt and leaned forward. "You *reek* of misery."

He was a Scire. Braids would know Perry's temper right now. How he hurt. How just breathing felt like work. It should have worried him, fighting someone who had the same advantages he did. But Perry heard himself laugh.

"You reek too, man," Perry said. "Like you've been chewing on cud."

Braids stood. He kicked the full bottle of Luster, sending it spinning into the darkness. The other men rushed over, their excitement like sparks in Perry's nose. He'd figured he would end up brawling tonight. He knew how people reacted at the sight of him. What man wouldn't stand taller after beating the spit out of someone like him?

Perry grabbed his knife and stood. "Let's get to it. See what you can do."

Braids squared off, flashing a wicked piece of steel with serrated teeth. More a saw than a knife. He looked steady and moved smoothly, but his temper was streaked through with fear.

Perry grinned. "You changing your mind?"

Braids came at him like a shot. Perry felt the bite of the knife on his arm, but not the pain of the wound it opened. A solid wound. The blood that poured from it was dark in the Aether light. For a second, all he could do was watch his blood leak out of him. Run down his arm.

Maybe this wasn't a good idea. Perry had never fought

anyone drunk. He moved too slowly. His legs were too heavy. Maybe it had worked for his father because Perry had been a boy. How hard could it be to hit a kid who'd stood there, wanting it? Looking for anything he could to make things right?

He choked back a sudden rise of bile, realizing the choice he'd have to make if Braids managed to get a knife against his throat. Pledge fealty or die. An easy decision.

"You're nothing like I'd heard," Braids said. "Peregrine of the Tides. Twice Marked." He laughed. "You're not worth the air you breathe."

Now was the time to shut him up. Perry spun the blade in his hand, almost dropping it. He made a move. A thrust that wasn't nearly as fast as it should've been. He almost laughed. Knives had never been his weapon. The movement brought another wave of nausea, this one powerful enough to double him up.

Braids rushed him as he choked back the urge to vomit. He drove his knee into Perry's face. Perry managed to turn his head. Took the brunt of the blow on the temple. He'd spared his nose, but he hit the ground hard. Saw the creep of darkness threatening to take him away.

The kicks kept coming, landing on his back and arms and head. They came from everywhere. Perry felt them dimly, shadows of pain. He didn't stop Braids. This was the easy way. Staying down. Perry's head rocked forward as a kick came from behind. The blackness came again, softening the edges of his vision. He willed it to come. Maybe it would make more sense if he felt on the surface as he did inside.

"You're *weak*."

He was wrong. Perry wasn't weak. That had never been the problem. The problem was that he couldn't help them all. No matter what he did, people he loved would still suffer and die and leave. But Perry couldn't do it. He couldn't stay down. He didn't know how to give up.

He swept his legs beneath him and sprang to his feet. Braids leaped back at his sudden movement, jumping out of the way, but Perry caught him by the collar. He yanked Braids toward him, the movement whipping his head backward. Perry jammed his elbow into his nose. Blood burst from his nostrils. Perry twisted the blade from Braids's grip, dodging a punch and driving a fist into his stomach. Braids folded, dropping onto one knee. Perry wrapped an arm around his neck and wrestled him to the dirt.

Perry snatched up the serrated blade from the ground and laid it against the man's throat. Braids stared up at him, blood pouring from his nose. Perry knew this was the moment he should demand an oath. *Pledge to me or die.*

He inhaled deeply. Braids's temper was red fury, all directed at Perry. He'd never submit. Braids would choose death, just as he'd have done.

"You owe me a bottle of Luster," Perry said.

Then he stood, reeling. The other men had gathered around. He breathed in their tempers, the scents both right and wrong. He looked for the next man who might challenge him. No one came forward.

A sudden twist in his gut had him vomiting right there in front of them. He held on to the knife in case any of them wanted to take a shot while he was heaving, like Braids had. They didn't. Everything came up at once. He straightened.

"Probably don't need any more Luster."

He tossed the knife aside and stumbled into the darkness. He didn't know where he was going. It didn't matter.

He wanted to hear her voice. He wanted to hear her tell him he was good. All he heard was the sound of his feet chasing the dark.

Morning came. His head felt like a door slammed closed on it, over and over. His body felt worse. Perry peeled off the shoddy dressing he'd tied around his arm. The cut was jagged and deep. Perry washed it, growing light-headed as it bled freshly.

He ripped a strip off his shirt and tried to bandage it again. His fingers were too shaky. Still too clumsy with drink. He lay back on the gravel and closed his eyes because it was too bright. Because darkness was better.

He woke to a tugging on his arm and shot upright. Braids crouched beside him. His nose was swollen, his eyes red with bruising. The other men stood behind him.

Perry looked down at his arm. The wound was well bandaged, tied off neatly.

"You didn't ask me to pledge to you," Braids said.

"You'd have said no."

Braids nodded once. "I would have." He took Talon's knife from his belt and held it out. "I'm guessing you want this back."

43

ARIA

A ria pulled her knees up. She'd woken hours ago in a cramped chamber, an acrid taste coating her tongue. A glove lay discarded in the corner. She'd watched the smudges of blood on the fingers fade from red to rust.

Her eye socket throbbed. They had taken her Smarteye while she was unconscious.

Aria didn't care.

The wall in front of her had a thick black screen nearly as wide as the room itself. Aria waited for it to open. She knew who she'd see on the other side when it did, but she wasn't afraid.

She'd survived the outside. She'd survived the Aether and cannibals and wolves. She knew how to love now, and how to let go. Whatever came next, she would survive it, too.

A soft crackling sound broke the room's silence. Small speakers by the black screen buzzed softly. Aria shot to her feet, her hand aching for the weight of Talon's knife. The screen parted, revealing a room behind thick glass. There were two men on the other side.

"Hello, Aria," Consul Hess said, his small eyes pinching in amusement. "You can't imagine how surprised I am to see you." He dwarfed the chair on which he sat. Ward stood quiet and serious at his side, his brow wrinkled.

"I'm sorry for your loss," said Consul Hess.

His words carried no tone of sympathy. She would never believe him anyway. He'd put her out to die.

"We viewed the 'Songbird' message from your mother," he continued. He held her Smarteye in his palm. "You know, I was unaware of your *unique* genetic makeup when I put you outside? Lumina kept that hidden from all of us."

Aria's gaze snapped to the glass. She understood. They saw her as a diseased Savage. They didn't want to breathe the same air she did.

"You have the Smarteye," she said. "What do you want from me?"

Hess smiled. "I'll get to that. You know what happened here in Bliss, don't you? You saw it in your mother's file." He paused. "You had a taste of it yourself in Ag 6."

She saw no point in lying. "An Aether strike and DLS," she said.

"Yes, that's right. A dual attack. External first. A storm weakens the Pod. Then internal, as the disease manifests. Your mother was among the first to study DLS. She was working toward a cure, along with many other scientists.

But as you can see by what happened here, we don't have an answer. And we may run out of time before we do."

He glanced at Ward, sending an obvious cue. The doctor spoke immediately, his voice carrying more passion than Hess.

"The Aether storms are striking with intensity not seen since the Unity. Bliss isn't the only Pod that has fallen. If the storms continue, they will all fall. *Reverie* will fall, Aria. Our only hope of surviving is to escape the Aether."

She almost laughed at him. "Then there is no hope. You can't escape it. It's everywhere."

"Outsiders speak of a place that's free of it."

Aria tensed. Ward knew about the Still Blue? How could he know that? But of course he would. He studied Outsiders, like her mother did. Like her mother *had*.

"They're only rumors," Aria said. Even as she spoke the words, she knew they might be true. Hadn't the rumor of Bliss proved to be?

Hess was watching her closely. "So you've heard of it."

"Yes."

"Then you're already on your way."

Aria's stomach twisted as she realized what he wanted. "You want *me* to find it?" She shook her head. "I'm not doing *anything* for you."

"Six thousand people died here," Ward said urgently. "Six *thousand*. Your mother among them. You have to understand. It's our only option."

Grief moved through Aria, pressing down on her. She

thought of the bodies on the black cart and the people on the cots in the triage room. Bane and Echo had died because of DLS. And *Paisley*. Would Caleb and the rest of her friends be next?

Her heart pounded as she considered returning to the outside. Was it the thought of seeing Perry that made her pulse hammer? Or maybe she felt she owed it to Lumina to carry on her quest. But she couldn't just let the Pods crumble.

"You can't return to Reverie," Hess said. "You've seen too much."

Aria glared at him. "So you'll kill me if I don't agree? You've already tried that. You'll have to do better."

Hess studied her for a moment. "I thought you might say that. I think I've found another way to persuade you."

A blue square faded on the glass. An image of Perry appeared on a small screen, floating between them. He was in the room with the painted boats and hawks. The room where he'd seen Talon in the Realms.

"Aria . . . what's happening?" he said frantically. "Aria, why doesn't he know me?"

The image faded, changing to Perry as he hugged Talon. "I love you, Talon," he said. "I love you." And then the image froze.

For an instant, the echo of his voice hung in the tiny chamber. Then Aria flew toward the glass, slamming her hands against it. "Don't you dare touch them!"

Hess stiffened, startled by her outburst. Then his lips turned up in a satisfied smile. "If you bring me the information on the Still Blue, I won't have to."

Aria put her hand on Perry's image, aching for him. For the real him. Her gaze drifted to Talon. She'd never met him, but it didn't matter. He was part of Perry. She'd do anything to protect him.

She looked at Hess. "I won't give you *anything* if you hurt either of them."

Hess smiled. "Good," he said and stood. "I think we understand each other." The door slid open and he left.

Ward followed but hesitated by the door. "Aria, your mother did leave us with an answer. She left us you."

It was night as she stepped into the Dragonwing with six Guardians. Aria wore her clothes—the ones she'd retrieved from beneath the black cart—and she had a new Smarteye slipped into her satchel.

In the dim glow of the cabin, she buckled herself into the seat. The Guardians peered at her through their visors with a mixture of fear and repulsion.

Aria met their stares and then told them exactly where to drop her in the Death Shop.

44

PEREGRINE

B raids's name was Reef.

Perry sat with him and his men that night around a fire, a jug of water in his hand instead of Luster. He told them about what he'd done. How he'd gotten into the Dweller fortress. How Talon and Vale had been taken. He told them about Aria in brief words, the pain of losing her too fresh, and explained that he was going home to claim Blood Lord of the Tides.

He talked until he grew hoarse and then some as the questions came. It was nearly morning when the last man fell asleep. Perry lay back and crossed his arms behind his head.

He'd won them all, not just Reef. All six men in the small band. He had inhaled and known the scent of their loyalty. Maybe he'd earned a chance with his fists, but he'd won them with his words.

Perry watched the Aether sky, thinking of a girl who would have been proud of him.

The storms came in force over the coming days, slowing their progress toward the coast. Funnels wheeled above constantly. The glare of the sky brightened nights and stole the warmth from the light of day. Winter had begun.

They traveled when they could, veering around burning fields. At night they found shelter and gathered around a fire, the men telling the story of his fight with Reef over and over. They embellished it, playing out their parts. Embarrassing Perry by slurring the things he'd said. They howled every time the story came to Perry vomiting with his knife held at guard. Reef earned Perry's respect again by accepting his defeat at the end of the story with good humor. He claimed he'd need his nose broken half a dozen more times before it looked like Perry's.

Perry had only known Scires among his family. Liv. Vale. Talon. Reef changed what he knew about his Sense. They spoke little but understood each other perfectly. He tried not to think of what this sort of bond would feel like with a girl. Whenever his mind tended that way, it felt like a betrayal.

One night Reef turned to him as they stood under a stand of trees waiting out a pelting rain. "It'd be a different life without the Aether."

His temper was calm and steady. Thoughtful.

The other men went quiet. Their eyes turned to Perry, waiting for him to speak.

He told them then about the Still Blue. For a while after he'd finished, he and Reef had stood watching the rain beat down on a charred field. Listening to the hiss it made. Perry knew he and Roar could discover this place. Reef and his men would help. Marron and Cinder, too. They'd learn where it was and then he'd take the Tides there.

"We'll find the Still Blue," Perry said. "If it exists, I'll get us there."

It came out sounding like what it was. Like he'd made a pledge to his men.

After a week of skirting storms, they approached the Tide compound under a night sky lit bright with Aether. Perry strode across a field that crunched like tinder beneath his feet, inhaling the familiar scents of salt and earth. This was where he needed to be. Home with his tribe. He had no illusions of the welcome he would receive. The Tides would blame him for Talon and Vale. But he hoped to convince them that he could help. The tribe needed him now.

A torch flickered to life at the edge of the compound and then he heard shouts of alarm, telling him they'd been spotted by the night watch. Within moments several more torches appeared, blazing spots in the blue night. Perry knew the Tides would think this a raid. He'd been a part of this situation dozens of times before. He would have been the archer on the roof of the cookhouse, where he now saw Brooke.

He waited for an arrow to pierce his heart, but Brooke

shouted down. He heard his name again, volleyed from voice to voice. He heard them calling, "Peregrine. Peregrine is back," and his feet stumbled. Within moments people poured out of their homes and clustered together, forming a mob at the edge of the compound. Tempers churned in the passing breezes. Fear and excitement, filling the air in bold, fragrant slashes.

"Keep walking, Perry," Reef said quietly.

Perry prayed for the right words, now when he needed them. When there was so much to explain and make right.

The frenzied whispers of the crowd fell off as he closed the final distance. He scanned the faces before him. Everyone was there. Even the children, who were half asleep and confused. And then Perry saw Vale come forward, the silver links of the Blood Lord chain flashing against his dark shirt.

For an instant relief crashed over him. Vale was free. Not a captive in the Dweller Pod. Then he remembered Vale's last words to him. Telling him he was cursed. Telling him to die.

Perry's legs twitched, unsteady beneath him. He didn't know what to do. He hadn't expected this. He could see that Vale was just as shocked as he was. Vale, always intent and cool, looked pale and shaken, his mouth set in a grim line.

Finally Vale spoke. "Back, little brother? You know what this means, don't you?"

Perry searched for answers in his brother's face. "You shouldn't be here."

"*I* shouldn't be? Haven't you got it backward, Peregrine?"

Vale gave a dry laugh and then tipped his chin at Reef. "Don't tell me you've come to make a play for Blood Lord with your little pack here? Don't you think you're a bit outnumbered?"

Perry struggled to make sense of things. "I saw Talon," he said. "I saw him in the Realms. He said you were there. He saw you in the Realms."

Darkness flashed across Vale's features. "I don't know what you're talking about."

Perry shook his head, recalling the way Talon had made Perry prove his identity. Talon couldn't have been wrong about seeing Vale. And he had no reason to lie about it. That meant Vale was lying. A sick feeling bloomed in Perry's stomach. "What did you do?"

Vale reached down to the sheath at his belt and brought out his knife. "You better turn around right now."

Perry sensed Reef and his men bracing behind him, but he just stared at the knife in Vale's hand, his mind churning. The Dwellers hadn't just been looking for the Smarteye that day on the beach. They had gone after Talon.

"You had him kidnapped," Perry said. "You set me up. . . . Why?" Then he remembered the Dweller dome with all the rotting food. So much. Enough to waste. "Was it for food, Vale? Did you get that desperate?"

Bear stepped forward. "Our stores are full, Peregrine. Sable's second shipment came last week."

"No," Perry said. "Liv *ran*. Sable couldn't have sent the food. Liv never went to the Horns."

For a moment no one moved. Then Bear shifted, his thick

eyebrows knotting in suspicion. "How do you know that?"

"I saw Roar. He's looking for her. He's coming here in the spring. He might have Liv with him by then."

Vale's face tightened with rage, the last of his guard vanishing. He was caught. "Talon's better off in there!" he growled. "If you saw him, you'd know he is!"

Shouts of surprise erupted around them.

Perry shook his head in disbelief. "You *sold* him to the Dwellers?" He didn't know why he hadn't seen it earlier. Vale had done the same thing to Liv. Sold her for food. Only it was justified by custom. *Archaic,* Aria had called it. Perry saw that now.

How many times had Vale lied to him? About how many things?

He caught sight of Brooke in the crowd. "Clara . . . ," he said, remembering Brooke's sister. "Brooke, he did it to Clara, too. He sold her to the Dwellers."

Brooke turned to Vale and screamed. She lunged forward, arms swinging as Wylan stepped in and held her back.

"Vale, is this true?" Bear's voice boomed.

Vale flung a hand at the sky. "You don't know what it's like getting food out of this!" Then he scanned the crowd, stunned, like he realized he'd lost the Tides. He turned back to Perry and drove his knife into the dirt at his feet.

Perry let his own knife fall. They were brothers. This wouldn't happen with something as cold as a blade.

Vale didn't wait. He charged low, slamming into Perry's waist, the power driving through him explosive. In the moment they collided, Perry knew Vale was the toughest opponent he would ever fight. Perry surged backward, his teeth slamming together, but his feet weren't quick enough.

They fell together, Vale's shoulder thrusting the air from Perry's lungs. The instant after Perry hit the ground, he took a blow across the jaw that stunned him. He blinked hard, unable to see, bringing his arms up to cover his face as punches hailed down on him. Perry couldn't gather his bearings. For the first time it occurred to him that fighting might come as easily to Vale as it did to him.

With his vision returning, Perry heaved up with all his strength. He grabbed hold of the chain around Vale's neck and pulled, driving his head up. Perry had aimed for Vale's nose but caught him in the mouth. He heard the snap of breaking teeth as Vale rolled off.

Vale pushed himself to his knees. "You bastard!" he yelled. Blood poured from his mouth. "Talon is mine! He's all I have left. All he wanted was you."

Perry rose to his feet. His right eye was already swelling shut. Vale was *jealous*? Perry felt like he was going to break. He remembered the Dweller with the black gloves chasing him into the ocean. The Dwellers had taken the Smarteye and Talon, but they had still come after him. They had wanted Perry dead.

"You asked the Dwellers to kill me. Didn't you, Vale? Was that part of your bargain too?"

"I had to get to you first." Vale spat blood onto the dirt. "I did what I had to do. They wanted you anyway."

Perry wiped the blood that ran into his eyes. He couldn't believe it. His brother had done all of this behind his back. He'd lied to the Tides.

Vale launched himself at Perry, but Perry was ready this time. He dodged to the side and wrapped his arm around Vale's neck. Perry pulled him down. Vale hit the ground face-first and struggled but Perry had him pinned.

Perry looked up. All around him he saw shocked faces. And then he saw his knife glinting on the ground. He picked it up. Perry pulled Vale around and laid the steel against his throat. They weren't brothers anymore. Vale had lost that privilege.

"Talon will never forgive you for this," Vale said.

"Talon's not here." Perry's arms shook and his eyes blurred. "Pledge, Vale. Swear to me."

Vale's body relaxed, but his breath still came fast. Finally he nodded. "I swear on our mother's grave, Perry. I'll serve you."

Perry searched his brother's eyes, trying to read what he couldn't scent. He looked over at Reef, who stood a few paces away, flanked by the rest of his men. Reef knew exactly what Perry wanted. He took a few steps forward and lifted his head, his nostrils flaring as he breathed in deeply, sifting through the hot stench of anger, searching for truth or lie.

He shook his head slightly, confirming what Perry knew, but didn't want to believe. Vale would never serve him. He could never be trusted.

Vale looked at Reef. He tensed with realization, and then grabbed for the knife, but Perry moved faster. He drew his blade across Vale's throat. Then he stood, Blood Lord of the Tides.

45

ARIA

"**W**hat should I tell him when I get there?" Roar asked.
They stood together in Delphi's courtyard. Spring
sang its chattering music into Aria's ears. Flowers burst up
all along the wall, the colors bright against the gray stones.
Winter had left broad bare spots on the mountain and the
smell of smoke in the air. Now it was time. After months
together at Marron's, Roar and Cinder were heading to the
Tides.

To Perry.

"Nothing," Aria answered. "Don't tell him anything."

Roar smirked. He knew how much she missed Perry.
They'd spent hours talking about Perry and Liv. But she
hadn't told Roar about her deal with Hess. Perry would have
enough to handle as a new Blood Lord. That burden was
hers.

"You have nothing to say at all?" Roar asked. "Better

have a look at her, Rose. I think she's ill."

Rose laughed. She stood with Marron by Delphi's entrance, resting a hand on her round stomach. Rose was due to have her child any day now. Aria hoped she'd still be there for the birth.

Roar crossed his arms. "Do you really think he's not going to learn you're out here eventually?"

"Well, *you* don't have to tell him."

"If he asks, I won't lie to him. It wouldn't help if I did."

Aria sighed. She'd been thinking about this moment for weeks and she still didn't know what to do. She knew Perry's fears. She wasn't a Scire. She was no different than Rose or the girl in his tribe. Perry could already be with her again. Just thinking that made her stomach tighten with hurt.

"Roar!" Cinder growled, waiting by the gate.

Roar smiled. "I better go before he gets angry."

Aria hugged him. He was close, his cheek pressed to her forehead, so she passed a secret message to him through her thoughts. *I'll miss you, Roar.*

"Me too, Halfy," he whispered, low enough that only she could hear. Then he winked at her and sauntered to the gate.

From the corner of her eye, the wildflowers along the wall caught her attention. "Roar, wait!"

Roar turned around. "Yes?" he asked, arching an eyebrow.

Aria ran to the wall, scanning the flowers. She found the right one and plucked it. She drew in its scent and imagined Perry walking beside her, his bow across his back, looking over with his lopsided grin.

She brought the flower to Roar. "I changed my mind," she said. "Give him this."

Roar's eyes crinkled in confusion. "I thought you liked roses. What's this?"

"A violet."

Two weeks later, Aria crouched in front of a fire, turning a rabbit over on a wooden spit. She couldn't see beyond the warm glow of the flames, but her ears told her she was safe in these woods, where only small animals scurried close.

She had left Marron's days earlier than she'd planned. She had missed Roar far more than she had expected. She'd even missed Cinder's surly presence. She couldn't stand to be in the same spaces without them, so she'd readied her pack, said her teary good-byes with Marron, and then set off on her own.

As she listened to the sizzle of the meat and gristle, she remembered the night she'd first seen real fire. How frightening and thrilling it had been to her in Ag 6. She still saw it this way. Perhaps more so. She'd seen the Aether set whole parts of the world to burn. She'd seen fire transform the skin on the back of a broad hand into something knotted and patched with scarring. But she also loved fire now, ended every day like this, rubbing her hands before it, letting it bring forth the sweet ache of her memories.

In the sounds of the night Aria heard footsteps, far off and faint, but she recognized them instantly.

She shot into the darkness, letting her ears guide her. She

followed the crunch of his feet on stones and small twigs, coming faster, louder, as his walk became a jog, then a run. She chased the sounds until all she heard was his heartbeat and then his breath and his voice, right by her ear, telling her, in tones as warm as fire, exactly the words she wanted to hear.

ACKNOWLEDGMENTS

Many people helped me create this book. I'm deeply grateful to Barbara Lalicki for her editorial insight, unwavering support, and boundless enthusiasm. Maria Gomez provided additional editorial advice. Andrew Harwell helped with a myriad of tasks behind the scenes with efficiency and a great attitude. Sarah Hoy and her team designed a cover that continues to stun me. Melinda Weigel turned an expert eye on the fine details within these pages.

To Josh Adams, a black belt in business savvy, thank you for running everything so smoothly. I think you're champ.

My sincere thanks to the international scouts and publishers who put their faith in *Under the Never Sky*. It's an incredible honor to see my story venture out into the world. For their support, Stephen Moore and Chris Gary also have my appreciation.

Two people aided me in shaping this novel from inception to completion. To Eric Elfman and Lorin Oberweger, my brilliant mentors and dear friends, my most heartfelt gratitude. Thanks also to Lynn Hightower whose mantras, *It's all about once upon a time* and *Every scene needs a heart,* have become my own.

Talia Vance, Katy Longshore, and Donna Cooner turned the solitary pursuit of writing into a team sport. I'm so fortunate to know you. Bret Ballou, Jackie Garlick, and Lia Keyes have each spent countless hours with me under the never sky. Thank you.

Friends and family, thank you for cheering me on over the years as I chased a dream. I couldn't have caught it without you. In particular, thanks to my parents for being the best role models a daughter could ask for. To my boys: pulling the pin on a love grenade and lobbing it your way.

Finally, to my husband: life is sweet, being rendered to you.